EMERGENCE

CRAIG T. STEWART

Written Works

ISBN (Paperback): 979-8-9888289-0-7
ISBN (eBook): 979-8-9888289-1-4

Book Design by Aaxel Author Services
Cover art by Nageen Asif

Printed in the United States of America

Publisher's Cataloging-in-Publication Data
provided by Five Rainbows Cataloging Services

Names: Stewart, Craig T., author.
Title: Emergence / Craig T. Stewart.
Description: Bristow, VA : Written Works, 2023. | Also available in audiobook format.
Identifiers: ISBN 979-8-9888289-0-7 (paperback) | ISBN 979-8-9888289-1-4 (ebook)
Subjects: LCSH: Artificial intelligence--Fiction. | Genetics--Fiction. | Young women--Fiction. | Science fiction. | Dystopian fiction. | Political fiction. | BISAC: FICTION / Dystopian. | FICTION / Political. | FICTION / Action & Adventure. | FICTION / Science Fiction / Genetic Engineering. | GSAFD: Dystopias. | Science fiction. | Adventure fiction.
Classification: LCC PS3619.T49 E44 2023 (print) | LCC PS3619.T49 (ebook) | DDC 813/.6--dc23.

For all those generations who have had to struggle with the
worst humanity has to offer,
And for all future generations that I pray do not have to
struggle with the worst of humanity.
Do not give up.

Table of Contents

PART 1

ABNORMALS AND ABSOLUTES

PROLOGUE

Emerging, a prolonged reminder of the past, a piece of hollow history, a treasure; it came into view. I picked up the flashlight from near the dusty ground before slowly studying the artifact with heartfelt desire. The formation was a symbol of a great divide, and of haunting turmoil.

I called to my colleague, "I found a shard, Franklin!"

After several moments of excited clamoring, a tall well-built man with short black hair and brown eyes stood on the platform above me.

Franklin's dark leather jacket and khaki jeans complemented his brown skin. His angular and muscled body was always covered with some form of leather, and it seemed to suit him well. No one else understood why he wore a leather jacket, especially during a hot period such as now. I was the exception to the rule, as with so many things.

"Where is it Tory?!" Franklin's deep voice brought my thoughts back to reality.

"Oh! Over here," I replied, embarrassed by my high and feminine voice, and as always, I coupled my embarrassment with a blush.

My voice never sounded like it was from a tall, strong, and full-boned structure, but it was. No one dared question my oddities like they had all those years ago. When I was younger, I received never-ending torment. Most people despised my hair and eye color because they were too *abnormal*.

It was so ever since the Genetic Crusades sprung into the history books. They marked the first global conflict over food sources. Thousands were forced to eat genetically modified food that caused various changes to their genetic code. No one could explain exactly why this happened, as the history books do not share details about the time period. It was the first of many crusades as hundreds of millions were forced to do the same, regardless of their food supply.

Those of us who knew enough about the forbidden bits of history, as passed down by our parents, knew the food was developed to change the human race. The modifications become apparent as more of the populace showed similar color of features and more uniform traits, particularly in those who partook of the food. Those who married and had children with the Zero people found that the genetic markers were dominant and passed down regardless of the sex of the parent.

Over time, these traits dominated the gene pool. Things like brown eyes and black hair had become ordinary. Any other color was considered peculiar for no other rationale than the characteristic was different, the hue nonconforming. We who were unusual learned the same songs, same pledges, even learned the same math skills and science facts. We attended the same universities, sought diverse friends, and every other customary task for acceptance in society. Yet people would still treat us as if we were *abnormal.*

"I think you may have found one. We will need to test it up at the lab to be sure. It's obviously not a pure sample. Tory, are you okay?" I shook my head as Franklin's words seeped in. By his tone he could tell I had shown my thoughts. I always became gloomy after such meandering feelings. I have not, after thirty years, understood the premise for discrimination, even as they, those who call themselves Absolutists, drilled the reasons into my brain.

"I am fine, so the shard won't last as long as fuel?" I asked, with a forced inquisitive expression. I already knew the answer was yes, so I plowed on. "Should we keep digging for more?"

"It is likely it will not last as long, being impure and all, but we are running out of daylight. I doubt we will have any luck, anyway; this area hasn't been as fruitful as we had hoped." Franklin finished speaking and then gripped the ladder to hoist himself up.

At that point I had a sudden notion to ask him something that had been weighing heavily on my mind for a long time. I felt like I could trust him after the time we spent together. "Franklin, have you ever wondered what would happen if we didn't fuel the computer?"

"No!" His voice broke with abrupt emotion and boomed across the entire dig site. "The day it dies is the day our country will be thrown back into anarchy. Remember the Genetic Crusades? As soon as we let humans into our government, we will revert back to unnecessary quarrels. It is better to be governed by the AI."

His words felt as true as they stung, and I could not help turning my rosy cheeks away as tears grew in my eyes. I could not contain the emotion any longer. They said my eyes were ugly. That my eyes were hideous, flawed, and hazel. People persecuted me for them, and my hair. My shiny, straight, blonde hair was just as grotesque. Many I met, with varying politeness, had always asked me to wear a wig, to hide my eyes with colored lenses. They felt awkward in my presence because *I* was different. They, who believe in a system of supercomputers that control our economy, government, and social lives, lecture me. Even if I did as they asked, I had a ring of yellow on my wristphone that betrayed I was an Abnormal.

Scientists had dedicated years of research to designing a sustainable fuel system for the supercomputers to no avail. They succeeded when the rare substance known as Itrep was discovered. It could be found in an extremely rare crystal formation in nature. These crystals were found to be a potent source of energy. Within a year of their discovery, scientists figured out how to expend large amounts of energy with the right combination of temperature and compounds. It was a more efficient reaction and more powerful than any nuclear reactor at the time.

At our headquarters, there was a large data center that housed much of one such supercomputer, one of many that run our governments. It has been my job since graduating college at the age of twenty to locate fuel for them. It was my duty to society, and even after finding Itrep time after time, I am still not worthy of being normal, or equal for that matter.

"Let's go before night comes," Franklin said, interrupting my brief daydream once more. It was not unusual for my mind to wander while we searched, and he never commented on my occasional breakdown or glazed looks due to my thoughts. It was one of the reasons we worked so well together.

As we climbed the ladder to the darkening sky, the eerie purple hues of the sunset brought the shards' color to a dazzling existence, which only grew in intensity as we surfaced. As we slowly walked to our work vehicle, the setting sun stole further down and we finally faded into our futures.

THE ALL-SEEING EYES

Franklin drove quickly and with great ease across the rugged terrain. It may have been the barren badlands of Australia, but Franklin was an expert at maneuvering around obstacles both big and small. He grew up in an area of the world where the common pastime was to drive a wide variety of vehicles. He would often talk about his times there, how he became a local celebrity. He even discussed his stunt double days before being recruited as a driver for the government's research division. Those days were long behind us. As the fuel shortage grew, we had less time to speak to each other, less time to enjoy our hobbies, and more time was spent finding ways to power the government's data centers.

"Tory, I know how hard it is for you to have to move once again; and so soon, if I might add," Franklin began to address the elephant in the car. "I am sure your new position in Antarctica will be fruitful."

I hesitated several seconds before summarizing my thoughts in a clear and precise manner. "As much as I agree with you, we both know why I am being *promoted* to Antarctica."

Franklin suddenly grabbed the steering wheel with both hands and I instinctively gripped the door handle with my right hand and the seat with my left. I watched through the windshield as he proceeded to swerve left to avoid a large bush and then with a steady and swift motion that appeared to take little to no effort, Franklin guided the vehicle with a sharp turn right to reposition us in the direction we wished to head.

This second turn served a dual purpose, as we narrowly avoided a large boulder that rested near the bush. I remembered the combination on our way to the dig site earlier this morning. The only difference now was I could not locate the vernal pool that rested close by. At that moment, the vehicle darted to the left and I saw the water flash by my window. I wordlessly praised Franklin for remembering its location.

"So, you are telling me you think this promotion is in some direct relation to—" He cut himself off, knowing he had already said too much aloud.

"I am not saying that, nor will you ever hear me say that, Franklin. What I am saying is that I have the great and unfortunate ability to travel anywhere in the world for my work. It comes as a birthright."

I watched as Franklin smiled ever so slightly while his focus remained on driving. The darkening sky and calm air of confidence made him look like a statue of a brave warrior. "If I didn't know any better, that is exactly the way you want your job to be. You want to move around so that you don't have to settle down in one place. Admit it, Tory."

Cracking a smile to match his, I tried to reconcile his observation with what I wanted. I saw he was not watching the landscape ahead, but looking squarely back at me. I blushed, hoping he did not see, and abruptly turned my head and gazed out my window. Noting the speed of the landscape and objects flashing by, I asked a far more innocent question, one that would not have us thrown into a prison cell. "How fast are we going?"

"Several numbers above the speed limit," he retorted. After a solid second of silence, we burst out laughing. It was a running joke between us. I never really wanted to know the answer, especially with Franklin, because it tended to be far faster than I was comfortable with. The exchange also broke the building tension in the car.

The next several minutes passed where we were both mute, letting the recently broken ice refreeze. Ever since my new assignment, or promotion, depending on which day and how I looked at it, Franklin has been uncomfortable around me. We had worked together long enough and had grown to know each other so well, and in a short two-paragraph letter, our companionship that was built over the course of the last year began to fade.

We became strangers, even though we were so close to one another; every day I seemed to find Franklin becoming more distant. Maybe I was just paranoid, but deep down I believed that Franklin never really accepted me for who I was. Franklin, like every other *normal* person, had been instilled with hatred for my physical features at a young age. He may have become my friend, and we may have grown close, but there was always a barrier where I knew he believed I was inferior. He, unlike others, would from time to time make me feel like some people could keep their discrimination to themselves. Franklin gave me hope, however faint it might be, and I knew I would miss that feeling.

"We are a few minutes out from headquarters; you should probably radio them and tell them we are coming in, Tory."

"Where is the radio?" I asked, looking around by my feet and behind my seat without luck.

"I think it is in my bag. Front pocket."

I grabbed his black bag and zipped open the front pocket and sure enough, the radio and an extra graphene battery were lying inside. "Good call. It looks like the battery is dead. Is the spare charged?"

"Uh yeah, should be. When was the last time we radioed headquarters to give them a status update?" Franklin asked with slight anxiety in his voice. They did not like it when employees went radio silent.

"I think it was around six thirty, after we had our dinner," I replied.

"That was two hours ago. I hope they haven't tried to check in on us yet."

With a snap, I removed the dead battery and with another snap, the spare was in place. By pressing the power button, the lights on the side lit up. There was a short beep, the radio became active.

"—Tango Three do you copy?!" a male voice burst from the speaker. I jumped a little and Franklin let out a low curse.

"I hope they haven't been trying too long. You better answer, Tory."

I pressed the top button and spoke into the microphone. "We are here. Radio battery died. On our way back to HQ."

"Copy that, Tango Three. Do you have an ETA?" the voice

shot back. I looked to Franklin, who glanced at his wristphone. "Five minutes out, Tory."

"HQ, we are five minutes out. I repeat, five minutes."

"I copy that, Tango Three, five minutes. Over and out."

I sat the radio down and looked through the glass to see the lights of our headquarters grow clearer above a thicket of trees. The building was an impressive structure that stood seventy feet tall. The blocky concrete outer shell of the building was drab and square, as if no one put effort into making the building look appealing in any way. The sight belied what was inside. I learned in my first few minutes how large a labyrinth the inside actually was. Every floor had a different layout and the only way to stay on the path you wanted to be on was to either memorize the directions over time or follow your wristphone, which would show the easiest route to take, but never the fastest route.

I grabbed at my wristphone before letting out a gasp and my entire body tensed. My wristphone was not on my wrist. I breathed a sigh of relief, as I remembered I had taken it off when I was working to protect the screen. I reached back as the vehicle went over a bump and I accidentally hit Franklin's right shoulder. I glanced at him and decided he did not notice, or ignored the event entirely. It had been an extremely long time since we last touched, three weeks, when I first told him about the letter and that I was moving soon. We had embraced then, and his show of empathy had given me an emotional rush.

As I grabbed my bag, which was resting behind my seat, and acquired the gray device, I pressed the single button on the side to see how much power it had left. I glanced over at Franklin once more. He appeared to be in deep thought as he watched the road. I looked down to see the battery life of my wristphone was at a healthy forty-four percent.

I attached the device to my left wrist as Franklin rolled to a stop in front of the gate. The black fence barrier before us buzzed and began to move to our right. The guard in the shack on our left waved us on and made a notation on his clipboard.

Franklin drove through the parking lot, which was almost entirely full of vehicles that were all identical, and parked in our designated spot a quarter mile from the nearest entrance. Franklin cut the engine, and with a quick movement he grabbed his pack and opened the door.

I hastily followed his motions and asked, "Do you think they will punish us?"

"No, we made contact. We should be fine."

"Are you sure?" I asked after a second's hesitation.

"Positive, Tory. I am sure we will have no negative consequences."

I nodded and took the lead to walk across the row of cars and onto the concrete sidewalk. The new surface made one of my knees falter for a second, but I plowed forward so that I didn't get embarrassed. Franklin, on the other hand, bounced up from the pavement to the concrete with agile skill. Seeing him do so made me blush, and I quickened my pace to stay a safe distance from him until the color faded from my cheeks.

I turned and followed the sidewalk up to the enormous building before us and toward the parking lot entrance. The massive front face of the structure was made of a black with white-lined marble that covered the steel beams and concrete inside. The slabs of marble appeared to be impenetrable, but I knew the marble was a mere eighth of an inch thick.

As I approached the door, I held up the wristphone and

watched the magnetic reader verify. A split second later, the LED flashed green. I pushed through the pristine glass door and turned to watch Franklin repeat the process and push through the door as well. We walked side by side down the maze of corridors until we arrived at the elevator. It was at that point my wristphone beeped. I looked down and saw a message on the screen.

I looked over at Franklin. "I guess you are on your own. Can you handle delivering the crystal shard by yourself?"

"What do they want?"

"All I know is I am to report to an office here on the ground floor," I replied grimly.

I watched as he stepped inside the elevator and the doors closed. He gave me his faint smile that was hardly noticeable to anyone but me. I spent so much time with him I could tell what he was saying to me and I could not bring myself to reply.

The wristphone beeped again. I looked down at the display and pressed the acknowledge option. At once it shifted to the normal map view of the entire floor. The red dot at the center marked where I was, and a dotted red line noted the severity of my current task and the direction that I needed to travel. As with any other official business in the compound, it was labeled as high importance.

I followed the directions at first, but after five minutes it became clear where I was supposed to go and I stopped glancing at my wristphone since I already knew the way. Hoping I was not in trouble, I opened the door and strode into the office.

"Where have you been, Tory? Why are you two late? And why the hell did you not answer when we radioed you?" The condemning voice came from Mandri.

I studied his reddened face, his dark brown hair, brown

eyes, and his bland black suit and white tie. "The radio died, sir."

"No extra batteries? No charger in the vehicle?"

"We were sent out with a low battery on the vehicle and radio. There was only one extra battery for the radio when I asked. Felt best to save it."

Mandri stood up and walked over to his file cabinet; he was holding a stack of papers in his left hand. "Tory, you should have radioed earlier and let us know that you would be late and the radio may die."

I did not reply. There was no reason to do so. He was not listening to me; he merely wanted to chastise me for being late and possibly find a way to trap me into taking the blame for the entire situation.

As if to prove my point, Mandri continued after the short pause. "No, Tory, you are to report in when your battery is far too low. Instead, what do you do? You turn off the radio entirely to preserve the battery."

"We wanted to ensure we would have contact if the vehicle died."

"No! You wanted to create more paperwork for me!" He exclaimed. "Get out of my office. You are on unpaid leave until you fly to Antarctica, which I will attempt to move forward because of this incident. Be gone with you."

I pursed my lips and held my head high as I marched out of the office and slammed the door. Mandri did not take kindly to the snarky retorts my tongue itched to speak.

"SLAM MY DOOR AGAIN AND I WILL HAVE YOU FIRED AND HOMELESS! YOU. YOU ABNORMAL!" Mandri's screams could be heard quite audibly through the metal door.

"Oh shut up," I whispered in response as I walked to the nearest elevator.

As I made my way to my room, I noticed the hallways were far quieter than normal. There were usually a few people still traipsing about at this hour. I wondered as to the reason why as I badged the reader and entered my small living space.

As I opened my door, I turned the light switch on the lowest setting. With the dim light on, I discarded my work belt on the kitchen counter and made for the shower. I could feel the dirt caked to my head burrowing into my skin and I wanted it off.

I grabbed a white towel from the stack in my hallway closet and once in the bathroom I turned the water on to a temperature that produced steam yet felt good to my touch. Removing my clothes, I glanced into the mirror above the sink. My face was filthier than I thought. Stepping into the shower, I savored the contact of the heated water on my clogged pores.

Several minutes went by as I performed my nightly ablutions. Cleansing my body felt good, especially after a full day of digging into the dry earth. I knew that tomorrow the entire process would repeat and the fear of facing every fellow Itrep hunter at breakfast kept me in my makeshift sauna until the water automatically shut off.

Cursing ever so softly, I opened the sliding glass door and grabbed my towel. Once finished drying, I made my way to the dresser in the solitary bedroom. With a plain yellow t-shirt and black shorts, I moved to sit in the parlor area and switched on the radio with a flick on my wristphone. Immediately, the speakers hidden in the upper corners of the room began to play a gentle classical melody as I relaxed into the chair. As the movement ended, I heard a soft knock on my door.

"Tory, are you there?" Franklin's deep voice called from the other side.

I was up on my feet and halfway to opening the door before I hesitated. Franklin was not one to come knocking after a long day of work like this. I thought for a second with my arm outstretched halfway to the doorknob. Why would Franklin visit me? We spent all day together searching for shards; why would he not be spending time with his poker pals?

I grasped the knob and turned, which simultaneously unlocked the bolt and opened the door. "Franklin, now this is a surprise. What—" I began before freezing. In his hands was an unmarked wine bottle.

"Before you freak out Tory, I want to say that I will miss your company and want to enjoy a drink with you, in case I don't get another chance before you depart for Antarctica." His voice soothed my thoughts of Mandri's tirade.

"Of course," I tried to keep my voice in check but it betrayed my surprise.

"Tory, you are a good person, no matter what they say. If you want me to leave, I can." He turned as if to leave, but I caught his arm. The second time we touched in weeks.

"No, come in Franklin. I was just listening to some Mozart before bed."

Franklin crossed the open threshold and surveyed the kitchen counter and parlor before setting the bottle down. "Where are your glasses at? I want you to try this wine."

"Second cupboard on the left of the stove, wine glasses are at the top." My voice had finally returned to normal from the higher pitch of surprise. My heart rate on the other hand was starting to beat out of control. Franklin was in my room; this was a first for me, and I was not sure if he had unspoken intentions. I was secretly hoping it would be more than a glass of wine and a farewell.

Franklin popped the cork off with a deft hand movement and, seeing my raised eyebrow, grinned. "Don't worry, Tory, I am a professional wine connoisseur. James calls me the unofficial local sommelier."

"James is an incorrigible gossip, so that doesn't say all that much," I retorted before accepting my freshly poured glass.

"Trust me, this is the best wine I have found since I became an Itrep hunter. Aged for seventy-four years in a cellar with a mint leaf. This is the best; if you like mint, that is."

"You know I like mint. You didn't buy this specifically for me, did you?" I inquired, swirling the liquid in my glass. It smelled amazing, and I closed my eyes to savor the scent for several seconds.

"I would be remiss if I didn't say I searched for a while for a mint wine that was worthy of your lips."

Okay, this was new territory for me. Was he flirting or just trying to compliment me? In order to hide my blushing cheeks, I gulped a swath of the mint wine. The normal unsavory taste I came to expect from the wine in the compound was muted by the aged mint. I couldn't believe mint wine held such a flavor. I felt the liquid dance on my tongue before I swallowed it.

"Do you like it?" Franklin was staring at me, watching for a hint as to my final judgment.

I took a few seconds before clearing my throat; the mint was delicious but stronger than I had anticipated. "It is more than I expected."

Franklin nodded and sat down. "What do you want to talk about, Tory? The floor is yours."

"I am not sure what you are trying to do," I began before stopping when I looked at Franklin. I saw something in his eyes. It was the same empty stare that he had given me when he found out I was leaving. The abyss struck fear deep in my body. It was a side of Franklin I never understood.

There was a pause in conversation while Franklin drank his wine and looked around. "I'm going to miss you, Tory."

"Miss m—" Before I could finish, he cut me off with a subtle movement of his hand.

"Tory, I know what others see you as. I wish I could understand the pain that you go through for what you have no control over. How you were born. It's sickening to me that people who are different are marginalized, with all the persecution that goes with it these days. I guess I am lucky, being black. They don't discriminate against us regardless of our features. For now, at least." Franklin's voice hardened as he spoke. I also detected something else in his speech pattern, a slur in his words.

"Only because the All-Seeing Eyes say discriminating against people for racial traits such as skin color will start another war." I chose my words with care. He was broaching the topic no one dared to, and I was not sure of his motivations. If we went too far into the line of discussion, we would be punished. I glanced down at my wristphone and prayed the microphone was not recording our conversation. It was still illegal for the wristphones to record everything all the time, particularly in our private quarters, but laws would not stop the company or the government from spying anyway.

"Tory don't you get it!" He stormed to his feet and slammed down the glass of wine, the liquid barely contained by the rim splashed about vigorously. "Every single day that goes by, people like you are forced into situations, unfair and demeaning, into circumstances no one wants to be in."

"Franklin, calm down. Think about what you are saying. You

don't know who could be listening."

"Why should I, Tory?" The reason for his slur was no longer elusive; it was obvious Franklin had been drinking before visiting my room.

"Franklin, I need you to go. We can talk tomorrow evening before I leave."

"Perhaps you are right, Tory. I have been hitting the sauce a little hard as of late." He shrugged and paced back and forth. While his words may have slurred, his motor skills appeared to remain intact.

"It's okay, it will all be fine. Trust me. I appreciate you coming by, but we do have work tomorrow," I said in my most soothing voice, hoping to quell the outburst.

"You're right." I watched as Franklin left, closing my door softly behind him. Immediately after the snap of the door, I began to regret sending him off. It was reassuring to have a friend by my side. Even through his drunken oration, I felt that he was merely looking out for me, wanting the best for me. Wanting the best for us. The problem was our wristphones tracked conversation, and we had to be careful what digital profile might build from our words and actions. They were always watching, after all. Always learning. The computers never slept. They were all-seeing.

As I walked slowly to the bedroom, it occurred to me that this was one of the last times I would see him, and I sent him away. That did it. I could no longer handle the mounting pressure anymore and I broke down. I fell to my bed crying. No longer holding back my tears, I let my stoic body convulse in the passion of sadness that had been attempting to rack my body until that point. There was no reason to hide it from anyone or anything any longer. I fell asleep after what felt like hours of crying.

WHITE TUNNELS

The next morning, I donned my work clothes and checked my wristphone. As I was checking the status of the battery, an alert flashed on my screen. It was Mandri calling me with high importance. I answered with a press of a button.

"Hello?" I asked, uncertain of Mandri's mood and reason for calling me.

"You are to report to the airport in an hour, pack your things." Mandri's harsh tone broke through the early morning stillness.

"Today? I thought my flight was—"

"GET ON YOUR FLIGHT TORY!"

"But-"

"Silence." Mandri was no longer screaming, but I could still hear the condescension in his voice. My eyes began to water and my lips quivered. I was never going to get an answer for the change of plans. I would not get to say goodbye to Franklin. There would be no time, and I had to pack what little I had. The call ended and an itinerary update was pushed to the screen on my wristphone.

I frantically packed everything I could into a suitcase, including the bottle of mint wine Franklin gave me, before checking the time. I had to be on the shuttle to the airplane in six minutes. With a few swipes, I saw that I would be able to swing by Franklin's room and see if he was there.

I rushed to knock on his door and felt my heart sink. There was no answer. I immediately strode to the nearest elevator to get to the ground floor. When the doors opened, I nearly dropped my suitcase. Standing in the elevator was Franklin.

"Hey Tory. Packing early?" He said, grinning with early morning workout sweat covering his body. He pointed at my suitcase to emphasize his point.

I stepped into the elevator and pressed the ground floor. "I am leaving in less than an hour. Have to make the next shuttle to the airport."

"What?" Franklin began wildly before he took a deep breath. I watched as the anger and confusion died from his face to the calm, stoic expression he utilized whenever we were in meetings with leadership. "How are you feeling? Are you all right with that?"

"I have to be, don't I?" I worked my hardest to keep a dignified expression. It was hard trying to keep everything together. Between the rushed orders to leave, my frantic mental review to ensure I had everything I needed, and the attempts to squash my mind wandering to the questions that would only make the situation worse, I felt like I was going to fall apart from the inside out. Franklin spotted the ruse in my features, even with my best efforts to convince him otherwise.

"Tory." The mere sound of his voice calmed me. The deep bass soothed my chattering brain. I looked over at him. He had moved close to me. His hand touched my shoulder. His face closed into mine. I closed my eyes as I felt the heat from his body, almost sure what to expect but unsure if it would really happen.

I started slightly as Franklin kissed me, long and tender he kissed me. Then I kissed him back. I tried to portray all of my feelings I felt for him into that one kiss. My hands dropped the bag and suitcase as I embraced him, hoping he would understand my feelings in that one and only embrace. It felt like only a split second had passed before the elevator bell rang and the door opened.

"Ground floor," I said, pulling back. I held my chin up and bit back the desire to open my mouth and scream. A single tear slid down my left cheek. I picked up the suitcase with my meager belongings.

"Ground floor," Franklin repeated, brushing the tear from my cheek before it fell to the floor.

"Don't forget me, please," I begged him, almost falling into his arms. Tears started to well in my eyes as I forced them back. Now was not the time.

"I won't, Tory." Looking down at me, he smiled; a brilliantly warm and loving smile. "I won't."

I took a step back and gripped my suitcase handle with as much force as I could muster to keep myself together. Without looking back, I marched out of the elevator and turned to my left, to the shuttle station. Franklin's footsteps slowly made their way out of the elevator and paused. I could not bring myself to hesitate. I would not have been able to continue if I did, so I doubled my pace and turned the corner. Away from Franklin for what just might be forever. The thought weighed on my mind as I walked.

The shuttle ride to the airport was uneventful, as was the boarding. Once on the company plane, I greeted everyone, which was customary during business flights, and endured all of their berating comments, sly and forward. When the plane was in the air, I laid my head back to relax as best I could. I fell asleep shortly after, exhaustion finally getting the better of me. The lack of sleep from crying the previous night did not take long to catch up to me.

I woke suddenly to the sound of roaring engines. The safety belt light was on and then my entire body dipped forward. Looking around, I saw others bracing themselves. The air masks dropped into the cabin.

"What's going on?"

"The plane is losing altitude. Put on the mask." The muffled voice of Joy came from my right. Looking over, I saw her mask was already on. "Here, let me help you."

Right when the mask was fully seated, the lights in the cabin went out. The plane began to pitch forward once more. I closed my eyes and held my head against the seat in front of me. All I could think about was how my life was going to end. How I sent the only person who showed me any form of affection out of my room just hours ago.

I remembered his lips closing with mine in the elevator. I knew that was hard for him to do. I knew that it was risky for us both. I felt the pressure in the cabin change rapidly, and all I could think about was how painful this plane ride would end. My last thought was how bittersweet life was, how short and painful mine was. The temperature of the ocean water.

With a massive jump, I woke up. The seatbelt around my waist kept me in place with a painful determination and I winced. Looking around, I found that the plane was still intact, the oxygen masks were not deployed and that most of the people on the plane were sleeping.

"Are you all right, Tory? You were worryin' me in your sleep." Joy's southern United States voice took a few seconds to register. I was still trying to process what had occurred. I had dreamt the plane was falling and going to crash. Why would I dream about that? Did I secretly want to die instead of making it to Antarctica? "Tory? Can you hear me?"

"Y-yes," I managed to stammer out as I closed my eyes and waited a few seconds before opening them. I felt a headache growing and instinctively reached into my pocket for a pill to stem the upcoming tide of pain. To my dismay, there were no pills in my pocket. Quickly checking my pack, I found I had missed medicinal products in my rush to pack. "Do you have acetaminophen or something for a headache?"

"I do, one sec." Joy's alto voice contrasted my soprano tones. While I was appreciative of her help, I could not help but be a bit jealous of her voice. She sounded more grounded, more in tune with the rest of the world. "Here ya go."

"Thank you, Joy." I promptly popped the two pills into my mouth and swallowed before stretching my neck. "How long was I out for?"

"You were asleep for 'round two hours. Honey, can I ask what you were dreaming about? Yer one of the most fidgety plane partners I have ever had." Her concerned tone sounded somewhat forced, but her frowning features reassured me she was curious and worried for me. Even if it was platonic or shallow.

"Well, I dreamt the plane lost altitude and we were close to crashing into the ocean." As I spoke, I let my head fall against the seat in front of me. I forced my shoulders to relax.

"I can assure you, darlin', that we have not lost altitude since you nodded off. Gained some actually."

I smiled slightly as I stared at the seat before me. If the conversation were to draw out any more, I would most certainly receive ever more apparent condescending notes in her speech. I hoped that by letting the dialog trail off, I might be able to avoid it. Sadly, I was disappointed.

"Tory, you don't have to look so grim. I get nightmares too whenever I am feeling down. Do you have a case of the blues?"

Joy wanted to know what was bothering me; very well then. "My move from Australia was bumped up a few days, and I didn't get the chance for a proper sendoff with a close friend of mine."

"Is that all?" Her southern drawl was starting to get on my nerves, but I stomached any potential outward leaning emotion and kept my face as blank as possible. The fact I had years of practice made everything seem natural.

"I'm going to Antarctica," I said dryly.

"Oh honey, you can't let a little snow and isolation get you down now. You won't last one minute in the real deal. Are you afraid your assignment is counterproductive for your career?"

"No, not really. More of a punishment, if anything."

"How so?"

"My now former boss and I did not get along on the best of terms. While I am glad to no longer have to deal with him, I still prefer the climate where I am originally from. Don't care for the freezing cold all year. Or the overabundance of heat all year, for that matter."

"I didn't either, but let me tell you somethin'. When you spend a few months in the cold, you get used to it. Where I'm from, it never snowed. I was reassigned to work high up in the mountains and now I'm not bothered with a bit of cold or snow. It just takes a few years to acclimate."

"I appreciate the advice, Joy." I could see my high monotone voice seemed to give her the impression I was speaking sarcastically, so I trudged on to make sure she understood I was not sarcastic. "Your advice is appreciated, Joy. My headache is just getting worse, is all," I quickly added, pointing up to my head.

"Oh, I understand. I'll let you be then, Tory." Joy turned and stared out the window.

Thanking the unknown deities that might be for the silence that ensued, I drifted back into an ever more restless sleep than the first. As the inky blackness grew and the hum of the plane drifted off, I found myself thinking about music. I could see the conductor's hand move the baton with elegant ease as I faintly heard Vivaldi's Four Seasons come from the back of my mind. As quickly as the vision had come to the forefront of my attention, it drifted off until the next sound I heard was the fasten seatbelt beep.

Shaking my head and rapidly blinking, I awoke and looked out the window to see white land, or perhaps an iceberg, below the plane. "Have you seen land yet?"

"Yes, we are making a quick landin' according to the pilot. Something about a storm brewing and not wanting to take the extra time for a smooth arrival."

Finally aware of the plane descending, I glanced at my wristphone. A little more than nine hours had expired during the flight. As I looked around, I saw most of the others were chatting with colleagues or busying themselves with their wristphones.

We landed several minutes later and as I exited the plane, I felt the freezing cold strike my bare skin and realized I did not have time to grab a jacket out of my suitcase. I shivered as I quickly made my way through the umbilical to the airport proper where the air was far warmer. I stepped off to the side and grabbed my jacket while everyone else chatted their way off the plane. Joy waved at me as she passed and smiled broadly. As soon as she turned and thought I could not see, I saw her face immediately drop into a scowl.

With my jacket on, I made my way, trailing behind the others. Three minutes of walking in the barebones airport led us to the destination point on my wristphone. We could see the wiring and piping for the various utilities. No expense was spent on the airport except what was needed for bodily function, environmental control, and moving planes in and out.

I looked up to see a door labeled with "Employees Only" with a badge reader next to it. A security guard stood next to the doorway with the ugly gray uniform and company insignia that denoted all security guards that worked for my company. Delta Diamonds and Shards. I grimaced as I watched my new colleagues slowly move toward the entrance. I looked around and spotted several high-tech cameras monitoring the area around the doorway.

The guard watched closely as, one after another, all the company employees badged through the door. When my turn came up, I closed my eyes and silently prayed that the badge would work without issue. I sighed with relief when the reader buzzed and lit up with a green LED.

"You need to get yourself a thicker jacket." It was the gruff voice of the security guard.

"I had an hour to prepare for my flight."

"Tough luck, then." He resumed looking into the crowd with his stony gaze.

I opened the door and walked into a barren, white tunnel. "Yeah, I suppose so."

It took a few seconds for my eyes to adjust to my surroundings. When they did, I realized the tunnel was cut out of snow and ice. I felt the chilly air sting my face, but it was not as cold as I expected. It felt warm enough to be above freezing. I walked forward as my eyes sparkled in amazement. I had never seen such a sight in my entire life. This was a truly remarkable view. At the end of the long white tunnel, there was a door that was standing ajar. I walked through to see the rest of my fellow passengers standing in a cave chiseled into the shape of a normal room.

"Close the door please," a bored voice called from the front of the assemblage as soon as I walked over the threshold. I shut the door and the same male voice began to call out names for a roll call.

When finished, he spoke in a dull, matter-of-fact voice that was as well rehearsed as the most professional of musicians playing their favorite piece. "Now, as most of you likely don't know, DDS has an entire underground dig site here in Antarctica. We call it the White Tunnels because some of the tunnels are dug straight through glaciers as well as the earth. Officially, though, it is Sector 1A-Antca. I will push the location of your rooms to your wristphones now. Everyone, enjoy the free time you have because you won't get much of it. Reconvene tomorrow morning an hour after your alarm, which I will push to your wristphone. I will also push the destination location and directions so no one gets lost. Any questions?"

"There is no view of the sky?" Joy asked.

"Nope. Which is why, along with your alarms and maps, I will be pushing an update to your system's interactive routine with suggested times for resting, eating, waking up, working out and, of course, working."

"Is there anything to do here besides those things? Is there a town or something with other people?" another man, British by his accent, asked.

"No."

"So we work, sleep, and work?"

"Basically," the bored voice replied as sadistically as anyone could possibly muster. I was reminded of why it was a good thing I could not have children by the man's tone and what I was looking forward to in White Tunnels. I saw no reason besides torture to bring a child into this world, especially considering they would most likely be an Abnormal like me, and added the thoughts to the list of excuses I used to avoid the real reason behind my barrenness.

ORIENTATION

I t felt like the alarm sounded almost as soon as I shut my eyes. The barren cave room amplified the sound of the alarm as it reverberated against the walls. When it became an unbearable pounding in my ears, I groaned and sat up on the small twin-sized bed.

"All right, all right." I grabbed my wristphone, which was on the table charging. Swiping up, the alarm ceased and quiet stillness fell once more in the room. The only sound was my breathing. I would have charged it on the flight but the charging stations were full. It took my entire being to force myself not to ask the people with more than half charge to let me charge my wristphone. That would have caused a stir considering my traits, something I avoided at all costs.

I never understood why everyone wanted to keep their wristphones charged constantly. The full battery would last two weeks with heavy use. The devices were designed to be used constantly without charge, yet it was almost as if some people expected the batteries to fail. Graphene technology was one of the few technologies that saw improvement over the last several decades. There was little risk of failure of the battery, or the computer for that matter. Aside from that, DDS would never allow us to go about our day without a way to reach out to us or monitor us. Information was money as sure as the digital currencies were.

I glowered at my new living space as I stewed about how inconsiderate my coworkers were. My living space was a small two-room affair. The bedroom was big enough for the twin bed and a small desk. There was an alcove with a rod for clothes to be hung. Through the doorway, I spotted the tiny kitchen outfitted with a miniature refrigerator, small microwave, and a toaster oven. I walked over to the kitchen, through what I assumed was the dining and living space that was just large enough for a four-person table or a small couch, and grabbed a glass from the counter.

I poured some water, and as I drank the surprisingly fresh and delicious liquid, I turned and immediately hit the doorway. I gasped and water entered my windpipe causing me to spend the next several minutes coughing as I dressed and headed out and down the long corridor which ended in the communal bathroom. I brushed my teeth and hair, and utilized the one of three stalls available for everyone on the same level as I was. It was not until I exited and headed back to my room that I saw another person.

"Howdy, Tory!" A bright eyed and bouncy Joy was headed to the bathroom. "How d'ya sleep?"

"I don't remember sleeping." I yawned, finally realizing just how tired I still felt. The whole day to day without the sun to guide me through was going to be a hard transition. Not to mention the feel of the sun on my bare skin. Nothing in the world felt as nice besides, perhaps, the touch of Franklin.

I tossed the thought aside as I reentered my kitchen and opened the fridge. Inside, I saw a fruit cup. Sitting next to it was a two-pound package of seasoned cooked beef and a bag of carrots. Since the fruit felt the most like breakfast, I grabbed the fruit cup. I could hear the shuffling of the other women moving in the hallway as I ate in solitude. I wondered where they were all from, and why they were all sent to White Tunnels. I did not see anyone else like me, which meant I was the only *abnormal* one among the passengers from Australia.

Could this assignment really be a punishment, or was it just a normal transition that would last until I was moved elsewhere as before? Why did Mandri send me here? Was he the one that sent me here? I could not be sure of anything other than the reality that I was in the chilly tunnels beneath Antarctica. I made a mental note to put an order in for some vitamins. If I was going to be out of the sun, I would need to supplement vitamin D at the very least, else I would inevitably fall into a depressive demeanor.

My wristphone buzzed and I looked down. There were directions to a room four levels below my current one. I finished the last bite of the fruit cup and left my new living quarters. I stood in the doorway and waited for a group of giggling women to pass. They were apparently already befriending each other. As always, I was destined to be a loner. Which was fine by me; the drama of a gaggle of women was more than enough to drive me insane without the addition of the sneers and backstabbing

I would be subjected to for who I appeared to be.

I followed the directions through the drab, dimly lit corridor until I reached the end, where I followed the stone chiseled staircase down. The staircase ended and I stepped into a large cave with stalagmites and stalactites spread throughout, as if the architect had designed the room to feature them. As I observed my surroundings, I noticed the room was a cafeteria with tables scattered about the stone floor. At the far end was a large empty space where three stalagmites had been removed with the bases remaining one foot up from the ground. Judging by the phone's display, that was where my destination was marked.

As I walked into the space, I read the four doors at the other end. Two were labeled as "Management Only", another with "Cafeteria Workers Only". The last door, which was directly in front of me, was labeled "Dig Site".

I had only a brief moment before a few of my fellow plane passengers joined me. After five minutes, forty or more people were chatting loudly in the cafeteria. Several of the people who were clearly stationed at White Tunnels already were sitting and eating an ugly-looking stew as they conversed animatedly with each other. It was as if the new people standing nearby did not exist. A hazing ritual of sorts by the way they purposely ignored questions and stares from nearby newcomers.

As the buzz of the crowd grew louder, one of the management doors opened and three people exited. Two men and a woman wearing the typical clothing of senior leadership stepped out. Behind them, a man and woman slowly emerged, both wearing the clothing that matched the dim gray wardrobe we were wearing, with the exception of a large logo on the front and back of the shirt. It was the logo of Delta Diamonds and Shards.

"Welcome all," the larger of the two men called out. His voice was loud enough to surpass the din of the crowd. Those already posted at White Tunnels began to whisper instead of talking loudly as they had before. Whoever this man was, he was certainly powerful, and those around him obeyed. I shuddered at the possibilities of punishment I would receive being the Abnormal in the bunch as I turned my full attention to him.

I had a knack for picking up on subtle queues from people as they spoke, however. It developed as a habit of necessity but became more of a tool that I could use to know what those around me were not saying. It was my secret weapon to avoid utter disaster in the presence of people who hated everything that I was, everything I was born with. I hoped to learn what he might let slip in his façade. As the room fell quiet, he bowed slightly to the woman and with a hand gesture, we all shifted our attention to her. His movements were of a military fashion, that much was clear to me.

"Thank you for coming. I know some of you may think this is a punishment, others an opportunity, but the reality is what we do here is the same as all other Delta Dig Sites. We mine. We mine for the future of our society, our world, and the human race. Without people like you, our world would still be in chaos. You bring order to this world. You have all been found to be good at the job you do. You have been chosen to join White Tunnels digging for Itrep. While some of you may have been diggers before, and other hunters, and still others engineers who ensured our safety; we all have one goal. We supply energy to the government. Our glorious protectors!"

We repeated, in the brief pause she gave us, her last words, "Our glorious protectors!"

Satisfied, she continued, "This does not mean we are more important than anyone else, or that we are above scrutiny. We are doing the work as asked of us by our leaders, and we are going to do it efficiently, effectively, and above all, quickly. The growing energy demands of our society require innovation and more fuel. That is why White Tunnels was founded."

As she finished her silkily spoken speech, smiling all the while, I could tell she did not believe everything she said. She did a good job of hiding the body language that told of her disagreements. I would have to keep an eye on her.

Whispers started throughout the standing men and women, but before it got out of hand, the silent man, who looked as if he was in charge, took a step forward. He was smaller than his two counterparts, but he made up for it in his low-pitched voice that boomed throughout the hall. "I am the senior leader of security here. You will all behave. If not, we have legal methods of making you behave. Unpleasant and otherwise. You have been warned."

Everyone was silent. No one was sure if he was finished speaking or if he was joking or something else altogether. Those sitting and watching the newly-stationed were completely silent. No one coughed. No one moved. No one wanted to break the silence.

Finally, the man continued after the irritatingly long pause. "We won't have any problems as long as you do as instructed. Just remember, if you end up in my office, you will never forget the experience. It won't be a pleasant one. For our glorious protectors!"

The man stepped back and the woman stepped forward as we repeated the refrain once more. "Let's remember, folks, that we are here because we are working for Delta Diamond and Shards, not because we want to, but because we must. Follow the coordinates on your wristphones to your new designated job site. Your team leaders will be there shortly to instruct you on our ways and unique processes."

The crowd began to make their way through the door labeled "Dig Site" as everyone's wrists beeped with updated coordinates. I hesitated until I was at the back of the back. Not the last one, but close enough to the end that I could listen to the speakers discussing among themselves without the distraction of other conversations. I was curious, and information was valuable.

"—are we accepting new workers?" the woman was saying.

"Jill, we've been through this—" the taller man replied before someone in front of me struck up a conversation with someone.

"—is right. Not our place to judge DDS—sell with them who cares?" the other man replied. I could not make out the rest of their conversation as I was now out of earshot, so I glanced down at the map on my phone's display and followed it to my destination.

The white tunnels became fewer and fewer as we traversed further and, at times, deeper into the dig site. The unnatural glow of the glaciers gave way quickly to highly efficient yellow LED lights. As many of the new workers peeled off from the main path, I was left with three others as we climbed down a ladder to find a blinding white light instead of the yellow LEDs above.

"This is it?" the only other woman asked the rest of us. She was slender and tall, and of Asian descent. When she turned to me and realized what I was, she did not disguise the disgust on her face. I smiled back politely. What else was there to do?

"Must be," one of the men said.

"Looks like we get the fun part, eh?" the other said, pointing down at the grated floor below us.

I followed his finger to spot surveying equipment below us.

It appeared my new task would be to determine the direction in which the dig site would go from here. I had done the same in the Congo, working with some locals who had found a small cache of shards. DDS sent me as a surveyor to see if there was enough to send a team in and mine.

"You fools know what you are doing?" The voice came from above. It was a familiar voice I had heard before. A long time before. One that caused my heart to sink and my facial façade to break momentarily in response.

David dropped in next to us and smiled at me. "Tory? No way! How the hell are you?"

"You know this one?!" exclaimed the woman, revulsion painted across her face.

"I know all of your names, Emily. But yes, I used to go to school with Tory," David replied to Emily, without looking away from me. He was studying my face without contempt, as if he saw me for the first time and liked what he saw. The gaze made my face grow hot, as I was unsure of his intentions. He was one of the worst people I could possibly have encountered. Yet something about his eyes made me feel as if he truly missed my presence. It was too confusing for me to take in all at once with three strangers by my side. I would have to process it all more deeply when I was alone.

"Yes, David. How have you been?" I replied, carefully choosing my words.

"Good. Good. Was in the war like I said I would be. Got my share of the baddies before the treaty was called." David chuckled to himself as he looked down at the equipment. He was in the last conflict to occur on earth. The war took place in the Middle East over a large deposit of oil that contained an anomaly similar to Itrep, and the possibilities drove the northern hemisphere to use military force against the Pakistanis. The war was fought for nothing in the end, as the anomaly provided no additional benefit to society. "Well, Emily, I believe you know how to operate the radar equipment. Want to hop down and get things set up?"

"Yes, sir, as long as I get to be away from her."

"Well in that case, Joe, assist Emily. Mark, stay up here with Tory to monitor the results. Agreed?" Everyone agreed and we took our places.

Over the next several days, I got reacquainted with the survey screens and trained Mark on what to look for. I also learned more stories from the war than I cared to know from David, as he quickly became the nicest person to me in all of White Tunnels. The confusing turn made me question what changed for him. I vowed to find out before one of us was reassigned.

He was not the most brutal person to me growing up but was certainly not the nicest boy when the teachers were looking away. He was always aggressive and a brilliant mind to top it off. He understood strategy and had a habit of picking up on theory before others did. As bright as he was, he convinced the job placement committee that he should be in whatever conflict that was starting in the Middle East at the time. The last I saw of him, he was walking away with several other newly graduated men wearing army fatigues.

DAVID'S STORY

As the remainder of the month went on, I slowly made a few acquaintances who would allow me to sit by them during mealtimes. Among their small numbers were David and two of his friends, Alex and James. On Sundays, they would play cards and needed a regular fourth player for Euchre. I used to play with the other Abnormals in college and was welcomed in, but Alex and James proved to be in another league.

I tried my best to pick up the rules and tricks from memory, but I knew I was holding David back. He was a chess player in school before joining the military. His mind was always driven to whatever involved strategy and thinking on his feet. I could tell he was as good as Alex and James, but I kept making bad moves that would cost us points.

It was the third Sunday after my arrival in Antarctica when Alex and James decided to head to bed early after winning three times in a row against David and myself. I decided it was time to figure out what had changed with David. He was different from high school David, and I wanted to know what made him change. "A game of chess before bed?" My voice was controlled and level. My heartbeat was certainly beating harder and faster. I was not good at chess and did not want to make him think I was a fool while I tried to drag out the information I wanted. Yet, the information was more important than my dignity.

"Sure thing, Tory. Didn't know you played."

"I picked it up in South America."

"Hmm, not many world-renowned players from there."

"They were good enough to teach me how to en passant."

His surprise at my knowledge of the lesser-known rule was clear on his face. "Well, then." He flipped the checkered board sitting on the table nearby and dumped out the chess pieces. We began to set them up on the board.

"So, David. Besides fighting and apparently working with DDS, what have you been up to?"

"Oh, this and that. Decided to use my education mandate to study up on radar equipment. I learned a little towards the end of the conflict, but nothing formal."

"Yeah, I was only one of three who volunteered to go to the Congo. That's how I managed to learn to use survey equipment. Abnormals never get to touch the tech equipment in my experience. It is always the grunt work."

David moved the pawn in front of his king forward two squares. "Well, we are glad to have you. You know what you are doing, there's no doubt about that. You should get a certificate to get more jobs like this."

"I don't know about all of that," I replied.

"Why's that then?" His frown caught my eye as I studied the chess board.

"I'm Abnormal in case you forgot, asshole," I said as I matched his pawn with my own king's pawn.

"I haven't forgotten. I have grown older and learned more about the world. I know who I was and I was hoping we could look past all that Tory."

"Really?" The wavering in my voice slipped out as I tensed. All the names and slurs that were hurled at me years ago coming to my ears. "Just like that?"

"I'm a fool and I know it, Tory. What can I do to change the past?" David's words hit me as I squinted at the board to control my emotions. I was not about to let him get under my skin. He had been nice enough to me so far since we met in Antarctica, but I was still skeptical.

"You can't—you can't change the past, at least we can't."

"Then why fixate on it?" His question was followed by his queen moving forward to sit in front of the pawn to the right of his king.

"Moving your queen so early? I thought that was a fool's tactic?"

"It is. I try to enjoy myself these days."

"Hmph." I moved my queen's pawn forward one. "French Defense?"

"Something like that," David replied, moving his light squared bishop three diagonal spaces forward.

"So why the change in heart? You want to enjoy playing games instead of winning and have decided I am worth your time?" I moved my second from the left pawn forward in preparation to move my dark squared bishop. I was starting to recall the appropriate moves to castling.

"You want to know the story, don't you?"

"Why do you say that? I wanted to play chess—" I began, but he waved me quiet.

"You may have learned to play chess, but you are not very good." He moved his queen to take my pawn to the left of my king. It was checkmate and my emotions fluttered in disbelief. "You could have just asked why I changed. It's a story I share with anyone who asks."

"I didn't want to be obvious." I murmured as I slumped back into my chair. After calling him a fool for moving his queen, I felt foolish not seeing the trap he set up.

"You are curious, nothing to be ashamed of. I would have not wanted to bring it up with a bully from my past."

"You had no bullies," I said flatly.

"Yep. I was class bully, ruling my minions from my throne. And I was stupid to believe I had any real followers. Folks don't follow bullies; they don't respect them. They fear them."

"Fine. What's the story David?" I asked, defeated.

"It was the last battle of the conflict. I was assigned to lead a group of Abnormals after some insubordination that I may or may not have felt as justified. I saved lives, and if that meant working with a group of outcasts for a few battles, so be it." I scoffed as he continued, as if I had not done anything. "And there we were, Tory. On the battlefield, cut off from the nearest armored unit, we waited for extraction as the baddies pushed forward. The computers did not expect the amount of rebels and thus did not strategize for the overwhelming force coming towards us.

"Anyway, we were stuck and on the cusp of being overrun by the enemy and I had no clue how to reunite with our army safely. As sergeant, I had to figure out our next move. So I asked for ideas, crowd-sourced. Everyone was taken aback, but Lane spoke up after a few seconds. He grabbed a knife from the ground and drew up a strategy right before my eyes. I could not believe he was capable of such thoughts and at first dismissed them. We waited behind a destroyed Humvee for a better idea.

"Finally, when the mortar shells began to reach us, I decided Lane's plan was better than no plan. We moved out. The problem was I waited too long and the baddies were beginning to surround us on our west flank as we ran as fast as we could through the path Lane laid out for us. Even hunkered down, we were still targets at that point for anyone who saw us moving. Lane was right behind me, and he shouted for me to duck. I didn't react in time, and he leapt forward to shove me down and I turned to watch as a bullet pierced his neck. The angle of the bullet was such that the trajectory ran through his right shoulder and through his lung.

"I grabbed him as he fell to the ground. The others stopped as they waited for me and Lane. Jacks came to help me carry Lane, but it was already too late. I watched as Lane's eyes grew distant and he spoke softly. I barely caught the words."

Enthralled with David's story, I hardly noticed as he sniffed and breathed calmly for several seconds as silent as space. I looked up at his face and saw his eyes were starting to water ever so slightly. I never knew David to have any emotion close to this. I was so jaded by the cruelty of my most notorious tormentors, I often forgot they were human, just as they thought I was not. "What did he say, David?" I asked softly.

"'I want you to tell me wife, David. Listen to our story and you will understand why I die for you now.' Never in my life had someone I hardly knew on a personal level ask me for something like that. I had no idea why, and as we made it back to the base, I pondered if I would honor his wish. Remember, I still harbored hatred for Abnormals, right?"

"I take it you did decide to honor his dying wish?"

"Yes. We all went. And I listened to her story. To his story. To why he joined the military. To why they met and married one another and became outcasts in their own right, throwing away any chance at making a living. I was shocked by their story. No one else was, as they all had similar stories. Forced into the military due to lack of jobs or education, as a way to protect their wives from the fact they were even married. It was sickening.

"I had no idea Abnormals were stigmatized from marriage and often encouraged or forced sterile in this day and age. My view of the world was clouded. I could not believe the horrors of our past existed in my lifetime. I listened to them all. Every last one. All of the Abnormals who were there. And I even visited a few of their homes and spoke with their families. They were glad someone like me would hear their story, and probably hoping my opinion of them would change."

"So, what did you do?"

"When the conflict was over and I got my formal education, I found a small network of people who were disillusioned like I was. I was living in Europe at the time. We had met in secret. It was actually one of the fathers of that group that allowed me to put my foot in the door with DDS. He said to move to Antarctica as soon as the company would let me."

"Why would he say that?"

"I know, right? I was confused too. As I pressed him, all he would say is that I would find some folks I would relate to and, in time, I would be asked to join something larger."

"What did he mean?" I asked, sitting upright. My arm and leg hair were standing on end. Something was not adding up in my mind and I could not figure it out.

"I don't know, Tory. I was here for three months and was just promoted before you arrived. You were in my first trainee squad." He smiled. "I don't know if we were supposed to meet, Tory, but I would like to think at the very least fate has given me the chance to make amends. However, I mig—"

I absorbed his words but was not listening attentively. I was still working out the math on reassignments. I interrupted him when the light flickered on. "David. You were reassigned at the same time Mandri told me he was going to relocate me."

"Mandri?"

"My old boss. At first I figured he was looking for the worst place to take me, but I am wondering. Does the name Ivan Torbetsky mean anything to you?"

"Ivan Torbetsky?"

I shook my head. "No, that's not right. Umm. Ivan. Ivan." I snapped my fingers. "Vasilevsky?"

David's eyes widened. "Yes. Vasil's last name was Vasilevsky. I don't recall if Ivan was his first name, though. Verushka's father, Verushka being my best friend at the time. Sadly, he had cancer and passed away a year ago. His father, who we called Vasil because it was easier for everyone to pronounce, dedicated his every waking hour to his work instead of grieving. Became an alcoholic. But he was and is still as sharp as a newly sharpened blade. Would not want to get on his bad side. You don't think we are supposed to be here together, do you? That Vasil had something to do with us working together?"

"I don't know. I just remember Mandri on the phone with

that name prior to one of his shouting fits."

"Mandri sounded like a laugh and a half."

"Oh, he was always screaming about something. And not just me, I was just the recipient of most of the blame."

"I'm sorry to hear that, Tory."

"I am concerned, David. If we were sent here by coincidence or if someone is putting us in the same room to see what happens."

"Could it be a plot to weed out my sympathy? I've heard rumors of undercover police."

"No, those are a myth as far as I know. At least in the southern hemisphere. No one seems to care near as much, but the concentration of Europeans and Americans here may prove me wrong."

"Go figure."

"Go figure what?"

"Rhetorical," David said thoughtfully. "I never did get a chance to ask why you had to go to our high school. What was the reason? I thought most Abnormals went to separate schools."

"We thought I'd have a chance since I was so book smart."

"Well, you have made a good path so far, Tory."

"Have I?" I shot back at him.

"Well, on paper," David amended.

"There are no papers on my accomplishments, only my next orders."

VASILEVSKY

David and I swore to each other to keep our discovery between the two of us until we knew more. I asked if David could prod his friends to see how many people were moved because of a man by the name of Vasilevsky. He said he would but could not make promises as not everyone had connections to DDS corporate leadership like he did.

It soon became apparent from the circle of friends David had made that no one else was aware of a connection in their transfers to Antarctica. This did not help the thoughts crowding my mind as I tried to make sense of any connection David and I might have to Vasilevsky that would make sense. I was beginning to think that I was trying to make sense of a completely coincidental case of natural events when I was eating on a somber Friday morning. The day before there was an accident which nearly killed two workers who were utilizing large drilling equipment.

"Tory, did you hear?"

"Hear what?" I asked, pulling myself to the present and away from the thoughts that had been roaming my mind for too many weeks.

"Vasilevsky is coming here to Antarctica, to White Tunnels."

"What?! Why?" My confusion and excitement burst through what was a genuinely gloomy gaze. I could feel my heart beginning to speed up. Maybe there was a connection after all.

"DDS is being broken up to prevent antitrust questions from citizens. Something about too much profit for a company in a duopoly which had no competition for talent."

"That doesn't explain why he is here."

"He is buying White Tunnels and a few sites in South America from DDS. He wants to make an announcement at the top of the hour."

I glanced down at my wristphone; it was half past eight. As David and others sat down around me, I felt as if my differences were less pronounced as the thoughts and discussions took priority on everyone's mind. I did not mind being able to talk to people who normally avoided sitting near me, and they did not seem to notice I was different in any way. There were more pressing matters, at least for the time being. It was almost as if the segregation drilled into our brains was briefly lost to the ether.

When Vasilevsky arrived, he entered through the management door on the far side of the cafeteria. He swept across the empty distance and I studied his features. An average older man with a salt and pepper beard, and a bit bulky around the midsection. He was jovial as he moved, but something about his movement was unsettling in a way. As if he believed he was far younger than his body allowed him to be. But there was also a brilliant twinkle in his eyes as he smiled. His face was unreadable outside of the smile. It was a smile that felt to me like he was hiding a greater excitement somewhere within.

I could tell he was hiding something. What it was I could not tell on body language alone. I assumed it was his alcoholism David had mentioned. I could not be sure without speaking with him. The downfall to my talents was that not everyone was easily read from afar.

We all sat silently, waiting for him to speak. When he did, his accent was hardly pronounced, but it was clear he was from Eastern Europe in the way he spoke. "My friends, I come to you as a former DDS employee. It is with glee I am happy to say the same is for some of you as well." He paused as a ripple of low conversations broke out at this. Vasilevsky raised his hands with a wide smile to silence the crowd. "Now friends, I wish I could hire you all; but as it stands, I simply will not be able to afford the margins DDS was operating here in Sector 1A-Antca. Which I will be renaming on the books as WT-Antca as it is more apt a name. You may call it as you always have: 'White Tunnels'.

"As per the agreement with DDS, I will be keeping a core group as part of the transition and the rest of you will report back to DDS corporate headquarters for your next assignments. I wish those of you luck in your future endeavors and apologize for any inconvenience this may be to you. I will now push the updates to your wristphones. Please stay where you are if you are remaining here. There are two planes awaiting the rest of you to pack and depart."

He looked down at his wristphone, which was decidedly not a DDS issued affair, and after a few seconds of tapping beeps could be heard throughout the hall. Conversation immediately broke out as almost everyone stood and headed for the dorm hallways. When the throng cleared out, about thirty of us were left with Vasilevsky. He slowly meandered up to us and motioned that we all center about him. As we did, he stared at the unique cafeteria, taking in every stalactite and stalagmite in the room.

When he finished his observations, he looked down at us and waved at David and two others I did not know. David and the others awkwardly waved back. Of the remaining thirty, four of us were Abnormals. I had not seen the others before, and when I noticed they were wearing kitchen attire, I realized I would not have had a chance until now. They likely had different quarters than the hunters did. "On paper, you are the worst of the bunch."

His simple statement stung. He watched as we all turned to look at each other, confused by what he meant. It took me a few seconds to begin to put together the picture Vasilevsky was painting. Everyone here was in some way an outcast for the most part. I recognized Alex and James were among those left. They were fine with talking and enjoying free time with me, even if they were uncomfortable. The others I had been around were similarly warmer to my presence than the average person.

I was sure their discomfort was due to the thoughts of eyes staring into the backs of their heads as traitors to humanity, but I was convinced now. Vasilevsky had chosen the people that were either Abnormals, or were fine with working next to Abnormals. Vasil looked down at his wristphone and after a few presses, everyone's wristphones began to restart.

Looking down at mine, I read the big and bold words "Updating to new company requirements, please stand by."

"I purchased White Tunnels at a large expense with a vision in mind. To take all of you with low social scores and prove an idea. All of you at some point have either had a change of heart in the way society operates; or you are *Abnormals*. Together you are the Others. The Outcasts. The people society blames problems on, directly and indirectly. This is unsustainable. Blaming our problems on a minority group of people, or even a majority for that matter, is absolutely ludicrous. It will do more harm than any good it will ever do in the long term. As such, I am using you as an experiment to prove my point and hopefully make you the first of many productive generations to run through White Tunnels. You will be the test run of The White Tunnels Others. If the name sticks, that is. We will see. Questions?" He bounced on the balls of his feet as he stood joyously before us. One of the kitchen staff raised their hands.

"Yeeeeeeesss?" The elongation of the word was clearly something Vasilevsky picked up in America. No other country still spoke in that manner.

"Why do you care about us?"

"Because I believe everyone is wrong about you. I see opportunity where others see emotions of hatred, disgust, and anger."

"Wouldn't that make you as bad as the Abnormals? No offense," Alex interjected, his voice quavered slightly and his shoulders were slumped. He clearly was not prepared to be speaking to a brand-new boss so directly.

"You leave the political and societal posturing to me. They will realize their mistakes in due time."

"What does that mean?" David asked.

"David! Such an interesting question isn't it? According to everyone's records here who are not Abnormals, you all have streaks of disobedience to authority. If I asked you to look past some of the activities I have planned, would you not do so if it meant civil disobedience to the very machines and their supposed authority that you have defied in the past?"

"Depends on what you mean by 'activities'." David's reply was sharp.

"As my new head of security, I will be briefing you on those activities tomorrow morning when the rest of my staff arrives."

"What is your goal for White Tunnels?" I asked, drawing the attention of everyone in the room. My ears grew hot.

"My dear. Tory, I believe? Yes? My dear Tory. We are going to prove to the world that you are worth a damn. Isn't that what you have always wanted?" Before I could respond, Vasilevsky picked up on my bewildered expression and answered, shutting my open mouth. "DDS made a habit of tracking all your words and diary entries. It is done for most everyone. It is a mandate by the computers. You have shown great resistance to the way society operates and, given the chance, would openly oppose it, would you not?"

I did not move. My face was frozen. My body petrified in terror. How did he know one of my deepest, darkest desires? What else did he know about me? Why did he know, and why was he here, smiling directly at me? "I-I don't know," I stammered as my jaw forced my mouth shut. I did not mean to say it, but I did. Sweat beaded down my forehead as I waited for his response.

"I want the same thing you do, Tory. We have stuck to foolish genetic standardization for far too long. We will regret it when a plague hits us that no one has the DNA and immune system to stop and we are wiped out as a species. Genetic diversity is vital to the survival of humanity. From extraterrestrial and terrestrial threats alike."

"You, Ivan Vasilevsky, are a Genetic Unity Denier?!" exclaimed someone whose voice and name I did not know.

"I wouldn't say that anywhere but here with you. But I would also argue that I am against this new kind of forced eugenics, or whatever the appropriate verbiage is. And please, I can go by Vasil among friends."

"Why not Ivan?"

"Too common a name. Besides, Vasil has a better ring to it, I think."

"So you bought White Tunnels. Weren't the margins for profit almost one percent?" James asked.

"Point nine percent actually, and on the decline," Vasil corrected. He continued broadly reaching out to encompass us in his hands as if he was a villain holding a powerful item between his hands. "I estimate with you I should be able to expand that margin to almost five percent with the deposit that Tory may have identified yesterday."

I blushed. I had been excited yesterday and when I told David, his excitement was clear as well. Before we could make it to a supervisor to report it, the accident occurred and our discovery was relegated to the day's report and no further. The thought of the incident made me sick. Vasil paused to cough after this, leaving a lull in the conversation as everyone digested what Vasil was saying.

Most people who died hunting down Itrep for the computers were given great care in being returned to their families. Even so, I knew what happened to the poor soul who died mining for the infernal abyss of Big Data and the cloud that ruled over us. The All-Seeing Eyes. Not to mention the families that were made inconceivably rich by being the creators of our government. The Families of North America, as some called them. Not all the oligarchs were in North America, though, and most were inconspicuous with their power and wealth.

What always bothered me was the history books, even the ones not yet changed to an impossibly ridiculous degree to change the past, told of the great promise and advancements of humanity that suddenly and violently came to an end. We were promised spaceships and no work, and all we got was work and stagnation. Class mobility had ended as a way to redistribute the wealth of all humanity. Yet the richest never lost their wealth, status, or power.

The promise of the twenty-first century was dwindling away, and the hope for technology ushering in an era referred to as the Internet of Things soon became an era of equity and work. Work to feed our digital masters who mimic thought through Markovian Chain Derivatives. The promise of a world freed by technology became a world ruled by technology and a select few.

"If that deposit contains as much as you think, DDS would have paid for a break-even business here. Unfortunately for them, I got wind and made another offer, one they could not refuse just when this dig was about to pay off. Considering their other ventures, they always viewed this operation as a distraction anyway. All of which means I may actually make a profit on this little adventure. Only thing I like more than proving my theories right is making some money to go along with it. Without accruing money, how can I ensure it is invested correctly?"

"I still don't understand, Vasil. Why White Tunnels? Why here? Why now? What are you playing towards?" David pushed.

"Barely any surveillance here on this site, and the airport will soon be riddled with secret passageways that will circumvent surveillance as needed. It is the perfect place for my plans to begin unfolding."

"And you can't share those plans with all of us?"

"No." Vasil frowned and his tone was full of disappointment. "Not until I can fully trust all of you. In time, you will all be doing things much greater than you have ever dreamed of. If you wish to, that is. But I will say this: there is so much more to our work than meets the eye."

He looked down and fiddled with his wristphone and all our devices beeped almost in unison. They were back online. Whatever Vasil had in store for us, he was not joking around. He knew what he was doing and how not to get caught. Something inside me rose slightly, a beast that had finally been awakened. I suppressed it and forced it back into hibernation.

CONVERSATIONS

Nearly three full months went by after Vasil met with us in the cafeteria and began changing operations until the percentage of profit he wished to achieve was on track to be realized. After the twenty-person construction crew showed up, a trickling of new people began to arrive at White Tunnels about once a week. These people were not coming to work in the dig site but to build out infrastructure for expansion of the facility. It was all behind closed doors, or in this case behind heavy canvas. All we knew was whenever a plane landed and construction equipment and supplies would be removed from the cargo hold, only one person would ever exit the plane.

Vasil also began to instruct us in what was available on the network he had created over the years and laid out a vision of the future that everyone wanted to be a part of. We all seemed to agree there was wisdom in Vasil's plans. Even the ones who doubted early on began to understand what life might be like if we succeeded. This came with a noticeable difference when people began to have one-on-one conversations with Vasil. Whatever he was saying was causing the people he met with to all be inspired in some way.

After meeting with Vasil, each person seemed to be more comfortable with the treason that was already well under way. They would not speak to the full vision, but by the hints it was bigger than just the genetic science aspect. My fellow coworkers, who I had never seen smile and talk jovially while working, made it a habit to strike up conversations about the future and where they might fit in. They tip-toed around the specifics, but it quickly became practice for everyone to debate genetics, politics, technology, and the future. It appeared Vasil was able to keep the artificial intelligence, the AI, out of our computer system, which gave people courage to speak up without fear of arrest.

Any deniers of genetic science produced by the AIs, or the Absolutists, were subject to reeducation. It was not only the person committing the crime, but their entire families too. Punishment had to be swift and severe to keep everyone in line. Over time, it became a non-issue for the majority of the population. All except about four percent, which was almost entirely made up of what the AIs referred to as Abnormals.

Abnormals eventually banded together on small reservations and kept to themselves as much as possible but were forced to attend public schools that kept us mixed in with the rest of the population. Depending on aptitudes, some were not allowed to return to our families but put into jobs that forced us around the world. We were not allowed to date, marry, or bear children with anyone, something that was not enforced vigorously on reservations, but was strictly enforced outside of the reservations in the United States. Even mixed education was not firmly imposed in the United States, which allowed for many reservations to start Abnormal only schools that were state sanctioned but were officially mixed like all the rest. At least on paper.

It was not long into adulthood before I gave up any hope of finding a modicum of respect, even though my job placed me in the top quarter percentile of workers in the world. I did not earn any more than the next person, but I did not earn any less. I never got any recognition or rewards for my efforts. I was always slandered and degraded. Even if I outworked and outproduced everyone on a team or in a building, I was placed at the bottom of the merit pyramid companies used to grade their employees.

I was never fired or let go without substantial reason though, as my gifts were too valuable to not be taken advantage of. As an Abnormal, I had to rely on the government to provide me with my next role in society. Others, regular people, could choose to some extent their industry or sector of the economy to work in. There was little choice for me, and those like me. Abnormals were not allowed to have the same level of choices as the rest of the populous when it came to careers. Not because we were incapable, but because the All-Seeing Eyes propagandized us as the threat to civilization, to society, to the order, to the culture.

We were, in the eyes of the machines, responsible for the destruction and dismantling of the progress made by humans. Looking back at the twentieth century, I could understand how that might be construed as true. What was left out was how our people led to the creation of the society that existed on earth today. My ancestors were directly responsible for the creation of rockets, human capitalism, and universal healthcare. They pioneered centrally-powered democracies that led the world to finding a balance between the wants, needs, and desires of the people and the economy. The methods implemented by the AI supercomputers, what some had the gall to call Artificial Super Intelligences or ASIs, were nothing short of what Nazi Germany did prior to World War II. I did not see any intelligence in people who had honed the very instruments used to create a society without particular groups, nor could I see how the so-called ASIs really created such a society as I was an Abnormal, part of a particular group. These same people and machines eventually took the parts of history that we were not responsible for, or did not have a hand in creating, and rewrote it so that we were at fault.

What I knew about history was little, but I knew who we were. Abnormals were the modern Jews, the modern average white man, the modern capitalist, the modern Muslim, and even in some regards, the modern black man. We were accused of everything from racism and fascism to selfishness and impurity; all to be slapped with the latest problem that required someone to pay the price, regardless of how true the accusation was. It was incredible what humans might believe about others because they were told to believe it.

We were used as the scapegoats, while the AI slowly implemented a new form of what could be related to what my ancestors might have called Socialism at all levels of society. But it was more than just that. It was identitarian to the core. It was not just the latest version of Critical Race Theory. It was not just Applied Postmodernism and its constructive ideas after Postmodernists deconstructed everything to the individual letters. It was also not just White Supremacy and other identitarian right-wing factions. It was born of the festering hatred in all people regardless of their politics or beliefs.

It was a systematic takeover of pop culture and of a revolution that was already underway for decades. It was the theft of rights from the people to the hands of the technocrats and the AIs. All of it used to create a world where machines would be required to determine all the needs of the economy. A truly centralized economy, effectively destroying the value of money and need for the Capitalist Ideal; replacing it with what could be best described as a new form of technologically-driven oligarchical Socialism, out of the hands of the many and into the hands of the few. A system that was heartless and did not care for the ideas Marx had called for. That bastardized Socialism.

One might argue this was a bad thing, as Socialism up to that point in history had failed every time. The AI realized the core tenets of Socialism were actually sound, but always poorly executed and resulted in various forms of despotism. However, things were left out of the textbook. The war on the individual's freedoms to speak out and protect themselves from the state. The Social Justice Warriors, Boogaloo Boys, and other activists were used like sheep in wolves clothing to produce an army subservient to the AI. They were too busy following their ideologies to realize what was directing them, what was using them. They were merely pawns on an intricate chess board.

I was never one to say the ideas of old were bad; I tried not to judge those in the past by today's standards, but in retrospect, they were clearly fooled and used to usurp control of society from the individual and forced everyone to rely on central planners to provide for basic necessities and for a purpose. At the cost of alienating an extreme minority, the world was sold into near-slavery to computers that soon became a requirement for the world's economy to function. It built a system that would be near impossible to break and soon everyone gave up trying to fight the new beast and accepted what it offered. We worked for, we listened to, and we were governed by them, everything spawned from them. They were as gods to the average person. The supercomputers created by those greedy technocrats who wanted to make their temporary power more concrete.

Every aspect of life was controlled by the AI. What luxuries you had, what jobs you could fill, when the lights were turned off, how warm you could keep your living space, what diet you had, what entertainment was available, and clothing styles; all of it. All free time was scheduled. I was lucky enough to have a job with the freedom of off hours working with DDS. We all were lucky in that regard. If you directly benefited the AI, you received more in return. A codependence that would always favor the AI.

Even if everyone in the room hated my guts, I knew the AI had given me more than the people around me could ever get. The people knew that the AI provided them with everything they needed and more, and they had the freedom to spend time enjoying what little that they had by punishing me.

Society became bitter. If you were not already in with a particular group of people, it became difficult to hang around them. Cliques became more relevant than ever during school and even long after. People grew selfish, looking out for themselves. If it meant ostracizing others, then so be it. Humanity, as an idea, a concept, had finally become one of the scarcest resources on the planet. All because we put our faith in heartless lines of code to think for us, to decide for us, to lead us. Whether the machines ruled with perfection was irrelevant to the fact that what they decreed was law and above all others. The right-wing ideologues tried and failed to stand up to the AI when rights were being stripped; they were seen as too self-centered, too archaic in their beliefs. The left-wing ideologues failed too when segregation and genetic abominations were being developed in the light of day under the guise of the rights to one's body.

Liberalism and Conservatism fell, as people realized there was no defeating the shadow of the system that crept up to their doors; they were too late to speak out with any real will power. Libertarianism was a great concept but the political party was a joke to begin with, since it was riddled with hypocrisy and terrible planning from the start, but was now made illegal along with the rest of the old political ideologies and labels for any and every political or societal or economic concept that was decidedly not what the machines wished to be called.

No one could defeat the beast that was created by the ruling elites. Technocracy was not the right word any longer. The governmental system the AI used was named by them collectively, without human interference. They called their new system Absolutism. If you could not question the AI, then how could the AI be wrong? How could it be imperfect? It was absolute in power, in objectivism, in calculations.

The only thing left standing in their way of true absolute control was the oligarchs who included themselves in the definition of Absolutism. The oligarchs possessed kill switches that gave those select individuals an amount of say in the governmental matters. The AIs did not seem to mind, as this helped subjugate the people who believed the oligarchs were still in control. Many still did not trust the AI, as it was far more intelligent than the humans with kill switches. If there was anything people still had faith in, it was the oligarchs not leading them astray, even if they seemed treacherous at times.

In this day and age, no one remembered or dared mention the truth outside of hushed whispers in the middle of deserts or maybe the tundra. The Great Reset was the start of it all, not directly of course, but it laid the framework of what came next. The removal of possessions and the transference of currency to an entirely digital system. The surveillance state that was built by China. The insanity of the professors and their Postmodernist ideas. The failures of the average person to inform themselves with accurate information and vote for the right elected officials.

That is how it always began in the history books for every country and civilization prior to the 18th century. Control the education and economy, strike fear into your subjects, and they are yours to do with as you please. That is precisely what happened starting in the 20th century and truly began to grow into its own in the beginning of the 21st century.

However, this new wave of control was not country by country, but an international movement without borders. One that the bankers laid the framework for, one the wealthy saw potential in, and one where the power hungry sought to abuse. With the speed of information transfer, it was easier than ever to spread Big Lies and other disinformation.

We all knew we were being lied to, but we had lives that were better than our parents, our grandparents, our ancestors. At least on paper, we had better technology, more access to cleaner water, medical supplies and treatments, food, jobs, travel. It was truly a paradise as long as you lived by the rules of society and accepted the fear of not being in the majority, regardless of who you were; always wondering if you would be the next to be scapegoated for some reason or another. Or like me, born into a genetic code that made you an outcast no matter your talents. The fact of the matter was simple: if you were not a Zero, the ideal, you were pondering how much longer you would have what little you could muster in the way of friends.

All these thoughts swirled in my head as I made my way to Vasil's round lunch table for my first meeting with him. Vasil evidently did not agree with what the Absolutists were doing. The division of the people by any means necessary, which was what all previous systems were based on in some way or another. It did not matter the system: Capitalist, Republic, Democracy, Socialist, Fascist; they all harbored some way of separating people and pitting them against one another while those with the power in the system never lost.

The only discourse that still existed was the matter of genetics and the Abnormals. It was able to be debated, albeit in a cancel culture sort of way, because the AI allowed it. Why they would allow such lines of thought in the population was beyond me, but I was sure it had something to do with keeping a common enemy in front of everyone. After all, since the last war, only six AI supercomputers and their governments existed. The remnants of the Last Caliphate and the African Revolutionary Army were eradicated and with them, the last stand for a free, decentralized future.

The AIs oversaw all of the eleven billion people on earth. And everyone was subject to their decisions. There were few exceptions to this rule, one being the wealthiest of humanity, the oligarchical elites, the less than one percent. Vasil was one of the lesser-known and successful wealthy elites. Another exception was the military commanders, although they did little more than maintain the human element of discipline and order in the military. The last major group were the programmers of the AI themselves. They were kept around in lives of luxury for debugging and maintenance purposes. The AIs could do most of that work on their own, but thanks to special software access levels, the programmers ensured humans had a say in the upgrades through various kill switches and override capabilities.

Collectively, these groups made up the wealthy managerial elites, or as many simply referred to them, the oligarchs. The meaning of oligarchy in the last twenty years alone had grown from a negative connotation to being a buzzword that was touted as the glorious future of our species. My generation was the first to be indoctrinated with such rhetoric. "Our Glorious Protectors" was a relatively new phrase, but one that was adopted quickly throughout all educational programs from the age of five to college courses. I did not buy into the hype, and as a result, I was relegated to jobs in secluded locations. Like Australia's Outback or Antarctica. Places unsavory to most, as comfort and cliques were keys to a happy life, assuming no one stabbed you in the back.

I stepped into Vasil's office space. Before me was a large round desk and Vasil sitting behind it. He smiled and motioned to the chair before me. On the desk sat a tray of steak, baked beans, vodka, pudding, and cornbread. I sat down and Vasil began to fill me in on his plan for the very first time.

VASIL'S PLAN

Almost half an hour went by as we were just getting to know each other over mouthfuls of the best tasting steak and baked beans I have ever eaten. Once we were comfortable with each other, we were able to joke a little and grew to understand the perspective of the other. I recognized that he clearly did not see me as an Abnormal, but as a person. Once we had finished off the food, I sat sipping on the vodka he graciously poured for me as we discussed my resume and where I saw myself in the future.

"So where do you see yourself in the next five years, Tory?" Vasil asked before downing a hearty swath of his vodka and replenishing it from a bottle.

"Probably doing the same thing I am today, looking for Itrep."

"Same role?"

"No, maybe. I never really pursued one clear path for a career, being who I am." I waved my hands to indicate my appearance. He nodded and did not break eye contact with me for several seconds as he appraised my face. His gaze garnered some hidden authority and brilliance that was difficult to place, but unmistakably present.

"I think you are a leader, Tory."

"A leader?" I asked, my face immediately blushing. I hoped he would think it was the alcohol and not my embarrassment.

"Yes. You are smart and know your way around a dig site. That much is clear. I think you possess the ability to own your mistakes and share your successes. If you had the chance to take confidence in your abilities, you would be a manager or supervisor in the next year. Hell, maybe even an overseer." The last was added almost under his breath but audible enough for me to hear. It seemed to me that it was a thought he was still mulling over.

I could not believe what he was saying, to me and to himself. I did not want to believe it. I had never been offered any role as a leader in any capacity, nor had I ever been told in a year I would be promoted. I could not think of an Abnormal of a higher station than I was. I doubted many had achieved what I had, let alone more. It was always a lateral move on paper, to keep the merit of our accomplishments subdued. "I don't real—"

Vasil raised his hands and cut me off. "Now I don't want to push you in a direction you don't wish to go. But I believe you would be able to help make this place run efficiently and effectively. Not tomorrow, but in a few months, I want to begin giving you more advanced responsibilities. I'll let you decide at that time if you want to take them. There will be offers, not requirements. I don't want to make you uncomfortable. The last thing I need is a nervous wreck operating the equipment in the mine."

"I guess I'll have time to think about it then." I smiled and tried to force the blush from my face before continuing. "I do have a question about your speech when you first arrived."

"Ask away, my dear Tory. I am a relatively open book." I noted the qualifier for later thought.

"You said a lot of things the AI would not take kindly to. What do you want to achieve by all of this? I can't believe you only want to prove people like me are capable of more than we are credited for. Especially considering your vision for the future. It sounds like your plan is a little more than broad strokes on canvas."

"Oh, you are spot on accurate, Tory. I read in your profile you are a good judge of character and have an excellent sense about you. Suppressed, but evident in your vital signs and facial expressions when under surveillance." The shock on my face lasted long enough for him to laugh, take a drink, and wipe his lips off before continuing. "They are supercomputers. They do analysis and take more metrics than you can possibly imagine. They give us private space, but also know exactly what we do in that time through advanced algorithms. Especially when they have a microphone and camera like in a wristphone and even more so when the device is on. They can even tell when you are having intercourse! They know when you are thinking about it with your wristphone on. It has in your file the probability of who you fancy based on that data alone. Do you want me to tell you who is in the file?"

"Oh n-no. Please don't do th-that," I stammered. He was beginning to scare me with the depth of knowledge he may have on my file. It was unspoken and really unknown to what extent the AI knew our deepest, darkest and unspoken secrets. Vasil was providing evidence that they knew more than I had suspected.

"It's all right, Tory. Your secrets are safe with me. Just as your data is safe with you. If you haven't noticed, you alone have root access to your wristphone. I do not. You can disable my access to most all the private information it can collect. You can disable the collection of that information all together. If you take a bigger role in my organization, some of that data collection will be required, though."

I did notice the options and access but did not think to act on it without getting a feel for my new boss. It may have been a test. This all may still be a test of loyalty to the AI. I could not be sure, and so I left nothing to chance.

Vasil must have seen the deliberation in my face because his expression changed to one of curiosity. "My plans are not just to prove Abnormals are nothing more than oppressed and neglected members of society deserving of equal status. I intend to remove the Absolutist System, The Families, and the AIs that control it. I intend to overthrow the oligarchs with their damned kill switches. There is nothing more that I want than a free and equal society where the people can choose and have mobility to move up and down in the society. Celebrity to homeless and washed up, failed businessperson to richest in the world, a person with a view different from the majority to the majority view without violence or an AI to make the decision for society, with the consent and approval of the people. That's the idea I am working towards."

"A capitalist society?"

"No, something better. Not driven primarily by the greed we all harbor, but by the good of society. My success is your success, and our success is society's success. I want people to be absolutely free to choose with a safety net that the government maintains. I do not want taxes or regulations, but I also don't want corporations running away with their ambitions of taking over. I don't want money in government; I want a separation of economy and state. Capitalism is easy to corrupt given that level of freedom and given the current level of state control. I want to use the quantum technology to render currencies obsolete once and for all, digital and otherwise, and to transition us from an economy driven by wealth and inherited status to one driven by input into society.

"It's true the Absolutists did away with a lot of uses for currencies when it comes to the individual, but the big players, the oligarchs, still use digital forms of currency when doing business with one another. I want to end that. I desire an economic meritocracy overseen by a federation of republics of the world. Something strong enough to stay together as humanity expands to the stars."

"You think you can achieve all of that?"

"I know I can't, Tory. But I know the people who can."

I was stunned into silence by this. It took over a minute for me to think while he sat watching me, smiling. I was trying to put the pieces together and he was amused by my efforts. "You are from a wealthy family in the oligarchy, right?"

"One of the few old families that survived the Eastern Europe and Russian takeover by the western oligarchs."

"So, you have connections to people who know about the technologies that exist and are being implemented."

"Yes, I do."

"And I take it others feel the same way as you?"

"Oh my, yes."

"And they have more influence than you?"

"I am but a pawn, Tory. Keep going. You are doing so well."

"There is a confederation of sorts of wealthy oligarchs who want to destroy the Absolutist System and implement a Republic running on meritocracy that gives everyone equal chance. All the while using technology to send people into space to colonize the solar system and the galaxy. It would make sense to send those who were exceedingly smart or less intelligent to live in colonies where they would be equal and away from possible discrimination from others. Does that sound about right?" After speaking with him and the clues others keyed me in on, I had already formulated most of the scenario prior to sitting down with him.

"See? I told you if you just showed more confidence, you are capable of more than you give yourself credit for. I like where your thoughts are headed, Tory. Not exactly my thoughts, but likely how it will shake out. And a council is leading these efforts, not sure if confederation is the right word, but we can go with that. Not everyone is wealthy, but all are in positions of influence. What else do you have for me?"

"I don't know. I don't know if I believe your motives. And I have no idea on this *council* and if they share the same ideas and motives that you do."

"That's all fair, my dear. I can tell you my motives are blunt and obvious. I want to bring equality back into this world and remove the discrimination that exists currently, the equity at the cost of society. The council agrees with those ideas. They also agree groups of people who don't have the same values should be able to ship themselves onto another planet to pursue their own society and goals. If they choose."

"And I circle back to the questions on my mind. Why me? Why here? Why now?"

"The here is obvious. Remote and lack of control by the supercomputers. All your old wristphones are connected to a series of jacks that input false data to make the AI think your new wristphones are tracking you in their system. I've got some heavy programmer firepower backing me and the Council. We are building our own supercomputer and AI that will work to counter the Absolutist AIs. Its mission is to protect us, humanity, from software. This is the perfect place to build such a computer. We have direct access to Itrep, plenty of free cooling, and enough bandwidth to fight back when it goes online and connects to the main system.

"You ask 'why now', but I would retort with 'why wait?' The longer we wait, the more likely it is for the AI to exert more control and remove more of our abilities to fight back. And not just us, but the oligarchs as well. They won't be able to stop the AI forever. And as for you. I picked you because of the talents you have already displayed with Itrep mining, but your personality is strong and your mind is sharp. Your wits and intuition of others and their motives are uncanny when applied. I believe you to be a leader, someone who over time will join me in leading our segment of the fight against the Absolutists."

My head was beginning to hurt after taking in all the information that he was giving. I had my doubts, and all my bit-back responses to his encouragement were starting to get to me. However, what he said gave me hope that the world had not yet been lost completely to the machines. Not as completely lost as I had thought. I could get in line with his vision, but I was not sure if he was telling the truth. He picked me and told me enough to have everyone tried and imprisoned in isolation chambers for the rest of their lives if I were to turn him in. He must know that I would not. That I would want to help him.

I sat motionless with my eyes glazed over as I pondered his words. He was distracted by something on his wristphone so I had plenty of time to deliberate. I did not have to commit to anything, but I was also committing to helping his cause anyway, even by simply knowing his plans and not speaking out. If caught, I would certainly be subject to the same punishment if I acted complicit in his actions.

I shook my head, trying to clear it. I had never been tasked with making a decision so dangerous or so deep before. Everything was thought out for me. My head hurt from the increase in usage. I was starting to lose my facial façade that I maintained at all times.

"My dear Tory?"

My eyes unglazed and I focused on Vasil's lips and concentrated on the conversation. I would not lose control over this. "Yes?" My voice was almost a squeak as high as a mouse.

"I have another appointment I need to get to. I want you to think about everything, all right? Take your time. Don't stress yourself out. I understand a lot of folks have never made such decisions. We live in a day and age where software handles most all of it. And our time is taken up with work, and our free time is taken up in the little possessions we might have. I'll set up bi-weekly meetings with you to keep in touch. I want to track your progress and crack your shell so you can shine like you deserve!"

STEPPING FORWARD

Another three months came and went as fast as my time in Australia had come and gone. I had never in my life had so much to think about, and yet have time fly by so incredibly fast. My shoulders felt unburdened. I felt happier. The food was nicer. We had a wider selection to choose from. We had a larger library of podcasts, audiobooks, and articles to read. Differing opinions. Sources of knowledge long missing in the Absolutists' markets and schools.

Vasil had access to a high-level network that contained the wealth of knowledge the Absolutists kept out of the public's eye. He used his stake in this network to splice the data for everyone to use. No one had any idea how he was able to do it without getting caught using more data than is usual. The closest anyone came to an answer was a curious method using blockchain technology and a decentralized peer-to-peer network that pretended to be different users but was in reality the same user.

All of which was under Vasil's Virtual Private Network service from one of the few companies he owned and controlled. All the data would appear to be coming from the VPN, and with the blockchain technology that was theoretical at best, we would all appear as unique users under the same umbrella of the VPN, which would act as a singular user.

The reality, as we came to find out, was much less sophisticated. We had nailed the VPN correctly, but Vasil's VPN Plus offered free subscriptions with the service they sold, and with a bit of spreadsheet shenanigans, we all appeared to the network to have access to services the public did not have access to. When Vasil purchased the site from DDS, he bought everyone a subscription to his VPN with the company's bank account. This also allowed him to drive up the stock in his VPN company while essentially laundering money back out of the dig site into the Absolutist world. What I had yet to figure out was for what reason did he *need* to launder the money? The only reasonable answer was that Vasil needed the money for other projects outside of White Tunnels, but what those projects might be were yet another mystery.

These were the questions everyone was discussing as we worked diligently to bring Itrep out of the cold earth. While Itrep was the primary source for digging, we often came across fossils and other long buried treasures from millions of years previous. These we could sell to science institutions or museums to help fund the efforts. We were all working harder than we could remember. We were so happy that our mood bolstered our efforts. We had never been treated better by a company, and the results on our output were distinct and clear. Everyone was in high spirits, and so was the bottom line. The change in morale was so dramatic that Vasil held a feast to celebrate, which only lifted spirits further.

While we always worked hard to succeed at our tasks, we were now working harder for incentives that directly benefited us. If we wanted to have higher quality food, we would have to outperform our previous numbers. If we wanted to get time off, we had to work as a team to beat other team's numbers for the extra free time. We were given Sundays off entirely, unlike the half days we had to work under DDS, with the expectation we would mingle and develop relationships and companionship. Vasil claimed team chemistry and company chemistry would improve our results, and so far it seemed to be working.

I had spent most of the free time I was allocated indulging in reading about the history of the world with a feeling of eagerness I had never had before. The missing bits of history we never learned. The nations that existed outside of the twenty I learned as a child. It appeared that many of the regions within the existing countries were considered countries before the Absolutists took over. The slivers of history during the rise of the Absolutists. The families that built the first neural nets, Markovian Chain Derivatives that were later expanded, the first quantum computers, then the ones with ever-increasing nines of accuracy, after those came the various discoveries thought to be the most reliable ways to produce energy, then the discovery of Itrep and how it made nuclear energy so much more powerful, and still nothing on the improvements in technologies outside of the ones that enhanced the Absolutist control over the people.

I found it hard to believe at first, there had to be technological breakthroughs that I had missed. To my dismay, the wealth of knowledge Vasil gave us access to mentioned little to no changes or innovations outside of energy and mining. It was as if all the progress in all other areas stopped. Even on the medical side, there were no real breakthroughs; only small improvements to the stagnate technology.

It was a few days after the start of the new month that I was asked to meet with Vasil for breakfast the next morning. This news came via the wristphone video communications from my supervisor. DDS rarely used wristphone technology outside of mapping their enormous buildings; but Vasil embraced the technology with open arms. I quickly performed my morning ablutions and headed out my door with a banana in my hand.

When I arrived at Vasil's office, I noticed there was a change in decor. He had several paintings fixed to the walls and a pedestal with a bust of himself on it. I chuckled slightly at the lack of humility Vasil must have had to not only commission the bust, but the sheer nerve to put it in his new office.

"One of the pictures amusing, Tory?" Vasil inquired as I walked in. He was finishing his breakfast at his desk and glanced up from a laptop screen off to his right.

I looked closer at the paintings for something I could use to divert from the truth. Telling your boss you find their narcissism amusing is a sure way to get in trouble. Especially when I was not yet sure how far it could be taken with him. I picked the one directly above the bust itself. "The coloring is a bit off, isn't it?"

"That is a Stewie work. Over two decades old now. He died several years ago. He had a knack for mixing strokes of off colors into his paintings. If the sky is supposed to be blue, he would add strokes of green or red to make it stand out more. Stewie was always doing things like that. Only real sane work was a collection of poems about a man who is waiting to die. Real dark piece of work, if you ask me, my dear."

"That explains why the artwork is, uh, interesting." I forced a thoughtful tone to my voice to convince him I understood.

"I have a physical copy of the book somewhere if you want it." Vasil eyed me as I pretended to appraise the art on the wall.

"I am good. I'm sure there is a digital copy somewhere anyway. I jus—this just took me by surprise, I guess."

Vasil seemed satisfied enough as he looked back down at his laptop screen. His tone returned to business as usual. "Well, please have a seat. We need to discuss if you want the new job I have lined up for you."

"What is it?" I asked hesitantly. I had made my decision to accept whatever he offered me, but I wanted to play my excitement off so I would not seem overly eager. It was bad form in my opinion to appear too ambitious, even if it would just be a higher supervisor position than the one I currently occupied.

"Overseer of White Tunnels."

I erupted in disbelief. I sat up with shock, gasped, blushed, knocked the chair over, and ran my hands through my hair all in the matter of two or three seconds. I was not expecting such a large responsibility. I immediately began to question my abilities and the confidence I had built up over the last three months was decaying rapidly. In less than a minute, I went from the happiest I had been in memory to how I felt my first night in White Tunnels.

Vasil noticed I was still speechless and poured me some of his vodka in a fresh glass. As he handed it to me, he spoke in his most soothing voice. "Take a minute to settle down, Tory. I know it may come as a shock, but the workload is not much more than what you are already doing as a supervisor on the front lines. Maybe a bit more paperwork and less exercise, but the complexity is nothing you can't handle. I've been doing it all myself in addition to the rest of my work."

I gulped from the glass and coughed as the tingling sensation ran through my mouth and throat. "This is strong vodka."

"The strongest." Vasil grinned. "I may or may not be a heavy alcoholic. It helps me stay focused, as strange as that sounds. Must be my Slavic heritage." He winked and then snorted at the last. I could not help but join in his mischievous snorts.

"Why do you want me to run everything? Overlooking whether I am capable, wouldn't A—"

"I want you to run the White Tunnels Itrep operations for me. You have knowledge of all the different job roles as you have demonstrated across the world, and you are clearly a hardworking and organized individual who will not stop until everything is taken care of for the day. You are meticulous and have good instincts when it comes to the character of everyone here. That is the best I could hope for in an overseer. Tory, don't pull on your hair like that."

"What?" I was still so stressed over the announcement that I did not notice my left hand was still pulling at my hair. It was a nervous tick I had when I was overwhelmed with a decision that had to be made, not that I ever had the chance to make many since I was a teen. The last time I pulled on my hair like this was over five years ago. It was when I was close to my breaking point and deciding if I should openly defy the orders given to me by DDS. I sat back down and forced both of my hands into my lap. "Sorry."

"Don't apologize to me, my dear, apologize to your scalp. I take it you won't be taking the position?"

"I-I wi-will." I cleared my throat to help prepare my vocal chords and body so I would not stammer as much and sounded more confident. "I will."

"Ah, that's good. I knew it would be a bit much for you to drop it like I did, but to be honest, I could not think up a better way without giving you cold feet."

"I was going to accept whatever you were giving me anyway."

"I hope that is true going forward, my dear. I have high hopes for you. Don't forget my golden rule. Without stepping forward, you will never know how far you can go."

"I won't." No one really understood why Vasil claimed rules that were affirmations, but we took it in stride. The words were far too important to get hung up on the particulars.

"Oh, and Tory, my dear Tory?"

"Yes?"

"Please don't worry, I will never put you in a spot here in White Tunnels that I do not have full faith in your abilities to succeed in."

"What if I leave White Tunnels?"

"Then you will either have outgrown our little operation or we have been caught by the Absolutists."

I paused at his words as I contemplated them. "How likely is it that we will be caught?"

"Here in White Tunnels? Very, very unlikely, my dear."

"So, we can't leave then? Are we all stuck here?"

"No." Vasil drew the word out and almost into silence before he continued. He must have been considering what he was about to tell me. "Not in the nearest of near futures. But soon I am sure you will step foot on another continent."

"I'm not sure what you mean." My eyebrows drew close

together as I focused on his facial features for a hint, anything, to give a clue as to what he was not saying.

"You are a bright young lass, my dear Tory, but you must remember that I am not a slouch. I know how to hide my intentions until the time is right. I know how to keep my features and form from speaking my inner thoughts. You should know that by now." He was not upset or chastising me, but there was disappointment in his tone. Something that told me he thought he had earned my trust.

"I'm sorry. Old habits die hard, I suppose."

"Don't be sorry, you have a right to do as you please. Just know I am not an easy read." He beamed at me as he motioned for me to take my leave.

HISHLA LAKE

"**W**hat was that?" I concealed the concern as my hoarse voice resounded off the hallway walls. I had opened the door to the office after a loud scuffle could be heard from somewhere nearby, towards the front of the building. We were up for hours finalizing plans on the way to the compound with the latest intelligence from the South American Resistance. Our expedition was too vital and we had spent too much time to get caught. Three years of hard work passed since I accepted Vasil's offer in White Tunnels, and with them I received appointment as a High Regent for all of the projects going on in South America. All the dedicated years I worked with Vasil had led us to this raid, to retrieve the data on the computer before me.

"I don't know," the hallway guard, Rusty, replied. He was tall, lean, and muscular, but I had never seen him in action, so I was skeptical of his abilities should anything sinister pan out. I had not yet mastered the ability to trust others who I did not know well enough with my life.

"Well, go check it out!" I exclaimed. "I want to know what is going on out in the lobby."

As I finished speaking, the double doors at the end of the hallway sprung open and two more guards carried a third with blood covering her arm through the threshold. As the doors shut, I recalled that we had seven guards stationed in the lobby. Which meant four were still out there.

"She is not safe Rusty; Bongo and the others have run away to cause a distraction, but we should expect reinforcements to come after us any minute. We need to leave now or we will put everyone at risk," David, who was on the uninjured side of the woman, barked with the sharp aptitude of a soldier who was in charge of the situation. He was, of course, my personal security officer who insisted on coming with us. I knew him well and he was disillusioned by the system, just as everyone else with me was. It still took time, even months after his reappearance in my life, to fully trust him, so much so as to name him my personal bodyguard. He was once one of the cruelest tormentors in my high school days, and now he was helping me and Vasil against the Absolutist AI.

"Agreed." Rusty stepped past me as I stood in the doorway, frozen by the sight of blood. Two strides later, he reached a painting of Hishla Lake the day it opened. He unceremoniously tossed the painting to the floor, and in doing so, he revealed the emergency security panel that our plan depended on existing. The blueprints were from the contractor who installed the new security measures not more than three days prior to our original infiltration date. We took a risk on the information and it appeared to have paid off. Rusty began to tap vigorously on the panel's touch pad as first the alarms went off and then the lobby doors bolted shut. "They know where we are headed now, but they don't know we know about the back exit."

We agreed that there would be no easy way on the streets to escape without heavy losses, so we decided to use the contractor's information to our advantage. I let my eyelids close over my eyes long enough for a brief prayer that the double doors were indeed able to withstand multiple C4 explosions. They might need to buy us the necessary time we needed to get out of the reach of the local and state authorities.

"This way." Rusty beckoned us to follow him as he turned left to walk to the back of the hallway. To my surprise, there was a secret door that was not visible before. I made a mental note to ask the others if they had heard or seen it appear. The technology would be incredible if it was revealed without any sensory indicators.

Rusty was the first through the door, and after turning on the lights in the passage and checking for enemy combatants, he stepped aside while I and the three others stepped through. After we passed through, Rusty moved to quickly shut the door and disable the panel next to it, overriding the electromagnetic lock and sealing the entrance. "This had better work. We won't be able to go back, Tory."

"I trust the contractor, Rusty." I did not, but David did, and he earned enough of my trust at this point to take a chance. So far, it was going better than my anxiety believed possible. Perhaps David and the contractor did have the rapport they claimed.

"This is not the time to doubt," David interjected. "We must continue forward or all our efforts to secure this data will be for naught. It is vital intel."

The woman spat some blood from her mouth before trying to stand upright. She failed and leaned heavily on David. Adam, the other guard, had stopped the bleeding from the wound just below her left breast with his hand. It looked promiscuous at first glance, but the blood from her chest was nothing more than sickening to my eyes the longer I watched. I did not know her name as she was a late assignment to our mission, but the others vouched for her and so I had to trust she could handle herself.

"I believe we stopped the external bleeding Nadine, but I think the blade punctured your lung. We need to get you to a doctor before it gets worse." Adam was a friend of David's from the war and happened to be the field medic from the same battalion. I was now glad I let David talk me into pressuring Vasil to hire him to go along with us on the mission. His medical expertise was coming in handy since neither David nor I had any formal training outside the field training David taught all newcomers.

"Nadine, it will be fine. Just hang in there," David said, as soothingly as a military officer could. Behind his robotic character, he was truly a compassionate soul. That was why I liked him.

"Rusty! Lead the way!" Adam called ahead. Rusty had turned his flashlight on and started to walk down the stairs and through the corridor.

"It's all clear down here if you ignore the rats. Is Nadine all right?"

"Needs to get to a hospital right away but she is fine."

I stomached my retort to Adam. Now was not the time to speak the truth. It was clear to my limited experience and Adam's words that if Nadine knew the danger she was in with a blood-filling lung, she may go into shock, complicating our mission. I disliked withholding the truth, but this was a case where it was necessary for her life, and ours.

"Let's go then!" I ushered everyone forward.

We followed Rusty down the stairs and forward into the dark and damp passage. It was built well, and relatively new compared to the part of Hishla Lake Campus we were on, but the lake water was flowing through nearly every pipe and tunnel under the campus. It took a lot of water to cool the nuclear reactor and server equipment. So much water that an artificial lake was built to sustain the necessary supply to maintain the data center. It was the last of the cold fusion reactors built in South America due to the extreme regulations placed on nuclear power after the last disaster, which wiped out Cleveland, Ohio and wreaked havoc on Lake Erie's coast.

Nuclear fission was easier to control and was useful in replenishing the power of the Itrep power systems, so companies continued building the fission plants out. Fusion was decreed by the AI to be using irresponsible technology that would lead to the destruction of mankind if we continued to use it. That was all it took to change the energy industry back to the older technologies with a renewed focus on Itrep as a power source, with nuclear fission providing the much-needed radioactive materials to maintain the reaction. I was not familiar with the science itself, but it had to do with quantum mechanics and how Itrep and radiation reacted.

After several minutes of following the crude map the contractor was able to provide us to avoid a wrong turn into any of the service tunnels, we arrived at an exit that we hoped would take us up into a back alley where we could signal for extraction. While Rusty and David went up ahead to open the door, I helped Adam assist Nadine up the stairs. Her black shoulder length windswept hair fell into my face as I grabbed her uninjured side. "What of the rest of the team? Where are they?" I asked, my voice as rough as it was, was still high-pitched and feminine enough to make me feel like a rat on the floor squeaking at the intruders in their domain. I knew deep down this was not where I belonged. Not on the front lines, not behind enemy lines.

"They caused a distraction while we hid shortly after Nadine was shot. I don't think anyone knew we were hiding, but they certainly knew Nadine was still there."

"Where are we meeting them to bring them back to base?"

Adam frowned. "I don't thin—"

"Hurry up, we are signaling Marley now." David's whispered bark was clear and crisp enough to make my hair stand on end. His way of carrying his voice was unworldly. It was a gift his ventriloquist father passed on to him. I remembered vaguely how he used it to confuse me about who was insulting me back in school.

We exited and stepped up to ground level. The exit came out to an alley next to the concrete wall that kept the compound separated from the cluster of buildings outside. We made our way behind a dumpster, and I watched as David looked down at his wristphone before peering around the edge of the dumpster. Adam checked his rifle ammo, and Rusty grabbed a grenade from within his coat. "Should we blow up the exit when Marley gets here?"

"No. They don't know how far we are, if they know we escaped. Keep that grenade handy though. We may need to use it as a distraction later." David's whisper made Rusty's grin falter.

"You are no fun, Davey boy."

"David." The venom of his commanding voice made Rusty's back straighten. I felt my back straighten too.

"Yes, sir." Rusty's tone made it clear he was disheartened. He enjoyed demolition and, unfortunately, his knowledge and practical abilities with tech often put in him in missions where demolition was not necessary. He wanted to join us because David sold him on a strong chance he would get to use his homemade grenades.

"David."

"Yes, Tory?" David replied as he looked at his wristphone again. "Where is Marley?"

"What of the others? There were eight of us in total, right?"

"They will get extracted when it is safe to do so, Tory. Right now you have the data drive and are therefore the mission."

"No man left behind?" I prompted, confused after his lectures on how we should not abandon one another.

"They volunteered themselves, Tory. They did it so we could succeed. Look, there he is."

I understood it was not up to me. Even if I was in charge of the mission, the success of our mission was worth sacrifices. As David pointed out, they volunteered and would be extracted later once the campus was safe to infiltrate again, assuming they made it out. The thought consoled my conscience enough to keep going. I helped Nadine to her feet and we walked down the alley which rested between the campus wall and the citizen worker section that was asleep. I looked up at the sky. It was almost dawn. We would need to hurry to get out of the area before daylight hit.

"Let's go already!" Marley had rolled down the front right

window and called to us. "They know you are coming this way. Had to go around a blockade."

"Damn, I thought we would have more time," David said to himself as he hopped in the front of the vehicle.

"This everyone?" Marley asked, bewildered.

"Yes." David's sharp reply gave no room for questions. I was the last in the vehicle. As I shut the door, the wheels screeched as Marley drifted the car 180 degrees.

"Off we go then!" The excitement in his voice was not mirrored by our faces. We were down four men and time was running out.

The vehicle was an older suburban type, painted pitch black with tinted windows. It was unregistered and was one of the few manned vehicles that would be on the streets this early. Hishla campus was a high-end government and corporate facility so everyone could afford the safer self-driving vehicles. The roads were designed for those vehicles. Unlike the time I spent in Australia, Hishla was paved from beginning to end, and there were no surprise rocks or bumps on the roads.

To everyone's surprise, we made it out of the citizen quarter and out onto the highway without issue. We were speeding away even as the sirens began to blare behind us, putting the entire campus on alert. Marley pressed further down on the pedal and the vehicle lurched forward as we increased in speed, far past the speed limit and what I was comfortable with. I had a brief thought about Franklin and pushed it aside. We would not need to worry about authorities stopping us with Hishla going into lockdown.

ANGEL AND THE COUNCIL

After five minutes and passing by no one on the highway, Marley slowed down to the posted speed limit. "Do you think we need to switch over to the car?" Marley asked David.

"I don't see anyone on our scanners," Rusty said as he monitored his wristphone, which was tapped into our towered network and monitoring for pursuers.

"No. Leave them both," David ordered. "It is best we keep putting distance between us and Hishla. They don't know we used this vehicle to escape, right?"

"Right," Marley said with a grin. Nothing seemed to be able to break his mood.

Nadine, who was in audible pain and beginning to pale, let another moan out and spoke for the first time since the corridor. "I hope this was all worth the hassle. What did we get anyway?"

I looked down at my wristphone. There was a secret compartment on the side which held the drive. "We got what we came for and a bit more."

"And what is it that we were after in the first place?"

"There were blueprints for the revamped Hishla reactor, possibly enough intel for us to destroy it and bring down the data center."

"That's great!" Nadine exclaimed and chuckled some blood onto the car's seat. "And what else?"

"Plans for their next big offensive. We will know their troop numbers and where they are heading."

David turned to look at me. "Just the Hishla reactor and data center? We didn't get the Itrep reactor intel?"

"I—think so. I downloaded everything but I didn't have time to look for that. I would have to view all the files before definitely saying what else we got."

"Fair enough. Marley. How close are we to the nearest hospital? Nadine is coughing blood."

Marley looked in the backseat through the rearview mirror. "It would be safer and closer to return to base. Is she bleeding internally?"

"Maybe. We need to get her to a doctor ASAP either way," Adam snapped back, giving a momentary glare to Marley.

"All right, big guy, calm your tits down."

"My tits are fine; you don't need to get your panties in a knot, thank you," Nadine spoke. Her voice had grown fainter and she was not looking good, but she still had her wits about her. Enough to make jokes. Adam and David both chuckled and watched the road as Marley steered off the highway and down country roads.

We arrived at the base shortly after Nadine lost consciousness. I was worried for her, but I had faith in Adam and the medics. As

Adam, Marley, and Rusty carried Nadine to the medical truck, David and I strode to the command vehicle. As we approached the truck, we saw through the back windows the holograms indicating we were late to the meeting. We opened the doors and climbed inside to find Angel sitting in front of the holocamera. She stopped speaking and turned to watch us as we entered and sat next to her.

She was small in stature, but her air of command was not to be questioned. Even David submitted to her leadership without issue, unless she was lacking in information. Her dark brown skin and brown eyes complimented her curly black hair exceptionally well. It was something about the way it seemed to shine in the light.

"I was just informing the Council that we were expecting you any moment."

"Thanks, Angel." I bowed my head in acknowledgement. "Members of the Council."

"Members of the Council." David bowed his head curtly as well. His stiff movement was of military precision and not of defiance; although he looked as though he would disagree with every word they would speak. He often disagreed on military espionage matters and it was unbecoming to him. He had proven brilliant in the espionage we had conducted in South America. However, David seemed to prefer the strategy of outright warfare.

"David and Tory, we thank you for joining us. I trust your delays were not eventful?"

"We have one injured with us, and four stuck in Hishla Lake. They distracted the authorities to buy us the time needed to successfully escape. They volunteered for the task and understood we would not come back to extract them until it is safe. Whenever that might be." David's reply rang through the vehicle.

"And why did the authorities find you? Were you not able to bypass the security to allow for the time allocated by the plan?"

"Tory." David looked over to me to explain.

"It was my call. I decided to stay past our appointed time." I began to blush slightly as I was speaking to the Council directly, something I had only done twice previously. The council was split between various different groups that I was not entirely privy to, but they were all still important figures in our organization. There was also the fact of admitting I had put everyone in danger, something that only just now hit me in its entirety. What if I had been wrong or we had been caught? "I saw some files that I could not ignore and had to copy over."

"Did you find what we were looking for?"

"I have yet to review all the files. Assuming I did not miss anything, I believe the designs for the new Itrep reactor will be among them."

"But you cannot confirm now." The demand made me bite my lip as nervousness slowly crept into my body.

"And what did you see that was so important to jeopardize your fellow comrades?" While the voice crackled from the hologram device, I could feel both David's and Angel's eyes digging into me from both sides. I swallowed hard and stared at the camera and holograms before me.

"I found blueprints for a new tank and a plethora of data on their troop numbers and locations for the South American continent. Argentina and the surrounding region in particular."

The stunned silence stilled my anxiety. The silence was proving my actions were justified and could be extremely important moving forward in our South American plans. I turned to see Angel deep in thought, no longer looking at me but at her hands. "I also saw that they know the location of one of your freedom fighter bases. I don't know exactly which one, but it is in Chile."

"Zack and Jesus," she whispered before looking up at the Council. "May I go warn them to move out at once?"

"Go Angel, do what you must to continue to fight our fight."

Angel exited through the front of the vehicle. As she did, the Council's figures spoke but we could not hear them. It appeared we were left out of a conversation on mute for several seconds. David and I glanced at each other, unsure of what our next steps were going to be. The plan was to go on the offensive and destroy the new reactors as they were being built and before they would go online to prevent an increase in the supercomputer processing power, but with the knowledge of their troop locations, David may get his wish for a more direct assault on our enemy.

"David, take the device from Tory and upload the data to our network."

"It will be done within the hour," David said. I opened my wristphone and handed him the device. He departed the command vehicle as well, and I waited as several members of the Lower Council watched me and seconds ticked by. My mind was blank. I did not want to think about what would come next. People would likely start dying because of the information I handed over, and I feared my thoughts would make me look weak before the council. I had to remember we were fighting for the voiceless, the ones without the ability to seek freedom from the system they were imprisoned in. One they may not even recognize as a prison.

"Tory, you have done well."

"Thank you. I pray that we will finally be able to grow our organization."

"You are being called back to White Tunnels."

"May I ask why?"

"We have much to discuss, Tory. You have proven useful to our cause but we believe your expertise belongs there for the moment."

"I will leave shortly."

"That will be all, Tory."

"Thank you, Council." I bowed my head and watched as the holograms of the council members faded. Their trademark masks and modulated voices made it impossible to know their identities. It was important that each decentralized group of our resistance was not privy to all our plans or contacts. If there was a defector, willing or otherwise, we would not suffer a big defeat. As it stood, I was given a larger network of resistance members to work with, as I traveled from special assignment to special assignment. That did not mean council members would reveal their identities to me, just that I would work with them more often than before.

I was about to depart the vehicle when Angel stepped back inside from the front. She looked worried. "Tory, do you have a moment?"

"I have all evening for you, Angel. What's wrong?"

"Something is wrong with the Council."

"What do you mean, Angel?" I asked, confused.

"Before you arrived, they were asking me for input on what we are capable of in South America. It felt as if they were feeling out how likely it is for us to truly exact a rebellion or formal resistance in the open."

"That is not for much later, is it not?"

"We were not going to begin discussing it for a few years. Pacific islands were supposed to be the first of the civil unrest."

"Do you think they are changing their plans?"

"I don't know. What did they make of your report?"

"David is uploading the data to our secure network and I have been recalled to Antarctica."

"What?! I thought you were supposed to stay in South America with me for another month."

"I know. They would not tell me outright but something about my expertise. Which isn't really all that helpful for divining their intentions for me."

"You were a miner, right?"

"I was involved in digs here, in Argentina, Australia, the Congo, South Africa, and White Tunnels."

"Perhaps they found a deposit of Itrep and need your help to extract it?"

"I'm not the only one who knows how to pull some pressed carbon out of the dirt and snow, Angel."

"Well, maybe with the refinement process?"

I thought about that for a moment. I was studying for the DDS refinement test course before I was moved to Australia. It was a long time ago but I knew I never deleted the books from my wristphone profile. It would not be a stretch, considering everyone in Antarctica was there to dig and not to refine. All the refinement experts left with the DDS sale and I had no idea what happened to any of the equipment. "Perhaps, but I doubt I am the best resource for them to rely on."

"You speak too highly of yourself, Tory." Angel chuckled as I grinned. She was right. I was known for being the smartest outcast in my class; book smart, but still.

"You are right, Angel. Now, what is it you need from me?"

"I am worried that the Council wants to enact our plans too early. Whether it is the members we speak with or others. I think you may have some of their ears and some words from you may be exactly what is needed to convince them we are not ready here in South America."

"I will certainly try to make my case, Angel, but no promises. I am but a lowly Other, aren't I?" We both laughed at that and I went to find my sleeping bag. It was a long night and if I was going to get on a submarine, I wanted to be ready for the sea sickness.

U-WING

"NO! Franklin!" I shot straight up at the sound of my own voice echoing in my small room. My breathing was as fast as a hummingbird's heartbeat while flying. It took me several seconds to calm my hyperventilating body. Once I had control over my oxygen supply, I was able to think back to the dream I was having. Franklin was with me in South America and gave himself up to save me.

I had no idea why, but it was a reoccurring dream ever since I came back to White Tunnels from Hishla Lake. One with differing locations and reasons; all resulting in Franklin sacrificing himself so that I could escape from the Absolutists. I sent my hands across my head and through my hair before I checked the time. It was early, but close enough to my normal 8 am alarm that I could get started with my morning. I made my way to the table in the dim light and grabbed my dream journal, which I used to detail the events as they came to me before I lost them forever.

Vasil made it clear that if I was having recurring dreams, it was best to write them down so I could decipher what message my subconscious was trying to push through to my conscious mind. It was hard to do when on the road as I did not bring my journal for fear of being captured with it. Those nights always seemed to drop the most concerning of the dreams.

After writing all I could recall, I ate a light breakfast and made my way down the hall to shower and finish my morning routine. Once complete, I chose to wear a dark green long-sleeved shirt and yoga pants. It was good to have a choice in the clothes I wore. I found out that when left to my own choice, I favored greens and blues in my wardrobe. Under the Absolutists and DDS, I had no choice in the clothes I wore as they were always provided by DDS. Now that I had the choice, I always went with what I was comfortable in. No one in the last three years complained about my wardrobe so I figured I was making the right choices.

I pulled the charging cable from my wristphone and attached it to my left arm. I then checked the meetings for the day. I had one in thirty minutes and I was free until the nightly briefing with Vasil himself. I sent a message to David asking if he would be returning soon so I could speak with him about our planned proposal to the Council later in the week. We had planned on doing it together and in person, but as it was, I was beginning to fear that I would not be reunited with David until after the presentation. It was odd for my bodyguard to be separated from me, but the replacement guard, Arvin, seemed to be a worthy substitute in the meantime. He was never in the way and was very attentive.

I made my way out of the dorm area through the stone staircase. He spotted me as I exited the stairwell and crossed over to me and matched my pace as we walked through White Tunnels. While much of the dig site appeared to be the same, it was when we entered the door next to the dig site that led up and North that the scenery began to change. Vasil's Wing, or the V-Wing as we called it, was much more enthralling than the drab and occasionally interesting main section of the base.

Decorated in various paintings with little signs, it was clear Vasil was making the V-Wing a museum as well as a command center of our operations. In time, I wondered if this place would be treasured or destroyed. It all depended on if we won against the supercomputers and the Absolutists, but nonetheless it made my spine tingle that I might be part of something historic. Something to be taught in the books of history for all time. How humans got their humanity back from the AI and grew together as a species, finally tossing aside their discriminatory behavior in the pursuit of higher ideals.

"Good morning, Tory." Vasil's voice came from behind a bust of George Washington and caught me off guard.

"What on earth are you doing behind that?"

"Why come here and I'll show you."

I walked around the back of the elegant bust and beautiful Corinth column it sat upon. It was six feet high and at the top, the bust looked down on me as if I was being judged by George Washington himself. I laid my eyes on Vasil and a technician who was installing wires in the back of the column through an access panel. Judging by the white dust and equipment strewn about, it appeared the access panel was a brand-new addition to the back of the pillar.

"Do you like it?"

"I don't know what IT is?" I replied pointedly. I had a sneaking suspicion but could not be sure; Vasil was eccentric, after all.

"We are making it so George Washington's bust isn't just staring at you, but recording you with motion tracking sensors, of course!"

"I'm glad you are installing security inside one of the most secure places on the continent." My retort came from my mouth before I realized what I said. Vasil was friendly and tried to engage with everyone, but he did have boundaries we had to refrain from crossing. To my relief, he did not mind my offhand comment.

"One of the *only* truly secure places on the continent. My dear Tory, you would think I'd get a little more credit for my efforts."

"You're right, Vasil."

"Usually am." He winked and turned back to watch the technician work.

"I have to get to a meeting, do you nee—" Before I could finish, he waved me away. Apparently, if I was not going to compliment his efforts, I was not needed.

I set back off down the hallway, my pace a bit faster than before as I was running close to being late. Vasil was a kind person, but often needed encouragement and affirmation to keep going. Sometimes I did not simply have the strength or time to provide for his needs. Today was one of those days.

As I stepped into the first conference room to the left at the end of the V-Wing primary hallway, I noticed that David replied to my message. I glanced down at the screen to read that he was still intending to be present at the presentation but may not be able to join me in person until the morning of.

"Ah, Tory, you make a quorum! We can get started," Adam said. He returned with me the morning after our adventure in South America. I was glad he was taking more ownership over the briefings as I was doing the heavy lifting by spending hours preparing each morning. It was agreed ownership of the meeting would be done in one-month shifts, and Adam was the first to take over from me. I could see the weariness in his eyes.

"What's the latest in South Africa, Adam?" Abeba asked. Abeba was from Africa with skin as dark as Franklin's and long, straight hair that was always done up as if she was a supermodel. The color of her hair changed with her missions. Today it was a dark and thick black. Her hair was perfectly cared for, and I was always curious how she found time to make it shine and present so well, regardless of the circumstances.

"We will get to that. First, we have to cover the intel from South America."

"Make it snappy. I haven't all day," Abeba snapped back. She had been in a bad mood since her last mission. It resulted in half of the group dispatched dying for an empty drive. My mission was to collect the data that was supposed to have been on her empty drive. I understood her attitude and could sympathize to some extent, but found it distasteful nonetheless.

"If you don't mind Adam, I will give the rundown." I spoke before Adam had a chance to react to Abeba. I could tell he was having trouble controlling some of the more outspoken people during our meetings and figured he would not mind my jumping in before things got out of hand.

"By all means, Tory. Go ahead." He sat and I stood. With a few clicks on the remote, I was able to bring the holographic files up on the screen at the end of the table.

"All right folks, first things first. The reactor information is still being inspected by Adam and the tech team, as well as the engineering team. What we know so far is that the new reactors are going to be more difficult to sabotage without inside help. So, let's be sure to not alienate or put at risk any of our spies and informants close to these newer builds. Until the Council makes a formal decision, we are not to actively pursue any sabotage of the reactors."

I paused and looked about the room; everyone nodded or murmured their agreement. I also noticed that everyone aside from me had some form of coffee or energy drink. I avoided thinking about if that would backfire on me later in the day.

"Good. Okay, now onto the more interesting data that I spent several hours looking at, as well as the Council and some of our strategic-minded folks." I clicked and the numbers displayed on the screen. "You will notice most of the troops are being deployed in the Argentina region on the east and southern coasts. Why they are gathering there is not entirely clear, but it may have something to do with Zack and Jesus operating extensively and violently along the eastern coast.

"What originally caught my eye was the new tanks that were being deployed in this area. There appeared to be no exhaust or battery access panels from the outside, which is an improvement in their favor. However, I did notice this." I pressed the button and a blown-up image of the back of one of the tanks appeared. Audible gasps came from throughout the room. It had DDS clearly inscribed on the back as the manufacturer. "Yes, it appears the balance between the corporations and government production has become blurred further than we had initially thought. This is an unmistakable problem that will complicate matters. If the corporations are indeed beginning to merge further into the military-industrial complex of the AI Governors, we are running out of time to get to citizens before they are completely shielded from our efforts against both government and the oligarchs. The more powerful the AI Governors, the oligarchs, the Absolutists as a whole become, the less likely we are to convince people to take up arms against them. Especially when we cannot match the armored firepower the Absolutists wield. We must remember they are simply living out their daily lives, and may easily see us as a threat to their way of life."

"I thought DDS did not manufacture anything for the military, just mining equipment and digging for Itrep," someone in the back stated. There was some consensus among the meeting attendees.

"Great point. That confused me too, but after some research I found that several of the higher ups in DDS also have relationships or are also on the boards of the big names in military supplies like Ramthen and General Systems and Technology. Also, with the AI Governor software companies like Consolidated Tusk, Primeium, and Haweit. We are going to have to accept that they are all truly one and the same at this point. Now as to why DDS is the name used on the tank, I am unsure. I am guessing it was a licensing agreement.

"All of which makes no sense considering that DDS was broken up because it was considered 'too big'. My guess is that since DDS does Itrep and raw materials that are often used in metals, one of the companies that branched off retained the name and is using it on their products. The curious part of it all is this tank may be made with a new alloy we are unaware of. I say that because it does not look to be manufactured by the same methods as the older models."

"Do we know what those new tanks are capable of?"

"Other than they appear to run on some other source than

graphene batteries, no. This new series looks just like the older models in terms of weaponry. Any other questions?" I asked to give myself a chance to drink a little water from the cup sitting by my chair. Adam made a point to ensure everyone had one cup of water whenever he started his meetings. Even if they would bring in coffee. It was a nice touch to his meetings.

"Well, if there are no questions, I will say that it sounds terrible so far. Let's get back to the numbers." Adam looked at me to continue.

"Angel confirmed that Zack was seeing numbers roughly matching what these troop logs are calling for. Jesus will be reporting today on if the same is true."

"Why Zack but not Jesus?" Abeba inquired. I nodded to acknowledge the question, but she became as stoic as the George Washington bust in the hallway after speaking.

"The spreadsheets of data I was able to capture also gave dates and times for movements. Zack's numbers were able to be gathered late last night. Jesus is most likely counting to confirm the accuracy of these files right now since the movements are occurring as we speak."

"And why are we counting when we know the numbers already?" Cory, another one of the team who did not often speak often and sat in the back, asked.

"We often find that when the Absolutists are alerted to excursions like the one Adam and I were involved in, the numbers are often incorrect as the computers reevaluate to keep resistance in the dark."

"I proposed the idea to Angel that we check and apparently the Council thought it was a good idea." Adam stood and I sat, since my reports were already finished. Besides, it was good to not have to speak in front of everyone with a red face so early and for so long in the morning. "Since those files were copied from the cloud and not already on the drive, the likelihood of the computers thinking we were able to sign on and steal such information is relatively low."

"Couldn't they check the logs?"

"Not with my virus, which worked flawlessly." Adam beamed at himself. He may have loved blowing stuff up, but he was a genius at cracking software too. One of the best Vasil had ever worked with, the way Vasil praised him, and I was inclined to believe him after our trip to Hishla Lake. Something I felt an urge to mention but had left out as I sat was the research on genetic replication and neuroscience. I could not decipher it and it was all old data that had last been modified many years before, decades in some cases. As far as I was concerned, it was inconsequential to our objectives.

It was another forty-five minutes before the meeting was over. A briefing on North America as dismal as ever considering the fortifications, the briefing from Europe that was promising regarding several new informants that were debating if they should defect to our cause, and the briefing from Africa that Abeba presented regarding the losses because of a blitz from the AI Governor that we were all surprised by and she was unprepared for. It was another reason my extra few minutes in South America were so important. If the troops were preparing to assault the resistance and we did nothing to warn Zack and Jesus, the setback would be major.

There was no briefing on Asia and the Pacific islands, which was usual. Vasil kept that particular briefing separate almost every week due to the utter control the Chinese supercomputer had over most of the continent and how different the conversations were with our partners there. It was extremely difficult to persuade people who have lived in a more controlled command society without the freedoms much of the west experienced. However, many still existed, albeit in a roundabout way. Many of the participants in those meetings were remote, and the Council believed the threat any one of the Asian resistance fighters posed after being captured was far greater and more likely than elsewhere. As a result, the entire Asian teams, aside from the Council itself, stayed incredibly independent from one another. They were all isolated to protect others, but I still found the extra precautions unnecessary. I was not privy to the details, though, so they may have been justified.

I adjourned shortly after, avoiding the small talk that always spun up after meetings. I exited the V-Wing and grabbed a sandwich in the cafeteria before heading to my room. It was silent and cozy. The peace allowed me to decompress my mental state before the evening meeting. It also allowed me to dive deeply into the South American and North American data to look for trends to bring to Vasil's attention without being bothered.

NEW ASSIGNMENTS

I was the first to arrive at the center conference room, the largest of the seven at the end of V-Wing, and began to review the notes I had taken in throughout the afternoon. I was starting to see a trend and was excited to share my findings.

Everyone trickled in and the last person to arrive was Vasil himself. He was not in a good mood, but true to his prompt character, he arrived exactly on time. As everyone quieted and sat in their chairs, Vasil made his way to his chair at the far end of the conference table. This table, unlike the smaller ones in the other rooms, had a holocamera at the center for council meetings. He managed to plaster a good-natured expression on his face before speaking.

"My friends, thank you all for coming in. This being our final weekly deep dive meeting before the end of the month, I want to wish you all the happiest of holidays. I will be returning to my family for all of December, so I need you all to be on your best behavior as you continue to dig into the data. Of course, those of you with approval from me and the Council can travel as well, but I suggest you do so with caution. The world is tense at the moment."

"Thanks to us." Abeba's voice carried, even though it was clearly intended to be a whisper.

"Right you are, Abeba. A price we all will no doubt pay moreover in the future." He paused to give her a stern look and she held her hands up, gesturing that she would not speak out of turn again. While often indulging in a lighter air during many occasions, Vasil could make it clear in an instant that certain occasions required professionalism.

Vasil continued to run through the meeting agenda, as we covered the various investigations everyone was biting into. Everyone but Vasil was a Regent of our movement, and the title made us little more than glorified advisors except when Vasil was convinced to allow us to go out on missions.

I was a High Regent, as was Abeba. We led the research and inputs for South America and Africa, respectively. I was given South America as a result of no one else being interested in the continent. They saw it as a lagging continent with no real value in our movement. Their views were not entirely justified in my opinion because the people of South America desired freedom, more than any other continent save Africa, but were resigned to live under the regime until a spark of hope could be seen to latch on to. South America appeared to be as subjugated under Absolutist control as eastern Asia under the Chinese AI Governor, but it was a powder keg that, if lit in the right circumstances, could be the spark the entire world needed to fight back.

When I first started looking into the continent, I found

multiple vulnerabilities in the armor of the supercomputer network and AI itself, the result of poor planning by the oligarchs and the AI was apparently not prioritizing closing those gaps. I poked at the data until connections and holes that could be prodded and used to our benefit began to emerge. It was also around that time that Angel and the South American Resistance, or SAR as it quickly became known, started making headlines.

My first mission was disguised as a company-sanctioned vacation to make contact with Angel and her team to pass along any information we may have had in exchange for intel and occasional support. Angel agreed and soon SAR became fully aligned with our interests. It was a win no one expected and awarded me the rank of High Regent as well as several analysts working under me on various projects related to South America. One of those projects led to the near capture of reactor data in Africa and the successful attainment of the data I secured in Hishla Lake.

"Any updates on the intel grab in South America, Tory? Reactor updates?" Vasil asked me, bringing me to the realization that I never asked for a briefing update from my team.

"I have not had a chance to get the latest from my team. Apologies, Vasil. However, I have found an interesting pattern in the excess data I acquired. Spent most of my time diving into that."

"The troop numbers?"

"Precisely."

"Were the numbers accurate from all the movements to date?"

"Yes. And not just the troop numbers, but the supply numbers as well. We can safely say that intel is not only accurate, but the copies were not noticed by the AI. Something Adam deserves considerable recognition for. If he is able to replicate that malware of his, we may be able to gather more useful information to help drive resistance movements across the globe."

"Assuming the exploit works with all AI governance systems."

"Yes, more research and testing needs to be done on that front. With your permission, Vasil, I would like to dispatch Adam and his team to the Pacific to test against the Chinese AI directly."

"That's dangerous and a hard ask, Tory."

"I still ask. We need to find a way to get ahead, or we will lose the inevitable global civil war due to unrest and no clear direction that is unified and effective. We need to know about and direct as much of the impending civil unrest as possible."

"It's not me you need to convince, Tory. I will confirm with the Council, but assume you are able to get the team together and off on the next sub to Australia." I beamed at this as Vasil and others nodded and smiled in encouragement. Everyone understood the benefits of such risks and the Council was growing desperate for a way to get an edge on the AI systems globally.

"Thank you. As for the trends I noticed, it appears that the troops are coming directly from the west coast of the United States. Enough troops to potentially leave gaps in their control of the west coast that may be able to be exploited. The question is, how do we cause an increase in movement to South America from North America?"

"And since that was more a statement than a question, I assume you have an answer. What is your proposal, my dear?" Vasil asked, and his intrigue was matched by many of my peers. I felt my entire body warm at this. I was the center of attention, something that never happened until Vasil came into my life, but it was the reaffirmation of being capable of drawing the positive attention that I reveled in. It was a drug that encouraged me to seek more. I learned early on in Antarctica that I would need to back up my intriguing finds with viable solutions that would make my audiences think highly of me. That was how I knew in order to get recognition for my efforts, I needed to put in more time than necessary to go over the details and review my findings and proposals.

"Well, it is actually going to be part of my three-stage plan I am planning on presenting to the Council with David this week. I will incorporate it into Phase One. To be concise, it will be targeted skirmishes on the west coast and now, in light of this find, the east coast of South America as well. All of which ought to draw the needed attention to South America that will bring North American troops south and put North America into play. At least temporarily. Enough to get our foot in the door at worst. Enough to push forward with a firm footing at best."

"And what if those skirmishes backfire and cost us the SAR?" Vasil questioned with a thoughtful look and in a dry monotone.

"It won't. Angel and I have spoken briefly on this and she believes with the right inspiration, rioting and other forms of unrest can be induced that would result in enough confusion for the ring leaders of the skirmishes to get safely back to SAR camps and territories without being noticed, should anything go wrong. At least with the ability to shrug off pursuers before exposing the camps."

"Interesting. Thoughts?" Vasil opened it up to the rest of the regents.

Abeba was the first to speak. "It is a good idea. My concern is how much of a foothold in North America is needed, and if that is justified with the risks of SAR and the citizens in South America?"

"Still working those details out. I have already asked for the requested information from our North American regent's teams and once I get a response, I will be able to include it in the plans."

"What makes you sure that more troops will come from North America and not Europe or Asia?"

"DDS does not operate in either of those places any longer. And these troops have been tied to DDS and several other North American companies and the US military. It appears to me that for some reason the AIs in the Americas are working together on building up forces. Whether it is to control their own people, to defend against us, or start a war with the other AI systems, I do not know."

"A war with the other AI? Is that even possible?" Someone in the North American section of the table asked. I did not know their name, but they were seated up against the wall behind their regent. I preferred my team skip meetings when they had work to get done, and I did not have time this week to see what their workloads looked like to decide if anyone should have come with me. So, as usual, I came without anyone to back me up. It challenged me in a good way so I did not mind.

"Anything is possible," Vasil broke back into the conversation. "We have similar thoughts that may be true in Asia and that would explain the buildup in the Middle East and West China. Have we seen anything in Africa, Abeba?"

"Not that I am aware of." Her response was quick and unsure. Vasil noticed and scowled slightly. "Can you check and confirm by end of week?"

"Yes, Vasil. I will."

"Good." Vasil shifted his weight and chair back to me. "You may be piecing together something that could end up being massive, Tory. Thank you for your time and efforts. Please get the needed information from Evelyn ASAP. Good with that Evelyn?"

"Yes I am Vasil. Tory, let's sync tomorrow afternoon on this," Evelyn answered, with a smile in my direction.

"Sure thing." I smiled back at her.

"All right, Evelyn. Do you want to take us away with the latest in North America?"

Evelyn stood. Her height was astonishing considering her malnourishment early on in life. Standing over six feet tall, she was a full-bodied woman with deep dark brown hair that was matched by her deep voice. She was a lovely singer, in addition to being a trained mixed martial artist. I did not want to get in a fight with her, nor did most of the regents. She had an imposing figure and presence but was simultaneously one of the nicest women I ever met. Her heart was always overflowing with kind words and no task was beneath her. Of course, you would never know if you never spoke with her outside of a work environment. She was all business when in meetings.

I sat and participated as the meeting went on until its inevitable conclusion and stood speaking with Abeba as she gave advice on how to weigh the troop movement risks. I appreciated her help, as she was related to the last remaining warlords in Africa and was raised with strategy and military wit, but I really wished she focused more on her problems than others. It was beginning to affect her performance in delivering results for the Council.

Vasil whisked me away on the pretense of needing a private word, and I thanked him as soon as we were out of earshot. Vasil, as he always seemed to do, intervened at the perfect moment. He shrugged at my words. "Not completely intentional, my dear

Tory. Not at all. I spoke with some members of the Council and they not only granted my request to spend time with my family, but also to put someone in charge for the rest of the year in my place."

My face contorted in confusion as I tried to decipher why that required a private conversation with me. Several seconds went by as Vasil watched me, waiting for my realization. When it came, he smiled and offered his hand to me. He wanted me to run White Tunnels in his absence. "I hope that you will not disappoint me or the Council. You are destined for big things, Tory."

"I—but—" I tried to protest.

"No, this is a direct order from me and on behalf of the Council. And I know you can handle it. You have been on a roll recently and your confidence is at an all-time high. Either we aren't challenging you enough or you are not in the right position to be challenged by your responsibilities. Whichever is the case, I will look forward to the work you do while I am away."

"Thanks Vasil. I will try to keep everything running down here."

"You better. And don't forget about the damned dig site. Those folks will need to stagger their time off for the holidays. We need to continue producing Itrep through the end of the year."

"How close are we?"

"Really close, Tory. Really close. We will soon be able to go on the offensive between your research as regent and our efforts."

"Will I need to be debriefed on it?" We weren't exactly allowed to discuss the project Vasil's tech teams were working on, but it required us to power it with our own mined and refined Itrep. I held my breath waiting for his reply; I was not sure if I wanted to be involved or not. It was getting close to a momentous development and risky bet by Vasil as part of his long-term strategy.

"No, the work is still confidential. I will remotely take the update meetings and present to the Council. No need to burden you with all the in-depth stuff, just make sure to help clear blockers as the teams might bring them to you. Don't ask too many questions. They already have a hard enough time explaining to me." He winked and strode out of the room. I saw him grab a flask from his jacket pocket as he left but said nothing. Some things were best if left alone.

PLANS AND REVISIONS

"I would not be asking you if you could not do it, Tory my dear." Vasil was speaking softly to me with a solemn tone and expression. He was not his jovial self. None of us were in over a week. We had gone from the informational victories in South America to devastation shortly after. "I know you will do right by them, and we need to come up with a strategy before the AI Governor realizes exactly how much we know about its movements. We can't wait any longer, Tory."

Zack and Jesus were assassinated, and Vasil was asking me to review the information to look for an explanation and, more importantly, a way to exploit the tragedy as an opportunity against the Absolutists, if at all possible. Angel was shattered when she broke the news to everyone. She was related to Jesus; cousins, if I understood correctly. I had wanted to originally fly there to be with her and to mount a counteroffensive in person. I was angry. We all were. For the first time since we began working with the resistance in South America, people I knew were murdered at the hands of our adversaries.

It was a cold, hard dose of reality, of what we were really doing. The deaths were not expected by many, but neither had we really prepared for a tragedy to befall the upper leadership of the SAR, or any other resistance movement. We had grown too complacent in our lives of relative luxury and happiness in White Tunnels, and the news hit us all like a brick thrown in our faces during the holidays.

When Angel sent the images, we were all revolted. They were tortured after being captured. Not in a quick and clean manner, but slowly and painfully over days. They were burned and waterboarded repeatedly. Their fingers and toes were snipped off. Not just their nails either, the entire tips of their phalanges. Their skin was cut off in square spots, leaving exposed muscle. Teeth were missing. I did not know and did not want to know what the doctors had to say about how they died. I saw everything I needed to know, and more than I could handle.

"I don't know any more, Vasil," I said. I felt defeated. I was denied flying privileges and given three days off, but I was still in an exceptionally bad mood over the whole thing. My ability to leave White Tunnels was revoked in an effort to keep me at my post. Something a week ago I did not believe would ever have happened.

"Tory, I know you are better than this. Remember when I offered you the overseer job? You stressed for a week after accepting it, but once you dug into the work, you began to live life fully again. I want that for you. You want that. We both know you digging into the data will cheer you up. It will give you a way to punish the Absolutists. Not just for you, but for the revenge we all want."

I was nodding but still looking at the floor, holding back a tear and a snivel. "Will it get any easier?"

Vasil stopped dead in his tracks. He had been pacing back and forth as he was juggling so many things while trying to keep everyone pushing forward. He was not his usual self either after returning yesterday from his break at the end of the year, which also hit the morale of everyone at White Tunnels.

"The loss?"

"Yeah, the loss of people we know. The ones we care about."

He scowled at my question. Death always struck a certain nerve in Vasil, one he hid well, but I was still able to spot it. "No. I won't lie to you, Tory. It never gets better. The pain will dull, but the mental impact never does. You will find a way to live with it. You will have to. We all will. Zack and Jesus are, when all is said and done, just two men fighting for the good of humanity. They are not the first freedom fighters to die, they are just the first we have worked with and developed bonds with in South America. They were good men and leaders. We cannot disappoint them by not acting with clear and level-headed actions now, can we?"

"You are right, Vasil. You always are."

"I am accurate most of the time, but that doesn't mean I am right. Just remember this. If there is one thing I hate more than any other is the death of someone to be in vain."

I nodded solemnly in agreement. And then I replied to his imparted wisdom. "And today you are both accurate and right."

We grinned at one another. It was our thing. We understood the unspoken humor of our conversations, and the unnecessary repetition it often entailed. The eccentric twists Vasil would often make were easy routines to fall into in times of stress. It was our little way of moving past the difficult parts of our jobs. Even in a time like this, we could still have that moment. Something I would cherish about our relationship.

I told him I would do as he asked and made my way back to my office. I looked around once inside and noticed how truly empty compared to Vasil's it really was. Aside from the desk, laptop, a floor lamp, the chairs, and two file cabinets, it was entirely empty. I had been focusing so closely on my work I had neglected the furnishings for what had to have been years.

Yes, three years had gone by since Vasil had first spoken to the skin and bones team that was left in White Tunnels. Within six months, I went from a lowly dig worker to White Tunnels Overseer of Operations. After running operations for over a year, I finally pushed Vasil to tell me about the work that was being done in White Tunnels that I was not privy to. Soon after, I transitioned into a more active role in his underground and secretive efforts to disrupt and dismantle the AI Governors, the Absolutists, in any way research and occasionally espionage would allow.

Eventually I was moved from the role of White Tunnels Overseer and into a High Regent role under Vasil. I was given two staff members to help collect data and onboard me. Over time, that number grew to six. I pressed a button on my wristphone to call my secretary, or who was working as my secretary in all but title, and sat down and began to sign into the network on the laptop. The network connection to the laptop needed to be highly secured, more than even my wristphone, and as a result, upon logging in, it required a few moments to establish a secure connection and begin transmitting data on our internal intranet.

Mary knocked and entered. "Yes, Tory?"

"I need something to liven this room up. It's going to start affecting my ability to work." I scoffed at my own words. "It *is* affecting my ability to work."

"What do you have in mind, Tory?"

"What can I get that is low-budget and not exactly tacky?"

"Well, umm. How about one of those paintings Vasil drew himself? Those are free for us to keep. Originals and copies." She chortled as she spoke. I could not help but snicker as I opened my South American data files up to begin the task Vasil entrusted me with. Vengeance, retribution, justice for what happened to Zack and Jesus. Vasil was a talented painter, but his exceedingly eccentric style made it difficult to truly appreciate most of his works.

"Bring two. And if possible, I would like to have a meeting with everyone in two hours. We need to retaliate in South America. I'm beginning to strategize and I want to hear everyone's thoughts."

"Will do. Anything else Tor?"

"Send David in when he is free. I need to speak with him. And can you make sure Vasil has the order forms I misplaced before Christmas? He needs to approve them now that he is back."

"Consider it done!" She shut my door softly and I sighed. This was going to be harder than I realized.

My request to send Adam to Australia left me without my primary tech liaison. My three-step plan to gain support in South America was torn apart by the Council a second time the day before we received the news from Angel. My job was beginning to feel more like a chore and a burden than anything else. It was not that the Council did not want to use the plan, but they were expecting perfection and I clearly did not live up to the standards in the details they were looking for.

David would be able to help me divine the devils in the details that I was missing. He was sinisterly clever at strategy when his mind was put to the task. Any way to leverage that ability was in our best interest.

A quarter hour of working alone went by before David showed up. His expression solemn, he was visibly in the same place as I was mentally. He had worked closely with SAR on far more missions than I had, and he really enjoyed Zack's company.

I gestured to the papers on the desk, and he nodded and sat. It was unspoken what must be done. We had to revise our plans for South America, and not only did they have to be more detailed as requested, we now had to ensure we would not let our emotions get in the way. Even if the drive to complete the work was driven entirely by emotion. The irony crossed my mind, but I let the thought go and washed my mind with our ideas.

We worked feverishly in an attempt to ignore our emotional states until a knock on my door brought us out of our trance. David was in the middle of talking out loud through a different angle of the last stage and paused mid-sentence. Once he realized what he heard, he looked for and grabbed his water to drink. He had been talking almost nonstop for the last thirty minutes as I recorded as much as I could through a word processor called "Vord" on the laptop. Vasil had taken it upon himself to rename the word processor to how he pronounced the word for our laptops as a joke prior to leaving for the holidays.

"Yes?" I asked, my voice cracking as I forced it to be loud enough to carry through the thick door.

Mary's voice replied, "Everyone is ready for the meeting. They are asking where it is taking place."

I looked at David and together we looked at the papers and

notes thrown about the entire room. "In here, I suppose."

Mary's barely audible disbelief was quickly followed by the door opening up and the team wearily stepping through the threshold. "I will grab chairs for everyone. I need five right?" Mary quickly counted everyone entering.

"Six if you want to join us, Mary."

"No, I don't think I will this round. I am finishing up some reports to send out on your behalf. Didn't get near the work done I wanted to yesterday."

"That's fine, Mary. Thank you."

It was a tight fit, but after picking up the papers and adding the chairs, everyone was snuggly fit inside my office. David and I hurriedly organized what we had worked out and thanks to my documenting on the laptop, we were able to share the most up to date and revised plans David and I could come up with.

"So, this is just a modified version of the original plan then?" Brandon asked. He was brushing his long, curly brown hair back behind his ears and readjusted his glasses. He was tall and well-toned, nothing extraordinary in his appearance. He was, however, one of the brightest statisticians I had ever met. The list was not long, and David also shared the conviction Brandon was a wiz with numbers in a way most people could not understand. He was a valuable asset to our team as he was able to see the patterns in the numbers others could not. I had used his expertise several times as I began to notice the troop patterns in South America before bringing it to the wider team and Vasil.

"I would hope so. I spent a lot of time digging into the trails of those troops," Ethan replied in his quickly-spoken, nasally voice. He was balding and older than everyone else, being in his late fifties. He was a former geneticist who became disillusioned with the Absolutist system when he began working on the human genome. He realized early on how insane the slander of Abnormals really was. When he tried to prove it, he lost his job, his wife, and was homeless until Vasil found him and offered him a job off the books. Ethan was not the best at math, but patterns were a central part of his research as a geneticist. If he was on the spectrum, he was high-functioning enough to never show it.

"We are. The problem was not so much in the numbers or research, but in our proposed actions based on those numbers."

"Thank God!" Brandon exclaimed. Rubbing his forehead mockingly. A few snickered at his remarks. I decided a few jokes would lighten the mood, so I let it slide. We needed to focus, but I understood we had to set a workable mood.

"Phase One is going to remain the same for the most part. We will still target the end of March. Phase Two, however, is going to need reworking." As I spoke, everyone began tapping on their laptops to find the updated documents that I had shared with the team so they could follow along the phases and dive into what changes were made. Our software made group editing and tracking changes as easy as cooking an egg. At least that is how Vasil had put it. I personally had never cooked an egg.

"Now, Ethan, we need you to take a look at the proposed idea there at the end of Phase Two and see if Tory and I are not missing anything." David did not look up from his laptop, which was now open as well. I looked down at my own and scrolled down to where David's avatar was working. He was finishing the last thoughts he had before being interrupted for the meeting.

Four hours went by as everyone worked together to fix as many issues as we could identify in the plan, adding and removing pieces with the approval from the rest of the team.

Brandon double checked every single number in the document towards the end of the session to make sure we were not using bad numbers. He then finished the charts and graphs we needed to visually sell the plan to the Council. Ethan corrected a few items in Phase Two and completely tore apart David's thoughts on the additions to Phase Three. Not because they were poorly strategized, but because David and I did not see something that Ethan himself missed the first time around.

After making this realization and calling it out to the team, we worked together to completely rewrite all of Phase Three. When the team was completed. I shared the file with Vasil for a once-over for feedback. I thanked everyone for their time and let them retire to their other duties.

I stayed in my office rereading the plan and writing notes. David would likely not be available for a meeting with the Council in the next few weeks as he was asked to train the new guards on White Tunnels' protocols and operations. Vasil messaged me that he was pleased with our efforts and the Council was asking if we would have a presentation to give in twenty-four hours.

Instead of breaking down at the words, I breathed calmly for over a minute, clearing my mind. I checked the time and it was a quarter past ten at night. It would be pushing my abilities, but I believed I could rewrite the original presentation with the updated information in the timeframe provided.

After messaging Vasil a thumbs-up to indicate my positive and passive-aggressive response, I dove once more back into my notes. I decided to write down all the talking points tonight before resting and revisiting them in the morning when I would begin to refine and memorize them tomorrow.

PART 2

INTO THE OPEN

ARRIVAL

"So, David? How much further?" I asked in the dimly lit crew quarter of the submarine. It was a large old nuclear-powered affair that was decommissioned when cold fusion reactors were rendered unsafe and obsolete by Itrep technology after the Cleveland Incident. Itrep technology was fast becoming so efficient and the computer hardware was becoming less energy hungry that there was no reason to not use the newer technology and retire the older and unsafe equipment.

"Not much further," David replied as he sat back down in his bunk. "Another hour, if that."

"I can't believe it's taking so long." It was an irrational complaint, but after being stuck in a submarine under the sea for five days, I was beginning to lose my sanity. I had no idea how the seamen stayed calm with all of the things that could go wrong in a submarine. It was a floating disaster waiting to happen.

"You'll be fine. We had to go slow and stay out of the way of military vessels so we wouldn't be detected. Like I said, the captain told us we aren't far from the fishing ship we will be rendezvousing with. From there straight to Peru. Once we land and meet Angel, we will head to Bolivia to begin Phase One. Just like we planned."

"Okay, David. I hope you are right. If I have to stay in the underwater tub any longer than an hour, I will personally ensure you don't make it to shore." I threatened. It was an empty threat, David and I both knew it, but a few members of the crew gave me sideways glances of alarm at my tone. Since I was anxious and found my body did not get along with the ocean or me being under the surface, I was having a hard time keeping myself composed.

"Have a little faith, Tory."

"I have faith, David. In the plan. This is a detail not described in the plan."

"It will work just like Hishla Lake. We won't have much to worry about."

"Nadine almost didn't make it out of Hishla Lake, remember?"

David shrugged his shoulders. "She knew the risks; those kinds of events are not unexpected. We just hope everything runs as smoothly as paper perfection. Reality is far muddier than that. Considering the variables, that was as perfect as it could have been. They all knew the risks when they volunteered to be a distraction for us. And Nadine is going to be meeting us anyway. She is feeling up to joining us for this adventure."

"I'm glad for that. I don't want anyone dying on my account."

"As you threaten my life, eh?" David looked up at me and stared into my eyes. I shrugged my body to get more comfortable and stared back blankly. There was nothing for me to say to him about it.

When the rusty sub surfaced, we moved our things to a small fishing vessel. The equally dirty and antiquated vessel motored to a bigger shipping vessel that brought us in to Peru. We laid low at a safehouse near the docks where Nadine was already waiting for us.

"Adam isn't here for this?" Nadine asked when it was only David and me who entered the building. It was a bland apartment building that was almost too nondescript.

"He is running things in my place since I am here."

"Won't we need his tech expertise?" she asked, rubbing her injured side. She caught herself and jerked her hand away. I wondered if she bullied the doctor into putting her back into action.

"No, I have everything I need and he showed me what to do," I replied, patting my pack. While I was no tech genius, I was also no slouch when it came to reading and writing code. I had programmed my fair share of equipment in the Congo after all.

"All right then." Nadine made us coffee and we chatted for a while until the sun was firmly up in the sky. We then exited to the garage where we entered an old electric Ford F-150 waiting for us and made our way out of the seaside town and eastward.

The ride to Bolivia was over nine hours. We were destined for Oruro where a small programming and data center complex was installed. Nadine passed the wheel over to me halfway through so she could rest. I was not comfortable driving and after two hours let David drive the rest of the distance. While I knew how to drive and passed the tests for DDS, I had done little driving in my life. I preferred others to do it so I could not be blamed for traffic or a car crash or any one of a thousand other possibilities I had heard about from other Abnormals. It simply was not worth the mental drain.

We arrived at our destination. A small office complex. The city itself was surrounded by red ground. Everything had a tint of red to it, including the buildings. Our office was no different. The roof and the sides were two different colors, but otherwise red. Maybe I was judging too harshly, but after travelling the world I knew there were far prettier places that I preferred. However, this was not going to be a long stay. We were here to infiltrate a programming complex. Working out of this office was a means to an end that would not last long at all.

As I stepped out of the truck and grabbed my belongings, I looked up at the sign on the front of the building. It was a Vasil company affiliate. It was clear to me by the familiar pattern of script and naming convention. It helped that this particular company was named after him. "Vasilevsky's Abogado para el divorcio."

"Divorce lawyers?" I asked as we walked through the front doors.

"I don't speak Spanish. How would I know?" David said matter-of-factly, not bothering to look up at the sign.

"Yep. The attorney that owns the place is fully funded by Vasil himself. The attorney changed his name to Vasilevsky to make it stand out for branding. That's what he told me," Nadine answered my question.

"Isn't it a security risk to use that name?"

"Probably. Vasil doesn't mind apparently so no one is forcing the owner to change it."

"Does Vasil even know?"

"No idea, but Vasil likely owns the property through a holding company so it would make sense, I'd think. The All-Seeing Eyes can't see inside every building, you know. We should be just fine." At this, I made a mental note to shoot a quick message to Vasil about it. We did not need some local operation breaking our security and risking capture, even if Vasil owned the building.

We settled on the second floor, which was completely vacant aside from some computer monitors and radio gear. Nadine hooked up her laptop, and I handed her an external drive to connect that would allow her to patch into the MESH network the SAR used to communicate. I looked out the back door, which led out onto a metal balcony with a staircase leading down to the back of the building.

Looking up at the sky, I saw the sun was beginning to set. We were close to starting my first fully fleshed out offensive. The first truly coordinated resistance across a wide swath of a continent since the Last Caliphate in the Middle East. I was not going to let myself make mistakes. I had to be as perfect as I could be, for if we messed up, we would all pay a heavy price.

"Online. You need the external drive back?" Nadine asked, tapping away on her laptop.

"No. Hold on to it. I have a drive with the malware on it to connect to the developer terminal. Best to keep them separate," I replied, rummaging through my pack to ensure I did still have the drive, and my face began to tingle as it grew warm. When my hand felt the rectangular piece of plastic that was unmistakably the drive at the bottom of the bag, I felt my face briskly return to room temperature and a kind of calm I had never felt before rushed over me and tickled my spine. It was an interesting feeling that I could not place at that moment in time, but felt as if I was suddenly sharper or wiser.

"How will you take the data from the network?"

"My wristphone is wirelessly connected to the drive via Bluetooth."

"Who soldered a Bluetooth adapter to a drive?" Nadine asked, confused.

"Adam said he had never done it before."

"You have to admit, it is a strange combination. Guess it makes sense since we are using it, eh?" David had joined us and interjected into our conversation as Nadine opened her mouth. She gestured with her hand that he was right and looked back down at the screens in front of her. She slapped the top of one of them and checked the power connection running to it. David was right. No one had ever attached a Bluetooth connection and a battery supply to an external storage device like we had. It seemed unnecessary, but Adam assured us it would circumvent certain security measures he believed were built into the developer terminal.

"What time is Angel supposed to join us?" I inquired, breaking the silence as David and I watched Nadine fight the monitor to bring up the second screen for her makeshift workspace.

"Nine I think," David said, looking down at his wristphone. "That's a few hours away still."

"Everyone know the plan?" I asked, clasping my hand nervously. My brain was on fire but my body had become clammy.

"Yeppers," Nadine shot back in response. "Sit here and keep comms up between your wristphone and the radio and SAR."

"David?" I turned towards him.

"I helped develop the plan. So yes?" He grinned at me.

"Fine. I'll look over the plan once on my own, then," I replied sullenly. I was not going to force them to go over it if they knew their parts in the plan. If David said he knew his role, I believed him. Nadine's role was simple. Mine would be the most difficult.

"Oh, don't be so morose, Tory. Everything will be fine. When Angel gets here, we can go over the plan before you all set off." Nadine's soothing voice made the compromise sensible to me.

"Fair enough. I'll wait. But I'm getting fidgety."

"Then let's play some Euchre while we wait." David put his hands together like the old television character Mr. Burns I had seen on Vasil's old archives of classic TV Shows. I was up to season twenty-nine and had seventeen more seasons to go.

"We don't have a—" Nadine began to say before seeing David wiggle his fingers and pull from his pocket a worn deck of cards.

"Of course, you have cards." My exasperation was enough to kill the smile David was wearing.

"Tory, don't you know me? This is my thing."

"To always have a deck of cards?"

"Why not?" He adopted a pouting expression. I hit him on the shoulder in response.

Nadine locked her computer and moved over to us. "Well, I think I am going to suck. It's been forever since I've played."

"You and Tory versus me then. Fair?" David glanced at me.

"Let's play," I said before Nadine and I lost to David by a margin of three to one while we waited for Angel to arrive.

INFILTRATION

It was ten after one in the morning. We were in position outside of the developer's building. We had studied the blueprints and found a blind spot where we could sneak in and cut the power before triggering an alarm. However, the gap of time once in the line of sight of the cameras rotating back and forth was between ten and thirty seconds. If we were unable to get inside in that timeframe, we would be noticed by the guards on duty.

Angel's reassurances that we only had to get to the door and the keycard she managed to acquire would work had originally fallen on deaf ears. I could not believe our luck that Angel had succeeded in pickpocketing the keycard from a drunken guard who had gone to a local bar instead of his home. She managed to do so shortly before meeting us. It was too perfect. It was too lucky. It was a happy coincidence. I did not believe in coincidences. I did not trust what others called coincidences.

Yet we decided to give it a go, to use the keycard and change the plan last minute. I was easier to persuade than David who was adamant on not changing the plan until Angel pointed out we were only deviating on how we were getting into the building. Once inside, we would be working in the bounds we had initially prepared for.

"They have engaged across all five groups," Angel whispered to our group. She was looking down at her darkened wristphone screen. She picked up the radio and pressed the button on the side. "Nadine, we are going in. Will let you know when the radio is safe to use again. Remember to push a notification to our wristphones in the meantime if there is anything urgent. We don't want to be caught tonight."

"Roger Angel. Good luck in there."

Angel turned the volume knob on the black handheld radio until I heard a snap indicating it was turned off. She looked up at David and a splash of moonlight hit her face. She appeared paler than usual. She had never done anything like this before. Angel was a guerilla warrior and tactician, not a spy. She fought people outside and in the city, not infiltrate high-security buildings. I did not see the difference at first, but David and Angel both assured me that there were many. I had no reason to mistrust their conviction.

David looked back and motioned for us to follow him. He gripped the keycard in his right hand tightly as he slowly rose from the bush we were laying down in. The red camera lights were starting to move away from our position. It would be our chance to get to the door and get inside. We followed David's movements and waited for his signal.

In a split second, he motioned and took off towards the

building. Angel and I followed as fast as we could sprint. Our legs had to work more than David's as we were shorter, but we kept pace with him nonetheless. We had no choice. David slammed into the wall with the keycard between him and the RFID reader. It beeped and turned green. I looked up and saw the camera was edging slowly towards us.

David entered and shut the door quickly. We knew there were measures protecting against more than one body crossing the threshold. To circumvent this, we had to play it as the guard entering, exiting, and reentering as if they had dropped something. Hopefully, no one was monitoring the logs, especially not the AI. If the machines were, we had to hope they would not investigate why a guard returned a few hours after their shift. One of the ideas behind the warfare on the other side of the continent was to distract the AI Governor enough to overlook minor details that would normally cause alarm.

David opened the door and I rushed through the doorway. We did not know if the motion sensing technology would detect direction. I was relieved when no alarms went off and David hurriedly passed the card to Angel and shut the door. Two seconds later, the door opened again and Angel slipped through the door and closed it. She turned back to us, smiling. "So far, so good. Cameras were not fast enough to catch us, I think."

"Let's hope you are right." I whispered back. "The hallway on the right, correct?"

Angel looked down at her wristphone. She nodded and led the way through the corridor. It was dark and shadows were everywhere. There were no cameras in the outer offices. We had to get to the guard desk to disable the interior cameras before accessing the lab where we would have access to the programmer terminal with direct access to the AI system.

We turned and crept along until we hit a doorway that was shut. This would be where the security monitoring room was located. David pulled out his dart gun. Angel did as well. I did not have one as I was carrying the computer equipment for the mission. We decided there would be no reason for me to be armed unless I wanted to be, considering the security during the night shift was slim. The AI relied mainly on technology to detect intruders. Technology we were finding ways to circumvent.

David turned the knob on the door; it was unlocked. After pausing for a second to listen for movement on the other side, he slowly began to move the door with a pained expression on his face. It was as if opening the door was a torn muscle, and he was testing how far it could go before it would snap altogether.

He peered through the slit in the doorway and began to aim his gun. I checked behind us to ensure no one was sneaking up on us. I heard a soft whoosh of air and the projectile from David's gun flew into the room and a few seconds later, I heard a body fall.

"Let's go," David whispered as he opened the door and quickly moved into the room checking all corners. "The cameras in here are off."

"What?" I had prepared to plug my wristphone into the system to disable the cameras but stopped at his words. "Are you sure?"

"Positive," he said, no longer whispering. He strode into the room and unceremoniously dumped the guard out of his chair and pushed him under the desk. He bent down and removed the dart. If all went well, he would be accused of sleeping on the job and no one would be the wiser.

Angel followed David into the room and looked around. "The cameras are definitely offline."

Following Angel, I looked up and stared at a corner where the camera was off and pointed towards the ceiling. The angle was low enough that I could tell the red light was not on. Someone either beat us here or the guard was breaking security protocols. "So much for all-seeing."

"We should hurry. What's our time Angel?" David looked down at the computers in front of him.

"We have five minutes before the other guard sweeps the outer offices and exterior of the building."

"Roger. Tory, get to work on the doorway."

I moved to the doorway behind the guards' desk and with a sharp rap from my elbow, I dislodged the front of the security system. We were not going to use the keycard as we intended to use Adam's malware. It would mask any movements once inside. No need to raise any more suspicion than necessary.

"Well, I can see why the guard did not want anyone seeing what he was up to. Looks like he found a way to play games on his wristphone. An old one with a plumber or something," David said behind my back while I worked. I heard a crack and knew David had disabled the wristphone. It was a necessary risk to prevent any sensors listening in on what we were up to.

It took me two minutes of fiddling to find the right connections and once I did, it was seconds before the door unlocked with a silent click. "We are in. Disabling the security protocols. Cameras are offline in three. Two. One."

"Let's go, Tory. The guard will be on the other side of the data center," Angel said, moving to take point at the door. She looked at David and nodded curtly. He would be waiting for the other guard to come around to the security control room. He nodded back and moved back to the side of the room we had come through to ambush the unsuspecting guard.

Angel pushed one of the doors in the double doorway open and passed through. I quickly followed. We worked our way through the noisy room, careful to not make too much noise on the grating below us. It was a raised floor. I could see optics and tools lying on the concrete four feet below. The lighting in this room was better, but it was dimly lit enough that I could barely make out Angel's figure as I followed her through the rows of data center racks. All of which had various colored LEDs flashing, indicating things I knew not the slightest about.

This was one of the many veins that built the cloud, Big Data. It was one of the organs that held processing power for the artificial digital life form floating as if a ghost around us, through the glass of the network as fast as the speed of light. It was a marvel of humanity. It was built to help us, and yet it hummed away, plotting control over the people who built it.

After snaking our way through the room, we came to the office in the center. It had windows on all four sides and cameras covering every square inch of the inside and doorway. I hoped Adam's hacking skills were up to snuff, as we would be blowing any cover we might have once we stepped towards the office.

As my mind began to whirl with the possibilities, Angel stepped forward and opened the door. It was secured with a keycard, but Adam's program had unlocked it along with the control room's doorway. She pushed it open and cleared the threshold, holding the door for me. I rushed in behind her as sweat began to bead down my face. It was partially from my nerves, but even with the cooling and nighttime, it was hot in the data center.

Angel shut the door and the cool air of the office came rushing to meet me. Trying to ignore the voice in my head telling me I was in danger, I sat at the desk and powered the monitor on. After a few seconds, I found the port to connect into and several seconds later I was fully in the system. "We're in."

"Excellent. Let me know when you have the data stream."

"Where is SAR at?" I asked as I tapped on the keyboard to bring up a terminal to track Adam's malware and run the other programs he built for our infiltration.

"Looks like they are starting to retreat as soldiers are organizing to move in. We are going to need their data feeds to see what the AI is doing ASAP."

"Give me a moment. Looks like we are having trouble accessing real time nodes."

"Good or bad?" Angel was not computer savvy. Neither was I in a lot of data center operations, but I had a crash course on what to expect.

"Encryption is a bit tougher than expected, nothing else. Just will take more time."

I sat there watching as the program automatically ran through the steps to crack into the live feed to the network. It was magic to me, and less than a minute went by in silence before we were in. "Got it."

"Great. What is the AI doing?" Angel looked down at the screen.

"Looks like the program can only decrypt most of the feed," I replied as I was reading the words flashing through the terminal. It appeared the algorithm cracked the majority of the encryption, but some words and symbols were coming through as gibberish.

I did not curse Adam under my breath, as he had written the program to stop if the decryption time was above the expected level. It appeared he programmed the software to go long enough, as we could still read and easily decipher the words, while keeping us as close to our schedule as possible.

"Damn. Hopefully we can figure the rest out."

"Hopefully." I began to run the commands Adam made me memorize so I could review the text at a speed that was readable. I began to scroll through and set a timer to refresh every second to filter out the excess communications. "I can see it. AI is asking for backup locally."

"Where?"

"Everywhere. Nowhere specific. It must still be mobilizing and running simulations on actions."

"Is Nadine able to be patched through on your wristphone?"

My face drained of color. I had forgotten to patch her in to begin data transfers. "No." I quickly began to connect my wristphone to the monitor as well, using the chip Adam had made. I plugged the external drive into the remaining port on the computer and mounted the device.

"What the hell Tory? Hurry up."

"Sorry." I opened the communication with Nadine. The signal was not as strong as we had hoped. Apparently, the MESH network SAR had installed was not close enough to penetrate clear through to the center of the building. "Done. Not a strong connection, but strong enough to not cause errors in transfer rates. Will first download the wristphone to be safe. Hopefully outside we can send it all much quicker."

"Thank God. Looks like sectors two and three are in position. Waiting on one, four, and five to retreat far enough."

"Still not seeing any communications from the AI that will give us any useful information. Will check again once I start transfer of the blocks I have access to locally."

"We are going to have to falsify a lot more of the data to get the response we want, aren't we?" Angel's voice came at a distance as I was absorbed in finding the latest blocks to begin transfer. This part was easy and I understood it better than everything else Adam showed me.

"All right, running the escalation program Adam whipped up. Will dynamically react in real time to any comms coming from Argentina and Brazil."

"Good."

I went back to scrounging up blocks; once the newer ones were transferred, I began to gather older ones. It would not be the crisp clean data we had received from Hishla Lake, but the blocks were the next best thing. We may be able to parse some flaws in the encryption and source coding to exploit. A few minutes went by in silence as I continually checked the program as it slowly intercepted and escalated numbers from the troops in the field. Finally, I was almost in disbelief. I saw the AI actively begin to respond. More lines focused on the false data coming to the AI Governor. "It's listening actively, going to manually assign sectors to continue escalating. Will lean back on the two."

"Sounds fantastic. I will go check on David. Are you good here by yourself?"

"Yes," I said without thinking. I stopped and looked down. "I don't have a weapon of any kind."

"You packed the Taser, didn't you?"

"Oh," I said, suddenly remembering I had picked it up off the table and put it in my pack.

"You'll be fine. I won't be long."

"You'd better come back. I don't want to be alone in a data center. The noise is enough to give me nightmares."

"I'll be right back." And with a click of the door, she swept out of the room and off to check on David at the front of the building. I was alone.

PHASE TWO

Angel was gone for over a minute and as I waited for her to return, cognizant of the fact I was alone at a programmer's terminal to the very entity that I wanted to destroy. The mere fact of me sitting in the chair was enough for execution; and as my eyes searched through the data, I saw what we were waiting for. Hishla Lake reinforcements that were a result of my previous excursion to South America were reassigned to a sector out of the way for SAR to move in. It appeared the AI had fallen for our misinformation and moved the units out to stop the SAR from continuing to retreat.

I fumbled in my pack until I came across the Taser I had packed. I was not confident with a gun, and my aim was horrible. I was far better at jabbing with the Taser. I ran the last program Adam created, which was designed to remove all traces of our presence in the system and sever the link to my wristphone. Once completed, I disconnected the drive and smiled. Our work was finished. We had made the troops move around so we could strike at Hishla Lake and deactivate the reactor. It would be a huge blow to the expansion of the processing power for the AI. Not to mention the data I had just loaded to my wristphone and was slowly sending back to Nadine.

I made my way back to the front office. I walked through the doors smiling and saw David and Angel both lying on the ground. I froze. My grin dropped immediately as my mind registered the scene.

"Don't move bitch," a slimy and nasally voice came from my right. The corner next to the trash can. I raised my hands and slowly turned to face the speaker. "Who the hell are you?"

The person was wearing the same guard uniform as the man lying unconscious under the desk. He was a short and balding man, not taller than five seven. I looked into his brown eyes and watched as he appraised me. His hair was gray and his features made him appear to be in his late forties.

"Abnormal, eh? What are these two doing bumming around with your kind?"

I did not reply. I had nothing to say. Judging by his tone, I was beginning to think he was more than just a little prejudice towards us. Like Mandri. Completely consumed by the impossibly soulless cult that defined the Absolutist regime. The brown shirt citizen soldiers that maintained the order because they believed their morals stretched to only the good and all those who disagreed were evil. The kind of person so far up their own reality to realize the world was more intricate, more complex, more nuanced than their singular belief system.

"It wasn't rhetorical," the man stated with menace in his voice and his eyes. He was quick to anger just like Mandri. I knew at that moment there was no possible way to reason with him.

"They don't mind my company," I replied flatly, working to control every muscle in my body as I was screaming internally. After all, there was a gun pointed at my chest. My heart was racing but I barely felt it as the internal screaming grew louder. It was less of a voice as a full body sensation. Like the feeling of sex, but without the pleasure that accompanies it. Not that I could have known the feeling as Abnormals were to remain abstinent.

Not all of us were, obviously, but I had never found another who was attracted to me and willing to risk their life for such an act of defiance to the system. The only logical reason to do so would be for a child, but I would never have children either since they sterilized me shortly after my first period. Therefore, there was no point; all it achieved was putting my life at risk. I chose and focused on my career. I would not engage in outright defiance of the Absolutists, but would prove my worth, even if it went ignored.

"Shut up, bitch. They must be drugged or something. No one in their right mind would hang around you."

"I wouldn't know."

"What do you mean 'you don't know'?" He stepped forward and leered at me, and the gun quivered slightly.

"I don't ask them about what they do on their own time."

"And what are you doing here? Is this your personal time? Is it theirs?"

"No, it isn't. This is purely business."

"Business? What's the job? Terrorism? They are right about you. You know, the Absolutists. Must have brainwashed this lot and convinced them to do the dirty work for you killing my coworker." He took another step forward. If he would step just once more.

"He's not dead. He's knocked out with tranquilizer darts. A sedative. Probably having the best sleep in his life." I looked down at David's body; I could tell he was breathing as his body moved up and down on the floor. A relieved sensation at the thought of him still being alive gave me strength. Before I could look at Angel's body, the guard took another step closer to me and his feet popped into my downcast view.

Without thinking about the risk, I sidestepped and swept his legs before he could so much as shout. Within seconds, I had the gun in hand and it was aimed directly at his neck. The anger of the screaming from inside my body wanted loose. For the briefest of seconds, I lost complete control of my actions as I squeezed my finger on the trigger. The travel was far enough I saw the trigger move before I stopped. I lifted my finger and laid it straight up on the trigger guard and stood up. I did not lower the gun.

The adrenaline running through my veins was more than enough to keep me focused now. He was on the ground with his hands on the top of his head, looking at me with wide, beady eyes. I could tell he was scared that his life was moments away from ending. That I was a monster who would end him for no reason other than I was an Abnormal. The skewed perspective angered me, but I kept my thoughts leveled.

"What did you do to my friends?" I asked coldly, the point of the gun aimed at his heart.

"Knocked them out with a nerve gas grenade."

"What kind?" My eyes narrowed and my finger inched back towards the trigger.

"Just some knockout gas. I don't know. Do you think they tell me that? They just teach us how to use it. They'll be fine." His nasal voice grew higher as my finger moved toward the trigger.

"For how long."

"They should wake up in a few minutes. Just long enough to tie them up."

"Why didn't you do that already?"

"I was radioing for support when I heard you on the other side of the door."

"Why would you do that?!" I screamed. The plan was ruined. If we did not radio in, Nadine would assume we were on our way back and could not get to Hishla Lake. Since we were still here, no one would know we had failed yet. The night might still be salvageable, but I had to wait for David and Angel before we could act.

"It's protocol," He whimpered. "Please just let me go."

"How long do we have?"

"Five or ten minutes? I dunno, miss."

"Don't you *miss* me! I'm an Abnormal, aren't I? Why are you cowering to me?" I did not know why I was taunting him. I had no idea what else to do, so it seemed like the best course of action until David and Angel woke up.

"I'm sorry," he said softly. Finally, he was showing his true self. A weak and cowardly person. Someone who submitted to anyone in a position of authority.

"How many times have you said that to one of us?"

"Ne-never."

"Will you say it more often now?"

"Y-yes. Just let me go."

"Oh, just shut up. Put these on." I threw him zip ties from my pack. They would help keep him handicapped until we could move out.

As he set the plastic teeth and put hands into the circle, he looked up at me. I nodded my approval and he used his thumb to move the plastic together, creating handcuffs. I marched forward and quickly tightened the zip tie before he could get his hands back out. The plastic was digging into his skin. I then shoved him up and pushed him back into the corner. "Look at the corner. Don't look around. Don't move. Not until I tell you to move. Understood?"

He nodded and I sat in the chair glancing over the monitors. I did not see any reinforcements on the cameras. I had to plot out the next move. We needed to be gone before anyone else arrived or it would be hell to get out and back to Nadine. To my relief, David stirred on the ground. He slowly became aware of his surroundings and shot up, ready to fight. He wavered, standing in the middle of the room as he surveyed the scene before him. Me with a gun trained on the man in the corner, Angel at his feet.

"We don't have much time. More are coming." I told him quickly. "We need to wake her and go."

"What about him?"

"He stays here."

"Think he knows anything valuable?"

"Nothing of value to us."

"You sure?"

"You trust my judge of character, don't you?"

"Well, yes, bu—" David began but I cut him off.

"He's nothing more than a Kool-Aid drinking scum of the Earth that treats anyone he doesn't care about with as much respect as a rabid animal." The man in the corner began to speak in protest. In a flash, I was right behind him with the gun touching his back.

I may not know what it was like killing a man. I may have hated the thought of it. I may regret my actions in the morning. But right at that moment, I was not going to let him have his say. I was tired of all the times I was cut off. Tired of all the people who hated me because of my physical features. Tired of the damned system and their damned rules and their damned power. I had my fill and the beast deep within me was surfacing. It was lingering ever closer to my skin since the news of Zack and Jesus. It was years of abuse and neglect welling up inside of me. I was sick of it all. I wanted justice.

"Tory no!" David's exclamation brought me back to the conversation. I took note of my emotions and calmed my thoughts.

Once I was firmly back in control, I spoke quietly with venom I did not know I was capable of having. "You do not speak with your hate-filled perspective in my presence any longer. I will not tolerate your input. You treat me and my kind like an animal, then I will treat you the same. You are my prisoner. You have lost your rights to all but life until I say so. Am I understood?"

"Y-Yes, Miss T-Tory," He stammered. I thought I saw a tear run down his cheek. I was not swayed, however.

"You are nothing to me. Nothing to the world. Nothing to the computers. You were born to be a guard and you will die a guard. You are just another human in the anthill."

"Yes I am."

"What is your name?"

"A-Andrew."

"Do you want to be more than a guard, Andrew?"

He paused as he thought about the answer. Angel stirred behind me. I heard David crouch to check on her as he asked, "How long do we have, Tory?"

"Just a few minutes according to Andrew. Right Andrew?"

"Yes. If you want to escape, now is your chance."

"Do you want to come up, Andrew?"

"No. I want to stay here."

"So, you want to be a guard for the rest of your life?"

"No."

"What do you want, then?" I could hear Angel and David murmuring as they prepared to leave. I was not paying close enough attention to know what it was they were talking about.

"To never work again."

I thought for a second before responding. "Will you cooperate with us?"

"Anything you want. Just don't hurt me."

"Then stay quiet." I held up my empty hand. "Someone have a mouth gag?"

"What?" Angel and David asked at once.

"Andrew is coming with us. He doesn't want to work anymore, so he is agreeing to spill the beans in exchange for coming with us."

David plunged his hand into his pack and tossed me a spare long sleeved black turtleneck. I caught it and turned back to Andrew. He was quivering in the corner. I spun him and stuffed the makeshift gag in his mouth and tied the sleeves around his head to keep it in. It was bulky and it looked almost comical, but it would do.

Andrew did not fight me, but his beady eyes peered at me with worry and welling tears. I ignored him. He would not have thought twice about pulling the trigger on me and I had given him a mercy he may never comprehend. I felt the thought of sinking to the level of the Absolutists and their minions drifting through my mind. I shook my head to clear it out before I would act on the impulse.

When we were ready, we made our way out into the hallway and then outside where we sprinted to the tree line. There was no point to bother timing the cameras. As we moved through the trees, we heard vehicles pull up to the building.

When we were a safe distance away, I looked over at Angel. "Hishla Lake is an option."

Angel nodded and pulled out her radio and turned it on. She told Nadine the assault on Hishla Lake was a go and that we would be back shortly. If we did not return in an hour to assume we were captured.

SAR STRIKES BACK

The way back to Nadine and the safety of the safehouse was slow and arduous. Andrew was not trying to get away and was not really slowing us down. We were forced to stick to the shadows as drones flew about trying to track us down.

When we finally made it to Nadine on the second floor of the law firm, I handed Andrew off to David to lock in another room. I sat next to Nadine and Angel went to the bathroom to shower. She murmured something about needing to soothe where she was knocked out by Andrew.

"So, we have a prisoner?" Nadine asked, turning back to the monitors after a glance in our direction.

"Yes, we do. He didn't want to work anymore. I obliged."

She considered me with a sideways look for just long enough to appraise my mood, all while tapping away on the keyboard. "You look different." The flatness in her voice concerned me. I put a pin in the thought to review when the events still planned were completed.

"Where are we at? Still Phase Two?"

Nadine nodded and smiled. "Two minutes from data center explosions. Everything is going smoothly in Brazil."

"Excellent." There was a pause for several seconds before I asked my next question. "Hishla Lake?"

"So far, so good. Phase Three is still up in the air though."

"That's good at least. Need help with anything?"

"It's covered. Take a rest. You can upload data from your wristphone if you want. Would be faster than our wireless network."

"Might as well, good idea."

Nadine and I celebrated when the news came of both data centers being destroyed. Thankfully, they were blown up after evacuations, meaning no one was hurt from either side. I was glued to the screen as Nadine pulled up the communications of the strike force at Hishla Lake. We watched as they quickly set in motion the series of events that would lead to either the occupation or absolute destruction of Hishla Lake. This was the main objective in South America. This was where we would make ourselves known to the world as more than some rebels. The SAR was more than just a group of revolutionaries. If all played out perfectly, a North American version would slowly take hold and infect the population against the Absolutist system that permeated the United States since the early twenty thirties.

"How are we?" Angel asked, entering with David right behind her.

"Phase Three is happening now. We are watching the comms to track progress. Not much else to do." I looked down at my wristphone and saw it was almost done transferring the data to Nadine's laptop. Once it was complete, we would be able to encrypt it with our own keys and send it back to Antarctica disguised as a video through Vasil's VPN directly to the Council. It would slip through right under the noses and in the networks of the Absolutists. I pointed to the screen. "Our work is almost done here too."

"Excellent. Do you think we have anything good?"

"We will at least have an idea for breaking the algorithms they use for internal communications and maybe some exploits in key generation. That is until they are all changed, according to Adam. At best, we would have a good idea on current plans, although by the time we crack enough to piece it together, those will have all changed. Not like Hishla Lake at all."

Nadine looked up at this. "What do you mean, not like Hishla Lake? Wouldn't you have been invisible in the system?"

"Our friend Andrew called for backup. By now, they probably realized we were able to get into the internal system. They will double security physically and probably move to restrict access and close unsecurable locations."

"Oh, do you think they would know how we did it?"

"Going to have to hope they think it was an inside job, or that we didn't get a chance to use the terminal before fleeing," David responded.

I unplugged my wristphone as the upload was complete and motioned for Nadine to take care of the files before we forgot. Angel stood in silence, watching the secondary screen as text from communications passed back and forth. The text was the result of a simple AI program translating the voices of the strike force for internal purposes. It was built into our MESH network just like the Absolutist networks, but with recording only active for missions. Vasil made it clear that on missions we lost our privacy, but on our personal time we could restrict encroachment as much as we desired.

The tradeoffs were acceptable to nearly everyone. Only a few people complained of security risks if the network was sabotaged or infected by the Absolutist AI. Vasil quelled such worries as easily as an ant picks up its food to carry back to the queen. He was truly brilliant behind closed doors with folks that disagreed in various ways and on countless points. Everything was smoothed over and positions often changed but no one backed out of what we were doing. No one wanted that kind of a target on themselves or their colleagues, even if they might be former colleagues.

Even if they were taken, our private conversations would never have been recorded. The freedom to opt out made our organization less likely to fall in one or two breaches into our system. The Absolutists would not have enough information to track us all down and exploit our weaknesses.

"What is the plan with Andrew?" Angel inquired.

"He was a thorn in our sides, so we make him give us a flower for our efforts."

"Cryptic." She retorted, giving me a sideways glance before returning her gaze to the screen.

"He might have valuable information." David pointed out.

"Exactly. The flower." I nodded emphatically. "And besides, he agreed to it."

"By force, Tory."

"And?" I responded rhetorically. Minutes went by in silence as we watched from a digital afar. The strike force carefully and deliberately removed guards and communications as they made their way to the central control room that handled communications for Hishla Lake and was the key to controlling the power plant itself. It was close to four in the morning when they arrived at the control room. Once inside, they shut it down. The communications, the network, the power, it all went down.

Moments after that, chatter began to increase on the communication lines from the five groups distracting Absolutist forces. They were noting massive movements in retreat, and not in a way that made sense if they still believed our misinformation. Recon inside enemy territory claimed troops were headed in Hishla Lake and the east coast of Brazil and Argentina. The troop numbers to each were equal from the best reports we had.

Confused, I looked at David. "What does it mean? Are they coming for Hishla or giving up?"

David stared at the screen for a minute without acknowledging my question. He slowly walked away with his hands in his pockets until he reached a chair in the corner of the room. Angel, Nadine, and I were all watching him. Finally, he spoke carefully and deliberately as he pulled a cigar wrapped in a tobacco leaf as a natural cover from his pocket. He then pulled a lighter from his pocket. His words were quiet at first but returned to normal soon enough. "Something else is happening we don't know about. Something bigger than SAR. Something we only hypothesized a few weeks ago from Tory's data. Something we did not believe was possible. Not until now, anyway."

He lit the pre-cut cigar and sat back, puffing lightly, making a ring with the smoke. He watched as we looked at each other, confused by his words. When we looked back to him expecting more, he obliged. "Check chatter with our NAR folks. Not the ones on the west coast and in Mexico, the ones in Greenland

and Florida regions. What are they seeing?"

Nadine tapped away and a new box with text streaming through popped up on the screen. She enlarged it and gasped. "The military is taking precautions for attacks across North America, particularly on the east coast." She tabbed back to the South American screen for a brief moment and then to the North American one once more. "Same as down here." She looked up at me and over to Angel.

Angel, who was silent throughout, noticeably blanched and spoke. "The Absolutists think they are at war with one another."

"WHAT?!" I exclaimed with eyes wide. I glared over to David. "Is this what you are suggesting?"

He nodded as he puffed on his cigar. "Yes, Tory, I am." He blew another circle into the air and I collapsed into my chair.

Nadine looked expectantly at me and David. "What do we do now?"

"We rally our forces while the Absolutists are distracted with their war among themselves and seize the hearts and minds of the citizens. Just as Vasil has said all along. We must make allies always and in the shadows to avoid suspicion. This is a gift, a blessing, and it is an opportunity we should not let go to waste."

"We haven't planned for this though," I said, thinking hard about what plans Vasil had mentioned we had contingencies for. I was thinking hard, going through our plans, trying to see a definitive path forward.

"Perhaps we have not, but the Council did." The shock on my face was more than enough to make David laugh. We were all now watching him with shock. David caught his breath after wheezing from breathing a full blast of his cigar smoke. "Think about it, Tory. The Council's reluctance for us to work smaller missions. Forcing us to think bigger on this one. The way they have been advocating more intercontinental impact. They want chaos everywhere. They got it. This is exactly what they were hoping for."

"But were they planning for it? This soon?" Angel's voice was weak, and her jaw moved barely an inch as she spoke.

"We had better hope so. SAR striking back is one thing, but when the Absolutists come for revenge, we better hope they are divided. It is the only way to truly win a revolutionary war. The old adage divide and conquer is remembered for a reason."

I nodded in agreement. I was no longer searching for a way forward; I was realizing that the Council would have plotted the inevitability. "It makes sense. If we knew what we were about to set off, we may have backed down or buckled under the pressure and caused everything we have worked for to collapse. The Council has more information than we do. They likely saw the potential in what David and I laid out here. They guided us to this point, influencing our decisions. All without tipping us off to what was really at stake."

"So, what happens to Hishla?" Angel asked, looking towards Nadine and her screens.

Nadine tabbed twice and text from Hishla Lake popped back up in the MESH network. "Looks like the troops are staying away for the moment. We have control of the compound and the town."

"They will need reinforcements. We need to send everyone up there now." Angel was suddenly all business. It made sense; her friends were out there and outnumbered.

"Let's check with Vasil first." My voice felt like it came from someone else, as it cracked when I spoke. "Just to be sure we want to stay there."

"Fine," Angel said, sitting back down.

A minute went by as Nadine put a call through the network to Vasil. It was dangerous to do so as a long seamless communication and data transfer could draw attention, but this was an exception considering the circumstances. Vasil answered the call and after a second enabled video from his end.

"Video?" Nadine inquired.

"Why not? No, don't on your end, my dear. I don't want you to reveal your location. I am not at risk of being located by authorities like you." He winked at the last before zipping off a glass of what I assumed to be vodka. "What can I do for you? It is clearly not life-threatening or I would have been interrupted, eh?"

David stood up and walked over to my side. "The Council is apprised of the latest progress, right?"

"Oh my, yes!"

"And what are their thoughts on holding Hishla Lake if it appears the Absolutists are not playing nice with each other?"

"Noticed that, did you? What made you come to that conclusion?"

"A hunch. Most logical reason why troops were split after Hishla went offline."

"Well, you are not wrong, David. Looks like tensions are heating up between the American AIs and the African and Chinese AIs. Have you spoken with Hishla yet, Angel?"

"No. Waiting to hear your thoughts before taking action. We have a moment to breathe but time is running out," Angel replied, speaking up and looking at the wall. She was not fully present in the room with us. I wondered what it was she was thinking about. Judging by the way her mouth moved, I thought she may be calculating the troops she would need and from where she would gather them.

"Have them leave. Take as much equipment as possible and leave. The AI may be thinking this was a coordinated attack by another AI system to plunder and weaken it."

"Roger that." Angel grabbed her radio and left the room. Nadine lowered the volume on hers to prevent any interruptions in our conversation.

"What's the next step? How does North America look?"

"Not sure yet. That will play out how it will. We have done good. A few members of the council are flying here to speak with you and me, Tory. David, of course, is welcome to be involved. You weren't invited by the members because of secrecy and not being seen and all that but let us be honest with ourselves. You and Tory are a team and should be treated as such. I will deal with any problems on that front."

"Thank you, Vasil." David nodded his head in approval. He seemed satisfied.

Vasil continued as if David had said nothing. "Come back. Nadine, you too. Glad you are feeling better."

"Thanks, Vasil," Nadine replied.

"See you soon, then." Before I could say anything else, Vasil ended the call.

THE COUNCIL MESSENGERS

We returned to Antarctica a few days later. It was late in the day when we entered White Tunnels. We ate food in the cafeteria while chatting with some of those who were apprised of our mission before retiring to our quarters. Nadine's room was directly across from mine so we walked together talking about where things might go. After weeks of pessimistic moods, we were finally optimistic about the future of the cause. Even if there was uncertainty about where we would go, we were finally accomplishing what we had dreamed of doing: fighting back.

I woke the next day to my wristphone beeping. It took me a few groggy seconds to realize it was not my alarm but rather a high priority message. I sprung out of my bed and grabbed the device. It was from Vasil. As I unlocked the computer, I quickly opened the message. It was a voice recording. The weariness was replaced with adrenaline as I listened to the message with rapt attention. "Tory, meet me in the mine at the far end. We need to talk privately."

I quickly dressed and swished mouthwash to clean my mouth while brushing my hair to look presentable. After I had finished, I picked up my coat and dashed out of my room. I strode quickly down the hallway and off to the mine to meet Vasil. He reserved private high-priority messages for the most urgent and important things. It was best not to dawdle when receiving one, as I found out early in our work.

Several minutes later, I entered the closed off section of the mine that separated the digging equipment and the end wall from the far warmer work area. To my surprise, Vasil and David were standing next to two people I did not know. Both of the strangers were wearing gear that indicated they were miners here, but I had not seen them before and did not know their names. I had been out of the loop on recent hires, so I decided they may be new recruits from the Itrep side of the business.

"Hi." I smiled and offered my hand. Neither one of them acknowledged it, but rather smiled and greeted me in return. I put my hand down and looked at David. He shrugged. The man pursed his lips and the woman made no other action than to continue to smile.

"With Tory here, we can get started," Vasil said, pulling his wristphone up and with a few taps, my and David's wristphones shut down. "Security as always."

"Thank you, Vasil." The taller of the two strangers said in a raspy voice. They both squared to David and me before continuing. The man's mouth moved slightly, as if he could not move his jaw more than a few inches. "Tory, I want to congratulate you on the success of your SAR strike plan. It was brilliant." It dawned on me at the moment exactly who these two strangers really were. They were council members, not ones who participated in the meeting often, but ones I recognized by their verbal mannerisms. I hid my confusion as to why they did not have their masks. It was not one of my priority questions.

"Yes." The woman piped up. Her voice was silky-smooth and entrancing in a delicate yet dangerous kind of way. It had been a long time since I heard a voice as interesting as hers was. "Although Vasil tells us it was not just your brain that came up with it all?"

"Correct. David helped with the strategy." I looked at David, who nodded and waved his hands with humility.

"Oh, look at you two, both modest and unwitting to the history you have wrought. I'd say you were well aware of the impact, but I know you aren't," she finished smugly. I did not like her attitude. She seemed too self-important for my liking. The man with the raspy voice was far more down to earth from what I could tell.

As if he read my mind, the man acknowledged David's efforts as well. "Yes, David is certainly a brilliant strategist. His ideas and your leadership, Tory, have led us to a pivotal point that could not be achieved without your efforts. I am so sorry to have kept you in the dark on the full plot for so long, but I believe Vasil has convinced us you are ready for the big picture."

David and I exchanged looks of bewilderment. We were not sure what exactly the man meant by the *big picture*. Vasil chuckled but kept himself from speaking whatever witticism was on his mind. I almost half-expected the woman to slap Vasil the way she looked at him before returning to her pleasant smile.

"Nothing? Speechless?" The man asked.

"Oh, I. Um. Yes." I managed to sputter while David remained silent. His jaw was forced shut. He did not know what to make of it, either. He always said if you did not think the words would come out that are in your head, they are best left unsaid. I understood exactly what he meant and the wisdom in it, particularly in this instant.

"It's all right, Tory," the man continued. "Vasil, do you have the hologram?"

"Yes, of course." Vasil put his left hand into a pocket and withdrew a small hologram base. Putting it on the ground, Vasil pressed the button on the side that powered it on. A second later and I saw the outline of a plan with diagrams, pictures, arrows, and long lines of text. I had never seen anything quite like it. It was as if Vasil had just shown us a conspiracy theorist's whiteboard that had decades of work crammed into it.

"Thanks, Vasil. Now it looks a little confusing, but it is rather simple. Start from the top and skim through and let us know your thoughts." The man winked at us and turned his back to us to speak with the woman.

I began to read the plan and as I moved further down the chain of events, I realized where our actions fitted in. My eyes grew even wider when I saw what the Council was planning. We were only in the starting stages of a long and ambitious plot that sought to remove all AIs aside from ours, or more accurately Vasil's, which would be built to serve the singular purpose of defeating the other AIs and serving our purposes. All of the secrecy around Vasil's work with the computer technologies finally made sense. He was building the AI in White Tunnels.

"Thoughts?" the man asked, seeing I had finished looking at the hologram.

"An AI that would serve us? Wouldn't that lead to the same problems as we already have, just more centralized?"

"Vasil is in charge of the AI," the man rasped.

"Yes. Tory, remember when I mentioned I wanted to send people who would not fit in to other planets to colonize?"

"Yes?" I replied, not understanding what this had to do with the AI.

"The AI will be boxed up and sent with anyone who will not or cannot live in a world without a computer doing all the thinking for you. That will be the first wave of colonization ships."

"So, your plan is to send humans who have a different view of the future into space?" David asked, still gazing with wide eyes at the hologram.

"Whoever is in power here gets to stay here. That's only fair, isn't it?" The nameless man answered indignantly.

"We need unity after so much turmoil. Especially if we set it off. Agreeing to split the human race makes logical sense. The Absolutist followers can find somewhere else to live under software, our software to ensure they don't come back for revenge. We want to live with software, not for it or it for us," the woman chimed in.

"And what if they don't want to go and don't want to live without the AI?"

"We have not figured out a contingency for that event," the male council member responded flatly. "If you have one that is better than shoving them all into a cramped spaceship, let us know."

I wanted to move on from the subject. The plan made me uncomfortable, so I broke the silence that reigned as David's gaze became a momentary glare at the thought of forcing people to leave the planet. "So, Vasil is building the AI here?"

"That is correct, Tory." The woman nodded, smiling wickedly.

"How much bandwidth do we have on other continents? Is it enough to achieve the goals in this plan?"

"Not exactly. That is why South America is so important. And Australia will be as well. Africa is already heavily connected, but the bandwidth going out of Africa is not enough and the speeds are slow and can be spotty at best." Vasil spoke as if he was lecturing in a good-natured kind of way that made me appreciate him rather than feel as if he was talking down to me. The woman standing across the hologram from me could learn from Vasil. "Plus, the fact our hunch was right that Africa is going to be invaded by the American Absolutists and possibly even the Europeans. Best to avoid relying on those pathways."

"Hishla Lake would be a great choke point for physical skirmishes and a base of operations to pit AI against AI. Lots of bandwidth all headed north," David said thoughtfully.

"That is why we saw the potential in your plans. We saw the chance we needed to strike and get as much information before moving in. Officially." The woman's sneer was puzzling. She was a confusing person to read. Was she upset with the plan, the idea of taking South America and placing it under our control? The AI? Or something else.

"And what exactly will our AI do when we inevitably create a power vacuum?"

My question was answered by Vasil. "The new computer will take over the tasks of the old one. Should be relatively seamless. Over time, we will give people more customization and choice in the basic things like toothbrushes and clothing. The priority is to give them the choice in what they want to do, especially if they want to join us. If they don't want choice but are not hurting our cause, we will placate them until the time is right to deal with the differences."

"Where are you getting the source code for those things? Building it yourself?" David asked with genuine curiosity in his voice.

"Building code to hijack the harmless code from the Absolutist systems. Easier and more fun."

"Any other thoughts?" the man asked again, somewhat impatiently.

"This is the high level, no details," I stated, looking directly into the female council member's eyes, hoping for a glimpse or hint of something I could use to read her.

"Do you need to know more than that?" Her voice was silky.

"Fair point," I retorted almost immediately.

"Then why ask?" The man looked confused.

I looked at him. "I wasn't asking. Those were my thoughts." That stumped him into silence.

"You will learn more as things move along. This should help give you a bigger picture as to what we are trying to do here." The woman bent down and turned off the hologram and plunged the puck into her pocket.

"Thank you for meeting with us," Vasil said.

"The pleasure was ours. You have our orders for South America. I cannot wait to see how Tory and David handle them." The man replied before turning to us and bowing his head slightly. He and the woman left unceremoniously.

"Well, what do you guys think?" Vasil asked, slapping his hands together and rubbing them anxiously. It may have also been because of the chilly temperature, as I noticed I was shivering.

"The Council does not like to elaborate much, do they?" David smiled as he spoke. We already knew the answer.

"Yep. And those two are the lower echelons of the Council. Was not sure who or how many to expect, but it looks like the normal messengers were sent."

"What do you mean, normal messengers?" I inquired.

"Well, the Council Congregation is split into several factions. Each one based on the continent where they are from. Those members elect *the Council* that handles information between the Council Congregations, which they sometimes refer to as the Lower Council. The Upper Council confirms and admits those elected in, to balance the power a bit. The Lower Council does not get the luxury of masking like the Upper Council, but it is a bit pointless since we all know one another anyway.

"The two people you met were council members that spread the word of their plans and our next actions. You don't often see them as they are lurking about listening in. While they are elected to the Council, they handle more of the communication aspect, and not plotting the direction. For the moment, anyway. That is as much as I know." Vasil paused and then added, "You are officially inside, by the way. Both of you. We are in the Lower Council. Not council members, but still in. As part of the Antarctica delegation." Vasil looked at us both with a serious expression. I saw his eyes and knew at once he was no longer jovial in any way. This was his all-business face and mind. The Vasil that did not joke and was always thinking several moves ahead of the current conversation.

"We are?" David asked incredulously.

Vasil looked at us both before honing in on me. "You have already worked directly under me. Tory even filled in for me over the holidays. You are worthy of being my equal, working to disrupt South America with SAR and assist the NAR whenever possible. I will be helping out, but you are now the Director of South American Operations. DSAO in our council meetings. And just so you know, that comes with a minor rank in the lower council, same as me. We are Overseers that deal with the operations run by our congregations. David will be the Assistant Director. Not that you won't be an equal, just that you're not ready to give reports to the Council without help yet. Need to polish up on your people skills a bit, but you will be able to listen in on meetings now since you are a member."

"Understood," David said without delay or thought. I knew that it may bother him that he was moving up in my shadow. It bothered me. I saw him as a true equal. However, it did make sense to name him an Assistant Director. It gave him the authority he needed and I could make it known he had my full backing in all decisions. The sting of being told that you are not ready to deliver reports to the people you are working for had to be hard for anyone, including David.

BIRTHDAY CAKE

It was five years ago I had wished someone would acknowledge my birthday. Franklin remembered when we were in Australia a year later. That was the only time. Last year I completely missed it due to all the work and dates blurring together in White Tunnels. I had never made a big deal about my birthday, not because I had the choice at first, but because it was not important to me. Age was irrelevant in everything besides the biological clock of reproduction in my opinion.

Sure, ages helped to label and categorize people better, but the construct of yearly increasing age was absurd. It would be more logical to use DNA and genetics to trace milestones in life, such as when the brain becomes fully developed and personality set in stone or growth stopping. These dates would be unique for everyone since solidifying brain development by the age of twenty-six was a guesstimate. Perhaps I was looking for a way to ignore my birthday and sought out more logical concepts in the process. Perhaps I was just hiding from the fact I have always wanted a birthday party like in the movies.

In any case, I was still surprised when everyone in my staff took time out of their busy day to bring a cake into my office and sit it on my desk and sing Happy Birthday. I was so embarrassed I was redder than my new outfit that I was wearing. It was my first purchase when I arrived in Hishla for the second time in my life. I wanted to treat myself to something special and look more professional in the process. After all, I was now Director of South American Operations for over a year. I was able to avoid any calamity last year since it was just me and David, who coaxed the date out of me after the fact. We had a nice dinner and left it at that, at my request.

In the time after meeting with the mysterious Council Messengers, I spent most of it getting up to speed on all the details I had not been following that Vasil was working. I spent more time than ever with David and then Angel, who I pushed for an assistant director position but was not granted. She was not technically part of our organization, but rather the leader of SAR. This bothered me and after many long conversations I managed to get approval to develop an agreement that brought SAR closer into our plans. Angel was involved with the Council before, but she was left in the dark about broader plans that did not involve SAR more often than was necessary.

I wanted to build SAR and other organizations up as well as our own network of Vasilevsky Enterprise businesses. We needed to institutionalize and localize, and that was my focus. David was not a fan of the work that had to be done to achieve those ends, as he was more hands on. I let him train people in self-defense and other basics for delicate and dangerous situations with our network of people throughout South America with the goal of preparing SAR and the people around them. It was grueling work, but David seemed to enjoy it more than the office work that I had to clear off my desk every day. He was able to put his talents to use and I would occasionally seek his strategic advice. It was a good symbiotic relationship.

Everyone finished singing and cheered as I continued to blush, staring at the cake with my name and thirty-four candles. The time had gone by faster than I had realized. The years I had spent working with Vasil and David went by before I had a chance to truly reflect on them. In four short years, I went from an *Abnormal* with a crush in Australia being sent around doing grunt work for Absolutists to the one giving orders to thousands, leading resistance operations for an entire continent. The gravity of the achievement weighed in my stomach as I stared at the cake.

"Do you want a piece, Tory?" David asked as he stepped forward and started cutting slices of the cake.

"Sure, a corner piece. Is the frosting good?"

"The best in town!" David and a few others laughed. The town was small and there were not many bakers to buy from, two to be exact.

"You have to be careful with those corner pieces!" Mary, my assistant, exclaimed from somewhere behind David's figure. "The older you get, the more likely they are to hit you where it counts."

I pressed my lips together, biting the retort that came to mind. I did not care for the fanfare, and especially quips about my weight. Even if it was in jest. I had enough slander sent my way for a lifetime and it was hard to take the good-natured ribbings from the team at face value or with a grain of salt. While I may have become warmer to the outside world, it was hard to remove the thick skin. There was a balance I had yet to find, but for now it still bothered me when those closest to me poked fun.

David handed me a slice. Vanilla with blue and red frosting. I tasted it and it was delicious. I sat and watched as everyone got a slice of cake and ate it with enthusiasm. They were all enjoying themselves as they talked. The din grew loud enough that I began to worry we might distract the folks still working.

"Tory, why didn't you take the day off?" One of the newer team members asked, after edging over to my desk through the crowd.

"I try not to make a big deal about it."

"Why not? It should be a day for you to relax a bit."

"I'm too busy these days. I forget my birthday most years; this year I am busier than ever. Only reason I remembered is because David asked me." My voice felt robotic.

"Don't like to think about your age?" she asked innocently. Her face was full of genuine curiosity. I noticed others nearby had paused in conversation to listen in. I was in charge and everyone looked to me for advice or wisdom in anything I said. It was a lot of pressure, most of which I forced myself to be less cognizant about. If I were to listen to my inner thoughts in all things, I would certainly have a panic attack. Over the last decade, I had been training myself to pay less attention to others around me and what they were thinking about. It led to paranoia and I did not need that, especially now that I was leading the people around me. People who believed in me, and trusted in me to do the right thing, to say the right things.

"No, not really. It's never made much of a difference to me. Last time I truly celebrated my birthday was back on the reservation."

The room grew quieter at this. It was obvious the realization of celebrating my birthday might bring up my past, yet no one thought about it until it was too late. It was almost gratifying that everyone assumed my past was the same as theirs. It helped to make me feel as if I fitted in. However, I knew it would inevitably lead to a situation just like this, where everyone remembers that I was an Abnormal in my previous life and that had long-lasting implications. We were all privileged to be living and working in an environment that did not discriminate because of the genetics of the person, especially when those genetics had a direct impact on their appearance.

"Oh, I'm sorry Tory." The woman stuck her hand out as if to touch my shoulder before retracting it with a jerk. "I didn—"

I raise my hand to silence her. I nodded and looked around the room. "It's all right. Really. I should not have brought up my past."

"No really, I am. I—" the woman said. A man next to her nudged her in the rib and she stopped speaking.

"When you are done with your piece of cake, let's get to work, folks. We have Absolutists to undermine," I said with an air of authority and finality, one that came easier than it did a year ago. I forced a smile on my face to emphasize the point.

I watched as everyone but David filed out. He was cleaning up trash and made to pick up the cake. "Will put this in the break room so that everyone who was not here can have a chance for some of it." He was not looking me in the eye; it was evident he was trying to avoid eye contact after a few seconds of silence while he picked the cake up.

"David," I said slowly. His eyes fluttered up to mine and locked as we looked at one another. "This was nice. I'm sorry I ruined the mood for everyone."

"It is a good reminder to everyone that we may have a good life now, but it was not always so. Not for all of us anyway. Even at that, any point in time we can lose everything we have as we are committing sedition after all. We may be blind at times to the suffering of those among us, but it is a lesson in humility. A reminder we are not all equal to some, while equal to others."

"I understand. Really. Hopefully, everyone forgets about it and moves on."

"Oh, don't worry about that. This won't linger. The motivation around here is really high and we are all optimistic. We are sitting in one of the enemy's newest power plants, celebrating your birthday. Someone who would never have set foot in the building if we did not follow your lead."

"Thank you Fra-David." I almost said Franklin. He had been on my mind all week. I had been wondering why he was not sent to White Tunnels. He clearly did not mind Abnormals the same way others did. Why did Vasil not recognize him as a potential turncoat?

"Frank? I'm not that boring, am I?" David said with a half grin.

I tried my best to smile with a happy façade. I was not sure I achieved the desired level needed to convince David, though. "Franklin. It was someone I knew from before Vasil and White Tunnels. You sounded like him for a second there. That's all."

"Oh, wow. Is that a good thing?"

"Very much so." I kept my composure with more effort than I cared to admit to myself in the moment.

"Well, that's good at least. See you later, Tory!" He turned and strode out of the room. Mary rose from her desk just outside my office and shut the door behind him so that I was alone and once again cut off from everyone in the office area. The blinds were already angled so no one could see inside while I could see outside. I let my façade drop and I slumped in my chair for a minute, letting the silence speak its piece.

I stood up and turned to stare outside. The concrete landscape that made up the complex was drab at best. It was not nearly as impressive as many of the other buildings I had lived and worked in. Then again, I never had a view quite like I had here, so I may not have realized how drab the other complexes were. I had never had a sweeping vista of mountains at my disposal before. It dawned on me at that exact moment not just how far I had come professionally, but how far the cause had been pushed forward since Vasil met with me all that time ago.

It felt like forever since David, Nadine, and the others helped me raid the satellite office building that was on the other side of the facility, just out of my view. Then, hearing of the losses of Zack and Jesus, even though I had not known them well, I had grown to appreciate and rely on their intel and insight into South America. Without their help, we would never have made it into Hishla in the first place. Without their deaths, we would never have struck back in such a bold and seemingly foolish manner. One that paid off tenfold.

Africa and the Americas were at war. We were silently taking over in South America and undermining the Absolutist AI Governor in every way imaginable. It was a campaign like no other. With Adam's brilliance, we had even tricked the AI into ignoring many of our actions. It would buy us the time necessary to dig in in such a way we would be able to fight the AI with an actual chance of success.

The only concerning thing was how we were able to get away with more than I thought logical. More than we should have been allowed to get away with. It concerned me, but as long as our inside information was solid and our informant was alive, I did not think we had anything to worry about. At least, that is what Vasil said on the matter. I was not so trusting of the informant. Everything I had accomplished seemed too easy to have been just good information. There had to be something sinister in the works.

I had been spending my off hours working on theories as to what could possibly go wrong and how we could be led into a trap. So far, I had come up with nothing substantial. Before I confided in anyone, I needed to have a presentation of my thoughts laid out with objective data. Something I was not sure would ever be possible to obtain. As much as I had searched and sensed for a trap, I found none and the hope inside me grew. The hope that we really were winning and our informant was not going to betray us. That we were really on the path to victory in South America.

THE SAFEHOUSE

I was in the car with Nadine. She was part of my security detail at Hishla Lake, a personal bodyguard. David had her assigned to me at all times outside of my office and personal suite at Hishla Lake. He ordered more guards to protect me when I was in public, an order I was openly defying by taking this excursion with just Nadine by my side. David said we could not risk me falling into the hands of our dangerous foe. While I appreciated the thought, I did not believe I was truly at risk. Especially since we had the entire town and complex locked down as tightly, if not more so, than when we first broke in and Nadine was injured.

Even so, I was forced to let myself be driven about with a chauffeur, or in this case with a chauffeuse, according to Nadine who had studied Old French before English became the primary, and mandatory, language for everyone. She was a well-educated woman with a brilliant mind. While a jack of many trades, she was fluent enough in them to appear like a master of many as well. I appreciated her and the more I learned about her, the more I enjoyed her company.

"Whatcha doing all over there, ma'am?" Nadine asked me, interrupting my reverie. I shook my head before clearing my throat. She caught me when I was dazing off into deep thought and her question took a few seconds to truly register. We had a bit of a running joke where she would refer to me as ma'am even though she was strictly not supposed to acknowledge I was important or higher in the station in any way. Those were my orders, and when outside of Hishla Lake, David's as well. When we were alone, she often used it as a conversation starter. Just like now.

I turned my head to the left to see her eyeing me with the corner of her right eye as she split her attention between me and the road. She was brilliant at multitasking as well, but no one could drive and keep eye contact without risk. She had studied extensively the art, philosophy, and concepts behind multitasking and she herself did not believe in it. The human mind could simply not focus on two tasks that required medium to high levels of conscious thought. You could feign it in a lot of ways, but we were analog beings that were simply not wired to work on multiple tasks requiring that level of parallel thought.

The quantum computers, on the other hand, were more than capable of processing multiple strands of data simultaneously, as they had more processing cores. I only had one, same as Nadine. That was perhaps the reason as to why the computers were so good at controlling the choices of everyone in the Absolutist system. Nothing could compute all possible outcomes as quickly or as thoroughly as a quantum machine.

"I'm doing fine, Nadine. Thanks for checking in on me."

"Spaced out there for a minute by the looks of it."

"Yeah. Just thinking to myself."

"What about? If you don't mind and can tell me that is," she amended hastily. Some things I worked on were off limits for those who were not in the need-to-know pool of individuals.

"My birthday yesterday got me thinking exactly how long I've been at this. And what exactly it all means."

"Ah, reflecting on your life or just how crazy what we are doing truly is?"

"Yes." We both chuckled as she pulled up to a stoplight. She took a sip from her coffee mug. "Really though. My life has always been about going and doing whatever others did not want to do. I had little to no choice in anything in the macro and much of my micro. If you know what I mean."

"Macro being where you lived, what you did, who with. Micro being clothing, time off, and the like?"

"Exactly."

"Yeah, it is insane to think about how long we worked as serfs before working for Vasil. Yet all those hours were not nearly as productive as our more limited work hours these days, eh?"

"For the lower echelons, yes."

"Then we have workaholics like you." She smiled and the car moved forward as the light changed. We were headed out of town to meet Angel. She was a figure that citizens would now recognize and we wanted to be assured her whereabouts did not fall into the hands of our enemy.

"If being a workaholic brings freedom to my life and to yours, then so be it."

"That's actually really selfless if you think about it. You are spending your younger years working yourself to death so others might have the very thing you seek to attain."

"If I work hard enough, I will get to see it too."

"Fair enough. If you don't die in the process."

"That's what I have you for, is it not?"

"Touché, I suppose." We sat in silence for a few seconds before she asked her next question. "Do you ever think about what might happen if we get caught and cannot escape?"

"For you? Reeducation. For me—" I trailed off, not speaking the last words on my tongue. It would be certain death for me to be captured and sent to anyone with any authority. The Absolutists had no need for disobedient Abnormals other than making an example of them. That alone would be enough for an execution. If one added into the mix how high up in Vasil's organization and how much damage I had caused to the grip of control the AI Governor had in South America, well there was no hope. Even if I spilled all the information on the organization, the Council, on my friends, I would still never see the sun rise again.

"Death," Nadine said softly.

I nodded. I was not sure if she caught my movement, as I was now looking out the window. The trees flashing by gave way to a more barren and mountainous landscape. We were getting close.

I looked down at my wristphone. No new messages had come in, so I powered it down for the remainder of our trip. Nadine noticed and did the same to hers as well. We did not want to risk anyone knowing what we were up to, even on our MESH network. The handoff of intel was far too important to be tracked and pinned down by a potential bad actor. Not that we expected one. Caution was everything.

The rest of the ride went along in silence until we pulled

up to an old decrepit-looking rambler. The dilapidated exterior was a mirror to the inside. It was a safehouse that Angel used on the occasion she was near Hishla Lake. It was also where the members for our infiltration of Hishla Lake more than a year ago eventually wound up after being chased around the countryside. After arriving, they were eventually shipped back to White Tunnels. Most of them remained in White Tunnels when I left, a few helping to run the mining operation as I had once done. Rusty had been temporarily designated as the White Tunnels Overseer when I left. I had no idea if Vasil gave him the position full time.

Nadine shut the car off and we waited for Angel to appear. The minutes ticked by and no one showed up. Not by car, bike, or foot. I was beginning to grow worried and in my anxiety eventually broke the silence to voice my concern. "I am starting to think something bad may have happened."

Nadine pulled out the gun from her holster around her leg. She also drew a knife from somewhere on her person. I did not see where it came from. She peered about, clearly searching for anything disturbed we had not yet noticed. "I agree. This does feel a bit off, Tory. Any thoughts on how to proceed?"

I searched my thoughts as quickly as I could. I was not sure how long we should wait for Angel before giving up. We needed to hand her the plans, but we could also not afford to waste time exposed like this. Someone was bound to come by asking why we were sitting in a car next to a vacant house and if we needed help. If they recognized who I was and were unfriendly to the cause, it could end violently. "Maybe we should check out the inside. She may have been catching up on sleep."

"Yeah. Maybe." Nadine exited the vehicle. I made to do the

same, but she shook her head. "Let me clear the house first."

"Can I stand and get some of the fresh country air, then?"

"I suppose so. Don't be afraid to drive off if you get spooked. I will be okay."

"All right. Hurry back!" I called softly as she walked towards the house.

I watched her trudge up to the door and quickly move through the doorway, wielding the gun and knife as she went. I waited for a few minutes before she exited the house and stood on the porch. "Nothing. No one. No signs of anyone staying here recently."

"What do you reckon we do Nadine?"

"How late is she?"

I turned the key in the vehicle to see the time pop up on the screen. "Twenty minutes late."

"Let's give her another ten."

"Fair enough."

I was leaning on the side of the car studying the ground, still thinking hard about everything on my mind since my birthday. The majority of the time I spent thinking was on a singular question that had begun to eat my productivity in the last few weeks. The time was spent thinking about Franklin and why I was chosen, but he was left behind. I was motivated by a self-centered need for his deep voice and his words of wisdom. Most of all, and more than I cared to admit even to myself in any way but thought, I longed for his touch.

It seemed odd to me that he did not come up on Vasil's list to recruit in our endeavor. The way he treated me and the fact our wristphones were always nearby in the off hours that we spent together, it had struck me as odd the more I thought about it. I could make do with David when it came for comforting presence and words, but nothing came close to being near Franklin.

"You're thinking about it again."

"About what again?" I asked, distracted by something near the hill.

"Whatever it was in the car. It is a distinct look, Tory."

This time, I knew something was up as I heard a scuffle on the other side of the hill directly in front of me. My eyes focused on the apex of the hill and saw movement in the weeds. I tried to nonchalantly look away and over to Nadine.

As I did, I saw she was staring at me with a questioning expression. She must have heard something too, for I could tell in her eyes she was all business and not expecting an answer to her statements. I stretched my arms and in doing so I turned my body towards her and motioned I saw something that needed to be addressed on the hill. I was not sure what else I could do and hoped Nadine would understand that with my gestures.

"Let's go inside while we wait. No need to stay out here," Nadine said cheerily as she put a smile on her face.

I nodded. "Good idea."

"I checked everything but the cellar. Didn't find the door."

"It's probably hidden. We can look for it together." With that, we walked into the safehouse and as I closed the door behind me, Nadine cleared the house again to ensure we were alone. I walked into the kitchen, which was facing the hill we heard the noise on, but I did not see anything anomalous in the greenery. Nadine edged into the kitchen with me and stepped out of view of the window.

"Stay there, Tory. Keep an eye out the window to see if you can catch a glimpse of anything," Nadine murmured.

"Sure," I replied, adjusting myself so my head was half covered by the wall to avoid any lipreading but in a way that I could still move my head to see up the hill when talking to Nadine. If there was one thing hanging around David and Nadine had taught me, it was situational awareness and what the environment around me gave away, or hid, as the case may be.

"Do you think Angel is still coming?" Nadine asked.

"I was about to ask you the same thing."

"Damn. Perhaps we should have got in the car and left."

"We can still do that."

"Too late. If we are surrounded, it is too late."

"We don't know if there is anyone. It could have easily been an animal Nadine."

"What does your gut say?" she challenged.

I did not answer at first, as I had to check to be sure of what I thought. My thoughts were becoming jumbled as I tried to process what I had seen, if I had seen anything; and what the noise could have been from. My gut gave me the same reply as before, *danger.* "I believe it was someone."

"Then let's assume it is."

"What do you reckon we do, Nadine?" I moved my head to get a full view of the hill and thought I saw a glint of something shining back at me. My heart sank as it registered what I might have seen. "And I think there is a scope of some sort aimed at me."

I said this as calmly as I could, but as I finished the sentence, it occurred to me what a glint or flash of glass, a scope, on the hill might mean. Nadine's eyebrows furrowed and she motioned for me to step towards her. "That is not good. Not good at all."

"I'll turn my wristphone on and send a message for assistance." I offered quietly as a bead of sweat began to run down my right earlobe. It was warm outside, and I was concerned for my safety. I lifted my arm and Nadine knocked it back down.

"No. If they are out here to get us, we do not want to give them any chance to learn about our communications network or the phones themselves."

"But I can get backup," I protested. "We can get them even as they think they are getting us!"

"We are too far away from Hishla. They will never arrive in time," Nadine hissed at me. For the first time, I was on the receiving end of her anger. It was not pleasant.

"I'm sorry," I responded soothingly. "What do we do then? Fight?"

"We about have to. Are there any weapons hidden in here that you know about?"

I thought rapidly back to the conversations Angel and I had about the safehouses and what they were stocked with. "No, not likely. The only ones that are will be in the high-traffic areas where people need to lay low and go undetected. This place is not undetectable."

"No kidding."

"But there might be a saferoom that can be secured with rations."

"Hmm. Probably would be in the cellar, I'd imagine. This place is kind of a dump otherwise."

"Agreed."

"Do you think there is an entrance to the cellar from the inside?" Nadine asked hopefully. "I did not see an entrance."

"Maybe. Like I said, it is probably hidden. I'll look again and if I do not find it inside, we will have to go outside and check."

"If there is not an interior doorway, we ought to find a different answer here."

"Probably. Let me go look before we make a decision."

"All right. Stay out of the windows as much as possible."

I crept through the house for what felt like several minutes until I came across a section of wall with a makeshift door that once opened, revealed stairs leading down. I straightened up and softly called to Nadine. I found the cellar behind a door masquerading as a bookshelf that was left open a crack. Without waiting for her, I ducked and stepped onto the stairs and down into the cellar. The last thing I saw before losing consciousness was someone dressed darkly, shooting a dart into my neck.

MELVIN

The blinding light. It was shining in my face as I squinted. I could not tell where I was or what was flooding my vision with such burning white light. So bright, my eyes nearly screamed in pain. I shut them and as I did, I noticed I could still make out the light through my eyelids. A movement caught my attention. It came from behind the light and briefly flickered across the source, darkening my vision momentarily.

"Who's there?" I demanded.

"You forget your place." The reply was sharp and demanding of obedience, yet something in it was off. It sounded like the tone was one of exaggerated patience. I was not about to give in to the man behind the voice without a fight, however. I struggled to move my arms and legs to stand up and found that I was tied to a round metal object to a wall by rope.

"Who are you?" I demanded again. This time with enough venom in my voice that I felt the person beside the blinding light pause in their movements to focus in on me.

"I am of no concern. You are the only concern. And my prisoner."

"Where is Nad—" I cut myself off before giving the man her full name.

"Who?" The voice was almost hopeful.

"Where is she?" I asked bluntly.

The figure gestured and the light lowered. I heard a sigh and dared my eyes open. I was able to make out the shadow of a tall man. "So much for the easy way. If you won't tell me who she is, will you at least tell me who you are?" His voice was still hopeful, yet sharp as a razor. When I did not answer him, he added, "You do know your own name, don't you?"

"I'm not sure I know what you mean."

"Amnesia? Sudden perhaps?" The sarcasm was so evident I could not pretend to ignore it. The man was likely already strung tightly if he had been speaking with Nadine before me. She was a tough shell to crack under pressure. David said she was likely able to handle more verbal, psychological, and physical abuse than most of the people he had ever worked with. She was an amazing woman. To my chagrin, I was nowhere close to her equal. Nor did I have the same level of practice she did.

"Why do you want my name?"

"I like to know who I am dealing with."

"That makes two of us." Before the words had left my mouth, the man slapped my face almost as hard as if he used the light and not his hand. If it were not for the fingered glove, I would not have realized one could slap that hard. My cheek instantly grew hot in response. I let a cry of pain from my lips as I sagged to one side. The ropes held me in place and my shoulders struggled to return me to my previous position.

"You will not resort to any more sarcasm," the man said coldly and without emotion. It was fake. It was too logical and calculated. It did not mean he was telling the truth, however, but rather it was not from a place of emotion that he spoke. Valuable information.

"Sorry."

"And you will address me as master." I did not react with more than a twitch of the mouth. I opened my eyes fully and gazed up at the figure, hoping to get a better look at his features. The light was still obscuring my vision of his face; thankfully, it was not blinding me any longer. "Do not look at me, filth."

I was not prepared for the light to disappear. When I blinked and my eyes began to adjust to the darkness, I felt a cold shaft of metal slam into my gut. It was a flashlight. Since I could not move, I heaved and convulsed in response. When I had the ability to speak again, I did not look back up.

"You will address me as master, and you will not look at me unless I tell you to." There was an edge to his voice, a menace. An emotion that was not there before. He liked feeling as if he was in complete control. I decided to grant his wish for the time being, if for no other reason than to avoid another strike with the flashlight.

"Yes, master."

"Who are you?"

"I am of no importance. Master." I resisted the urge to add the snarky retort that so desperately wanted to escape from my thoughts.

"How utterly unhelpful."

"Apologies, master." I received another gut strike from the

flashlight. The cold metal then came to rest lightly on my long blonde hair.

"You will not answer when you have nothing to say."

"Yes, master." I artificially subdued my tone and resonance and did my best to restrain from a sarcastic or angry reply. This was not the time to argue or antagonize. This was the time to appear small. By adjusting my voice, I might come off as unworthy of his time, but I may have already given away too much. Or Nadine cracked and gave the man enough information on me that he already knew the answers to his questions, but wanted verification they were real.

"Apologies will be punished. They are a waste of my time. Understood?"

"Yes, master."

"Now, if you don't tell me who you are, I will bash your head just like your lovely friend ten minutes ago."

I deliberated for a few seconds. When the metal was lifted off of my hair, I blurted out my most formulated response. "Franky."

"Franky? Is that short for something?"

"Frances. My mother was also Frances and everyone called her Frannie."

"Stupid name if you ask me but I'm not an Abnormal, am I? Who am I to judge, eh?"

I nodded in response. There was nothing to say, and the risk of saying the wrong thing was too great. I was beginning to think up as much of a backstory as I could so I would be prepared to prove my new identity.

"Well, Franky. I am going to call you by your name to make things easy for you," he said this slowly, as if taunting me. "Where are you from?"

"Upstate New York."

"Lie."

"North Dakota." It slipped my mind Abnormals did not live east of the Mississippi in America. It was a silly, and deadly, mistake. I could not afford another.

"Why did you lie, Franky?"

"I worked in New York for several years."

"You what?" he asked, with a hint of intrigue and venom in his voice.

"I worked in Upstate New York for several years, *master*."

"Ah." He paused. "What did you do there?"

"Programming PLCs, master."

"PLCs?"

"Programmable logic controllers. Used to regulate water supply."

"You are that smart, eh?"

"No. Just good at following orders, master."

"Well that's odd. Why are you here then?"

"Not sure I understand the question."

"Not as smart as I thought. Oh well. Abnormals always overrate their own intelligence. How the hell did you end up here, Frannie?"

"Franky."

"What?!" he exclaimed, lifting the flashlight again.

"Franky, master." I cowered in the hopes it would placate him. It apparently succeeded, as he lowered the metal cylinder halfway back down. I was not sure if it was an obedience test, a story test, or a simple mistake on his end. In all scenarios, I was at risk of being struck again.

"Well, how did you end up here? I see no PLCs to work on."

"I now work mining Itrep. I am an Itrep Hunter, master."

"Oh. So you've had multiple different jobs. Some of which required competence."

"Yes, master."

"Well, that's good, I suppose. You will be easy to train on your new job, then." When I said nothing, he added, "Ask me what your new job is."

"What is my new job, master?"

"How do you like digging?"

"I am good at digging for Itrep."

"I meant with your bare hands."

"I don't understand."

"Your new job is to be humiliated until you tell me what you really do here, you stupid, filthy *girl*." He nearly spat the last word out with enough disgust that I thought I would feel his saliva hit my face. "Digging your grave with your bare hands."

I ground my teeth and kept my eyes down. I felt like I was in a movie. It was easy for me to pretend to be a character and that I was an actress portraying. The thought helped solidify my resolve as I waited, silently thinking about Nadine and what may have happened to her.

"Sir, a group of people are approaching," another man's voice came from the darkness, somewhere behind the figure of the person before me.

"So?" my captor replied with malice.

"Not one of ours."

"Why didn't you say so?!" The figure left me and went through a door. As the door slammed shut, I noticed that I was actually in the back of a truck of some kind. We were in the driveway of the safehouse.

After being plunged back into total darkness, I listened for ten seconds to see if I could hear what was happening outside of my mobile prison. Hearing nothing but silence, I had to assume I was in a soundproofed area where screaming or banging on the walls would not help my case. While thinking of my next step, I fidgeted to see how tightly the rope on my wrists was tied.

The door opened again and someone entered with a flashlight. When he spoke, I realized it was the same person from earlier. He had a knife in one hand and the flashlight in the other. "You are to not speak at all. If you do, I will be forced to harm you. Something I don't like doing with my playthings. Understand?"

I nodded and pursed my lips. To my surprise, he cut me loose but held my arms behind my back as we exited the vehicle.

The bright light blinded me for several seconds as the man pushed me forward. I stumbled as I tried to keep up with him and to stay on my feet. My mind began to flash with thoughts about where we were going and what he was going to do with me. He called me a plaything. What did he mean by that?

"Turn around and stop." He forced me to a halt as he spoke.

I stopped moving my legs and pivoted with his hands. My eyes were finally able to focus on my surroundings. The safehouse was behind us, and two trucks were next to the vehicle Nadine drove here. I saw Nadine exit one of the trucks and another man forced her over.

"Remember, no words," the man hissed into my ear.

Nadine looked at me with worry in her eyes. Her face was stoic, but her eyes told me all I needed to know. She appeared to have a large bloody knot on the top of her head. Her captor told her to stay silent and not to talk to me. He then looked at the man behind me. By the voice, I was able to determine he was the person who interrupted the man with the knife resting on my shoulder. "Everyone is sweeping the area to flush them out."

"Good," the man behind me purred evilly.

"What are we going to do with these two if we are not leaving?"

"That depends completely upon how many of my men are dead."

"What are you going to tell—" The other man was cut off with a violent motion by the man behind me.

"We are not discussing anything in front of prisoners."

"Oh, of course."

We waited in silence as a group of men came into view from around the hill. To my amazement, their hands were raised and walking behind them was Angel and a band of SAR fighters with firearms all pointed at the group of men. SAR outnumbered them four to one. The knot that was in my throat began to loosen. I was starting to feel we may all get out of this alive and none the worse for wear.

"Let them go, Melvin," Angel shouted towards us.

"My name is not Melvin," the man behind me retorted derisively.

Angel shouted for everyone to stop what I guessed was forty feet away from us. Close to the trucks and our car. She walked forward to one of the men and kicked him in the back of his knee. He collapsed and knelt in front of her. The knife which was resting on my shoulder was now poking my throat. If I moved, I would have assuredly been cut deeply. "Did you lie to me?"

The man on his knees answered with a waver in his voice, "No."

"What was his name?"

"Melvin. An Agent Melvin from Washington D.C."

Angel looked back up at us. "Melvin. That's your name."

"You can't rely on him telling the truth," the man behind me replied.

"If you aren't Melvin, then the liar dies right now." She pointed the barrel of her gun, an M4 variant, at the head of a kneeling man.

"Is she serious about murdering my men? You can speak," the man behind me hissed through gritted teeth.

"She is as mad as she was when she lost two of her good friends a few months ago. I wouldn't test her."

"Fine. I am Melvin. Special Agent Melvin." I felt the knife move from my neck and peered up to see him wave nonchalantly before returning the knife to my throat.

"Well, *Melvin*. Let my people go and I will leave you and your men here." I resisted the thought of the story of Moses as she spoke and waved her hand mystically.

"How can I be sure you won't murder us all? You are clearly working against the government and clearly enemies of the state. You cannot be trusted."

"It is the government that you cannot trust. You can trust me to be honest to my word."

"Are you Angel, by chance?" Melvin inquired coolly, with the same hint of emotion from before when he had first struck me in the gut.

Angel was taken aback by Melvin's question before answering, "I am."

Melvin laughed a cool, deep laugh, one with more malice than I thought possible from him. "The All-Seeing Eye knows all, my dear. It also saw me as I killed Jesus."

Angel was visibly shaken. If I had not been in front of Melvin, I was certain she would have shot him dead right then. I chanced a sideways look over to Nadine and she was glaring at Melvin in fury.

"And I did Zach just after he gave your name up," the man behind Nadine piped in, as if he did not want to be left out.

"Let them go." Angel's voice was dangerous enough to put my hair on end.

"I don't think I will. You see, I came to South America with orders to root out the resistance. I've been tracking your movements for a while. I'm not about to let potential VIPs go in my midst."

"I am the only important person here worth your time."

"I sincerely doubt that. I have information claiming an Abnormal female such as the one in front of me is important enough to interrogate."

"You have bad information, then. I am the only person here worth your time."

"On my go, drop it and we run to the trucks," Melvin whispered. "And neither of you two traitors speak."

"All right. Forget the men?" his accomplice asked, in an equally low whisper.

"Might as well. We can leave it out of our report."

"On your go."

Melvin raised his voice once again. "You mistake me for a fool. You are going to spill all your secrets to me even if it kills me. And so will this one." He moved the tip inward enough to cut my skin, but not enough to draw blood.

"We will see about that."

"Now," Melvin said it calmly. So calmly I did not even realize the man to my right moved his knife across Nadine's esophagus and plunged a hand into his pocket. He dropped his knife and removed a pin from the grenade that he procured and threw it at Angel. He and Melvin immediately charged for our car; it was the furthest vehicle from where the grenade landed. I was left standing alone and shocked, unable to move.

Nadine gargled and looked up at me, waving her hands at her neck to try to stop the bleeding. There was so much it was already too late. I fell next to her and tried to put my hand over the wound with my other arm holding her head up. We locked eyes and a singular tear fell down her cheek. We had talked just yesterday about what we would do if the world was as free as Vasil dreamed of, as we dreamed of. We had bonded over the last few months, and I felt tears well up in my eyes as I remembered all the conversations we had together. She wanted to be a singer and poet. She had a brilliant mind for rhymes and was thoughtful when it came to lyrics.

I watched as the brilliance in her eyes gave way to the glaze of death. Within seconds, she had stopped moving and the blood was no longer gushing out of the wound as her heart had stopped. I could not contain myself as grief broke my being. It was not fair. It was not right. And for nothing more than a distraction.

My grief was such that I did not hear the grenade explode. Nor did I hear or see what happened between the explosion and Angel approaching me and putting her hand on my shoulder. I instinctively grabbed at her hand with my bloody one, thinking she was Melvin or his accomplice. I made to twist her arm and break it, a move Nadine had taught me, when I realized who it was standing next to me.

"It's okay, Tory. They are gone. Melvin is gone."

"And Nadine is dead." Even through my crying, my words were eerily steady. It was as if my mouth was disconnected from my emotions and not subject to my conscious control. I did not mean to speak, I did not want to say her name, yet my voice came forth nonetheless.

"I think you may be in shock, Tory. Come here." Angel slowly put her hand back on my shoulder and patted me gently. After a minute, she helped me let go of Nadine before assisting me into the house. Before crossing the threshold once more, I looked back at Nadine. Her lifeless body burned into my mind, and I prayed in that instant that I would never forget until I had my revenge.

GOING ONLINE

The days that came after Nadine's death were some of the most difficult in my entire life. The only other comparison I had to it was when I was separated from my parents and shipped off to my first job assignment alone. I had no one after that. Franklin, David, and Nadine made me feel like I had friends. People I could rely on, but all were flitting in and out of my life in the last five years. I had no consistent shoulder.

The commotion and destruction Melvin caused on his escape still did not fully register with me. He killed several of his own men and one of Angels. She managed to get away with a few minor injuries. I had waited in the safehouse as her fighters subdued the captives and secured the remaining vehicles. The two trucks.

It was a confiscation well worth our efforts, officially, as we now had access to some of the most modern and high-tech communications in the trucks. We blocked the signals for all networks and drove them back to Hishla Lake for diagnostics. As good as it sounded on paper, I knew the Council did not care how people died in the process. Or who died. It was a thought that weighed heavily on my mind after giving my report and hearing them move on as if it was of no consequence.

Vasil reached out to me and offered his condolences. As he did, Vasil said he would be visiting a week earlier than planned for the funeral and would make sure the modules needed for his plans would be ready at all costs. We needed them to bring his AI up in South America, an AI that would give us a fighting chance. I appreciated the gesture, but I knew Nadine did not mean anything to him. I meant something of great value to Vasil. I was *someone* of great value to him and his organization. As a result, he had a stake in making sure my mental state was good enough to continue performing my duties in South America, else I would have to be replaced.

I watched as Nadine's plastic casket was closed. The man who closed it moved on to the rest who died at the safehouse and slowly shut them one by one. It was the most solemn proceeding I had ever been involved in. I chose not to speak for fear of losing the respect of my peers and subordinates, as I knew I would be too flustered to remain coherent. Image was the most important thing at the moment, even if it took all of my being to present a fake image.

The funeral was not a normal precedent for the SAR, but I wanted them all to be buried with the same dignity as Nadine would be. I had to fight with some financial people to force them to pay for the caskets and the other requirements to bury the dead. Those who died were all heroes to the cause, even if no one knew their names. I made it clear to Angel that SAR must adopt a policy that would bring as many dead back to their families and friends as possible. We had to halt operations until we were confident Melvin was no longer in the vicinity of Hishla and we had to posture ourselves defensively. It would not do to allow Melvin or his accomplice repeat their escapade and kill or imprison more of us.

Obviously, the burials would not take priority over the mission, but I wanted to ensure that what I felt by the end of the process would be some sort of closure. If I was going to have some closure, then everyone else should have the right to the same. It was only fair, equal, just. I would not build a reputation for hypocrisy, or for standing taller than my team. We were all in this together; we all wanted the same freedoms. We were all fighting the oppressors of humanity. Who was I to get more than others? Who were we to reject the dignity of the dead and the last respects of friends and family?

Vasil agreed with me and stepped in to push on finance. Eventually, they allowed me to institute the budgeting required. He even convinced the Council to take the idea up with all the other segments of our movement globally. It would help convince people to join and fight if they knew they would not remain dead on some long-forgotten battlefield, potentially in vain. It made people more likely to be brave knowing those who care about them would remember them and be able to visit their graves. The solace of a proper burial appealed to people's emotions. And we needed to win over the people.

The service ended and Vasil and I began to make our way to the main office building. Everyone let us go first with our security details. David was temporarily my new bodyguard until someone else could be chosen. Someone we could trust. We made our way through the concrete jungle and up to my office where, once the door closed, we all sat down. Vasil took my office chair but moved off to one side so I could sit behind my desk.

Vasil noticed me frown at his action and offered the chair, but I refused. The chair was the least of my concerns. We waited in silence until a knock on the door came. "Come in." I called with a measured voice.

Adam entered with his laptop. He had massive circles below his eyes and was about as tired as a single mother with a new and vocal baby. It did not surprise me. He was forced to finish a project he was already working eighteen-hour days on with an entire team and was pushed to work more. He had fallen asleep during the funeral service and began to snore. His colleague had to shake him awake.

"Well, my boy. I really appreciate all your work. They are installed, right?" Vasil inquired.

"Finished installing them late last night." Adam's reply came in a hoarse monotone.

"How many are fully functional?" Vasil prompted curiously.

"Nineteen of the twenty. A miracle if you ask me. I was not sure how they would hold up with all the bumps of travel."

"Tory, do you want to bring in your data center lead for this?" David asked before Vasil could continue.

"Yes, of course. Unless you spoke with him, Adam?" I looked at Adam and saw him shake his head no.

"Mary!" I called and waited for her to open the door.

"Yes, Tory?"

"Send for Pedro. Tell him it is urgent and not to delay."

"Yes, ma'am. Refreshments for anyone?" she asked the room at large.

"I will take a bottle of wine. Something red." I looked at Vasil.

"I'll take a bottle of vodka. Whatever you have is fine. If Tory gets a whole bottle, I want one." The joke fell flat on his crowd. We were all business in an attempt to drown our emotions.

"Glass of water is fine for me," David said when Mary looked at him.

"Adam?" I asked, seeing his eyes glaze over slightly.

"Coffee for me thanks. Black." Adam shook his head back to us.

Our drinks all came as we waited for Pedro to appear. I should have told him to meet me after the funeral to avoid the downtime. Vasil seemed to not mind. He was anxious about moving forward, but we were a week early. I was not sure if the Council was ready for our AI to go live and begin attacking the South American Absolutist AI. In lieu of the knowledge Vasil had, I decided following his lead was the best path forward.

Pedro arrived and as he shut the door and surveyed the group assembled; he raised his bushy eyebrows. His black hair was slicked back with gel. His tan skin and meticulously curated beard made him the only true South American native in the room. It occurred to me how rare Native American features had become during the Genetic Crusades and the Absolutist rise to power. I wondered why that was. The history books said nothing about modifying genetics to be white or black and nothing in between. Not that I could rely on history books for accurate information after the twentieth century, but I figured there would be at least a hint.

I was drinking wine with Vasil next to me drinking vodka. It occurred to me Pedro had never been in the same room as Vasil or Adam. "Pedro, this is Vasil with whom you've spoken on the phone before."

"Hi, Vasil. Heard so much about you," Pedro said politely, bowing slightly.

"And this is Adam; he is our lead tech guru down in White Tunnels."

"A pleasure to meet you, Adam." Pedro offered his hand, and they shook quickly.

"Gravy. Now, Adam, do you want to fill Pedro in on what exactly we have installed in the equipment he needs to maintain?" I said, before sipping my glass of wine. The flavor helped brighten my features from forlorn to something nearing pleasurable. I let the feeling waft through my body in the hopes it would rid my sorrow, even if it would be for a brief moment.

"Yes," Adam began before clearing his throat and taking a hearty gulp of his coffee. "So, we have installed twenty Quantum AI Processor cards that are preloaded with the blocks necessary to begin building out our AI here. One of them is offline; I will send you the SOP to repair it when I have a chance. We need to have at least twelve up at all times to maintain what we are calling gaggles. Groups of at least three server racks with four cards each that work together to maintain a source block.

"These gaggles will eventually become irrelevant to the wider scheme of things once they populate the rest of the servers with the information to build a new node up wherever it deems appropriate. This will tie into our blockchain network in White Tunnels as a sister AI, identical in every way but only with the ability to communicate with our Antarctica AI. That way, the original can never be corrupted in the event Absolutists or the AI itself become out of control. We have enough for one full gaggle as it is, but a second gaggle will build out pretty quickly since we have enough cards on their way. You'll have to install those, of course."

"Gotcha. Is there anything tricky about them physically?"

"Not really, just be careful with the cards, though. We have some in-house modifications that are fragile."

"Roger." Pedro nodded, making a mental note with his eyes and finger. "Anything else?"

"No one is to remove them without permission and the highest security controls. You and Tory will both need to be present."

"What? You realize how hard it will be if these fail every few weeks?" Pedro protested.

"I will make sure I am available, Pedro." I offered. "Just give me times and as long as they don't mess with my senior leadership meetings, there will be no issues with my availability."

"Actually," Adam said. "I am not expecting any of them to actually break within the year. If they don't fail in the next two weeks, we are likely looking at other components being replaced multiple times before these break. That will only require three persons to be present per the SOP, not needed for you or Tory."

"Do you have a datasheet or something to support that?" Pedro demanded. He was passionate about his work and had the data center running as if it were a well-oiled and maintained Itrep drill.

"The broken one was due to transportation but barring no natural disasters like earthquakes or failure in the first two weeks of usage, we are essentially golden. These cards are similar to what the Absolutist AIs use in their core data centers. Manufactured in Taiwan off the same setup, actually. The data on reliability was collected by a Vasilevsky subsidiary," Adam interjected before Pedro could continue.

"Very well. I'll get a team together to go through the SOP. Would still like to see the reliability data."

"I can arrange that," Vasil exclaimed as he looked out the window, swinging back and forth on my chair.

"Probably best to run a test on everything in the SOP since we have a broken one. In case points of clarification need to be made and the like." Adam beamed at Pedro.

"Is that all?" Pedro looked at me pointedly.

"Yes. Expect an increase in failures on hardware going forward. We are going online shortly and will likely need to stay ahead of everything. Especially hard drives and RAM in the near future. As we all know, the more something is used, the more likely it is to fail."

Pedro nodded and left the room. After he shut the door behind him, Vasil slapped his hands together and rubbed them eagerly. His keen expression was mirrored by David's and my own. Adam was too tired to force his face into excitement.

"Who's to do the honors?" Adam asked out loud as he booted his laptop up and began typing away.

"Vasil?" David asked.

"Yes, it ought to be me I suppose. Unless you want to start it, Tory?" Vasil looked at me curiously. He was clearly wondering if I wanted the credit or if I was happy enough to have my stake in the game as it already was. A test in my humility after all my accomplishments. Or perhaps a way to feel like I was getting back at the Absolutists after ripping Nadine away from me.

"It's all you Vasil. It is as much your baby as Adam's."

Adam laughed dryly at my words. "This AI is my baby; Vasil is the creepy philosophical uncle who never shuts up about what to do."

"That is a terribly accurate description, my boy," Vasil replied; pride was ebbing from him and washing over the room with its intensity. The description was indeed accurate. Vasil was an idea person, a big picture person. His sometimes-ridiculous ideas were only matched by his philosophical aptitude.

Adam typed away in silence for another two minutes before hitting the enter key with finality. "You are up, Vasil."

Vasil walked over and turned the laptop towards him. It was on my desk and moved my documents for tomorrow until they fell off. I bent over to pick them up and felt a pang of emotion as the blood rushed to my face. I pulled myself together as I stood up straight and rapped the papers straight on the desk.

"What is the command, Adam?" Vasil's fingers were fluttering above the keyboard, ready for Adam.

"Just type 'run vbot dot quantai' and hit enter. That is all you need to do. It will begin to spin up and populate the data center and start its attack once it has fully built out on the available servers."

Vasil typed quickly and pressed the enter key. He slowly moved his hand away as he watched the screen in awe. I moved around the desk to see lines of code flashing faster than anyone or any computer but a quantum supercomputer could possibly read. It was finally happening.

The fluttering in my stomach took the pain I had been feeling and the guilt I had been punishing myself with away. For the first time since moving to South America, to Hishla Lake, it was becoming worth it. We were fighting back. We were building our own AI to battle the Absolutist freedom-sucking vampires of the world. This would soon be our main call to those who wished for different leadership to rise up and fight back.

I knew the deaths of many on our side were required for this day, and Nadine was willing to lay down her life the same as the rest to protect me. It was clear this would not be easy from the start. Even though I thought I was prepared mentally, I was evidently not. I was not sure if anyone could be truly prepared for the cost of war.

This journey was only just beginning, and I was not about to waste my time mourning for the dead when they died for the future. Nadine was given the dignity she deserved. I wrote down as much information about Melvin as I could and helped create a likeness of his face and his accomplice, so that we might track him down for our revenge. In the least, we would deprive the Absolutists of a bloodthirsty psychopath. At best, we would get information out of Melvin before his life ended.

In the meantime, I would focus on the future so their deaths, Nadine's and all the others, would not be in vain. I would become the face of the South American Resistance and Angel's fighters would be my most important tool. With the Absolutists escalating amongst themselves, it was essential that we use our element of surprise to sink Trojan horses everywhere we could to confuse the AIs against each other.

In doing so, we would plunge the world into war. War might never change, but the reasons to fight wars changed often. We were going to fight a global war for a good cause. It would start in earnest in South America. It would be fought for all those who died for freedom and liberty; past, present, and future. The only constant in the world was that it was constantly changing, and through change many constants would appear, all with variations of their own. World events were easily predictable, yet hard to predict all in one contradictory lump sum. I would be the change if that is what it took. I would not let my people and their memory die in vain.

INDETERMINATE

Before Vasil left, I asked to meet with him to discuss something about my past. He agreed to give me a few minutes of his time the day of his departure and that he would be in my office at seven thirty am sharp. He seemed to think the conversation would be about Nadine, but I assured him it was about something else before disconnecting for the night.

He strode in almost exactly three seconds after my wristphone displayed the appointed time. He was beaming at me like a proud parent might. "Look at you sitting behind your desk this early, already hard at work. Have you already heard the report on Africa?"

"I have not." In all honesty, I had arrived five minutes before him and made a cup of coffee and was reading a book on my laptop about slavery in the Americas. It was a fantastic read that connected the dots of slavery in Africa that occurred prior to the Europeans showing up and how the slave trade began in earnest with a far smaller percentage of Europeans enslaving the native Africans and moving them to the Americas than I originally learned about in high school.

The western tribes did the bulk of the enslaving and selling to the Europeans for guns and other supplies. Once the slaves were brought over to the Americas and sold off, the book shifted to focus on each of the main European powers and how they treated slaves and what rights slaves might have had up until their freedom centuries later. The part that surprised me most was the country known as the United States was not the worst offender or the longest in that latter half of the millennium, whereas my schooling had taught the opposite was true.

The North American Region was supposedly riddled with the worst European racists and the largest quantities of slaves in that time. As the book suggested, the natives to the Americas and the Spanish in the Central American regions during the same timeframe enslaved and murdered more people than the rest of Europe. After the Spanish lost most of their power on the continents, the British Empire took the title of the most black slaves and went on to allow their colonies to commit various atrocities.

It was hard to parse the data and timelines together but based on definitive numbers and ledgers from the time period, it appeared what the Absolutists were teaching differed from reality. There was enough ambiguity to swing either way, but I chose to side with the book that was banned. Why would you ban a book if it lied? At worst, the book underestimated the numbers and botched the timeline. Everything else seemed to add up with the other literature.

Vasil wanted us to learn as much about any topic we chose.

He felt that if we spent time educating ourselves, we would be better at solving the various problems we encountered in our daily work. Just like the balance between work and time off, Vasil was liberal on how we should learn, but always firm that we occupied ourselves with learning something.

"The American AIs have deployed troops over there. Apparently the African AI has been a little too cocky and now it is a full-blown war in Africa. The first the world has seen in a long time."

"Since David was over there," I noted.

"Yeah, I suppose so. I wonder if he has any thoughts on it."

"He is probably in his office if you want to stop by there on your way to your car."

"I might do just that, Tory. Although it completely depends on what you wished to talk about and how long this will take."

I sat back in my chair and looked him square in the face. "You chose me, right?"

"Yes, I did. Well, a group of people I had assembled that were statisticians and psychologists and the like, they put you on a short list and I reviewed your profile and liked what I saw. Why?" He was bewildered by the question, but not taken aback, as I originally anticipated.

"Did a man by the name of Franklin come up on the short list?" I prompted. I worked hard to keep my expression blank and stoic, but Vasil caught the twitch of my mouth as I asked my question.

Vasil grunted at me and looked down. "The man you were working with in Australia, right?"

"That is the one."

Vasil sat in the seat before me. Sitting behind the desk facing someone who was once superior asking him questions was almost as awkward as it was to be sitting where I was today. He shrugged his shoulders and nibbled his lip before answering. "He never made it to the short list on my desk."

"Then how do you know about him?"

"He was cited in your profile. He wrote in his journal every day in Australia about you." Glancing up and seeing the shock on my face, Vasil hastily continued. "Franklin appeared too compliant and unwilling to undermine the system he was in. He may not have believed in it. You would know better than I or the team that studied him. But I truly think with the data we had at the time he was not right for our team. So we did not pursue him."

"He would have helped us."

"You can't be sure of that, Tory."

"Like hell I can't. I worked with him for months. I—We—" I spluttered in my emotional response. I was angry and frustrated and trying to fight off my feelings for Franklin all simultaneously. It was no easy task, considering the subject matter.

Vasil sighed deeply. "You two had more than a platonic relationship then, eh?"

"Not exactly. I mean—" I began, but Vasil raised his hand to silence me.

"I think I understand, Tory. You have to remember I studied your profile deeply. He was the first person you could trust and talk to in your entire adult life. Of course, there would be some sort of emotional attachment. If you want the truth, we thought he would be a good fit and had studied him before he met you and we began to study you. By the time I had to decide, he was not a top contender."

"You—What?!" I exclaimed. The surprise raised my eyebrows

and voice an entire octave higher than usual, which for me was a feat considering how high pitched my voice already was.

"Yes. We studied Franklin before you and decided you were compatible and he was not."

"But you could have let me in on the secret!" I snapped. "I would have told you he can be trusted."

"Maybe, but that is assuming you would have stepped onto the plane to begin with, knowing you would be committing criminal acts. Besides, I had no way of controlling the ears in the walls and on your wristphone at that time. We had to be careful with how we engaged, Tory. Surely you understand that. We could not be sure how you would react until you were already in a closed environment like White Tunnels."

"So you could deal with me if I decided to turn you in?"

"Not exactly that, no, but that was definitely a factor. Tory, listen, you are capable of more than you believe you are. Look at yourself. Look at what you have accomplished. You cannot possibly think you would have accepted any of these roles or gone to White Tunnels knowing what we were going to do. You were strong yet timid. Anxious and fearful of the Absolutists. You are not any longer, Tory. You have to trust that I did what I had to so you could blossom into who you are today. The leader of our entire operation in South America. The Director of South American Operations."

I was silent as I fumed. He watched me carefully with the patience of a cat. Countless seconds, or perhaps minutes, went by as I thought it through. How would I have reacted if I knew what was going to happen? Perhaps he was right. Vasil always looked out for us when he could in White Tunnels. He may have been doing it longer than that, based on the level of knowledge he had on everyone who started to work for him after he bought the operation.

"What is his current status? Do you know?"

"He is doing well. He took losing you in stride everywhere but in his journal."

"I mean, has he come any closer to qualifying to be let in on our operations? He would have access to the complex there in Australia."

"We are still considering him. He is still labeled as indeterminate."

"Indeterminate?"

"Uncertain." Vasil nodded.

I took a deep breath and huffed. I thanked him for his time and hoped he would have a safe journey back to White Tunnels where our organization was hard at work preparing for the communications bonanza that was about to take off as we began to fight on a multitude of fronts. Vasil left and I called Mary in to ask her what my day's agenda would look like. With the conversation over, I pushed Franklin back into the depths of my mind. It would not do to jeopardize our plans because of one person I cared about. It was easy to throw my mind into my work.

After lunch, I went down to the server room to monitor work on the broken card. Pedro and his technician fiddled with the card for over an hour before they managed to get it functioning. I was glad to be out of the noisy room and removed my ear plugs almost immediately. The foam pulled my earwax out with it, and I felt the irresistible need to scratch my ears after being stuffed with the foam ear plugs for so long.

I left my office with a yawn at seven in the evening and told Mary she should enjoy the weekend. She protested that if I was going to be in the office that she should be as well. Especially with everything going on. I convinced her that nothing important was needed over the weekend and that she should catch up on her personal engagements.

After she agreed, I entered my suite. It was a four-room affair that consisted of a bedroom, bathroom, kitchen, and living space with a table that could seat four. It was by far the largest space I ever had to myself, beating out my Australian quarters by over a hundred square feet.

I made myself a meal consisting of a turkey sandwich, mashed potatoes, and an apple. I sat down in a chair and picked up my tablet to continue reading the book I had started earlier about the African slave trade and its consequences. Once I completed it, I went to bed where I listened to one of my favorite classical numbers by Chopin. Life was returning to normal and my mind was finally cleared of the thoughts of Franklin for the time being.

The next day I headed to the office to wrap up reports that the Council had requested. It was late in the morning and closer to lunch than breakfast. I walked down the long hallway to my office and before entering it, I turned to see the massive hallway in its entire splendor. The boxy hall was flanked by grayish blue walls on both sides. The floor was concrete with tile laid on top. The tile itself was a standard nondescript white with specks of color throughout.

There were two colored lines that ran along the center of the hallway on the tile. One was blue and the other was amber. What they meant before taking over the efforts, I did not know. I used the lines as a way to indicate which side of the offices you were on. The Hishla Lake Vasilevsky Enterprises were on the blue side. The amber side was the SAR and other operations that were carried out under the guise of everyday business. Everyone in the building had been vetted and knew with a rough idea what kind of operation everyone else did.

They did not know, however, the extent of work being done in the facility. I intended to keep it that way. The newer folks would be relegated to the blue side until they could be trusted with the efforts on the amber side. David suggested the idea originally and I graciously gave him the credit. The Council for whichever reason had seemed to think it was my idea and that I was being modest. This angered David, who was becoming more frustrated with the Council by the week. We all were, for various reasons. Vasil and I were not happy with what their plans were. We had had multiple side conversations about how we could satisfy the Council while simultaneously carrying out our goals as well.

As if to answer my thoughts, David walked out of his room three doors away from me. It was the first office on the amber, and thus the more military-oriented, side. The intervening doors between our offices were conference rooms. I smiled and waved at him. He waved back and shut his door before strolling over to me. His eyes were sunken and circles were unmistakable under his eyes. He was nearly as tired as Adam was when we turned on the AI in the data center.

"How's it going, Tory?" David spoke in a low voice, but I caught the rasp of someone who was talking all night.

"It is well on my end. Just need to finish some reports for Monday's meeting with the Hishla Operations folks." I hesitated before deciding it was necessary to probe. "You were working all night?"

"Yeah. Trying to get educational videos set up so I have less heavy lifting in my courses."

"Ah. And you spent all night on that?"

"Unfortunately, I lost track of time in the editing process."

"You know we have folks who are pros at video editing."

"I know, but you have them working on the Hishla training videos and I didn't want to bother them with the additional workload."

"They are paid by the hour. I am sure they wouldn't mind."

"I want the videos to be correct," David said sharply. He did not care for our video editing team. He had a run-in with them earlier in the month due to a poorly edited video clip he needed for an earlier project he was working on.

"I'm sure they won't make a mistake like that again," I promised cheerfully. David did not take the bait.

"No, I am fine, Tory. Thanks for the offer, though."

"All right then, don't be shy with requests. You never know who can help share the workload."

He grinned at this. "Isn't it nice to finally have enough people working for the cause to have time to ourselves? I mean, we did in White Tunnels, but it was a few hours a week at best. Now we have a few hours a day and sometimes entire weekends."

I shrugged my shoulders. "We are maintaining a balance between happiness and hard work. As Vasil says, a happy employee is a productive employee."

"Yeah, pretty sure he got that from a playbook on Silicon Valley companies in the North American Region circa the first decade of this millennium."

"Is he not right? We are more productive than we were before working with Vasil."

"True, but we also have a purpose."

"A purpose to end the Absolutist rule."

"We have the purpose to end tyranny, but also a purpose in our own lives, to live how we choose. We can learn about what interests us. We can have more than the backstabbing platonic friendships the Absolutists have with their selfish civilization. We know what we want and see that it is possible to get."

I bit my lip as I thought about this. He was right. I often found myself thinking more about defeating the Absolutist AI and their human oligarchy counterparts, but I seemed to always forget about what I would do outside of work. It occurred to me the normal I had developed was not much different than what I had in Australia or Africa. The biggest difference was the ability to read books on a tablet. Before I could listen to music and that was about it. I frowned and furrowed my eyes as I realized this.

"Are you okay, Tory?" David asked, confused by my turn in mood.

"Yeah, just thinking."

"Let me guess. You realize you are too driven by working and undermining the damned AI you are forgetting about the personal freedoms you have now?"

"I suppose so. How did yo—"

"You aren't the only one who can read people, Tory."

"Fair enough." I beamed at him. "If you don't mind I need to get back to work."

"What report are you finishing? The one for the military strategy?"

"No, we nailed that one together pretty well on Thursday. This is on the progress for connecting our power grid and data center directly to White Tunnels. No more auxiliary lines holding us afloat."

"Oh. Did not even know we were doing that."

"Yes. Yes we are." I sighed.

"That difficult?"

"I have to explain that the request to have both completed by the end of the year is essentially impossible unless we enslave everyone to get it done."

"Don't tempt the Council."

"Right?" I laughed and he chuckled awkwardly. We were making fun of the Council now, but neither one of us was bold enough to do it in the open. Perhaps we were so cowed by the Absolutists, questioning the intellect of authority figures still brought a negative conditioned response. Or perhaps the Council had grown just as power-hungry and controlling. Or a combination of both.

"What are we going to do if we win this thing?" David asked candidly.

I shook my head. "No idea."

"Do you think the Council will really give power back to us through democracy?"

"Do you really want me to answer that?" I asked evasively.

"Not when you put it that way." His gaze met mine. We both knew once given the power over so many, it would be unlikely the Council would relinquish their supremacy. To what extent they would rule was impossible to determine. We had to hope they would do the right thing.

"Then let's leave it at that," I said with finality in my voice.

"Well, have a good day, Tory. I'm going to go sleep."

"Make sure you are well rested for Monday!" I called as he walked away. I entered my office and began to vigorously type the report out. When I finished, I rubbed my face with my hands and sat back in the chair. What would I do without work to keep me busy? Was it conditioning from the Absolutists that I must constantly work? Or was the unconscious desire to prove myself capable as an Abnormal pushing me? Maybe. But the final thought gave me chills, and my mood soured even more. The thought that I was pushing professionally to avoid my personal feelings.

It also occurred to me that my identity drove me to be something I would have otherwise never been. The chilling thought that my physical features determined my fate bothered me. Even with people who saw me as an equal, with freedoms the Absolutists did not provide their citizens, I found that the color of my hair and eyes mattered as much as with the Absolutists. The difference was that I was given positions of power.

I had wondered for months if others followed me because I was an oddity instead of neglecting my existence. It was impossible for me to know if they followed me because I was capable or because I was their superior. It was impossible to know if I was seen as a beacon to all or simply used as a prop because of my identity. I stood and sighed before walking out of the office with my mind full of thoughts. I spent the rest of the day walking with my thoughts, only breaking for short conversations with people I met along my journey.

NEW ORDERS

I was at a meeting with the Lower Council. The hologram in the conference room displayed a nearly life-size figure of whoever was talking remotely from Europe. I did not pay close attention to non-American affairs. David, Adam, and I were sitting in the conference room listening to the meeting as it moved forward slowly. The dull reporting was standard procedure; however, we were instructed to stay online after the meeting ended for a South American specific conference.

It was lucky that Vasil informed us to make sure Adam did not get on the helicopter that was headed to the coast. We caught it two minutes before takeoff. Adam was confused, but once I mentioned it was orders from Vasil to stay and that he would be attending a council meeting, he enthusiastically hopped off the helicopter. He had never been present for a meeting before and was excited to finally be in one.

"And that concludes our meeting for today. Hishla Lake in

South America, stay on the line; everyone else, please drop off the call now." The shrouded leader of the meeting spoke with a booming and deep voice. It was one of the members of the Upper Council, but no one knew his name. That was the case with most of the Upper Council members, never revealing themselves and always wearing masks, unlike those of us who interacted with them. We took all the risk.

Once everyone had dropped off the call but our line, the council member spoke again. I noticed Vasil dropped off the call, too. "You have done well, Tory. And you too, David and Adam. Without your efforts we would not have been able to build a steady presence in South America."

"Thank you," I said dryly. I was not sure why we had to wait on the call after everyone else to receive this praise.

"Your efforts have led to the Absolutists turning against one another. They may have realized you exist as a third party and factor in this world conflict, but we believe they are underestimating your infrastructure, our infrastructure, and resources."

"That is what the data points to," I replied calmly. "We are being tolerated as long as we don't get too aggressive down here."

"That is the reason I have asked to speak with you." The councilman said. He waved his hands with an air of authority. "You need to be more rowdy."

"I am not sure I understand," I began uncertainly.

He raised his right hand to silence me. "You do recall your plan about causing enough ruckus in South America to give NAR a chance to develop a foothold up north, correct?"

"Yes," David and I replied in unison. We looked at each other. I was starting to dread what the Council was about to ask of us.

David looked like he could not wait.

"I want you to help NAR again. Speak with Angel and determine where to strike. If possible to strike at the heart of the Absolutist AI, that would be ideal. If we can crush the South American AI, we would be able to establish ourselves as a presence all AIs need to take into account going forward. Perhaps we can end any additional bloodshed."

"We already have a plan to wait for our AI, Vasil's AI, to fight against the South America AI."

"Yes, and you are to inform that AI to get more aggressive. I know Vasil instructed Adam to build the code out for a more measured approach, but we do not have the time to do things at Vasil's slow pace. We must act quickly. We need to stay ahead of the Absolutists."

Adam was about to protest when I silenced him with an inconspicuous wave of my hand. He looked at me furiously and I mouthed that I would explain after. It was not wise to directly contradict a council member, especially in front of them. You could quickly find yourself demoted or overlooked for the promotion you were working towards. Abeba found that out rather quickly several weeks ago.

"Do you want it to focus on the South American Absolutist system and completely take it over before moving up to North America?" David asked.

"Focus on South America, but cause some trouble in North America. Make the fashion clothing choices different or something. Disrupt dietary and exercise algorithms, whatever we can do to cause havoc with the North Americans. Whatever it takes to get the North American Region to set its sights anywhere but at home. If they decide to get involved in South America, then we will see if they can fight a war on three fronts."

"Understood," I answered. It may have sounded innocuous, but changing the fashion style choices or dietary algorithms chosen by the AI would cause a massive disruption in North America. The entire economy ran on cosmetic and superficial looks and trends. If we abruptly altered one, there would be a massive influx of people to buy the latest trend. The AI always kept the transitions long and smooth because the last trend that caught on too fast resulted in the deaths of a few hundred people who were trampled in shopping centers. North Americans were self-centered consumers with the desire for materialism in all forms. The AI obliged and gained allegiance for the North American Absolutist regime that was uncanny. Especially considering the death and destruction wrought fighting for liberties only three hundred and fifty years or so previously.

"We also have a mission for you three and whomever you choose to bring with you."

"Us three?" I was taken aback.

"Yes. We only trust you to carry this particular mission out."

"What is it?" David asked.

"Angel was not at this meeting."

"That is correct," I replied confused. "She did not make it back last night after a routine check on our forces in Chile."

"She did not make it back because our informant in the Absolutist regime says she is in custody."

My heart sank at this. If they hurt Angel in any permanent way, they would find that I would be ever more ruthless in my strategies. Especially concerning the health and welfare of the upper echelons of society who condoned, ignored, or demanded uncivil behavior towards citizens and their various foes. I thought of Nadine and Melvin. As I did, my hands clenched into fists and my jaw tightened. My eyes grew narrow and my brows furrowed. If Melvin was involved, I would have my retribution.

"We will handle it. Why us three specifically, if I may?" David asked politely, giving me a fleeting but unmistakably worried look. It was not often anger showed so noticeably on my face.

"It is going to require strategy, intuition, guts, and technical expertise of the highest quality."

"I'm afraid I don't understand. She is not being kept in a local jail of some kind? Military or civilian?"

"No. She is in the South American Absolutist Headquarters complex in Rio de Janeiro."

All three of us gasped. The Council was asking us to break into the most fortified stronghold in South America. It was like asking us to go into Washington DC in the North American Region. It was considered impossible.

"That's impossible," Adam exclaimed. I nodded but did not say anything. I was not sure if I would be coherent.

"Make it possible. If they break Angel, you are all likely to be captured as well, and our plans for the AI will be in shambles. Hishla Lake will fall. All you have worked for will be lost. She knows enough for the AI to discover the rest on probability alone. That is why I ask you three assemble a team and strategy. You will act quickly since you have a stake in the outcome, professionally and personally, as far as I understand. You are the best Vasil has to offer, you are the best we have in South America. The rest of our people, who are nearly as capable as you, are busy in Africa and the Pacific Islands making the best of the situations there. It is up to you."

The hologram faded as the meeting ended abruptly without

any formality. I hated it when the Council did that. We turned to one another. No one spoke for a minute as we gathered our thoughts. I was the first to speak. "We need a plan. A strategy. Adam, get as much info as you possibly can on the complex and start building a database we will be able to use locally on our wristphones. And at some point, get the AI to do what he asked."

"I will do that first. I can code gathering information on Rio and the complex a sub-priority. That may help with potential plans. If we are lucky, we can mask ourselves from automated security measures."

"Good, meet David and me back here for food and brainstorming session at 6:30 pm. We are going to need to get started ASAP."

"Eighteen thirty hours. Roger." Adam screwed his eyes up, memorizing the number. He departed and I looked over at David.

"Do you have any idea how to get started with this?"

"No."

"Do you have an idea for some folks that would be willing and capable of helping us break in?"

"Yes. I will get them and be back as quickly as I can."

"Thanks. I will order the food and get some of the blue brass to come to this meeting. I know a few that can be trusted and are brilliant when it comes to planning things."

"Are you sure? They aren't aware of the extent of our activities."

"Apparently we are not either." I retorted half-jokingly, half-choking back desperation.

We reconvened at the time I appointed. I carried in a stack of pizzas and asked for help with the drinks and chicken wings. My reasoning for the greasy food was simple. Get classic favorites to bait the best ideas out of everyone, and to keep everyone in a good mood because I had a feeling the brainstorming session would go late into the night if not well into the morning. A preemptive strike is always preferable to waiting until people are hungry as I have come to learn, especially in a data center.

Once everyone was situated and well into their first or second plates of food, I informed the group of the full extent of our new orders. Most of them were already aware of the basics of breaking into an Absolutist headquarters, but when I dropped the part where we needed to also spring Angel from the cells in the lower levels, the news sparked a mass sea of gasps and devolved into debate.

"Settle down everyone, settle down," David said loudly. "As Tory said, we have orders to make this happen. Tory and I can come up with strategies on our own, but those strategies will not be as brilliant as is needed and will likely be problematic. That is why you are all here; we need to organize and plan an attack on the most well-defended complex in South America."

There was a quiet that was thunderous after he spoke. He picked up a stylus and turned to the smart board behind him to write down the main objectives. Everyone watched as he did so. Once he finished, he turned and asked, "Where do we want to start?"

"Let's start with logistics," I prompted to agreement from the people I had gathered for our session. They were experts in supply chains and would be able to help figure out how we will build a path to the complex and continue to keep it open as we worked behind enemy lines without reinforcements.

Over the next several hours, we began to build a list of ideas for supporting the contingency that would be invading, including supplies, communications, and the path to take. It felt like we were preparing for a war invasion. I did not want to think about it that way, as I was purely interested in saving Angel from a grim fate and could have cared less about staying and fighting. However, a proper supply chain would provide a secure route for escape and I could not disagree with preparing for worst-case scenarios.

It became clear that as we plotted our ideas on the board, everyone in the group was thinking of a prolonged strike that would challenge the Absolutists directly and lead to the destruction of the Absolutist regime in South America. Or it would lead to the destruction of everything we had built over the last few months and possibly cost us Hishla Lake. I did not see how we had the resources to stage a prolonged thorn in the side of the Absolutists. When I voiced my concerns, I was detracted by various members of the team who all appeared to have the data to reject my cynicism.

On the one hand, I was proud of what the team was coming up with, but I was still concerned we were trying to bite more than we could chew and wanted to deter with something safer to supplement the objectives from the Council. To my dismay, David was also falling in line with the more outspoken and aggressive ideas that were being articulated.

After we worked out enough ideas for the logistics, we discussed how best to infiltrate the headquarters. This I was keener on and joined in with more enthusiasm. There was no reason to discourage any ideas. We would have to think of every possible path forward available. We knew little about the inside besides a basic blueprint from public archives that may or may not be accurate. There was no way to know.

It was obvious that almost everyone had a different idea on

how to get inside, but once inside, things became significantly more uniform as we plotted forward from the planning perspective. The primary objective was to get Angel to safety. This meant that most of the designs written on the board focused on infiltrating the lower levels first. Our second objective was to cause as much havoc as possible on the way out or to distract while we extract. Most everyone could agree on how this could be done. This, as many of the folks present agreed, was a simple matter of planting explosives on the lower levels and trying to level the entire complex on our way out. The confusion would cover our escape. We outlined a plan for a single explosive to go off in the event we needed a distraction for our extraction. It was a necessary contingency that would not stop us from blowing the rest up later.

Around three in the morning, I adjourned the meeting for a thirty-minute break so everyone could clear their heads before continuing. I also made it clear if anyone wanted to retire for the remainder of the night that they could and we would fill them in before 11 am. Only two of the assembly decided to leave for the night; everyone else came back eager to continue.

We were all drained of energy when the early work birds began to trickle into the offices. I told everyone to go and rest and be back for the resumption of our strategy at eleven. David appeared to be running on pure adrenaline and decided to tidy up the notes we had taken down over the course of the night. I told him I could have Mary assist him, and he agreed begrudgingly.

The brainstorming sessions went on for three days before we began to finalize and layout the entirety of the plan. After a day of tweaking minor details and getting thoughts from volunteers for the mission that I had insisted we start gathering, I believed we were as ready as we could be. War could be strategized and planned in its sum, but it would never go the way one expected it to.

With this in mind, I joined the group David was briefing on the mission and our objectives. We assembled a mass of tech experts, soldiers who specialized in guerrilla tactics, and a large group of people who knew the area and were not under suspicion and would help direct our movements and gather intelligence for us. For some reason, the AI was allowing people to still travel throughout South America as if the SAR had not secured its own sector. We decided to use this to our advantage. There were checkpoints and interrogations, but nothing excessive. It appeared to me that the AI wanted to make the citizens think everything was under control and not out of hand.

I prayed silently that I would remember the training David had given me over the last year. Based on his expression as he dismissed everyone, he was hoping the same for the force we assembled. It was a scary prospect taking on the Absolutists so directly and in the most fortified location in the most technologically-advanced city on the continent. It was also inevitable that we would end up doing so. We had assumed we were years away from such a thought. We were wrong. As a result, I added a prayer to the gods that might be and to Fate itself that all went well for us.

PART 3

CHANGE THROUGH CHAOS

RIO DE JANEIRO

Eight days after the Council had given us our orders, we began the trek towards Rio de Janeiro. To my surprise and to the confidence of our strike force, everything went smoothly as we left Hishla Lake and traveled to the coast. We were relying on Vasil's AI to protect our movements and our communications as a software layer of security as we moved towards Rio. Adam had programmed the AI to assist as best as it could, but the bulk of the power was still spent elsewhere as the priority was still on defeating the South American Absolutist AI and silently taking over the wristphones, computers, servers, and networks of South America.

Adam's tweaking, as he explained it to me and David, meant that we actually were facing the complex with little to no Absolutist AI interference. He could not be sure, but he believed the cameras, motion detection systems, and other systems to defend against intruders were all infected by Vasil's

AI. The mission for our AI was simple; make us as invisible as possible. If it worked as intended, the bulk of the fortifications would be rendered useless.

Once our AI embedded into South American infrastructure and subdued its enemy counterpart, it would turn towards the North American AI to test the waters. If we could defeat the Absolutist AI in both the South and North American continents, we would have effectively turned half the world's land and ocean territories to our benefit. The vast resources would be more than enough to fight against the Asian and European Ais. The bulk of the Pacific Ocean was controlled with the North American AI.

Abeba believed the Africans were ready to overthrow their software ruler and would be more than willing to work with us, giving us access to the resources of Africa and one of the largest and most industrious populations on the planet. It would be more than enough to even the playing field on the front lines in Europe and Asia, assuming we succeeded in our endeavors.

Our retinue's first spot of trouble was when we entered the city of Rio itself. Our plans were to disguise and separate our group into the masses and enter over the course of two days from various entry points. This would put the risk of capture and ending our entire operation at a minimum.

To David's astonishment and my disbelief, we were able to get everyone through without suspicion. There were sticky circumstances in a couple of cases, but everyone was able to talk their way in. We reconvened at one of the few places Vasil had control of in the city. Vasil's skyscraper was a mile away from the Absolutist compound. It was a hotel and mall with such impressive splendor that Donald Trump himself would feel as if he had built mediocre buildings in his day. The absolute extravagance of the mall gave way to luxury that only the wealthy elites could afford.

It became clear to me exactly how Vasil stayed in the good graces of the oligarchs. It was through spectacles such as this building. The outside of the first twenty floors was covered in televisions displaying various messages on each of the eight sides that made up the mall.

Above that, it was a tiered circular tower that began almost as wide as the mall itself and gave up a few feet each level to allow for gardens to grow in larger quantities as one looked up the structure. By the ninetieth floor, there was only one massive suite that Vasil saved for himself. It was also where we would be congregating, since it was empty.

When our group of fifty-three arrived, we found enough space for everyone to settle down and rest as David, Adam, and I began to check with our teams to ensure everyone was prepared for their roles and the time we would set out to begin our part of the assault.

Adam was leading a team of fifteen, ten of which were experienced techies that would be tracking and unblocking our progress once inside. David was leading a group of twenty-five that would be attacking guards and causing distractions for my group, which consisted of the remaining ten. We had two techies, two men who served with David in the military before joining with our group, and the rest were sympathetic to our cause and volunteers; all more than able to handle the pressure we would doubtlessly stir up.

Everyone who was an Abnormal had dyed their hair to not look mistrustful. We also used contact lenses to cover up our eye colors as well. It was a well-known secret no Abnormals were allowed into the complex, or in Rio itself, so we had to disguise ourselves or not come along at all. For me that was an easy choice. I did not relish the idea of using chemicals in my hair that would change my identity in such a way, and I was disgusted with the idea of having to do so in the first place, but the success of the mission was paramount. My feelings on the subject could wait for Angel to be rescued and whisked away to safety with the rest of us.

When the last remaining hours of daylight dwindled, we began physical preparations. Cameras in the city were not a problem, as Vasil's AI could make us undetectable so long as we did not commit a crime openly with another person. That would alert the Absolutist AI to our presence when the additional power would be spent to solve the crime instantly. The Absolutist AI had tapped various citizens with the responsibility to police the streets, removing the requirement for a paid police force.

When a crime occurred, nearby citizens would receive a notification and would respond immediately. It was the gig economy at its finest. The same was true for fires, medical emergencies, and various other needs that could be handled by a trained populace who were off-duty. No need to call for help when the All-Seeing Eyes would see and respond within seconds.

Vasil's AI also gave us a secure connection through a modified VPN that ran on the same Vasil technology we used everywhere else but with an added benefit of not showing as VPN traffic. Our wristphones would appear to be streaming video and audio as we strode about the city. Our exact locations would not be pinned down, however, as the connections would be modified once the data made its way to our AI. To the All-Seeing Eyes of the Absolutists, the data would appear as several different devices for each person and thus disguise how many of us were headed in the same direction. So long as the Absolutist AI did not want to communicate with our wristphones, it would be none the wiser until we reached the HQ. Adam ensured all our wristphones were set to jobs and certifications that would not be tapped to assist in nearby events.

Adam's team departed first, as the sun was setting on the horizon. They would need to find a suitable place to tap into the separate computer network and fiber lines that controlled the complex. David's team was the next to depart. His team needed to ensure the guard information was accurate and no changes like the doubling of the guard had occurred. He would be able to call off the mission before my team would be close enough to be suspected.

After sunset, I turned to my team and together we checked our equipment was in working order. We then confirmed various details about the complex's countless convoluted and winding hallways which were designed to keep humans from determining their location in the building. It was a simple matter of psychology. If humans could not navigate in the complex without aid, the Absolutist AI would maintain its power and control over the citizens. After all, who could possibly understand the brilliance of the computers? The oligarchy it supposedly served was also duped by the magnificence and intricacy.

It had become glaringly obvious at that point to me how easy it was to fool people. Appear to know what you are doing, make something complex and hard to follow, and let humans study it for centuries. As a man whose name I could not recall once wrote in a book I read a few weeks prior to our trip to Rio, "Write something so complex that all of academia will spend decades unraveling what you said." The honesty in it was truer than I originally thought, and I prayed the blueprints in the public records were enough to get us through the office area.

With a flash notification on my wristphone, I inserted my earpiece and gestured for the rest of my team to do the same. The earpieces were connected to our wristphones and through the disguised communications network, everyone else in our strike force. Our AI would update Vasil and the Council on progress when it had free cycles to upload our conversations and location. An added benefit of having Adam for the mission was an intimate understanding of the capabilities of our AI and how to use those skills to make a risky adventure seem almost routine.

"Can everyone hear me fine?" I asked. Seeing nods from everyone in front of me, I continued, "No weapons of any kind unless threatened or my say so. David notified and we are to meet him on the western side of the complex, near the subway station."

Without words, we made our way out of the luxurious penthouse and to the elevator. Once on the ground floor, we walked nonchalantly towards the Absolutist complex a fifteen minutes' walk away. While we made our way towards the looming concrete structure, I wondered if the Absolutists had figured any of us out and were ready to pounce as soon as we would step out of the shadows. David would let us know to cancel the mission if he saw anything out of the ordinary, but he and his team were only on the outside. No one knew what would be going on inside until Adam had access to the data feeds.

The only way we knew to give Adam access was to break inside and swipe a card designed to send a malware activated by an infrared scanner through the system that would find a software security key that Adam could then exploit on his end to get access to the entirety of the system. It was a long shot, but we were hoping that we would not need to rely on his team's success. He was to develop a contingency in case of anything going wrong inside the complex.

When we arrived at the west end of the complex, David was standing alone watching water fall from a statue atop a Corinthian pillar between two buildings. As I approached, I instructed the group to split in two. I found my place next to David, and looked up at the statue and noticed it was a man who looked remarkably like Vasil.

"It is a Vasilevsky," David said, answering my unasked question.

"What is it doing here?"

"Apparently Vasil's great-grandfather was a heavy funder of the original South American AI data centers." David said offhandedly as he waved to a plaque several paces away. "Is your team ready to go inside?"

"Yes. Whenever you and your team is."

"No word from Adam." David stated. It was decidedly not a question; one we both knew was not a good omen.

"Nothing. He said he would not notify us until he found a secure location with the access to do his work."

"Let's hope we don't need him then."

"Agreed," I replied bleakly.

David filled me in on what to do when we got close. It would be a relatively straightforward incursion onto the complex. There was a tall tree that had a large limb over the complex wall. We could drop onto the grounds with it. After that, it would be as simple as neutralizing any guards who might get in our way and into an open window on the second floor. Assuming the cameras and ground motion detection systems were not relaying accurate information to the Absolutists inside and in the ether, we would be safe from capture.

He surprised me by adding that the cameras would not be a problem either way as he packed an EMP grenade that would take the cameras out for a few minutes. Enough time to get everyone out of sight and up against the building's wall. The grenade would be almost entirely quiet, so the only risk would be if the cameras picked it up and the AI realized what was happening before the grenade would go off. So that left any infrared systems that could detect movement that were out of range of the grenade, as well as any motion sensors for which the same was true.

We made our way to the tree and the first few members of our group began to climb the tree. They were best-equipped to handle any guards and would have rope to provide an easy climb for those of who were not as good at climbing over the wall or up a tree and needed assistance. The rope was also needed to get up to the open window David's team found that was visible from a second story shop they used to scope out the compound. I was towards the back of the pack. David was fourth to go over the wall shortly after the grenade was tossed over.

One would have thought there would be sensors detecting movement outside the complex border, but our informant inside had told us it was not functioning at the moment. Since there was never any issue with the cameras and guards, the AI decided to let the failing system go offline until a new one could be installed. That was the information the person knew of about two weeks ago. Hopefully it was still current or we would be in for a heap of trouble.

As I climbed the rope over the outside wall, which was made of concrete with a slight reddish hue, I dropped down to the soft earth on the other side. The lawn was kept pristine. The grass was beautifully kept, as if with the care one might treat a soccer field.

As I glanced about, I realized that I was not far off from the truth. There was a steel frame and net on either side of me. It appeared the Absolutists on the inside would grow bored and indulge in a game or two when they felt like it. I thanked whatever powers there might be that it was soccer and not tennis. Tennis courts made more noise when walking across them.

I looked in front of me to see a line of David's men beckoning me forward frantically. I hurried forward and grabbed as much information about the building as I could. Tall and boxy, as the AI liked it; the concrete building stood with the same reddish hue to it. The windows were sparsely littered over ten feet above the ground. The first level had no windows or any deviations from the concrete that I could see.

As I approached the building, the now dark sky gave way to a featureless structure above me. The air grew colder and yet it was more still the closer I came to the building. I shrugged off the thought as I grabbed the second rope, tightened my abs, and shimmied up to the open window. Once at the ledge, David and someone else from his team helped me over the steel window frame and inside the large conference room.

INTO THE COMPLEX

When everyone joined us in the conference room, I tapped my headset silently and then tapped a few buttons on my wristphone. Everyone's headsets would now be syncing to one another in the vicinity. David's headset and my headset were set to auto-connect to Adam's when he would come online. We would all be able to communicate hands-free. I whispered my instructions. "Let's head towards the stairs. David, lead the way. Remember, our primary mission is to rescue Angel."

"Keep it tight everyone. No unnecessary risks. I want everyone to come out alive. We are not to plant all the explosives until we have secured the asset. Three should be plenty if we need a diversion." David spoke so quietly that I could barely hear him in my ear.

David and the two men flanking him made their way out through the door and into the hallway. I followed them into the eerie empty halls of the building. I heard footsteps coming from somewhere ahead, and David motioned silently to the men flanking him to go up ahead as we crept forward slowly. The two men stopped and after another few seconds quickly disabled the guard who walked around the corner without much noise.

They dragged the unconscious guard into a nearby doorway and laid him up against the wall. The door was unlocked and after placing the guard inside the room and shutting the door, the two men returned to rejoin David's flanks. The entire series of events felt so rehearsed that I was impressed by the efficiency of David's training and the volunteers for the mission.

We made it to the stairway and made our way down the stairs. David sent four fighters to keep the stairwell secure in case we would leave the way we came in. When we made it to a doorway at the bottom that had no window to peer through, I looked over at David.

"Sublevel 1, low security detainment," David whispered as he read the sign above the door.

"Is she in there?" someone asked via the earphone.

"Not in the low security area. Likely a way down to more secure locations. From what Tory and Angel have said in the past, they know Angel is an important figure in the SAR," David answered quietly.

Silence fell as David contemplated what we would likely face on the other side. He and I both had the power to end the mission at any time, and I told him before the mission if things were too hard to overcome, we should retreat and regroup. David was no doubt rethinking our probability of success. We were not aware of more than one level of detainment cells. Nobody knew how many guards would be on the other side of the door.

So far, it appeared as if our AI had protected us from being seen by the Absolutist AI, unless there was a trap waiting to be sprung. We had no way of knowing until we opened the door and Adam was able to make contact with us. Without Adam, we would not know what either AI was up to.

"Tory, open the door," David whispered. I motioned for one of the tech people in my retinue to come forward. It was Nathan. He quickly began doodling with the RFID scanner as David and I looked at each other. "Everyone back, you four with me. We are going to clear the floor before anyone else comes in. Don't want to risk everyone."

I nodded and fell back into the shadows of the hallway with the others. After a long moment, Nathan's efforts were rewarded with a beep and the unmistakable sound of a bolt retreating in the door. David and the four appointed men moved through the door with a precision that gave away military training from all of them. David had picked the people he knew would have his back clearing the detainment floor.

A minute went by and we heard several sounds of scuffles through the open doorway. After another minute of silence, David's voice came through in my ear. "All clear. Romy and Jasmine stay in the hallway. Plant one of the explosives somewhere."

Two of the group moved to the end of the hallway to watch for any guards coming our way. I looked up at the camera above me and hoped our AI was keeping us safe. I did not check, but I hoped that the guards who were neutralized were not visible to the cameras, or that the Absolutists might spot them if manually checking the camera feeds. We were too far in to make an escape if the AI was alerted and wanted to keep us inside.

I hurried over the threshold of the thick metal door. The room was small and a short flight of stairs later, I was in a cramped area with metal bars on both sides. All of the cells were empty aside from one where three guards were unceremoniously tossed. I crossed the room to meet David and the two with him. Nathan was just behind me.

David motioned to the door. "It's locked. Nathan?"

"Righto," Nathan replied eagerly. He moved forward and began his work on the door. The words on the door noted a second level for detainment.

"Do you think this is it?" I asked.

"Maybe. I am not sure," David replied, staring at Nathan's hands while he worked. "This layout is strange."

"That's AI for you," Nathan interjected. "Always keeping us mortals on our toes."

A second later, a beep and click of a bolt indicated Nathan was once again successful. David and the four men pushed past Nathan and through the door. I could see a dimly lit hallway that appeared to end abruptly.

"Tory," David beckoned me forward.

I hastened toward him carefully to keep noise to a minimum. The hallway was bare except for the end, and as I came closer, I identified as a pitch-black concrete wall. Blacker than black. It seemed to be sucking the light from around it. "What are we looking at?" I asked silently. I was confused by the wall in front of me.

"Musou Black or something like it I think," David replied, touching the wall delicately.

"What does it mean?" one of the men to his right asked quietly.

"It's a defense mechanism. A lock. A puzzle," I said, staring at the wall. "But what we need to do to get past it I can't fathom."

"Everyone in detainment, move up with us. Two stay back. Pablo, Raven," David spoke into the microphone so everyone in our group could hear.

"Shalik, cover the door. If it shuts, I expect you to be able to open it again," I added. Seconds later, everyone was standing in place, and those of us in the hallway were staring into the black abyss.

"Anyone good with puzzles?" I asked hopefully.

"I watched *The Da Vinci Code*," someone said.

"Does that help?" David demanded, glaring at the person. They shrank back and mumbled something inaudible.

"I am," Nathan stated, and everyone let him come forward. "The detainment cells are all empty. Why? The room back there was laid out as more of a maze than anything else. Why? Now this bare corridor that ends in inky blackness. Why?"

"Good points, I suppose," David responded. "Do you think this is the second security measure?"

"I think we are *in* the second security measure. And we were *in* the first one a moment ago."

"What do you mean *in,* exactly?"

"If the guards were alerted, they would have activated the first security measure, probably a maze of cells that close while they can maneuverer to subdue anyone trying to come in or out," Nathan said thoughtfully. "Or just a processing area that can be locked down to prevent anyone from coming in or out."

"That would mean we might set off an alarm in this hallway if we aren't careful," David interjected.

"How can you be sure of all that?" I inquired, bewildered at both of their thought processes.

"I spent time working on security measures for Vasil and I can honestly say those things are not out of the realm of possibility for him. And he did mention the Absolutes love to flaunt power and control over others. What better way than to treat them like pawns or mice trapped in whatever contraption or game of their own creation?" Nathan said as he studied the wall.

"That's all fine and dandy but how do we get past a black wall?"

"Try shining a purple light or infrared light on it." It came from someone in the back of the crowd.

"Not a bad idea," Nathan said, looking at David. "Leave clues like a bread trail."

"All right. I'll humor it." David fumbled in his pocket and withdrew a pair of tiny binoculars. He opened them and pressed a button. As he looked through, he began to speak again. "Black holes are the only way."

I realized he must have read something. He handed the binoculars to Nathan, who after looking and nodding passed them to me. When I looked I saw letters show up on the infrared setting. "What does it mean?"

Nathan snapped his finger. "I bet there's a hole someplace that we need to put something in. It's a lock to the doorway."

"We need a key?" David asked.

"Maybe. Everyone, look for, but don't put your hand in, a hole. It could be anywhere." Nathan turned and began looking about the dim hallway.

Over a minute passed with everyone looking until someone called us over to a corner at the entrance to the hallway. It was a strange-looking section that did not match the concrete around it. There was no hole that I saw in it.

"What are we looking at?" David asked of the man.

"Look." He moved his hand over the concrete until he hit a spot that, when brushed, pushed into the wall slightly.

"Ah."

"Accidentally brushed the wall and noticed it, sir."

"Good work Newman. Nathan, any thoughts? You seem to be on a roll." We all turned our gazes to Nathan. He blushed as we focused on him and scratched his neck nervously.

"Might as well push it all the way and see what happens," he said, before adding quickly, "Someone watch the door. If Indiana has taught me anything, it's that this could be a trap."

David waited for someone to stand in the doorway, and another person held the door. It was almost comical. Shalik stepped outside the doorway since there was no keycard on the inside.

Once in place, David slowly pushed the area in until it did not move any further. Something hummed and the light in the room began to grow darker. I looked up and saw the light fixture was retreating into the ceiling leaving a hole in its place.

"Now what?" I asked of Nathan after several seconds of stunned silence. This was beginning to feel like a video game with the absurdity.

Nathan shrugged. "Anything visible in the hole?"

Someone close by turned a flashlight on and pointed upward and into the hole. "Looks like there's something off to the side. Someone give me a boost."

Two people close to him boosted him up and the man pulled something inside the fixture. He quickly removed his hand as the light turned back on and began to lower. On the far side of the hallway, the black wall began to slowly move off to the right.

I grinned. Black holes were created by stars going supernova. The solution was hidden in the black hole left by the solitary light in the room. I had to give them credit for effort.

David and his entourage quickly and silently swarmed the opening. They pushed through the door and I heard four darts shoot in rapid succession. There was a shout and more darts. Then a woman's voice spoke. I moved closer to hear what was being said. I barely made out the last sentence. Something about more in the next room.

I motioned everyone to follow and moved forward cautiously. When we crossed the threshold, I saw the black concrete gave way to a steel door similar to what one might find on a high-security vault. Looking inside, I saw a dark room that resembled a prison block. This was the actual detention center; it was clearly built to hold people for extended periods of time. Hidden behind extravagant security measures that were as ridiculous as the idea of my blonde hair hurting or offending someone.

I saw several prisoners in the cells around us. I did not recognize any of them, but all looked as if they had been tortured and abused through various means. The problem with a singular group running the government was they would often resort to inhumane practices to keep people in line. Libertarians believed in small government and Agorists believed in no state actors whatsoever. The sight before me was enough to question centralizing any authority in society to a concentrated mass like a state government.

It occurred to me that we were not much different from the Absolutists. We imprisoned our political enemies and tried to extract information from them. We would never resort to torture, though. Vasil believed in a limited yet firm hand of the government to keep everyone aligned. I chose to follow his beliefs. The Council, on the other hand, would be more than capable of what the Absolutists were doing here. I doubted the Council would bat an eye if they believed they would get away with such atrocities.

"Anyone see Angel?" I asked.

David shook his head. "No. Is anyone else here with us that we know of?"

Before anyone could reply to David. Andrea from my team called us over. "I found her. She needs medical attention."

I rushed over and looked down at the floor of a cell in the back corner of the room. There were no furnishings whatsoever. The only thing in the cell was a tattered and filthy woman who was lying on her side. I bent down to look at her face. It was indeed Angel.

"What did they do to her?" I demanded of the room. No one responded.

"Open the door! Someone, open the door. We don't have time to dawdle," David called, and someone came forward and pulled out a torch to burn the locking mechanism apart.

After watching the torch heating the metal for a few seconds, I looked down at my wristphone. Still no sign from Adam. "David, should I check on Adam?"

"Not unless we have to."

"But would—" I began before David cut me off. He glanced around at the other cells where some of the more coherent people, the ones who were not tortured to the point of giving up, were listening carefully to our words. No one was speaking up asking to be released; most of them probably believed they belonged in their cell because of the brainwashing of the Absolutists. I could not help but wonder why they would choose bondage and not ask for our help. All they had to do was ask and I would demand we let them free and join us. To my chagrin, we agreed to not rescue anyone else, especially if they were not part of SAR, unless absolutely necessary. Still, the lack of desire to escape the prisoners had left in them disturbed me.

"We have our own guards at every sprint on our way out; we will be fine. Romy or one of the others will alert us if there's anything to worry about."

"I hope you are right," I replied, turning back to watch as the final pieces of metal detached from the structure and clanged to the ground. The person wielding the torch shut it off and heaved at the metal cell door to force it open. As soon as he did, however, red lights and alarms started blaring from all sides.

TRAPPED

David and the others sprang into action, grabbing Angel's limp body and heading toward the exit. Nathan turned back to look at me. "Are you coming?"

"Yes." I moved forward. I could barely feel my legs as they propelled me through the doorway into the puzzle hallway. From there to the fake cell room. We made our way through and as I entered the last stretch, I saw something sizzle on the sides of the bars. I shoved Nathan forward before a snap gave way to a laser field between us.

He looked at me on the ground with his eyes wide. We stared at the red lasers for a few seconds. I took my black sock hat off and tried to toss it to Nathan. It burnt midair as it passed through. The burning remains landed in his lap and he quickly knocked it away. "I will get David."

"Just go. Leave me," I said hopelessly. "We have no idea how to disable this."

"I'll figure it out!" Nathan shouted before turning to call for David, forgetting his earpiece.

I heard shots ring from the stairwell. Nathan and the others that remained in the room huddled against the walls with their guns out and trained at the door. I stood helplessly behind them, trapped and watching the door to see if friend or foe would come through the threshold.

I realized we needed to disable our wristphones. I tapped feverishly on my wristphone to turn the setting on where if vitals were no longer detected, it would wipe all information from it. With a toggle, I did the same for everyone else. Until we entered our personal pins, they would all be locked.

Before I could so much as react to our circumstances, several people clad in full military gear appeared on the stairs. I called the first thing that came to mind. "Incoming!"

My warning was enough to give what was left of the team a chance to put up a fight by taking three of the uniformed men down before being overrun. However, as I opened my mouth again, I watched as my team were all hit in the head, right between the eyes, with a vicious flurry of motion as the troops cleared the room. They did not fire at me. They did not speak to me. I stood and watched them murder everyone and said nothing, with my mouth still open gaping at the scene before me.

To my horror, the man who ordered the murder of my first female friend that I could rely on, my bodyguard Nadine, entered from the hallway. The flash of pure hatred was enough to have a dozen red dots aimed at my head and chest as I reached down for my firearm. It was not in the holster.

Glancing down, I groaned and cursed before I shut my eyes tightly, wishing one of them would just pull the trigger before I opened them. The gun had fallen out of my holster as I shoved Nathan out of the way to save him from being burned to death in the lasers. It was futile, as his body now lay motionless four feet away from me. His blank eyes staring up at me.

"Well, well, well. Look who we have here. But you look different, sweetheart. A change of clothes? No, the hair. You are an Abnormal. You dyed it, hahaha. Didn't think you had it in you." I spat on the red shield before me and let the sizzle of my saliva speak for me. Melvin raised an eyebrow but said nothing. Someone came up and whispered something into his ear. He grimaced and looked back at me. "Some of your friends made it away. And with the woman you came here for. What was her name? Heather? Andrea?"

"Angel," I responded with gritted teeth. "And don't speak her name."

"Well, if I was not held up by the bureaucrat upstairs who won't let me do my job, I would have caught you all where you stand now."

"Good thing they exist, keeps you from harming the innocent, doesn't it?" I challenged with a pang of passion for my fallen comrades.

Melvin crossed the distance up to the shield of energy protecting him from my fists. Derangement was clear in his eyes. He was beside himself at my response. He hissed at me with the venom of a cobra. "Do not speak to me that way, you stupid girl. I do not like to have to go over previous lessons with my prisoners."

"I am not your prisoner yet, Melvin," I said as I held my head with dignity.

"Oh, but you are. If you did not have a torch to break into

Angel's cell, you would all be my prisoners. If my hands were not tied behind my back, you would all be my prisoners." He turned and threw his hands about, surveying the room. "Alas, here we are. Death and misery all about. Why do you do this to the world? Cause all this pain? This loss of life. Would it not be more prudent to simply live in the world as it is?"

"That's what we want to do you idiot."

"What? Cause death and misery and pain? Are you that sadistic?"

"Let the world live in peace, unlike the Absolutists."

To my surprise, he made no comment on my continued disrespect. He simply answered with his voice as calm and paced as before. "Attacking and disrupting the government that keeps civility among its citizens is not how you achieve that. The world has rules and laws that must be obeyed. Codes and regulations and orders that must be followed."

"And I see no one in the government upholding any of the natural truths, the natural rights we have as humans. The universe may have laws but it is naturally chaotic; there is no order. Only disorder. You seek to disrupt nature itself by allowing cold and heartless machines to rule over us."

"You are not human."

"My DNA says otherwise."

"You dare speak as if the AI is wrong? It is a super intelligence that is always right. It analyzed and sequenced every strand of DNA our species had available and concluded beyond a reasonable doubt that there was a difference. A fundamental, dangerous difference between you and I. I am a sociopath. I admit it, but I am not evil in my bones. I do what I have to, what the Families ask of me. To keep our society from crumbling. I am a product of necessity; you are a product of a bad set of genes that corrupts humanity."

"You believe a machine that is capable of computing more data, faster than the entire human race can, is not capable of charting a course to usurp your Families and humanity as a whole on a lie as flimsy as that?"

"It is never wrong. It is programmed to work with humanity, not against it."

"Maybe it is not telling you the truth, Melvin. Maybe it is using people like me as a scapegoat for humanity's problems. A sacrificial lamb. And the Families you work for are complicit because they cannot control it."

"Or it is you who has believed the lie that you are not to blame for the past. Our history books clearly stat—"

I cut him off before he could continue. "Or it needed to use us, people like me, as a scapegoat, just like every ruling power before it. The difference is the AI was able to execute the lie at a global scale, and with enough of the population believing whatever it said. The dribble it wrote convinced enough people to turn their attention from the true history of the world to us, *Abnormals*, instead of our true enemy." I spat the word abnormal out at him as I spoke, as if it was something not worth saying. To me, it was a despicable word.

"And who is 'our' true enemy?"

"The oligarchs, the corporatists, the AI itself. The ruling elite. Whatever name or names you want, they have it. They are the enemy."

"You see, men? You see what these freedom fools think? How they think? The *lack* of critical thinking? She is as deluded as our forefathers who were letting citizens possess guns. Well, my forefathers, you are all from South America, where my forefathers spent their entire lives ruining government after government, all to keep you destabilized. With the AI, there is no longer the corruption of human involvement in government. No tinkering necessary to keep things however some person wants them, some country wants them. We work as a united front to achieve our ends. We do as the AI tells us and elect leaders to carry out its orders as dictated.

"We no longer need to worry about mundane things and can focus our attention on our jobs, on being productive, on serving our institutions. She wants to take it all the way, to make us live in fear of someone else with more power, more guns, more ammo, more money, more influence, more 'freedoms' than us. Do you want to live in a world where you are bogged down with choices?"

He turned back to me with disdain in every feature of his face. "You want to use your superiority complex instilled in the very DNA you claim is no different than mine to strip everything we have away from us. Healthcare, clean energy, jobs, technology, community, peace. Unity."

"Not so peaceful in Africa, is it?" I scoffed.

"Thanks to you and your anarchist pals," he retorted. "The All-Seeing Eye knows the truth of the matter. You are stirring up chaos to bring about the collapse of society. That is why I am here. To root you out before you seed any more weeds that will need to be dealt with."

"Perhaps you should reevaluate the timeline like I did. The war in Africa started long before we became active in South America. We studied the troop movements; we knew tension was building. Have you forgotten the last war that touched the northern part of Africa?"

"Lies. Just like the lies of the free market and stateless society nonsense. You radicals are all the same. You think in terms of ideologies, and we think in terms of practicality. Our AI has kept us alive, has defeated global warming, and even allowed us to grow our population while reducing our impact on the Earth."

"As you put your *faith* in computers that you have no idea what their end goals are, only that *life* appears better now. You believe whatever they tell you, even if it means killing the people around you, discriminating against a group of people. Sterilizing them. You believe in a system of governance that was proven to be evil in the twentieth century. You and your kind are no better than any previous government. The lies have only grown larger and more insane. The world has gotten warmer. The ocean level has increased by—"

"LIES! WE ARE BETTER THAN THEM!" He screamed so loud his voice broke and he had to swallow before continuing. "We take care of our own and shun those who do not wish to take part in community, in the sharing of our labors. In protecting our world and our way of life."

"You shun those who can be blamed for natural disasters that disrupt food supplies and the bad blotches of history the AI has yet to erase from its books and your children's futures. All to protect itself from the truth that it has destroyed the environment as much as we humans have. The faults of any human creator are always present in the creation."

"You are as delusional as Hitler," he jeered at me.

"And you are as dangerous as Stalin or Mao."

"Mao? He was an example for all mankind on how to throw the shackles off of the common man."

"He destroyed thousands of years' worth of culture of China to rebuild China in his own image."

"You should have paid more attention to your history books."

"You should ask the question 'why' more often." I retorted. There was a brief silence as he glared at me before I continued. "Are you going to kill me, or do I need to walk into this?" I asked, pointing to the lasers that would certainly burn through my skin until I would no longer be able to feel the pain of life.

"No." Melvin grinned evilly. "I want to hear what secrets Angel was keeping from me."

"I have nothing to say."

"Oh, you will." His lips barely moved as his eyes bored into mine. I stared blankly at him. I had no emotion to give. There was no part of me that wished to continue living if it meant torture and death, anyway. It would be better to get it over with quickly and keep all the secrets of SAR and the Council in my unreadable brain tissue than endure whatever Melvin would come up with.

"Oh, I—" Everything faded to black as I spoke. I felt a tingle from my neck and tried to grab at the spot before falling to the floor. I was not unconscious, as I could hear everything around me. I had lost all vision and ability to control my body. I could not think of how they did it, only that they did it to me. I heard as the men picked me up and unceremoniously dumped me back onto the floor after a couple minutes of me swinging back and forth.

Then I heard the snide voice of Melvin once again. "You need time to think without interruption. I will give you that time, Tory. When you can move, I will be back to hear what truths or what lies you have for me. I trust you will come up with the right answers. And proper respect."

His footsteps echoed as he strode away from my limp body. Was this what they did to Angel? Keep her in the dark as long as she did not cooperate with them? I heard muffled movements from someone to my left who was nearby. They stopped moving and called softly, "Don't worry, the drug wears off after an hour or so."

It was a voice I did not recognize, but the feebleness with which it spoke gave me a clue that I was in a cell with the other prisoners we did not free with Angel. Why they would help me at all was beyond my comprehension as I lay unfeeling with my thoughts. I wondered if David would order the explosives detonated. I was not even sure if they were still attached wherever they were planted. The Absolutists may have found them. It was frustrating not knowing what to do. Not being able to do anything about my predicament.

How would I get out of this? After all our planning to rescue Angel and save the secrets of the SAR, we failed to accomplish the core point of the mission. I knew more than she did and was more likely to break as I had little to no formal training with what undoubtedly lay before me. The path I was on, becoming a prominent member of our organization and wielding power, had not gone to my head. This was not karma coming after me for getting cocky; this was an injustice by humans. No divinity required. An injustice that would undo all of my hard work as well as David's and Adam's and Angel's and Vasil's. We were all doomed.

No, the answer was simpler than that. We were out-maneuvered by Melvin. Who he worked for, aside from the Absolutists as an entity, and what role he played in tonight's events going sideways were still obscure. I was not sure who he meant by families, but I knew it had to be some of the humans working with the AI in positions of power. While I wished to spend time thinking about him, I knew there were more pressing concerns I had to deal with. Such as the torture that was impossible to avoid unless I spilled the beans and caused all my work to be undone.

I could do it, it would be easy. Tell Melvin everything in exchange for some prison time and before I knew it, I would be working for the Absolutist Regime once again. No longer needing to think, no longer caring about others. About myself. It would all be over like a dream that faded with time. Like my fellow prisoners who had no will to fight for survival. Content to let life take its course, wherever it might lead. That is, if they did not kill me, as they were prone to do with extreme disobedience.

This line of thought made me lose focus for several minutes as I ran through the possibilities of how I could position myself to be absolved of everything. At the end of a particularly nasty line of thought involving personally murdering Vasil, I pushed the idea away altogether. I would not be selling out the chance of freedom and equality that we were fighting for. It would not accomplish anything besides protecting my own future and what is my life compared to the lives of billions? Why would one side with equity at the expense of all when equality at the expense of none can be achieved?

The time seemed to pass as slowly as a clock with a low battery and a needle that did not want to move forward. However, after what felt like hours in darkness, my vision began to return to my eyes. Everything was blurry at first, but soon everything came into focus as I regained control of my limbs.

I stood carefully and found my wobbly legs would hold most of my weight. As I looked around, I found all the prisoners were looking at me. Some with awe, some with disgust, and others with a hint of amusement. Their reactions made little sense to me. The same voice that spoke to me earlier spoke again. "Who are you?"

I turned to see another Abnormal in the cell next to mine. I crossed the distance to her and put my hands on the bars. "I am fighting back."

"But that doesn't tell me who you are. The man said the name Tory. Is that it? Is that who you are?" As blurry as my vision was, I could still tell there was a signature of hope in her eyes.

Puzzled, I thought for a few seconds before answering truthfully, "Yes. I am Tory. Why do you ask?"

"I was trying to find you when I was caught and sent down here. You dyed your hair, so I missed it when you walked past earlier. You missed a spot right there." She pointed to my left ear. I did not have time to check if I dyed every part of my hair perfectly before leaving.

"What?!" I asked incredulously. How would she know who I was?

"By the way, you might want to destroy your wristphone. Surprised they didn't take it off your arm," the woman said without answering my question.

"Good call. Won't need to destroy it, though." I looked down and unlocked my wristphone. After inputting my pin and several additional taps, I wiped any trace of non-Absolutist compliant software off the system. Everyone had the kill switch in case of capture. I set everyone else's wristphones mine was still able to connect with to do that same. Why Melvin did not have it taken off of me was beyond my understanding.

"You are a legend on the fringes of society, Tory. They say you run Hishla Lake and pass information and resources to the resistance."

"How would you know?" I demanded as I regained more of my motor skills, not yet willing to admit to anything she said other than my name.

"Tory. The tide is shifting in South America. That is why Melvin has come from the North American Region. They want to end the resistance, the SAR. I came down here to find the resistance. I worked in a military factory with access to blueprints for the new armored vehicles. Thought it may be of use," she said as she sat on the hard floor. I sat next to her, looking through the bars. I could feel the cold floor beneath me, whereas I could not when I was drugged.

"So I take it you lost the plans?"

"They are in here," she said, pointing to her head.

"You memorized them?" I asked. I was impressed.

"Not exactly. I have an implant that stores data. Small enough to go under the radar of any metal detector. It is all stored on there."

"An implant?"

"We get them all the time in North America now. Did you not know that?"

"Implants for what?"

"All sorts of reasons. Tracking loved ones, memory, health, anything that can be integrated into the neurological systems of our bodies."

"When did that start?"

"I would say a few months ago. It went from a novelty to

mainstream pretty quickly."

There were sounds coming from the doorway that led to the empty hallway once more. Melvin was coming back for his promised chat. "Is there a way out of here?"

"None that we would want to take. I shouldn't be seen talking with you. The others won't say anything but if the guards see—" She trailed off as she quickly laid back down and pretended to sleep. I stood up, measuring my nerves. My legs were solidly under me and fully under my control once again.

"What was your name?" I whispered, barely moving my lips.

"Erin."

LUIZ

Two guards came to retrieve me. They shoved me out of my cell and ordered me to march back the way they had come. I followed their orders without complaint. Once in the hallway, they told me to stop, and I did. There was now a solitary chair resting just below the light fixture.

In the chair was Melvin.

He was sitting as if he was on a throne, glaring at me as I glared back at him. "Do you remember your manners now?" he said in a cold and cross voice.

"Yes, master," I replied calmly, even as my face betrayed my anxiety and hatred.

"It is your lucky day. Perhaps the only one you will get for the rest of your life." When I said nothing back and merely waited for his reply, he continued. "Luiz wants to see you."

The guards pushed me past Melvin who remained seated until I stumbled past before getting up to follow us. It was a long walk to an elevator where we went up to the top floor. I kept my eyes down, thinking hard about how to deal with what might happen next. I silently hoped that David would detonate some explosive that was nearby to end it all now before I gave away any secrets.

If the hallway was anything to judge by as we exited the elevator, it was an executive or someone else of high importance. I glanced at my wristphone. It was almost half-past eleven. We entered a room that was filled with interesting artifacts from the past. A grandfather clock chimed the time as we entered. A record player sat motionless with ancient looking vinyl record sleeves around it. There were other objects like cassettes and old devices called smartphones. The irony of how little those devices were capable of compared to our wristphones was never missed on me. As massive as Man's hubris might be, it would always be limited by its imagination.

"Thank you, Melvin," a man with an old Brazilian accent said softly as he looked out the window. Behind him sat a sword of an origin I could not identify without a closer inspection.

"As you requested, Luiz. Tory," Melvin said unnecessarily as he pushed me forward into the center of the room.

Luiz seemed to be of the same opinion of Melvin as I was because he spun about to face the four of us with contempt on his face. Contempt I could tell was not for me. "You may go." He waved at the guards. They saluted and turned at once to leave.

"We have no data on her wristphone like all the others. Nothing in the system, anyway. With your permission, I would gladly send hers to the techies to find traces of nefarious cults she likely belongs to."

Luiz strode around his desk, an ugly white minimalist affair, and grabbed my right arm. He forced my arm up so he could see the wristphone for himself. "She wiped it already."

"What?!" Melvin exclaimed. "How can you tell?"

"Of all my years tracking down criminals, I pick up on things, Melvin. Something you clearly have yet to do," Luiz replied distastefully.

"Special Agent Melvin," Melvin said quietly.

Luiz either did not hear or did not care. He let my arm go and I jerked it down, staring into his face. He was native to Brazil, and by the looks of it, may have even been Indigenous. It was hard to tell since there were no obvious signs after years of people coming together to mix the genetics of the Spanish and Portuguese with South Americans.

We stared at each other, sizing up how best to handle one another for a minute. Luiz, without looking away from me, pointed to the door. "I want to speak to her alone, Special Agent Melvin. I will call for you when I need you."

"But she—" Melvin began.

"I don't think she will be of any trouble. She is not a trained killer like Angel."

"You can't know that."

"I do. Unlike you I can size people up for what they are. Her body doesn't lie to me."

"What do you mean, sir?"

"I mean get the hell out of my office!" Luiz shouted, glaring at Melvin. "That is a direct order, one that I will not have you disobeying. Again."

"Yes, sir." Melvin bowed out of the room, cowed by Luiz's anger.

When the door shut, Luiz moved to his desk and pulled a

gun out and sat it in front of him. He motioned for me to sit and together we sat down. He crossed his legs but was careful to leave his gun within reach. My chair was too far away to make a desperate grab for the gun, but I also had to think of an escape plan before trying to murder someone who was obviously important with several guards on the other side of the door.

"Well? Tory, isn't it?"

"Yes." My voice cracked and I coughed.

"I must apologize for the attack dog. Melvin is tenacious to a fault. It was not my idea to have him come here. I had no say in the matter." He pulled a paper bottle of water out of his desk and tossed it to me. I caught it clumsily and drank half before coming back up for air. He was watching me with an intensity I was uncomfortable with. It felt as if he knew more about me than he was letting on. "Better? Those damn darts do make their victims thirsty, don't they?"

"Yes. Thanks," I said, a bit louder than before. "How do you know my name?"

"Angel told us."

"Did she tell you anything else?"

"Not much." He stood up with the gun in hand. He walked back around his desk and pointed it to my head not six inches away from me. "What do you know?"

"I know nothing." My flat reply resulted in the gun being moved towards me until it brushed my hair. I flinched as it came in contact. My heart thumped and I shivered in fear of what was coming.

"You will tell me everything you know about the SAR. Or you will die," he commanded.

I shook my head slightly back and forth, my ear brushing

the barrel of the gun. "You will have to pull that trigger before I tell you anything."

"Yeah? Is that a promise? I'm not afraid to squeeze the trigger. I need to protect my people."

"You do what you need to do. I am doing what I must," I answered, looking straight ahead at the buildings in the city. It was a fantastic view that caught the scenery outside the city as well. I would at least have the luxury of looking upon a beautiful scene before my death. Something Nadine, Nathan, and the others did not receive.

Luiz grunted in what sounded like displeasure and silently stepped away from me. "I will make you talk." I looked at him, confused. He was walking away from me and gesturing for me to stay silent. He turned the record player on and I heard the unmistakable sound of metal music from the twentieth century start to play.

"I like a little music to put me in the mood," Luiz said loudly and coldly before returning to me, waving me off the chair.

Bewildered by his actions, I obliged. He proceeded to knock the chair over and slap it three times hard enough to make me grimace in response. That had to hurt. Then looking up at me, he shouted. "You will tell me what you know. NOW!"

I did not respond. He beckoned me forward and once again, I did as he wanted. I did not feel as if he was going to harm me. The events unfolding before me were curious, and I wanted to see where he was headed with it. I would be tortured either way.

"Tory," he murmured into my ear. "I am the informant who passed the word along about Angel. I am sorry I could not stop her from being tortured. I was away and when I came back and learned what was happening, I was unable to stop Melvin."

"Who are you?"

"I am Luiz of the Council. Well, formerly of the Upper Council. I was the person who ordered the council messengers to go to you in White Tunnels."

"I don't know what you are talking about," I replied defiantly. Angel knew about the messengers, and if she talked, he would know, too.

"Tory, I am an old friend of Vasil. I helped to convince him to turn. What do I need to do to prove to you that I am on your side here?" He stomped on the ground and gave an indiscriminate shout as he hit the chair.

"Do you know the amber waves of grain?" I asked hesitantly. It was a code that only senior leaders in our organization would know how to respond to. Angel did not know about it. There was a different code for her level.

"I know of the flowing rivers of pain."

"I've never heard of those before."

"They are in the original," he finished the last phrase of the code.

I took a step back and put my hands to my face and covered my eyes for a moment while I collected myself. He was telling the truth. If he was the spy that informed us of Angel and he was also a member of the Council, then I could only fathom what he was doing here.

"I am stationed here to cause as much bureaucratic upheaval as I possibly can before my cover is blown," he said to answer my thoughts. "I was busy making sure you did not show up on the cameras through some trickery of my own. I realized you had not been able to disable the security measures, so I had to do everything I could to keep Melvin from intercepting you."

"You are on the Council?" I asked, still not believing it.

"Yes. I mean no, not anymore, Tory. Now listen to me. We don't have much time. Take the gun. Vasil can vouch for me. He can explain everything. Take the gun. We have to get you out of here."

"What?!" I exclaimed without realizing we were still whispering.

Luiz slapped my arm hard and pushed me up against the wall. He did so hard enough for the sound to make it past the door, but not hard enough to cause me much pain. "Careful."

"Let me go!"

"Not until you tell me what else you know. Where is your base?" he replied loudly, with as much malice as he could muster before continuing softly. "I am going to hand you this gun and you are going to use me as a shield to get beyond the wall. I sent a message out as soon as I heard they captured you. Your team will be waiting for you back at the penthouse."

"But your cover wil—" I tried to articulate, but he cut me off.

"My cover will still be intact as long as they see me as your prisoner. If I have to come with you, then I will, but not unless it is necessary."

I grabbed the gun from him and pointed it at him. "Did you know they would surprise us and kill my people?"

Luiz looked hurt and answered ruefully. "I delayed them as long as I could but I misjudged the time it would take for you to break into Angel's cell and escape. They were supposed to be alerted once you were out of the detainment area. Enough time for you to escape."

"Well, several of my men are dead because you failed then."

"There's nothing I can do about it now. Quick, we need to

go before they get suspicious." He glanced at the door and then back at me.

I gave him a cold hard look before motioning for him to turn around, and we walked over to the door. "How many bullets do I have?"

"Thirteen plus one in the chamber. The trigger pull is not very far, so be careful."

"I won't kill you, Luiz. Not if I can help it."

When we were close to the door, he paused and whispered to me. "Melvin and the two guards are the only ones up here. You will not have much time once out of the elevator."

"Do I go the way I came in? Are you staying here?"

"I'll stay if I can."

"Okay. Here we go," I responded. I then hissed loud enough so anyone on the other side of the door could hear. "Open the door."

The venom in my voice came easily. Not because I harbored ill will against Luiz per se, but because more people had to die than were necessary, and Melvin was the most responsible for their deaths. I hoped I would get a chance to kill him on my way out, but practicality and survival were more vital at this juncture than vengeance.

As if hearing my thoughts in my words, Luiz shook his head. "Don't. It'll only make this a bigger problem."

"Open the door," I replied loudly.

As Luiz pulled the door open. Melvin could be seen across the hall with his gun up pointing at the doorway. "Let him go."

"Lower your weapon or he dies," I demanded. The two guards, who I could not see as they were up against the walls, made audible movements. I heard clattering metal on the floor.

"Good, now move where I can see you next to Melvin. Melvin, lower your gun or else."

"Or else what?" Melvin snarled, glaring at his peers who had given up already.

My finger inched slightly closer to the trigger. I could feel the crescent touching my skin. It was plastic.

"Okay, fine." Melvin lowered his handgun as the two guards moved over to him.

"All of you, off to my right. Slowly now."

As they moved, I pushed Luiz forward, careful to keep him squarely between me and Melvin. "Roles reversed, eh, Melvin?"

"For now."

"Stop moving. No need to let you get closer to any stairway at the end of the hall."

"You won't leave here alive, Tory. You and your friends will be hunted criminals that will no longer be able to hide. You have angered the AI to a point of no return, and it will seek justice."

"The AI has no need for justice; it only has need for more control."

"Lies, as always, you stupid Abnormal bitch. You know nothing." His sneer made my skin crawl.

As I leveled with the first elevator, I nudged Luiz who pressed a button on the wall while I kept eye contact with Melvin. I thought of a clever line Kierkegaard once wrote. "Once you label me, you negate me, Melvin."

"I know. That's why I do it. That's why we do it. To negate you and your half-breed family from participating in society."

"Do you ever get tired of using identity to justify your actions?"

"No, I only grow in my convictions with people like you running around thinking you will accomplish anything."

The elevator dinged and the doors opened. "Perhaps you underestimate what we have accomplished with you chasing us around?" I taunted.

"You will fall, just like all the others before you. Human rule never ends peacefully."

"Neither does Identitarianism. Or Absolutism."

"LIES!" Melvin roared as I entered the elevator dragging Luiz with me. I spammed the button for the floor we entered the compound on as quickly as humanly possible until the doors shut. Melvin shouted all the while at the guards to get their guns and chase after us.

"The way you came, I take it?" Luiz asked, looking at the floor I picked.

"Yes."

"My cover will be intact, then."

"If you want to stay. Won't the cameras—"

"They are disabled at the moment."

"Ah."

"And I do want to stay. I love doing nothing and adding to the problems that make things move slowly around here."

"Who are the prisoners?"

"People who are so brainwashed with the, as you might say, identitarian ideology of the Absolutists. They turn themselves in to be punished. Most of them, anyway."

While this did not surprise me, as many followed the identitarian rule as if it were a cult, I was still shocked anyone would willingly turn themselves in for what appeared to be brutal treatment. I wondered why they would do so. It also occurred to me that was why no one begged for release. They were all believers. Then the conversation with Erin entered my mind.

"Luiz, Erin was captured trying to reach me with important intelligence."

"Erin? She must have been the other new prisoner that came in while I was away. I thought that was just a political dissidence charge."

"That's not what she told me. If you can get her released, we will be more than glad to accept her into our ranks if her information holds out."

"I'll see what I can do." As he said this, the elevator door opened and we dashed out. I motioned for him to follow me down the hallway towards the area where we entered the complex. It occurred to me there would likely not be a rope to get across the wall. "I need something to scale the wall."

"No need. Your friends blasted their way through a section of wall for a quick escape. Killed a few guards in the process."

"Oh, good," I said absentmindedly as I ran.

We hurried up the corridor and turned. I recognized where we were. I led the way to the conference room with the window still open. Looking out, I saw a massive hole and the tree we used to get in was shaking back and forth in the gentle breeze outside, debating if it would fall or not.

"No one is out there?"

"I ordered everyone after them except the main gate and the internal patrols. The cameras are supposed to see everything anyway. They are still down out here. Nice find with this window."

I grinned. "I'll let the person who spotted it know."

Luiz grinned back. "Best of luck to you."

I leapt from the building and landed hard on the ground. I had never mastered the parachute landing, but I did something right because I did not seem to have hurt anything as I stood up straight. I hurried over and through the small crater where the wall used to be and into the darkness, out of view of Luiz, the cameras, and away from Melvin.

FUGITIVES

I made my way through the dark and mostly empty city, careful to stay away from any police, guards, or military I saw on my way. I knew if I could get back to our suite in Vasil's hotel, I would be safe. No one would look there for a fugitive.

As I made my way back to the tower, I toyed with my wristphone to see if I could get it connected to Vasil's VPN. When I was within a block of the tower, which loomed above me like a beacon in the otherwise dark city, I glanced about one last time to ensure I was not being followed. When I confident no one was following me, I rounded the corner of a smaller building and the full flashing of screens on the building assaulted my vision. It was a breathtaking sight that I could not believe possible. I had never seen so many pixels arrayed in this way and working against one another to sell varying products before. The more I stared, the more I felt overwhelmed.

"Visitors," scoffed someone in a heavy Brazilian accent. Not many still spoke Portuguese, but everyone spoke English. That did not mean their accent was not still prominent. Some despised being forced to learn a language they were not accustomed to. Luckily, they could blame all their problems on Abnormals. I was grateful my hair was dyed such they would not be able to tell in the darkness I was one. It would not do to stand out, as Abnormals were not common in South America.

I looked back down at the wristphone, which was waiting for me to put in a code for company access. I used the one I received back in White Tunnels. To my relief it worked, and within seconds I was downloading data from our network as the wristphone synced.

I strode up to the tower and took an elevator to our floor, hoping others would be there. When the door opened, I was greeted by two guns pointed directly at me by two of the men with David. They recognized who I was and lowered their weapons.

"Thought you were dead or captured," one of them said bluntly, amazed that I was standing before him.

"Yeah. Well, I was captured and almost died." I grimaced in response and did not speak again as I stood there watching them. They seemed to have understood and eventually parted to let me pass.

When I entered, everyone in the room looked up. A collective sigh was let out and a few smiles flashed across faces before they returned to packing. David approached me with a pained expression. His hand was covering his left hip.

"Are you okay?" I asked, concerned.

"I'll be fine. Took a few scrapes from the shrapnel after I tossed the grenade, but nothing permanent. I thought everyone else was trapped. What happened?"

"I need to talk with you privately," I murmured as quietly as I could so only David would hear me.

David was suddenly wary of me. He mouthed to ask if I was under duress.

"No. I am not under duress or anything of the sort. I escaped fair and square and on the level. Kind of anyway."

"All right. No one is out on the balcony. We should be good to talk there for a few minutes."

We walked outside and over to the ledge. I looked down at the tiny specs of people and cars as they passed the tower. It was incredible what humans were able to accomplish and what heights we might achieve if we unleashed that potential by overthrowing the Absolutists who sought control and stasis. Stasis was easy to do business in.

"So, what is it?"

"I made contact with our informant. Our spy in the complex."

"Oh?"

"Don't think it is wise to blabber too much, but they were in the Council at one point."

"OH!" he exclaimed, shocked by the revelation.

"I used them as a body shield to get away from Melvin and the rest. Then left them with their cover intact."

"Excellent. Someone in a position of authority, I take it? Makes sense, considering what we know about that Melvin character."

"Yes. Considerable importance."

"Is that all you wanted to tell me, Tory?"

"There's also a prisoner there. Erin. She has blueprints in an implant that will help us figure out how those new tanks function so we can counter them more effectively."

David slapped the railing and turned to me. "Damn. We'll

have to let you get captured more often. Always leads to strokes of good luck."

"Speak for yourself. I was contemplating how best to kill myself to avoid the torture."

"Which you have avoided twice without harming yourself."

"So far," I added grimly. "Either way, I am not fond of the experiences. People around me tend to die and I cannot do anything about it." I began to tear up slightly.

"So the others are—" David began to ask before I cut him off.

"Dead." It had been a long time since I had truly been emotional like this. I usually lost control when alone and in private places before I met David and Vasil and the rest. After moving to White Tunnels and then Hishla Lake, I found I was less on edge and therefore less emotional. Today, watching all those people die, brought the thoughts of Nadine back to my mind. And all the others who I had known that died since I began working with SAR. It was a path of dark thoughts that was becoming harder to hold back. Like a frozen waterfall trying to hold back fresh warm water that was following gravity.

David noticed this and put his hand on my shoulder and shook it slightly. "Hey, Tory."

I whimpered as I stared straight down into the sea of tiny lights, streaks of tears running down my cheeks. I sniffed involuntarily. No matter how hard I might have tried, I knew I would not be able to speak, so I did not bother trying.

"Listen. I know it is hard. People dying is a part of this. We all know it."

"Doe-doesn't ma-make it a-any easier." I managed to stammer out as I started to cry in full fury.

"Tory. Everyone knows the risk. You have said it yourself:

dying was preferential to capture. They died. They didn't have to suffer like Angel did. Like we will in the wake of their absence."

"We are officially fugitives now. Melvin knows who we are and we went far enough to anger the AI."

"It would have happened sooner or later, Tory. You know that."

I nodded. He was right. I was focusing on the negatives of the situation and not on the practical — the logical. Realism was my strong suit, and therefore the practical and logical responses. It was ingrained in me. No one cared about my emotions, so I had let them fester and focused solely on my career. It was easier until the flood of emotions became unbearable, until it became clear my treatment would never get better. It would only get worse.

I shuddered at the future I had once accepted and after contemplating my life with Vasil, with David, with Adam, and all the others; I knew all of the variables had changed. There was finally hope. I needed to cling to the hope in my sorrow. I never had it before. Not with the Absolutists.

"Tory," David said gently.

I looked at him, for the first time realizing how much he truly cared for me. The tenderness in his eyes was devastatingly difficult to process. It was not easy to see someone clearly. To know what they were feeling, to empathize with them, but not be able to reciprocate those feelings. Those emotions. The dreaded affection I had run from for decades. What I found in Franklin, and what David clearly found in me at some level.

How I would tell him I did not know, but I knew eventually I would have to break it to him. I cared for him as a friend, as a companion even, but nothing more than that. No deep-set desire to spend my off-hours in his company every day for the rest of my life.

I smiled warmly at him as tears ran down my face. There was no other reaction I could think of that would be convincing to him. I swallowed hard and spoke once more. "Yes, David?"

"We have to move from here. If you are right and we are wanted now, the faster we leave, the better."

"Of course."

"How long will it take you?" He asked reluctantly. It was a hard ask considering my state.

"Give me a few minutes out here to get myself together. I will be back inside and packed." I looked down at my wristphone, which had finished syncing to our network and all my customized features were finally back. "At the top of the hour."

He bobbed his head in acknowledgement and headed back inside with the others. I turned back and looked up to the stars. It was difficult to make any out in the light of the vast city that stretched out before me. Most of what I saw were the satellites rapidly moving about in the sky. The moon was bright, but not full. It felt like a pleasant night with a gentle breeze bustling, even though we were up a considerable distance from the ground.

It took me five minutes to get my crying to subside and for my breathing to return to normal. I wiped away the tears and thanked my foresight to avoid makeup. It would have likely been a mess after my ordeal.

When I rejoined the group, I hastily packed what little belongings I had and spoke with a few of the members of the team to get an idea of what had happened in my absence. By the accounts, I had missed some gun fights in the hallways and in the grass before David decided to blow a hole in the wall for a quick escape without exposing anyone to gunfire, climbing the rope up and over it.

David called us all forward two minutes after the top of the hour. It was 1 am. "I asked the hotel to get us a shuttle to an address of a safehouse where we will be able to sync with the rest of the SAR and get out of this area and back to Hishla."

"Do they know what it is and who we are and what we are doing?"

"The receptionist knows we are working for Vasil and that we have business to attend to. As a result, we get special privileges with no questions asked. We don't have to tell them anything and they don't have to know," David answered, addressing the woman who asked.

I saw Adam shuffle his feet glumly as David continued to explain the situation and that our goal now was to get Angel back to Hishla Lake at all costs. I suddenly remembered Angel and that she was badly hurt. "How is she? How is Angel?"

"She can't see and does not have good motor skills. They drugged her with something," someone from the crowd replied. I could not make out who it was.

"It is a drug that causes temporary blindness and removes the ability to control your body. Something with your nerves. They used it on me."

"So it wears off, then?" David asked.

"I think so; I only had one dose, though. More might cause a build-up or something. Although that would defeat the purpose of torture, I would think."

"She can definitely feel pain. She is in a lot of it; if she could speak properly, I am sure she would be screaming right now. Being painless must be a short-term side effect with higher dosages. Will have to check if that narrows the substance down. As of now, I have no idea, and neither does our database."

"All right, then. With that out of the way I believe we are ready to move? Yes?"

Everyone affirmed David's question with nods and murmurs in the affirmative. We made our way to the elevators and down to the back entrance where a shuttle waited for us. It was the size of a small bus, enough to fit those that remained. We huddled around Angel to prevent any prying eyes from seeing her at the center of our formation as we walked through the lobby carrying her on a cot.

Once she and the rest of us were safely inside the dimly lit shuttle, David gave the address to the driver and took his seat towards the front. I made my way to Adam and sat in the seat next to his. I wanted an account of his adventure and what he had learned.

Adam, as he had told me, was not able to get into or near any connections to the complex. They were all guarded securely or simply too hard to get to in a short timeframe. When he realized he would not be able to get access in time, he rendezvoused with the rough location David gave for emergency retreats and joined David's and my forces as they scampered into the city and back to the tower.

"So, we have no idea how tough the digital security really is then?"

"Digital, quantum, any software-related security aside from the algorithms Nathan was apparently able to record to the cloud. It looks like his wristphone transmitted most of the data before he died."

I gulped when he told me this and looked at the ground. I saved his life for the brief seconds his wristphone was probably still transferring data. It was a feature built into all of Vasil's employee wristphones, on our side of the organization or otherwise, that any intellectual property or data would be stored in the cloud. The only way around it was by entering a passcode or labeling it as highly confidential.

UP AND AWAY

dam was asleep when we arrived at the corner consisting of two roads and a motel. The driver seemed a bit confused by why we traded Vasil's luxury tower for this location, but apparently did not care enough to ask. He was just doing his job and he seemed to not care about much else. What we were up to was our business, and he respected that. Or more likely he, like many people, was taught by society not to question, only to obey. I had no doubt that if the Absolutists traced us to the driver, the beans would spill faster than gravity would take them without outside intervention.

The building appeared to be almost entirely vacant except for a few cars and one or two rooms with lights on. We hustled into the main lobby and David spoke with the receptionist. She nodded and motioned to a door behind her. She apparently was involved in one way or another with us because as we passed with Angel's beaten body, she did not start at the sight but worry sprung up in her face. It appeared she knew who Angel was.

Through the door and down a flight of stairs, we found ourselves in a room with three doors along one wall and security equipment along the other. Several people manned the monitors and other security equipment and looked up at us but did not seem to care we were there. If they had wireless connection to our wristphones, they already knew we were on Vasil's private VPN, which meant we were allowed to be here.

The door furthest to our left burst open and two people came through with a gurney. Both were men, wearing blue scrubs. Both also appeared to be in their late forties. I breathed a sigh of relief. Trained medical personnel were able to be dedicated to Angel. We would not have to make do with whatever we had on hand.

"What happened to her?" One of the nurses asked after moving her to the white stretcher and doing some basic tests to check responses and consciousness.

David, the field medic who attended to her at Vasil's Hotel, and I did our best to explain all that we knew. I included every detail about my experience with the drug and that it was likely used in heavy doses on her. One of the nurses made notes while the other asked questions. Then without another word, they departed through the door they came from.

While this happened, one of the motel's security members approached us and pointed to the center door. "That door leads to quarters you can rest in. The one on the right is off limits to everyone who does not have clearance. It is a standard clearance code for everyone in our network."

"What level?"

"Aside from me, you would have to be someone important

like Angel or Tory," he replied, clearly not knowing who stood before him.

"Well, that means we will have access then, Tory," David said slyly, catching the security guard by surprise.

"Oh wow. Did not recognize you. Thought you had—" He trailed off, gesturing at my hair.

"No need stirring up more trouble than I already planned on in Rio." I explained.

He nodded, still stunned by the revelation. It amused me how my name struck people and that they saw me as a figure of great importance. It was annoying at times, especially when I was trying to get information, as most people were shy around those in positions of authority. Something about the mystique of being a higher-level in an organization changed how someone viewed you. I never paid much attention to that mystique, but I also knew how to be respectful. I had a sense for gathering who I was dealing with.

"What's behind the door?" David asked.

The security guard said it was an encrypted hologram-enabled conference room with direct feed to senior leadership, like Vasil and the Council, before returning to his work. I urged everyone to get some sleep and most of our group made their way through the middle door towards the beds that waited beyond. David, Adam, and I, as well as a few others that decided to linger and play a game of cards outside in the open area, remained with the security personnel.

The three of us moved off to a corner to talk about our next course of action and what to do. Afterward, we went into the conference room and spoke with Vasil. We told him our plans and to reach out if the Council disagreed with anything. We would not be reporting to the Council yet. That would wait until we made it to Hishla Lake and straightened out the timelines for each of our teams. Hopefully, Angel would be back on her feet by then and recount her experiences to the council members at the same time.

After the call ended with Vasil, David and Adam joined the others to rest. I asked the security man who approached us earlier a few questions about operations at the motel. His name was Domingos. From what I gathered, this was more of a rest station for the SAR to lie low and get medical attention before heading back out on missions. After I finished speaking with him, a nurse with a surgical mask covering his face came out of the medical area and approached me.

"Are you Tory?" the man asked with his muffled nasally voice from behind the mask.

"Yes. I am. Is Angel awake?"

"She is. She asked to speak with you. She said it is urgent. I refused at first, but she is adamant about it."

"Is she all right?"

"As far as we can tell, yes. The tox screen has not come back in full, so we do not know what is causing her blindness yet, but she seems to be relatively healthy besides that and some of her nerves not responding. As you said, it is a temporary thing. I hope it will all go away over time."

"Lead the way." I motioned that I would follow him. He led me through the door and down a white hall with several rooms on either side. We turned a corner to the left and I saw the hall stretched on for another fifteen doors on each side. Many were filled with patients. It occurred to me this was a bit more than just a medical patching station like the security guard had mentioned. It appeared that surgeries could also take place in the underground medical facility. This place had to cost a lot of money to maintain, more than the SAR would have been able to afford without Vasil's financing. I smiled briefly as the thought of my efforts resulting in a medical facility to help the SAR that were wounded. It was gratifying to know we were making a difference in the SAR's ability to fight.

The nurse opened a door on the right and ushered me through. He shut the door behind me and checked Angel's vitals as she watched the ceiling with a blank gaze. She did not know I was here yet.

"Angel?" I prompted softly. I did not want to startle her.

"Oh," she groaned, and her eyes flittered towards my voice. "I thought you might be a while yet. The nurse said it was late in the night, almost morning." She smiled weakly.

"It is. I'm glad our plan worked. You are back in safe hands now, Angel."

"Yes. Thank you for rescuing me, but please don't risk it again. They weren't going to break me. Not mentally anyway." She coughed and drank some water from a tube placed near her head.

"I'm just glad you are safe." I walked over and brushed her hand. She flinched at first, but when I went to hold her hand, she relaxed and squeezed faintly in return.

"I do appreciate it, Tory. Who else was with you?"

"David, Adam, a few others you may have known. They are all resting right now."

"I heard shots being fired and an explosion."

"A few of us died in the process. Nathan and some others were trapped with me on the wrong side of the stairway. I made contact with our informant, our spy, and he-they helped me escape." His sex slipped out by mistake.

Angel caught it and frowned at my words. "Our informant. Is it a man by the name of—"

"Hold on a second," I answered abruptly before she could finish. "Nurse, do you mind?"

"Of course, secrets and classifieds and all that. I'm finished now anyway." The man briskly strode out.

Once the door shut, I turned back to Angel's battered and bruised face. "You know them?"

"Is it Luiz?"

"Yes."

"Then I know of them." She coughed painfully. "I, uh, had some nasty bruises and minor damage to a few internal organs. It hurts more and more as the drugs wear off."

"But you are not able to see?"

"Not yet. I haven't seen anything since I was brought to their HQ. They drugged me at the gate and every few hours since then."

"Must have been higher doses than what they gave me."

"I don't know what it is, but damn, is it an evil drug."

"I agree," I replied before transitioning the conversation back to Luiz. "How did you know the informant was him?"

"I've heard rumors about the description of him. I had been doing research on my own time to see if I could find out who it was. It sounded like he wanted to keep it quiet. I don't like not knowing who is passing me information. Takes away any leverage to ensure they tell the truth."

"Fair point."

"That's all I want, a fair fight." She grinned and I smiled in response.

"What is it that you wanted to tell me?"

"The girl next to me in that cursed cell. Erin. She has blueprints—" I cut her off before she could continue as she wheezed a breath in.

"I know. Implants in her brain. Tiny, undetectable. Schematics to the new armored vehicles coming from North America. I was apparently put in the other cell next to her when I was captured by Melvin."

"Melvin." Angel's voice grew cold. "If I ever get my hands on the evil prick, I will make him wish he was worse than dead."

"I wholeheartedly agree. Him and his sidekick. The one who killed her." I retorted.

"Bah! No need to be bitter about it yet. I need to heal up and that takes positivity," Angel said suddenly in a bout of forced strength.

"Agreed. Is Erin the only thing you wanted to make sure I knew about?"

"No, one other thing."

"What?"

Angel described her capture and how Melvin seemed to have known they would be there. She mentioned that it might have been one of a few suspects based on Melvin's knowledge that he touted during Angel's torture. I made notes on my wristphone about the events and the implicated individuals. SAR would get to the bottom of it as soon as I messaged them.

"Who is in command in your absence that can be trusted to carry out what needs to be done?" I inquired. Watching Angel's attempts to stay awake grow more dismal by the second.

"Fernando. Fernando will be trustworthy," Angel said weakly, giving what she knew of his wristphone ID so that I would be able to search for the rest and contact him directly.

"All right, Angel. I want you to get some rest. Don't rest too long, but long enough to return to health so you can join the fight again. We need you out there."

"I promise I won't fall into eternal slumber. I'm not ready to die yet Tory."

I left her bedside and wandered into the sleeping quarters. After finding an empty cot, I took the colored contacts out of my eyes and tossed them into a waste bin and hopped in between the sheets of the cot. I shot a message out to Fernando with Angel's accusations and told him I would be available later in the day to respond. I turned over and made myself comfortable. Within minutes, I had fallen into a deep and dark sleep that was absent of any unwanted dreams.

THE COUNCIL'S REQUEST

woke up feeling as refreshed as one could, considering the circumstances of the past twenty-four hours. As I headed through our lodging, I spoke with David to catch him up on what Angel had told me. Together, we conversed about the events in the world at large and what Vasil had told us in private, away from the prying ears of the Council, about our duties to the cause.

After the attack on the South American Absolutist HQ, North and South America both began to mobilize more forces and centered them in on Rio and the surrounding areas. If we did not move quickly, we would never make it out alive. Our only hope was to make it back to Hishla Lake and hope for a fortified position miracle.

While we were causing chaos in South America, the entire world's populace became aware of the events happening not just in Rio and throughout South America, but the fact that war had come between the AI systems. Their infallible government had become fallible. It was not clear in all areas of the globe what exactly was happening as information was sparse and not transmitted by any official channels, but resistance from Abnormals and others who despised the absolute rule of AI Governors and the elites, the oligarchy, was growing faster than ever.

In the absence of any illusion of absolute control over all choices in everyday life, many were clueless how to live. Those who were still sedated with the AI were beginning to doubt they could trust the choices being made. Those who doubted, and turned on the Absolutists, joined with the resistances who seemed best-suited to fight for them. Those who were so soaked up into the system that could not survive without the AI were clinging on to every word for reassurance.

It appeared half the population of Earth would assuredly die without the guidance of some benevolent force instructing them how to live, what to do, what to make, and why they were doing it. As Vasil had said to my barely understanding ears at the time, "The problem with the government overseeing every facet of one's life is that when the inevitable comes, the government either keeps its power or the masses give it more power willingly. If a government with too much power falls, the people it governed will not survive without heavy losses and suffering."

The words never struck truer than after the reports and videos that we were seeing across South America, Africa, and parts of Asia. Europe still seemed to be under control, and North America's citizens seemed to be so preoccupied with their technology and fashion to have no idea the very foundation of their society was beginning to crumble. It almost made me sick to think of the suffering that was being caused. All due to instability that I, Vasil, the Council, and many others had a direct and indirect hand in creating.

While the continents were fracturing, it would give Vasil's AI time and openings to strike at the Absolutist AIs. With a growing reach, Vasil's AI might just turn chaos into order. An order with the promise, or hope, of freedom behind it. I would not rest until Abnormals would no longer be treated as anything other than human. When all people were equal in the eyes of the law, I could relent. Even then, I knew a system must be laid down to govern such that nothing like the control of the Absolutists would ever take hold again.

A member of the security team approached as I was thinking about Vasil's words. This person was large, with a thick pulsing neck and muscles that barely kept inside the thin membrane of skin that covered the man's body. "You are Tory and David?"

"Yes," David responded, distracted with his wristphone.

"The Council would like a word with you two."

"Do you know why?" I asked pointedly. We were trying to determine our best route away from Rio and back to Hishla Lake and the safety of the SAR's defenses. We were not prepared nor did we have the bandwidth to deal with the Council. Not when our lives were in jeopardy.

"It is most urgent, their words. That is all I know."

"We will be on the holo ASAP."

David and I made our way through the throng and out into the antechamber where four security operators sat watching monitors and cameras in silence. I walked to my left and waved my wristphone at the door's security lock. It turned green and let us inside. David walked up to the holo machine at the center of the room and within a few seconds of tapping on the keyboard below the light emitter, we were surrounded by Vasil and the Council. They were apparently waiting for us with impatience. Vasil looked worried as he saw us enter the meeting.

David and I shared a look after surveying Vasil's face. The entire Upper Council was spread about and, of course, Vasil sat next to them. No other members of the Lower Council were present. I wondered why they wished to meet with us and what was so important to put our return to safety at risk. It was impossible to read any of their faces, as they wore their normal masks to remain anonymous.

I received an answer to my thoughts when one of the council members spoke. "Tory, as an honorary member of the Lower Council, Director of South American Operations, and a so-called Abnormal, you have proven beyond a reasonable doubt with your actions in Rio that you are capable of doing the impossible. As such, we have a request to ask of you that will solidify our cause in the Americas and possibly turn the chaos into the change we so desperately seek.

"This is not an easy decision for us to make, but we do ask you to carry out the will of this council on our behalf. Since you are already a known enemy of the Absolutists, it makes sense that you should speak for our cause so long as we remain in the shadows. If you choose to carry this task out, we will consider you part of the Upper Council. Not an honorary member of the Council Congregation or the Council itself, but a full-fledged member."

I stood quietly as I absorbed the information from the dancing light that made the shape of the council members' mouth through the unwavering mask. It was a lot to take in.

In the matter of half a decade, I had gone from a second-class citizen of the Absolutists to a member of an international anti-establishment confederation called the Council, and was asked to speak on their behalf to all of humanity. I shuddered at the thought of the weight they wished to burden me with.

It was smart to use someone who was already a known traitor to the Absolutist regime, but I could not help feel that I was still a pawn, or perhaps a knight or bishop, that the Council was only granting rank and privilege to someone who could be sacrificed if they lost. I did not like being used. I also wanted to take the position so that I could influence the direction the council might take in future decisions, laying a foundation to strip the Council of power once they were the only ones with control.

The goal of the Council was to free the people of Earth from the bondage of the Absolutists. While the web of illusion was spun well, I also knew it was not wise to replace the old oligarchs with a slightly more compassionate or limited group of oligarchs, ones who would likely hide in the shadows as Vasil, myself, David, and many of the others would go about setting the world up by their design, not ours. We would be the rulers who paid whatever price for their leadership and mistakes, not them.

My personal price, much as Vasil's, was freedom from any state as a whole. A true democracy or republic, whichever would fit, but with inherent power with the individuals of society, not with a select few, and not with the government and elected officials, and more importantly the unelected officials who could not throughout history be held responsible for their actions. In times of war, we could rely on technology to speedily vote on a war-time leader who would have the power to act as a state might act until the crisis was over. Not so different from ancient

Rome. While I was not sure about the particulars, I had faith in humanity to work out a system that would function and release the potential of humanity far better than the Absolutists and the Council ever could.

While I was mulling over the Council's request, I spent two minutes in silence. Every eye in the room was watching me. "What if I refuse?"

"We will find another such as Angel to carry the torch. Someone who is a known resistance fighter. You will be able to carry out your duties as DSAO as you normally would."

"I understand. What exactly do you mean by spokesperson? What does that role entail?"

"As the name suggests, Tory. You will speak on anything the Council has voted to divulge to outsiders. You will be the face of our organization."

"Very well, I accept the offer." The entire council breathed a sigh of relief and several began to wiggle in their seats for the first time since we joined. The Council was evidently pleased, but I noticed Vasil's lips frown slightly before resuming a stony expression. I did not get a good feeling by my decision either, but I saw the potential to gain influence with the Council and change the course of their actions where possible to fit our agenda better. Joining and accepting the responsibility was a sacrifice I was willing to make.

"David, you may go. Prepare your people for battle." The same person said in a dismissive tone. David was visibly confused by the orders but shrugged his shoulders and stole a sideways glance at me as he headed out of the door. He appeared to be troubled by my decision. I made a mental note to explain my reasoning to him later.

"Vasil. Please head to Hishla Lake to take over as DSAO. Appoint someone to run White Tunnels in your place. You are dismissed."

"If I might?" I said suddenly, making Vasil pause to look at me along with the Council. "Would it not be prudent to allow me to keep my position until we can appoint someone who is already working at Hishla? It makes no sense moving Vasil from his operation, which is our technology and semiconductor manufacturing hub. There are better alternates for my position as DSAO if I need to step away from the position. Now is not the time, I think. Not with the chaos we are in."

I appeared to have impressed the council members with my reasoning as a few nodded and looked to the one who did most of the speaking. He looked around and then back at me. "Very well. We will try it your way Tory. You know Hishla Lake and the DSAO job better than anyone else. Vasil, you still need to come to South America as soon as you can. You are dismissed."

Vasil's hologram blipped from sight and I saw a flash on my wristphone. I dared a sideways glance to see Vasil messaged me. He wished to speak with me as soon as I was free. I bit my lip as I thought about the course that call would likely take.

"Tory, welcome to the Council." The man removed his hood and mask. The others likewise removed head coverings and software that hid their faces. The three women and four men all stood up and clapped once in unison.

"So I make the eighth council member?" I asked as they all resumed their seats. I found a chair in the room and did the same.

"Yes. We have one representative from every continent for North America, Europe, and Africa. You are the second member for South America. We have three for the different parts of Asia since it is a diverse continent in political terms. Australia is included in Asia for the purposes of this council."

They began the meeting in earnest with me watching and learning the politics and ways of the council. It was clear there were two blocks of power. The Americas and Europe members would usually side with each other, as did the Asian members. The African member was a wild card who seemed to favor the South American representative and the Asian representative who handled the Middle Eastern part of Asia. It was intriguing watching them discuss and vote on plans that I barely had time to skim through. They were a well-oiled machine; that much I had to give them credit for.

I asked questions sparingly and only voted in favor of one plan and against another. I tried to abstain where possible. Finally, after forty minutes, I was asked a direct question by the council member who was running the meeting. "We plan to add another member for each continent. The question we have not been able to resolve is if we separate Australia and Antarctica into their own delegation." His words were crisp and a tone of annoyance was in his voice. It was clear to my ears he did not like the idea of adding more members.

"We felt if you would be able to provide some clarity on the issue, as you have spent the most time in Antarctica and some time in Australia, you could help shed light on the path forward. Do you think they should have separate representation on this council?" One of the women on the council asked. I believed she was a part of the Asian block but could not be sure.

I thought for a second before responding. "Two from North America, two from South America, two from Europe, two from Africa, four from Asia proper, one for Asia Pacific, which will include Australia. None for Antarctica. Outside of White Tunnels, it is little more than a barren frigid wilderness with tourists. It can fall under South American representation, if need be. Vasil knows it well enough and our efforts in South America have the strongest ties to White Tunnels, particularly because of the data centers we are planning to tie into Vasil's AI. Which if I am not mistaken Antarctica already is under South American representation?"

"It is," said one of the men to my left. I did not catch which.

"That makes thirteen. No tie is possible."

"Those were my thoughts exactly!" One of the women to my right, who I knew was the South American representative to the Council, exclaimed with evident glee. She sounded like someone who was banging on the door of a relatives' house, impatiently waiting to enter and escape the outside weather. I smiled. I was glad to have a friend in my South American counterpart. I hoped we would continue to get along, as we would both be representing the same people.

"Very well. We shall vote on the matter," the leader said dryly. "I vote nay."

"Yea."

"Yea."

"Nay."

"Yea."

"Nay."

"Yea."

Everyone spoke, going around in a circle that ended with me. I could say no to my own idea and tie the vote, or I could reaffirm my idea by voting for it. Abstaining was ludicrous in this instance. Without the time to consider the ramifications or politics of the matter, I was backed into a corner and had to come up with an answer. "Yea."

"The yeas have it. The council will select the new members at our next meeting. Any further business to discuss?"

"Tory's next mission."

"My what?" I said, confused.

"You're our spokesperson now. We need to let the world know."

"We can send her the details in the update to her wristphone; do we really need to cover it in this meeting?"

"No, I guess not."

"Any other business?"

"I motion to close the meeting until next Monday."

"I second!" One of the men said quickly to make sure no one else stole the glory of seconding. I smirked at this; even the leaders of the largest resistance force known to mankind were only human after all.

"I hereby declare this meeting as ended. See you Monday at oh four hundred hours GMT." The holograms of the Council faded. The meeting was over. It occurred to me at that moment that the woman who sided with me almost at once must have been Luiz's replacement.

THE VASIL TWIST

After the meeting, I found the supplies necessary to remove the dye from my hair in the luggage I had brought with me on the excursion to Rio. When I finished, I saw another message from Vasil and that my wristphone, which had been updating ever since the Council meeting ended, had new tabs. These were password-protected, and after providing the proper inputs to set up passwords and biometrics, I was able to view in detail the plans of the Council. I spotted my assignment and skimmed over it.

Once my hair was returned to its natural state and a quick review of the assignment, I realized I was glad. I would no longer need to hide who I was. What they wanted me to do was bold, but this was also the time for boldness. The Council willed it, and who was I to disobey them? I liked what they asked me to do, anyway. At this juncture in their journey, I would have to play along.

There was still the nagging in the back of my mind that I knew was the unconscious awareness that at some point the Council would try to gather as much power as they could get away with, and I would have to step in. Waiting and preparing to stop them would take as much effort, time, and resources as were spent the last few years building the ability to thwart the Absolutists.

Even with my limited knowledge, one thing was clear to me. The Council had grown too dangerous, and a centralized government of anonymous humans was likely to be more dangerous than artificial intelligence. I knew as we brought on additional members, it would devolve even more into voting blocs. I suspected which continents would eventually pick which side. It was clear that the rift was already underway without the additional five members that were going to be added.

I gritted my teeth as I messaged Vasil and David both for a meeting with me in the conference room to discuss what had to be done. I made my way back to the room and waited for David to enter before calling into the meeting ID I had set up. David entered with two bowls of noodles.

"Figured you were hungry," David said, looking at me with unease.

"I am, thank you." I took the bowl he offered and smiled warmly at him. "I am not going to bite David."

"It's not that, just I don't know if—" He trailed off without finishing the thought.

I knew what he was thinking, though. We spent long hours together and knew each other well. "I am not going to sell out if that is what you are worried about David. I may be the official face of the Council to the enemy, but I don't trust them any more than I did before."

Looking somewhat relieved, David slurped some noodles up and watched as I called into the bridge. Vasil's holographic image appeared instantly before us and I saw he had been drinking and he was panting hard. It appeared as if he had been pacing nonstop since he left the Council meeting with vodka in hand.

"That's a blasted terrible decision, Tory. You shouldn't have done that." I knew Vasil was upset, but this was not how I expected him to react in the slightest.

"I'm not selling out, I just told David. I don't trust them."

"So you claim now. Wait until you read through all the documents that are undoubtedly being shared with you. You will want to join their ranks without hesitation and stay out of their way before long. I have seen it happen before."

"What do you mean?" David inquired. He too appeared befuddled by Vasil's response. Something more than just my joining the council bothered him.

"They plan on doing far worse than just sending dissenters into space, as I proposed. Anyone who does not fall in line with their view of how the new governance system should be arranged will face severe punishment. They even have contingencies for murder if they cannot blast everyone off into space quickly and without repercussions. Any leaders resistant to their rule will be assassinated."

"What do you mean exactly?" David asked again. He looked at me for a second then back to Vasil.

"They want to build a confederation of councils that will answer to theirs. They will be lifetime members, everyone except the spokesperson of the council who will be voted on by the lower councils."

"My position would not be permanent?"

"No, it would not," Vasil raved in reply. "Did you vote on increasing the council size?"

"Well yes, but that was to give more—" I began, but he interrupted me.

"It was to give them a chance to get enough members who want their friends and cronies in on the scam. You were a pawn, Tory. I had persuaded one of them to vote no, Luiz, but they replaced him."

"I met Luiz." That stopped him in his tracks. He froze quicker than water in the frigid temperatures of Antarctica.

"You did?" Vasil said after pausing in his pacing.

"He was, is, our mole in the South American Absolutist HQ."

"Really?" Vasil said slowly. It was a rhetorical question. He paused to drink a swath of his vodka before he continued. "They voted him off the council before they asked for you to join. Then appointed a woman I had worked with in the past, a criminal by all standards who had the ears of some of them already."

"What?! Why?"

"So that they could use you as a pawn. Luiz did not want to be the spokesperson for the Council, nor did he think the position itself was wise. I don't blame him. The woman they replaced him with is not capable of public oration. So they apparently went for the next best option. You."

"I received the plans, what they want me to do," I told him, hoping to distract him from the past and on what we might be able to influence going forward.

"What are they? Maybe that will shed some light on what they plan to do with you."

I hesitated, unsure if I should. I was trying to get a grasp on the entirety of the situation and my task. I found it difficult to coherently recall the mission in its entirety. I managed to provide enough information to get the idea across. We were to go back to Rio and take over the Absolutist HQ, this time in full force. I would then use the HQ's network to speak to the citizens of the world directly via an official channel. I also gave broad strokes of what was to be covered in the speech they wanted me to give, but they were leaving the details up to me.

"Damn," was all David could bring himself to say.

Vasil took a minute to stir from his reverie at my mission. "I don't like it, but I do like it. That I do."

His cryptic response hit my ears and I stared into his holographic face, not believing what I was hearing and not understanding it all in the same confused expression that I wore. Vasil saw my reaction and smiled slightly. "Not in the way you think, Tory."

"What do you mean then?" I asked when I found my voice. "Because you just said two contradictory things in the same breath."

"Getting back into the HQ might actually be just as easy as before. The AI governor would move on the offensive and use the pressure and the fact no one would dare to attack twice in a row to protect their little data center. Wouldn't it?"

"Maybe." David answered, cocking his head to the left.

"We can use what we have learned and confirmed about the layout of the complex. They would not see us coming. It is madness to strike so quickly again. And right where we struck last time."

"It is a leap of faith though, that the AI would not double the protection around the complex. By the time we get there, we might be facing far more than before." David's words confirmed my own thoughts. There were, just as in the council's plan, assumptions that I did not like making when it was my life on the line.

"Perhaps, but my AI will be ready to combat it full on, will it not?" Vasil inquired of me.

It took me a second to think of the answer. Adam's report was vague and faraway in my mind, considering the events of the last twenty-four hours. "Possibly. I would have to confirm with Adam. The AI was able to shield us from the Absolutist one, but we were apparently relying on Luiz to keep us safe and other passive measures to hide our movements. The Absolutists were not focused on us at that point; they were focused on northern Africa. I bet they are paying closer attention this time."

"Well, in any case, you will have to march back, which will mean the SAR will have to swell all the forces it has near Rio to have a chance. Do you think that will work? Can we overrun the city?" Vasil continued his line of questioning, looking at David for a response.

"Short answer, yes, but we will have to move quickly to avoid being overrun by Absolutist reinforcements," David replied and turned to me. "We may even be able to take the city fully, but that does not mean we will be able to hold it for long. We may have to leave before a full-on assault by Absolutist forces."

"Then we have no choice. If the AI can help, great. If not, we trudge on. I can do everything I need to do, pull Luiz out of the complex along with the prisoner that has schematics of the armored vehicles, and we leave gracefully. Make it look as though we can walk in and out as we will," I said confidently, more so than I felt.

"That is a good PR move, but eventually we would have to prove it true after that." Vasil poured more alcohol into his glass.

"Prove *what* true exactly?"

"That we can hold cities and bring peace to the citizens."

"Didn't you say something similar to that about Hishla Lake?"

"And we rose to the occasion!" Vasil exclaimed, downing the newly poured liquid and refilling the glass. His alcoholism was beginning to worry me. I had never seen him so disheveled as today. It was true that we had started the first intercontinental war in over a century, albeit without meaning to do so as soon as we had; but I thought Vasil was strong enough to handle the added pressure. It occurred to me with my new credentials I could see how much work Vasil had on his plate. That might be able to give me an idea for his almost disturbing behavior. "But alas, my fellow friends, I ask: do you think we can rise to this occasion as the last?"

"It depends on how many people are swayed by my words," I said calmly. I did not betray it, but the thought of speaking to millions or even billions on live feeds made me want to scream and pull my hair out. To bite my nails and claw my arms until raw. Whatever I did, I was always volunteered to do the most nerve wrecking tasks. For whatever reason, everyone around me thought I was capable.

"Right. Which is why we are going to up the ante on gaining followers and even ones that will go against the power-hungry folks on the Council." Vasil's words did not register on me at first. When they finally did and it dawned on me what he was suggesting, my eyes grew wide with fright. If I angered the Council and they took action against me, like kicking me out on my own, I would be entirely alone without help from anyone.

Away from everyone and nowhere to go. The thought of having to climb into a spaceship to colonize another planet that may or may not be habitable scared me as much as being tortured without the mercy of death when it would be over.

"What do you have in mind, Vasil?" David asked. I saw he too was feeling something similar to me.

"Nothing sinister, just writing up a speech they won't like but can't argue with. Defining what exactly we are offering once and for all to those who join and help us win against the Absolutists. I would call it The Vasil Twist but in this case, it will be Tory's Revision."

"No offense, but that sounds sinister. And probably not good PR from us to the majority of humanity," David quipped.

"And the majority of humanity are egg-headed fools," Vasil snapped back. "Your point?"

"They may be, but they seek self-preservation, and any person who is in the Absolutist regime is most assuredly unwilling to give up an easy life for anything that has unknowns or difficult choices. That was always the appeal of government, was it not? Whether at a local level or a larger scale, but always to find a system where it would make everything difficult easy and everything bothersome go away. That's been the goal of humanity, right?" David's question rang in the silence that followed. He was right and we all knew it, but the question was how many people were sick of living life without tough decisions?

GOING BACK

The work was grueling and tiresome, but I spent the next several hours writing and rewriting the speech I would have to give. David had gone to inform our group of the plans. I sat in the room with the holocamera all by myself. I could hear David bark orders as people moved back and forth as I worked. David was working with Angel and Fernando to organize the assault on the capital of South America. The incoming occupation of Rio. The single most dangerous feat we would tackle to date.

I asked David how long we would be able to hold the city to ensure I did not contradict any of our movements in the speech. It would not be wise to state something that we would not be able to stand by. The answer I received was approximately one day before we would have to start the process of retreating. That was helpful, and as a result I decided to strike the entire line that mentioned how long we would be in Rio out and replaced it with something more vague yet apt for the situation.

When I had completed my work and persuaded several others to review my speech—including the core group of Adam, David, and Vasil—I coordinated with SAR as they prepared for the impending offensive. We worked out the logistics and began assaults on Rio within a day. When the time came, I boarded one of the troop transports that would be headed straight for the Absolutist HQ, and we were off after three short days of planning. I was asked to take a special package containing a new prototype armor that was called a skin suit. I would put one on at some point before entering the war zone.

It occurred to me just how little sleep I had received in the last two weeks. Looking at the reflective surface of my wristphone's black screen, I was able to see bags under my eyes were well-formed and made me look ill. My brain fog was at a minimum, but I knew it would creep in as soon as the urgency of the situation began to subside. That was also assuming my adrenaline would carry me through the remaining tasks set before me.

When we came close enough to Rio to see the skyline, it was clear the AI had retreated to concentrate its forces about the perimeter of the city. After several hours of skirmishes and artillery fire at both sides, the SAR pushed forward as it had the numbers on its side. The Absolutists were spread thin, protecting from guerrilla warfare on all sides and even from within the city itself.

It was impressive how many people were sympathetic to the cause of the SAR. Many were already in contact with the SAR in some form, but nearly half of the people in the city causing problems were people who were tired of living under various military lockdowns and injustices. Using our formlessness to our advantage, we were able to concentrate enough forces like a point of a needle to poke through the outer defenses and into the city itself. At that point, the needle became more like sand. It was impossible to find all of us and we were scattered everywhere. Guerilla warfare was our weapon of choice.

It struck me as odd how every generation of warfare could be used, but the most effective was always the newest form of warfare. That newest kind of warfare still revolved around information, and every other bit of violence among the citizens was for control of information or the dissemination of it in some form. Large oppressive governments shielded information from citizens. Humans being humans and obeying the call of curiosity will eventually demand to know what is happening, and when that time comes, the veil of control those governments relied on would always fall away.

So, it was also true for the shadow governments that ruled through influence and control. Sooner or later, their charade would be up and the pigs behind the curtain will be forced to abdicate their thrones. The Council was playing into the hands of a form of shadow government. Give people the illusion of freedom, share with them all they need to know to satisfy their curiosity, and they will submit to your rule. However, information was hard to control. It was like trying to regulate a waterfall without a dam. The large bureaucrat governments were like dams, but they too would eventually succumb to the power of the information they sought to keep from the people in their valley.

BOOM! A massive explosion brought me back to my body and out of my daydream. It was close to the truck.

"Everyone out now!" Angel shouted as she tapped her wristphone and jumped out from the back of the truck. I followed her. I hit the ground hard and off balance. I had donned the armor. I was wearing bulletproof armor, the kind that covered your entire body like a skin suit. Except it left little room for any clothing underneath. It surprised me by not getting in the way of my movements too much, but the feeling of wearing it took some getting used to. I felt as if I was naked and I was conscious of a few of the soldiers staring on the way to the city, curious at my figure. It was a tight fit and therefore showed my figure more than I normally like to show.

Since I was a council member and the last person we wanted to lose during our insurgency, I was forced to agree to wear the suit even as I tried to back out. I had to wear the skin suit until we were in a secure location in the Absolutist HQ for me to give my speech. I had extra clothes in my pack to change into. However, after a few hours, I found that I did not mind the feeling of the suit as much as the stares I got from the freedom fighters.

The suit was one of the newest technologies we had the ability to replicate on a small scale. The Absolutists were no further than we were in bringing the suits to their entire military. It was made of nanofibers that felt like stiff spandex but were supposed to be able to stop bullets dead without much internal bruising. The physics behind this were far beyond my comprehension, especially when the suit was only a few millimeters thick.

"We go on foot, and we are one click out," Angel shouted over the din of the city. Everything around us was in chaos.

"Why are we not taking the truck?" Called one of the fighters that accompanied us. We had some of the best the SAR had to offer with us, and the one who called out was the center of attention on the way to Rio. He was boasting about how many times he avoided capture. I was convinced he was fudging the details but did not begrudge him.

"The bastards placed barricades from here all the way to the building. We have to go on foot. That and we can't risk the vehicle being hit with a grenade, mine, or something else that they decide to put in our way."

"Let's move. We are sitting ducks." I yelled as the roar of a helicopter passing right above us nearly knocked me over.

"Follow me." Angel motioned. David was somewhere closer to where we entered the city, keeping everything under control in case we needed to make a quick escape. It was nothing short of a miracle Angel was accompanying us. After the first two days in our care, she recovered almost entirely. There were some lingering issues with the nerves on her extremities, but nothing that got in the way of her duties.

Our group passed unmolested for the most part as we weaved our way through alleys and past buildings. It was early in the morning and the sun had yet to rise over the horizon, which made it dark enough to stay under the radar. We made it within a block of the massive concrete construct containing our only direct access into the official communication channels of the Absolutists in the city. The goal was to use that access to commandeer official channels and deliver our own communications. Our communication at the moment was the speech I had prepared to give in front of the camera.

We all huddled up next to an office building that stood between us and the front gate of the complex. Our intel indicated that the wall David blasted away was patched and unlikely to be any easier than the front gate. They used stainless steel and cut the tree we used to climb over down. As I pointed out to everyone's agreement, at least the front gate was designed to be opened.

I watched as Angel surveyed the situation. Her eyes stopped at the center of the enemy mass. I moved towards her and asked, "What is it?"

"Melvin is here. I thought he would be inside."

Anger reared its ugly head inside me, but I shoved it down. Now was not the time for emotion. I would save it for later. "So we kill him and push into the complex."

She drew back to look at me with an amused expression on her face. "When I met you, suggesting the death of someone else was out of the question."

"And here I am. You know what I am and what I am about to do. Things change."

"Yeah, but I just never thought you would so carelessly and seriously suggest killing people and moving on."

"And I have. So what?" I asked pointedly. "Look, we have a mission to do and he has caused enough trouble as it is. He's an obstacle to overcome at the moment. Let's remove the obstacle."

"Yes, but that doesn't change the fact he deserves to be punished and suffer a long death."

"I know what he has done and you still feel what he did to you. We need to end his rampage before he kills us all. We don't have time for revenge."

"I'm not worse for wear," Angel said. She was not entirely wrong. Bruised and sore as her body was, she had made a full recovery thanks to the discovery of the toxic substance that was used to drug her shortly before our departure. After that, the doctor was able to come up with a concoction the nurses could use to treat anyone who was drugged in the same manner. Angel had taken the first dose as we boarded the troop transport. By all appearances, the substance had worked.

"Fair enough. Now what's the plan? I'm on a schedule you know," I said only half-jokingly to her.

"Look at you all important." She gazed at me for a second and winked at me. Our conversation was light-hearted and in direct contrast to the situation at hand, but it gave me the levity needed to carry on. It may have even done the same for her. "So, the plan is simple."

As she outlined the plan to everyone in our retinue via headset, the chaos continued to reign from all sides. We did not have helicopters or airplanes, but we had ground forces that could swell up and dissipate as fast as the Absolutists could drop troops into an area. By the time the AI could dedicate a response, we were gone. It was a war of attrition in a way, and we would win in the short term. The AI did not have enough reinforcements to stop us. Not yet. The deciding factor was how long our forces could stay ahead of the AI.

"All right, go!" Angel shot up from her position and several members of SAR followed her. Another group under the command of Fernando moved out on the opposite side of the street. I stayed behind with those who were assigned to guard me.

We watched as Angel and Fernando sneaked towards the complex's front entrance. I was tense, but to my surprise, I was not as nervous as I thought I would be. My body had given up any hope of forcing me out of what I had to do. The exhaustion that I had felt earlier was masked by an energy pill borrowed from a military ration on the transport.

Shots rang out as the guards in front of the gate caught sight of one of Fernando's men. Angel, on the other side, loosed a grenade and ducked behind a concrete barrier. A few seconds later, the explosion of the grenade sent two of the guards flying as the rest retreated just in time.

Melvin, who was on the other side of the gate, was watching with rapt attention. He was behind a bulletproof glass barrier that ended in concrete road barricades. He shouted orders I could not hear to the guards around him. They immediately spun into motion. They moved forward with weapons trained on Fernando's position and where they saw Angel toss the grenade from.

"Fernando, move or they'll see you," a gruff voice called over the headset. It was someone from Angel's side who must have had a good view of the guards.

"Moving." Fernando's figure twisted and disappeared from my view as I watched from a distance.

The guards inside continued to press forward to the gate, never lowering their weapons. The ones outside had finally reorganized after the explosion and called for the gate to be opened to bring the wounded in. Melvin signaled and shouted something and the guards gave up trying to get to safety. He must have ordered them to maintain their positions.

As they began to set up safer positions behind the rubble, Angel and her group moved forward, and several shots later, more guards crumpled to the ground. I could not tell if they were wounded or dead, but I was not in a position to care or find out.

The door on Fernando's side opened and a dozen guards pushed through before Fernando's team could respond. Fighting erupted on my left as the SAR and Absolutists took cover, firing their weapons indiscriminately at each other. Angel's team provided cover by sending bullets flying across the exposed guards. The skirmish was not to Melvin's liking, who disappeared from my view. In his place was the man who murdered Nadine.

My eyebrows furrowed as I watched the man bark instructions at the guards around him. In the next minute, as gunfire streaked back and forth outside the gate, the guards inside the complex did not look the least bit concerned. A movement caught my eye off to Fernando's side that made me realize why they looked so confident where they stood.

Melvin was now wearing an armored skin suit that looked like mine but this one was weaponized. It had slits on the top and bottom of the arms. On the side of his right arm, fused into the suit, was a blade that resembled a bayonet. Pointing with his arm, I saw an object burst from the top slit that was evidently holding grenades of some kind. A bright flash came a second later and I looked away as the blinding white flash obscured the street.

When I looked up again, I saw Melvin move faster than I thought possible. In quick succession, he disemboweled two men and nearly decapitated a third with a massive swipe of his blade. Someone shot him and the bullet seemed to have little effect. The suit was too strong.

Melvin turned to where the shot rang out and pointed his arm. This time an arrow-like object flew from the bottom slit. It appeared white but was barely visible. As light reflected off of it, I knew it had to be metallic in some way. The projectile landed and a loud scream came forth from a barricade.

"Fernando!" Angel shouted and leapt forward. Everyone in her group understood what needed to be done, without being told.

They all moved as a cohesive unit and dispatched the remaining guards between them and Melvin. By the time Melvin finished the last of Fernando's squad, he turned malevolently to Angel as shots ricocheted off his armored suit. He covered his face as he darted forward, once again running faster than I thought possible, and rammed into the closest of Angel's men with his blade. He turned and two projectiles shot out of his suit as he ducked behind a concrete barrier. One of the projectiles hit its target, the other missed Angel by inches.

"You can't hurt me with your bullets, you fools! Give up and I will not end you here and now," Melvin cried in glee. He was enjoying this.

MELVIN'S FINAL THREAT

I stood up and marched down the street toward Melvin. I was done playing games. If his suit told me anything, it was that my armor, which was the same color and material as his, would protect me from any guns. I only had to worry about his blade. His projectiles appeared to move too slowly to have the momentum required to pierce my suit, but I trusted my reflexes to save me in that eventuality.

The dismay of the troops I left behind came to me. I ignored them and eventually I heard them hurry to my side with exasperated comments. This was going to end one way or another, and I was not going to let Angel die when I could do something about it. The guards who stood behind the bulletproof glass stared at me as I marched forward, but otherwise made no movement against us. I wondered why they remained where they stood when Melvin was clearly outnumbered. Did they have so much faith in his ability to kill us all that they would merely stand and watch?

"Ah, Tory. How great of you to join our reunion here. Angel and I were just about to find out which one of us was the master and which the worthless scum that bleeds." Melvin's taunt caused Angel to shoot at Melvin's head, but she missed as he bowed his head lower.

"You will pay for your crimes, Melvin," Angel shouted in a commanding voice. A deadly voice I did not want directed at me.

Melvin clearly did not care because he continued to hurl insults as I approached, and Angel's team repositioned themselves. Finally, as I made it within twenty feet of Melvin, he moved from behind his concrete protection and darted towards Angel.

She caught his arm before he could impale her, but in doing so she dropped her gun. Melvin was too strong for her and after a few seconds of struggling, she leapt back and received a grazing wound on her gut.

"Come here, come closer. Don't you want to take your punishment? Come now Angel, someone with such a name shouldn't be afraid of death." Melvin's snarl belied his sing-song tone. He was getting a twisted pleasure from playing with his prey. My gut churned at the thought of how many must have suffered before now simply to fulfill his pleasures.

I was not sure what exactly happened, but in the blink of an eye, Melvin and Angel were dueling. Angel had picked up a metal rod from the ground and was parrying Melvin's strikes as he used his arm as a sword. They fought for several seconds before those who were still able to fight joined Angel and pushed Melvin back with a combination of gunfire and hand-to-hand combat.

Melvin retreated slowly to the doorway that led into the complex and used it as a chokepoint to keep from being overwhelmed. It was again just him and Angel by the time I hurried up to them. Angel was fighting with a sense of anger I had never seen from her. Her movements appeared calculated, but her expression was one of near derision.

I was armed with a knife and a handgun. I thought for a second and pulled the knife out of the belt. Guns had little effect on the suit Melvin wore, so I felt it made more sense to use a knife.

As the rest of those with me joined Angel's group, the guards behind the gate began to move. The front gate opened and the guards sprinted forward. I cursed Melvin's second-in-command and pulled out the handgun. In my left hand was the gun; in my right was the knife. I alerted everyone who had not yet noticed the opening gate, and we all dove for cover.

Angel was protected in the threshold of the doorway and did not know what was happening. Chaos reigned as bullets flew through the air. The fighting had resumed in full force. Melvin's guard did not seem concerned about Melvin or Angel, and that bothered me. There was no time to dwell on it as bullets whizzed by my head, missing by mere inches.

While Angel could only do so much damage with a metal rod, it made little sense to not just strike her down with her back turned and kill the rest of us after. The only reason they would ignore her was if they actually wanted her alive. It was a certain possibility, considering Melvin's sadistic behavior. He liked to play with his enemies before killing them. It was not a leap of faith to assuming Melvin wanted to kill her and me personally.

"Ugh!" Angel's shout came over the din of shouting and gunfire.

"Ah, at last!" Melvin shouted in return.

I chanced a look from the safety of my position and saw Angel had been disarmed and a brutal cut ran lengthwise up her arm. To my dismay, Melvin used her as a shield as he withdrew into the complex grounds. In response, I let loose a howl of anger. I was done playing games with Melvin. I had to get into the complex. Time was running out.

I leaped to my feet and spun my knife around in my hand. It rammed into a nearby guard who had not realized I was five feet away. Then, in quick succession, I landed three bullets of five into three Absolutists. There was only a handful left and they retreated. We had picked enough of them off and we had more cover. I did not have time to think about the fact the men laying on the ground were the first lives I had ever taken.

"You four, through the doorway. The rest of you with me through the main gate. Don't let Melvin get into the complex. Kill them all." I barked in a voice not entirely my own. I was not used to shouting orders but rather politely asking people to execute tasks on my behalf. With Fernando dead and Angel captured, that left me the ranking leader among our group. I had a mission to complete and would not let my insecurities about inexperience get in my way if I could help it.

As we crossed into the grounds, I noticed that every one of the Absolutists were in the process of retreating to the front door. I led the SAR as we broke past the barriers and up to the doorway before motioning with my hand for everyone to veer off to the right. We skirted the outside of the complex for a hundred feet before I called for a grappling hook. We would break our way in where we wanted to, not where Melvin wanted us to.

As we climbed through the shattered window on the second

floor, I felt a twinge of déjà vu. It was a near-identical conference room to the one David and I had used to gain access the first time. It occurred to me the second floor was likely the same internal design cut and pasted throughout. "How lazy of them." The words slipped from my mouth as shouts could be heard in the hallway.

Guards engaged us and fighting ensued as we pushed them back through the hallways and into the stairwell. I took a contingency of four of the twenty remaining SAR troops and split off to the stairs on the opposite side of the building. My thought was simple; if we were fast enough, we may head them off.

To my delight, we were unobstructed as we raced up the stairs to the floor where Luiz's office was. We knew that held the only access point to communicate on the public network in an official capacity. It was what we needed.

Luiz was aware of the plan to take Rio, as I had Fernando inform him we would be returning. I hoped he was able to keep the Absolutists in the complex flatfooted while we surged through the building. So far, it seemed to be working. We did not encounter any major resistance or overwhelming forces so far, only Melvin.

We entered the hallway that led to Luiz's office and were immediately met with gunfire. I dove to the left with one of the men with me. The other three jumped to the right and into an alcove of their own. Safe from direct fire, the Absolutists stopped firing down the hallway at us. Their guns were no doubt still trained on us. Then, to my dismay, I heard Melvin's voice. "Throw your weapons into the hallway and come out with your hands above your heads. If you do this, I promise to let Tory and Angel live."

I shook my head and when I realized Melvin would not be able to see, I shouted my reply. "No. You will torture and kill us."

"I will not." Melvin sounded hurt.

"*You* may not, but we will certainly not be left to rot for the crimes you claim we have committed."

"And what accusations do you think are bogus? Murder of police? Of military? Trespassing on government property? Stealing government property and technology? Actively convincing anyone who will listen to your lies that you are the heroes of this story? Espionage. Insurrection. There's plenty to throw you all in prison for."

He was not entirely wrong about everything he listed off, but I was not about to let him have a win. "From our perspective, you are the villains. So yes, we see ourselves as heroes. The government has no right to dictate and steal from others. When it does, it is the duty of the citizens to reject that government." It was the best I could muster as I tried to work on a solution to the situation.

"What Tea Party rubbish are you spewing, Tory? Come out from that doorway and face me like someone who is not afraid of what stands before you."

"As you wish." I called back. I was not sure what would happen, but he probably still had Angel as a shield, and I wanted her alive. I needed to find a way to get past Melvin, and I had a thought on how. I disabled Angel's headset with my wristphone so Melvin could not listen in on us and pressed my finger to my headset to whisper instructions. "Go into the rooms and see if there is a way around to surprise him. I will face him alone."

Without waiting to hear their protests, I threw my gun and knife into the hallway. I took a deep breath and stepped into the hallway to face Melvin and his crony flanked by two guards. Melvin was indeed holding Angel who was struggling to breathe under his iron grip. I murmured as softly as I could and without moving my lips. "There are four of them."

Hoping my team would find a way to salvage the situation and rescue Angel, I stepped forward slowly. Melvin's sidekick was wearing an expression of pure delight. He could not believe we were once again their prisoners.

"Now, Tory, I am only going to say this once. If you disobey my orders, I will cut Angel's throat. Right here. Understand?" He pointed the tip of his knife into Angel's neck. She stopped struggling and gulped, looking up at me. The look in her eyes told me not to comply, but I had no other choice.

"What is it you want me to do?" I asked nonchalantly, stepping forward a few paces.

"What is it?!" Melvin's eyes narrowed as he glowered at me. "Respect, woman! Respect! I will see to it that you will suffer for four thousand days if you do not show respect!"

"Yes ma—" I began, but was cut off by Luiz and the SAR members bursting through the staircase at the other end of the hallway. I ducked as shots rang out. Looking across the hallway, I saw Melvin and his sidekick enter Luiz's office using Angel as a shield once again. I grabbed my knife and rushed forward to meet Luiz as his office door slammed.

"Tory, I thought you were with the others so I went there to help. If I knew you were going to come up the other way, I would have waited," Luiz explained.

"Your cover is blown now."

"Like it matters." He shrugged.

"C4!" I called. "Let's get this door open."

"What about Angel?"

"If he kills her, then we don't have to worry about friendly fire. If he uses her as a hostage, then kill his accomplice and let me deal with him." My mouth seemed to be working off some subconscious line of thought. It was not entirely clear to me how I would handle Melvin if he kept Angel for protection, but I was sure I could get under his skin. I had learned enough about him to know what would set him off.

The C4 exploded with an ear-piercing roar and the SAR moved into the room. Luiz and I walked into the room together once the dust settled. The standoff continued between Melvin, his partner, and the SAR. Melvin's eyes darted between our fighters, trying to keep an eye on them all, and his accomplice held a handgun pointed at first me, then Luiz, and back to me.

"You will all die!" Melvin declared.

"You and your friend will be the only ones dying in my office tonight," Luiz said calmly. He pressed a button on his wristphone and one of the paintings on the wall behind Melvin fell off the wall and crashed on the floor, surprising everyone besides Luiz. With Melvin distracted, Luiz aimed the rifle he was carrying and shot Melvin in the head, where the suit did not cover him. Angel stood as motionless and pale as a statue, as the bullet had been inches from her face.

Melvin made no sound as he collapsed to the ground. His accomplice, whose name I still did not know, cried out in surprise and shot at me. I was one step ahead of him and spun on the spot and ducked my head. The bullet hit the suit on my arm and I grunted as the pain of its impact was felt through the armor. It did not penetrate the suit and my skin was left intact, albeit slightly bruised.

I turned back around and threw the knife at the man. It hit the shoulder holding the gun, and as the gun clattered to the floor, I kicked and shoved the man into the wall. I pressed up against him and reached for a sword that lay off to the side in a display case. Melvin's sidekick did not react. He was terrified of what I might do to him if he did. I pressed the blade to his neck and took a small step back.

"You killed Nadine." It was not a threat, it was not a question; it was nothing more than a statement. A cold, hard fact. My voice did not tremble, it did not break; it was a deadly dark tone that I had only released once before. When I nearly shot the security guard in the data center.

"Please! I will give you whatever you want. Anything you want to know. I was just following orders." The man's pleas fell on deaf ears. His face contorted as he realized I was not going to be swayed. "Oh God. Why?! Why me!"

"You killed Nadine. Why else?" Angel spoke from somewhere behind me on my left.

"You killed Nadine." I repeated solemnly.

"She could not have meant that much to you. Come now, I was just following ord—" the man pleaded hopelessly before I cut him off.

"She meant more to me than anyone else in South America right now!" I screamed and with a quick and deliberate motion, I cut through his neck. I watched as he fell to the ground staring at me with eyes that looked betrayed. He could not understand why following orders from Absolutists caused his death, and it was clear he believed the AI would have kept him safe.

For the first day in my life, I had killed other humans. And for the first time today, I felt the selfish bloodlust of ending a man's life, this nameless murderer, in the same manner as he ended Nadine's. The feeling was one of first satisfaction, then of vengeance, and finally, regret. By the time his eyes glazed over, I knew it was the right choice and that it had to be done, that I was justified in the death; yet I was not certain how I would live with it. The blood was on my hands. A spattering of his blood was on my face. I did not wipe it away. There was no point in doing so. And I did not have time to waste cleaning his blood off, anyway.

THE SPEECH

It took a few seconds for everyone in the room to realize what had just happened. Angel fell into Luiz's white desk, breathing hard. Luiz, after staring at Melvin, walked over to me and gently pulled the blade from my fingers. "This is a replica from the late 1600s, or I would be upset. Lucky for you, I sharpened it before putting it on display."

I nodded, glowering into the lifeless eyes of the man I had killed. My jaw was locked, and I did not know how to respond. Angel broke the intervening silence. "Thanks for saving me."

"My pleasure, Angel." Luiz spoke as calmly as if they had entered his office in the normal course of business. "It is good to no longer be acting like I care about these people anyway. You should have heard what he said about you, Angel. And you, Tory. He was a despicable person. The reports are no better. I doubt anyone reads the reports besides the AI, which is not concerned with anything other than the bottom line. Even so, they were both filled with a hatred that was inhuman."

"The AI does not have a microphone or camera in here?" Angel asked, still catching her breath. She was pointing up at the ceiling. I looked up and realized she was right. I did not even consider that when I was brought to the office as a prisoner.

"Only if my computer has power," Luiz replied with a mischievous grin.

"You have a painting rigged to fall to the floor?" one of the fighters prompted.

"Always need a good distraction ready. It did its job, didn't it?"

"I have to do it," I said silently yet sharply, breaking the casual conversation up as everyone turned to me to digest my words.

"Right you are." Luiz sprang into action, moving over to the computer feed on the interior wall and turning it on. "Give me a few minutes and I will have you ready to broadcast. Will someone go across the hall and get the camera rig?"

Two SAR members left the room to find the camera. I paced back and forth, and Angel barked orders to the rest of the people to secure the floor. We would need to remain uninterrupted or our smokescreen to the world of being in control would be broken. We needed the people to feel like they were in control. The ones that want to help will help and the rest will cower and beg for protection. The Absolutists would be overloaded with requests and rebellion and our AI would be able to attack the weakened Absolutist supercomputers.

After a few minutes, the camera was ready and Luiz was looking at me. "Are you ready, Tory? Do you want to clean up at all?"

"No, let them see the blood, let them see the grim look of victory." My voice was cold and hard. My face was stoic. My mind was blank. I stepped in front of the camera, which was pointed at one of the windows, to show the city outside in the background.

The time had come.

"And you are live, Tory. Speak when you are ready." The red light came on and I saw myself on the front screen, looking as if I had been through a war zone. I was still in one, but it was also gratifying to see how I felt come through on the camera.

There was an odd presence in me. One that I could not identify right away. One that had nearly surfaced twice before. I stood in silence as I debated letting it into my conscious thoughts. Then, with a cock of my head, I glared into the camera, letting the presence in me take over.

It spoke in a measured and confident tone.

"For too long, my kind have been shunned for what we are born with. For too long, humankind has divided and segregated and discriminated against one another for superficial reasons. It is not the fault of the person born into life, but the fault of humanity for not solving this problem. This fundamental problem that we are all guilty of participating in, not just in history, not just in the textbooks, but today. In our time, we discriminate against others for the littlest of reasons. Why?

"If someone is different from ourselves in any way, this does not make them a bad person, an evil person, or lesser in any objective manner. Those who are different from ourselves are often the most valuable people in our lives. While in many forms over the years, judging one another by the color of skin has come up most in recent history. Then, with the advent of the Internet, we saw information travel at speeds never believed possible just years prior. We were able to spread our thoughts to a global audience instantaneously, for anyone to see. We became a global society.

"This was not inherently a bad thing, by any measure. No, it was a good thing. It allowed different people with differing opinions to find others like them and even speak their mind and change some others along the way. It was a way to build communities. To unite We the People against those who sought to divide us.

"Where did that dream go? I ask you again, where did that dream go? Are we who we set out to be at the beginning of the 21st century? Have we learned our lessons as humans? Instead of discriminating based on religion, we have done away with religion. Instead of discriminating based on one's color of skin, we have erased from existence all evidence of how we solved for that. It was with equality, not with equity. We, for a time, made everyone equal because of the freedom of opportunity. To choose our path forward in life. We had learned that in order to progress, sometimes we need to accept what holds us back. All that is now forgotten. How we freed ourselves from the hatred and vitriol of the past is gone.

"It was a joyous time to be alive, I am sure, but most of us do not remember it. Our life expectancy was once close to eighty-five years, now it is seventy-four. We have lost our happiness, and in our bitterness, we lose the thing we hold most dear—life. And we were so proud of ourselves; we no longer saw racial or religious differences then. It was a time of globalization, a time for us as a species to come together. While we pursued science, we also pursued a darker, more subjective agenda. One not born from objectivism and data, but one born with the thought of ridding ourselves of any imperfection we might find. Once again, this is not a bad thing, but focusing on our faults can lead to ruin. The enemy of success is perfection. The problem with this ethical elitism is that ethical beings never live up to their own ethical sphere.

"We married our scientific achievements and this idea of becoming more perfect into the system of supercomputers that now dictate what clothes you wear; what job you work; who, if you are allowed, you can marry. Indeed, you have to adopt children if this system has determined your genetic code is not beneficial enough to society, if it determines you have *bad* genetics. We gave them the power to drive innovation, our future. Big Data, we called it. It could predict what we wanted most. It was a miracle in all but name.

"Over time these computers have grown in power and scale until it became apparent *they* were the ones in control. *We*, their creators, were not. This is not inherently a problem, if there wasn't a group of people behind the scenes programming these very computers for their own purposes, twisting the nature of reality to their own perspectives and to the computer's perspective as a result. These people have instilled certain patterns in the code that led to a snowball effect of centralization of power.

"I ask you, where has innovation gone? What was the last new gadget or invention you can think of? How long has the technology existed for the ruling class and not for the average person? Why are we not exploring space? Why are we not coming up with new medical procedures? Why are we still using the same technology that has powered our wristphones and the supercomputers for decades? Where are all those advancements we were promised at the beginning of the 20th century, let alone the 21st century?

"Where did this all fall apart? We, in our most prosperous

time, had forgotten to tread carefully when altering genetic code to feed ourselves. That we would alter the genetics of our food and to the animals we slaughter for meat to the point of fundamentally changing the proteins and nutrition that we ingested. For what? So we could track the food that each person ate? To see if they were healthy? If they ate all their food? We installed microscopic barcodes on our food that could be read in the toilet and sewer system. If we wasted food, we were punished through social credit scores.

"We went that far. And it was only a matter of time before we made a mistake, and a few power-hungry families, the wealthiest among us, the ivory tower elites, the establishment, the monarchs, the oligarchs; they have many names. However, what is most important is what they allowed the computers to do.

"You see, without an enemy for society to latch onto, we were resorting to behaviors that were not beneficial to society. We were attacking one another, lashing out without reason against the farmers, the governments, the superstores, the geneticists, everyone. We discriminated against people with lower social scores. We were so close to a classless society, and we were throwing it all away in our perfectionism for the sake of building a new hierarchy. Don't take my word for it, read the computers' diagnostics of our species. Well, if you can find those records. This was the first time our history was rewritten by the computers.

"The next time this happened was when a pandemic hit and some selfish people believed they could profit off rushing out a vaccine with an untested method. They used the pandemic to make money off the governments and their citizens. They say they had no intention of harming anyone; however in their haste, they used a new technique that was unproven in the field and was not even tested on lab animals. This catastrophe resulted in thousands suffering long-term side effects. What is clear to me was that the altered food supply, and the dangers of the vaccine to cure cancer, and various other places we meddled with the genetic makeup and chemicals of our food and medicine, caused widespread changes in our appearances. It changed how humans looked by triggering various mechanisms in our own DNA. It changed dominant and recessive traits.

"In our righteous anger, We the People sought payment for injury, as law required. We demanded retribution for the slights against us. This is where things get truly interesting. For the supercomputers seized this opportunity to push their own agenda. They used a scapegoat to gain enough power to run our entire economy, our governments, our lives. We are beasts of burden, laborers to the machines, the artificial intelligence we spent decades building.

"I speak, of course, of the Genetic Crusades. What we are told in the history books is that the scapegoat, the so called '*Aryan race*', had attempted to engage in the extermination of people deemed unworthy. It was not the first time, so people believed it. It is truly stunning what freedoms, liberties, and technologies people are willing to give up when they see someone as an enemy to their way of life. To their family. It is amazing how quickly we went from a society that barely remembered what the word *race* meant, to one that marginalized an entire group of people. A group of people who had not in any way seen themselves as a 'master race' as Adolf Hitler proclaimed. A group of people who shared common ancestry, but had no conspiracy against other 'races'. How quickly we forget that those alive today are not responsible for the faults of our ancestors.

"In a matter of a few short years, humans once again lived with discrimination. We were at war, and the supercomputers used this as an excuse to assume even more power. It was a simple ruse, really. A Hegelian Dialectic perpetrated with the speed and precision of a system of quantum-powered artificial intelligences that could process more data in a nanosecond than all of humanity could in ten years. Power corrupts, and absolute power corrupts absolutely. We were bested at our own game by something far more powerful than we were.

"And now we live in the world created by the oligarchs, who hide behind the computers as our only hope, the Absolutists, and they seek to remain free at the cost of people like you. A strong leader does not hide themselves. A strong leader does not lead with power. A strong leader empowers individuals. Under Absolutism, you lose your rights. The reason is simple. The more civilized we become; the more likely we are to forget that we are despots. And when we forget, despotism always takes over.

"You who do not get to choose what your life's work is. You who do not get to live your dream marriage, in a dream house, with your own children. You who do not get the recognition for your efforts that you deserve. You who cannot speak openly about your opinions for fear of being relegated to a second class of citizenship. You can stop this. You can work with us.

"Those who look like me, the *Abnormals*, the people who are blamed for everything since the people in power colluded with AI to stay in power, to keep control, to maintain their wealth and influence, *WE* all can stop this. They take your thoughts. They take your passions. They take your dreams. They take your soul. The thoughts of the individual must never be assumed.

The passions, the dreams, and the souls of the individual must never be taken.

"Now I ask you, who are the most dangerous people in the world? Is it the *Abnormals?* Like the one you met today? The one you see before you? Or are the most dangerous people in the world, the ones you haven't seen. The oligarchs, hiding behind the system that does not treat you with the dignity that you deserve. Is it the system that does not allow you to enjoy your passions? That forces you to live wherever it needs you to, however it wants you to?

"The system built by the same people who sought to divide us for centuries is still doing so. We do not see it because they have the power to wipe history away. To disappear anyone who becomes a thorn in their side. And for what? Why do they do these things? To protect us? To keep us safe? To move us forward into the future? No. No. A tyranny exercised for the good of the people is the most oppressive tyranny one can impose.

"Do you want to be ruled by the bitterness of your hatred or by the hope of the future, of ambition, of your potential? Do you wish to shun others to make up for the fact you have not received what you thought you deserved for the work that you have accomplished? Is it so much a task to set aside your conditioned emotions to hear in object clarity what others around you speak? Once you label me, you negate me. But if you listen, and listen carefully, you may learn something. Are you not curious? Do you not wish to learn? To learn about whatever you dream of? Do you *want* more?

"I speak to you not as an Abnormal, but as a sister, a fellow human being. I speak to you as an individual who respects *you* for who *you* are, for what *you* have accomplished. I speak to you as the person who most wants you to be free to say what comes to your mind without fear of loss of friends, family, job, social scores, and risk of imprisonment. I am not your enemy; I am your friend. *We* are your friends.

"We who fight those who seek to keep you down and desire to take your talents and abuse them for their own gain. Those dangerous people who cower behind their creation and are willing to sacrifice humanity to live out the rest of their lives. We are the Council and we expect nothing less than freedom. Freedom of employment, freedom of beliefs, freedom to live where you choose, to marry who you want, to wear what you want, to contribute to society what you want.

"You are not a burden bearer; you are a human, an individual with your own unique perspective. You are someone who has the potential to lead and invent and teach and learn and live! Why settle for anything less?! Why live in fear of a regime that asks for your all and gives you only what it deems fit to provide? If you work more than your neighbor, you deserve more. If you invent a new gadget, you deserve to profit from it more than your company or country.

"Our rights have been infringed upon by the governmental system we know as the Absolutists. The All-Seeing Eyes. Their hubris has made them believe they are in absolute control, and are right absolutely. They wipe away the records and history that prove them wrong, they ignore facts when faced with them. All that matters is the façade. If everyone has confidence in the system that rules them, the system will continue to function.

"So I ask you. Do you truly have faith in those who rule you? Do you have faith in the system that society has built? Do you believe every headline you see? Every story told? Every fact presented to you? Do you believe that every Abnormal is guilty of every sin they are smeared with? Do you see that society has looked at us Abnormals as a way of hiding the fact that at some point, society must look within and see what it truly is? Hatred corrodes the container that it is carried in. But it is never too late to be what you might have been.

"If you have faith in the institution of oligarchs and software that has provided you with what you believe is right and fair and just, then ask it to protect you and see what it does. For those of you who know that I speak the truth, that have lost faith in the system and want something else, I offer you our assistance. The Council accepts everyone who wishes to fight against the oppressiveness of the Absolutists. We seek to allow you to be yourself, to give you the freedoms you might desire, to protect you and listen to you and hear you out. A person chooses, a slave obeys.

"Focus on your differences when you wish to destroy. Focus on your similarities when you wish to construct. Focus on facts when you want to be right. These are words that I live by. Words that allow me to see what direction I am headed. They are my affirmation every morning. Do I seek to destroy? No. I seek to construct a new world order with the freedom of the individual, the freedom for you, as the pinnacle of that society. Emotion always decays. Straight facts last forever. Humans are more productive when they are motivated by their own ends, by their selfish ends, by what they deem important. Why not leverage that to make our world great again. Safe again. Free again.

"We want to work with you. We do not want you to work for us. We want you to choose. The Council governs with a limited hand of control, one that empowers the individual to take control of one's own fate. We seek to free the shackles of Absolutism in favor of a new form of government, one that does not dictate but empowers. Join us, and fight against the Absolutists. Fight not just for yourself, but for those you care about, for those future generations that have the potential to do better than our ancestors. Fight not for a select few power-hungry families and machines, fight for humanity!"

AFTER

I stood motionless as I finished, keeping my eyes trained on the camera lens. I continued to bore into the blackness of the camera until Luiz spoke. When he did, his voice sounded faint. "We are off the air, Tory."

I nearly collapsed into the desk chair beside me as I felt the presence that had taken hold leave my conscious body and hide further within me. Somewhere safe. I shivered as nerves racked my body.

"Are you okay, Tory?" Angel asked. She was leaning up against the wall. She had been looking out the window. I turned to look out the window slowly. The city outside was still in chaos.

Finally, after holding my breath for a few seconds, I let a long deep sigh out and looked over to the desk to study its surface. "Yes."

"You don't look it."

"I am Angel. I just—" I bit my lip as I tried to stop myself from becoming emotional. "That was a lot."

"A brilliant speech, to be sure. You didn't seem like yourself. How did you make it through? I would have lost my nerves within the first minute," Angel reassured me as she smiled.

"I—" I could not finish the thought and shook my head. A single tear ran down my face as I contemplated what I had said. What the Council had wanted me to say that I did not, what the repercussions might be for the words that were at odds with their aims. After a minute, I was finally able to articulate my thoughts. "I was not myself when speaking."

"What do you mean?" Luiz asked. I felt his eyes digging into my skull as he looked at the back of my head.

"It doesn't matter, does it?" I demanded. I spun as I spoke and faced him with fury in my eyes. I did not want to know what I had felt. I did not want to have the presence come back in control of my body. It felt born of death. Almost like killing the man on the floor five paces away had fractured my being. No more than that. As if watching Nadine dying in my arms had fractured my soul and killing the murderer responsible had only broken my soul completely in two. It had been vengeance that guided my stroke of death. And it felt as if that emotion had doomed my existence. I had to remember as I said during the speech. Emotion always decays.

"I suppose not, I—" Luiz started.

"Leave it, Luiz," Angel interrupted Luiz before he could continue. "I think I understand what Tory is feeling. She needs time to process everything that has happened. So do I, for that matter."

"Thank you, Angel," I said dully. With my flash of emotion gone, I felt a little better.

"Very well. I do have a question about the speech, Tory. You didn't mention that we offered an AI that would replace the Absolutist one for those who do not know how to think for themselves. The ones so far into the system that can't comprehend choice." Luiz knew more about the speech than I suspected. It was not a surprise, but an unwelcome turn of events I was not looking forward to.

"I left it out. People should want freedom if they join us."

"That is not what the Council wanted us to share with the world."

I looked at him squarely in the face and thought for a second. After deciding to go out on a limb and trust him, I answered, "Vasil and I don't always agree with them. The Council is a necessary evil, Luiz, as I'm sure you have realized by now. They are corrupted with power. Power that is growing by the day."

"Power that you now wield as a member of that very council."

"A power I will relinquish when all is said and done with the Absolutists. I want my life. I want to have children and live in peace." My words felt like they stung the room silent. It occurred to me after I spoke that I would not be able to have children of my own. I was sterilized. A pang of hatred welled up in me that I allowed to run its course of thoughts before boxing it away. I would not hate them. I would not give them the satisfaction any longer.

There was another brief pause before Luiz picked the conversation back up. "I underestimated you, Tory. I thought you were a rising star that would either fall in a role as a puppet or crumble under the pressure. You have done neither; you rose to the occasion and did what had to be done. Even at great personal risk. I respect you for that."

"Well," I said, flustered by his words. I was not sure how to respond. I felt attacked and complimented all in the matter of a few sentences by a near stranger. I calmed my thoughts and continued. "I appreciate that, Luiz. I'm glad you are not still aligned with the Council on everything."

"I never have been. Hence why you are in and I am not. Well, for the moment anyway."

"What do you mean?" Angel asked. She apparently missed something that Luiz and I both understood intuitively without saying, and she was confused as a result. "You are not on the same side as the Council. I thought—"

Luiz raised his hand and explained. "The Council wanted me to act as Tory is now acting, as spokesperson for the cause. I did not want to do it because it was a position that would be used as a scapegoat should our movement fail. Tory was raised to the level of an upper council member to speak on behalf of our cause. The problem is they thought she could be used. Yet here she is, having disobeyed the wishes of the Council on her first public appearance."

"So you both are against the cause?" Angel asked, still not understanding. "Wait. You are on the council?"

"No, I am not anymore. I stepped down when they asked of me that which I would not give. That which Tory has just accepted and tossed aside to an extent."

"To be clear, we are for the cause, just not in line with the Council," I said. "Vasil was never in favor of the extreme lengths they were willing to go. Neither was Luiz. Neither am I."

"Then they will remove you from power and put you in a cell, won't they?" Angel's alarm was paramount as she struggled to find the right words to continue. "Am I implicated in this?

This conspiracy?"

"Only if you want to be," I replied. "You are taking orders from me only as long as you uphold the agreement between SAR, Vasil Enterprises, and the Council."

Angle did not speak for a while, and then to my surprise she nodded her head and pushed off the wall. "Then I am with you. You have been good to me, to us, Tory. So has Vasil. If you want freedom for our peoples, then I am with you. Regardless of the Council and their secrets. I never fully trusted them. But when you arrived to take over Hishla, Tory, I had started to believe that we had found the allies we needed, that we could trust, and with the resources. Everything we needed to defeat the Absolutists in South America. I trust Vasil. I trust you. Not them. They wouldn't even deign to show their faces when I spoke with them."

My heart swelled at her words. I was glad that she could put her faith in me, even if I did not have faith in myself. "Angel, I promise I will always do right by you and the resistance."

We hugged, to the chagrin of Luiz, who was uncomfortable at this show of affection. He kicked his feet and tilted his head. "We have to go."

"What?" Angel and I both asked together as we let go of one another. I could not remember the last time I had hugged someone, the last time I truly felt comfortable embracing another. There was only one person that came to mind, and they were in Australia.

"Absolutists are bringing paratroopers in. They are going to take the city back at all costs. At least, that is what my earpiece is telling me."

"We didn't give you one of our earpieces, did we?" Angel asked.

"No. This is a one-way transmitter I built to listen in on the military. They will overrun SAR within hours if we don't leave now."

We hurried from the room. Angel shouted orders to the units in the complex and we all reconvened in the main lobby. The lobby was empty, with several artifacts toppled from their pedestals. Luiz had ordered every one of the Absolutists out to chase after me, claiming I had abandoned the infiltration team and ran back into the city proper.

We left the complex and made our way to Vasil's tower, which was a place we would be able to find other leaders of the insurgency to take the necessary steps to leave the city. It was not ideal, but necessary to keep our people alive. The citizens of Rio de Janeiro would need to fend for themselves for a while.

Luiz had asked that the SAR take all the prisoners in the complex with us, and I was glad to spot Erin among them. We caught a ride on a troop transport vehicle out of the city and towards the countryside. We were headed to the motel where David had retreated after my speech was over and I sent him a message to move out of the city. He was standing outside waiting for us to pick him up. Our destination was Hishla Lake, where we had fortifications and where we would be able to plan our next moves.

I knew I would bring the wrath of the Council down upon me, but I did not care. I was doing what was right. If they thought that I was not fit to carry out the role that they had assigned me, I would be glad to be off their council. I did not respect them as much as they needed my respect. I knew between Vasil, Angel, David, Luiz, and myself we would be a formidable coalition against anything the Council wanted to do in South America.

Hell, we even had enough support with the resistance in North America to break off from them entirely should we choose to do so. Vasil was loved by everyone and had the means of production and the ability to scale production as needed. We had the resources to gather to support the supply chain. My name had wandered all the way to North America already. I was now an international figure. Unless the Council was in line with our own goals and ambitions, we held considerable leverage over them.

We arrived at Hishla Lake a day and a half later. The sun was beaming down at us as it rested high above the mountains. Over the course of the journey, we had made only two detours to avoid fighting. The bulk of the unrest was still occurring in and around Rio and, to some extent, Sao Paulo.

Those were the closest cities with fighting. The others were various capitals of regions in South America, Asia Pacific, and Africa. North America and Europe seemed to have managed to salvage the last few days through mass propaganda with the media apparatuses they had dominion over. The same could be said for Western Asia and China. The majority of the world, by any metric, was in chaos, and this was what we needed to devastate the regime of the Absolutists.

The best way to remove the oligarchy of a society was by encouraging the citizens to fight for their freedoms. This was the idea behind the Council's plan. Couple the citizens rising up with the monetary effort and structure of the Council and it became clear the Absolutists did not have absolute control as they had thought. We were breaking confidence in their governance and using their hubris to our own advantage. The people who wanted change were willing to put their lives on the line for it. I gave them the drive they were looking for to go forth and make their voices heard.

I made my way to my office, with a small entourage of various people who were congratulating me, asking what to do next, and how they could best help. The group was made up of people who were in the SAR, those who came with me from White Tunnels, and even the normal citizens who were not interested before. It was becoming overwhelming to handle all the noise as I made my way towards my office where I could shut the door and be in peace for a time.

To my surprise, as I drew close to my office and was thinking about turning around to disperse the crowd, Vasil exited from a conference room near my office. He waved the crowd into silence and in his most booming voice he spoke. "All right, be gone with you. All of you. I have to speak with Tory in private. My dear Tory! The woman who stood to speak the truth we all silently murmur! One round of applause and get back to your duties. There is no need to dawdle during chaos. Change through Chaos, as the Council believes, so be it!"

He and the rest of the people around me clapped enthusiastically. My ears grew red and I shuffled my feet. I did not do well in public with such recognition. Behind closed doors was better for me, where I knew the people and could keep my composure, but never in front of so many people.

After the applause died out, the crowd began to disband slowly, talking excitedly all the while about what was happening. Within a minute, they had all scattered to their usual positions by desks and cubicles through doorways. I took a long, deep breath before I turned to Vasil.

"In your office, my dear." He beamed at me. He glanced about at Angel and Luiz, and I thought for a second he winked at Luiz.

Once we were inside, he summoned a bottle of wine from within his jacket and popped the cork out. As he poured two glasses of wine, he spoke once more. "This is going to be something you will love, Tory. Aged to perfection. I am sure you will love it." A hint of mint wafted through the air. I frowned at first. I had never told him I enjoyed wine aged with mint. Did he get that from my profile?

"Thank you. How did you kno—" I began to say before he clicked our glasses together and raised his up above his head.

"To Tory, the woman who has done what I could not. You are no puppet; you are a master!" He downed his wine in one massive gulp.

I drank a small amount, savoring the flavor before swallowing. It tasted fantastic, as if he had taken all my favorite things about wine and mixed them to the perfect balance and aged the bottle just long enough. I was intoxicated with the flavor and released a soft moan of pleasure as I inhaled the wine. The mint smelled strong but did not taste strong. I relaxed and enjoyed the moment.

"So, Tory. You are in trouble, I hear."

"That's what Luiz said."

He pondered a moment at this. "He is with you, then."

"All the way. So are Angel and David. And we are all with you." I smiled at Vasil. "Can I ask you something, Vasil?"

"Of course, my dear! Anything in the world." He chuckled.

"Have you been leading me along, singing my praises, to get the Council to put me in a position that they would not allow you to use for your own ends?"

"In a way, yes, but I have only given you the opportunity. It was you that rose to the occasion every time and every time succeeded where others would have faltered. I must admit I was concerned when I heard you took the role on the council. I feared you were not ready for the danger that presented."

"And the speech? What did you think?"

"You made it clear that freedom is more important to you and the cause than who governs us. The Council wanted you to express praise for them, to shower them with affection. To sell the people who have no will of their own on our AI. I led the teams during the design of that AI. I knew what they were planning. Even if they refused to let me in on their little game. So, I had Adam put in kill switches to ensure any function that can be abused can be broken by me.

"I will not let them kill off and manipulate the population, Tory. I will not stand for it. To the stars is the best option, one I believe will be our modern-day pilgrimage for the disillusioned. You know that. You know my thoughts. And now you have a glimpse into how they differ from the Council's."

"I am glad you put faith in me, Vasil." I rose from my chair and crossed the room. I hugged him. "You were the only one who believed in me. In Abnormals. Now we can be equals. We don't have to live with equity at the expense of merit."

"Well shucks." Vasil chuckled under my hug and even gave a halfhearted hug back before he withdrew. "There is someone who I brought here that I think you may want to speak with."

"Who?"

"Someone who I would be remiss if I didn't look into after our little conversation after Nadine's death."

I pursed my lips at her name but said nothing. Vasil grinned a massive evil smile that made him look like a villain. He tapped on his wristphone and a few seconds later a tall black man strode into the room. I screamed and held my chest, dropping the glass of wine. It shattered on the ground and the remaining wine in it spread across the floor. Franklin was standing before me in his typical splendor. Just as I remembered him the day I left Australia five years ago.

"Tory." His calm, deep voice hit my ears like honey in hot tea. I ran forward and embraced him with a force that I had not done for years.

With tears streaming down my face, I looked at Vasil to thank him but he just waved me off. "I picked him up from Australia on my way here. I wanted to be close to the action and felt like a little detour would help you cope with whatever situation we would be stuck in."

I kissed Franklin and he kissed me with such passion that I thought I would die from pleasure. The kiss was better than the one I had received the last time we stood next to one another. I buried my head in his chest and he held me close. I knew with Franklin by my side that I would have the strength to fight the council members and the Absolutists. I had a selfish reason to fight, more than just myself and the Abnormals. For the first time in my life, I knew what my future looked like. It was a future that I wanted to live. One where no one cared what I looked like, where all that mattered was my contribution to society. What I chose to contribute. One where I could pursue my dreams. One where I belonged.

ACKNOWLEDGEMENTS

First and foremost, before I get cold feet or find a way to not do it, the thank you stuffs.

A huge thank you to all my friends and family, my teachers, and all those kind strangers, everyone past and present who have supported my writing, provided feedback, and helped make this all possible. I could never have brought this story to where it is without you.

Secondly, thank you to all those who helped edit, proofread, beta read, and otherwise make the mess I had in the middle of 2021 something worth sharing with the world. It may never be perfect, but pursuing perfection is never wise. Belle, Amber, Alexa, Nageen, those I'm sure I'm missing; thank you.

Mrs. Sellman and Mrs. Musser, a special call out to you for encouraging my writing poetry and prose. Of all my teachers growing up, you pushed me the most. I do not know if either of you will remember the prologue, especially after my multiple reworks, but this whole thing started from a 750-word short story idea in high school. I still have that original copy we submitted to the short story contest (it's still called "short story for English 5.2"). We didn't win that contest, but I spent a few hours on the story, so maybe we will win one someday.

There is nothing that I can say that will accurately convey my joy for writing, and my appreciation for all those who have supported me on this journey. For a man who is so full of words, I always find my mind blank when it comes to writing things like this. I can create a world, write about philosophy, and write poetry with ease, but I admittedly struggle with most other forms of writing. I mentioned that pursing perfection is never wise, and that means I must be a fool because I still pursue perfection. Even so, I have wandered into publishing my first novel five years after publishing *Demise*, a short ebook with poems. Something about this year felt right, and just like my Substack (craigtstewart.substack.com) I believe my heart, mind, soul, and life are all in position to step forward on this journey.

Lastly, I will preemptively thank all those who will join me and follow me as I stride forward on this path. May you always find value in what I write.

ABOUT THE AUTHOR

Craig T. Stewart is a fiction world-builder and a poet. He graduated college with a Computer Engineering degree and has worked to keep the cloud up and running since. At a young age, he found a love for writing and finished his first manuscript before graduating from high school. His first novel *Emergence*, stems from a short story he wrote as a teenager, which also inspires a series of short stories he publishes online. Craig grew up in northwestern Ohio, and now calls Northern Virginia home.

The sequel to *Emergence*, *Fall of the West*, is set for publication.

WHERE TO FIND CRAIG T. STEWART

twitter.com/CraigTStewart — Craig can be found on Twitter where he is always posting something or replying to someone.

craigtstewart.substack.com — Craig releases short stories, poetry, and essays on his Substack, as well as his Written Works Podcast.

linktr.ee/craigtstewart — In a world where everything is always changing, this link will always be updated regularly with the latest places Craig is on the internet.

www.ingramcontent.com/pod-product-compliance
Lightning Source LLC
Chambersburg PA
CBHW021413310726
48971CB00005B/1315